FIR...
UN...
MI...

MELISSA McCLONE

AND

A MARINE FOR
CHRISTMAS

BY
BETH ANDREWS

MILLS &
BOON

Dear Reader,

Once again I find myself in Hood Hamlet, Oregon. I wanted everyone in the quaint mountain town to experience a little Christmas magic this time—but most especially Leanne Thomas!

Leanne made brief appearances in *Rescued by the Magic of Christmas* and *Christmas Magic on the Mountain*. She also appeared in *Snow-Kissed Reunion*, my online read. Each time I wrote about her I thought she would make a great romance heroine.

Leanne Thomas is a mountain rescue volunteer with Oregon Mountain Search and Rescue (OMSAR) and a paramedic with Hood Hamlet Fire & Rescue. Whether at work or play, she's surrounded by men. She tries hard to be 'one of the guys'. I wondered what kind of man it would take to break through Leanne's tough exterior and melt her heart.

As I researched women firefighters, I learned quite a few marry other firefighters. I thought a firefighter might be a good match for Leanne. Enter Christian Welton—the handsome young rookie at the fire station, who is also a rock-climber.

Neither asked for love when writing their Christmas lists, but sometimes what we want isn't what we need. And, no matter what's happened in the past, it's never too late to believe in Christmas magic and happy endings.

Enjoy!

Melissa

FIREFIGHTER UNDER THE MISTLETOE

BY
MELISSA McCLONE

All the characters in this book have no existence outside the imagination of
the author, and have no relation whatsoever to anyone bearing the same name
or names. They are not even distantly inspired by any individual known or
unknown to the author, and all the incidents are pure invention.

First published in Great Britain 2011
by Mills & Boon, an imprint of Harlequin (UK) Limited,
Eton House, 18-24 Paradise Road, Richmond, Surrey TW9 1SR

© Melissa Martinez McClone 2011

ISBN: 978 0 263 88929 1

23-1211

Harlequin (UK) policy is to use papers that are natural, renewable and
recyclable products and made from wood grown in sustainable forests. The
logging and manufacturing processes conform to the legal environmental
regulations of the country of origin.

Printed and bound in Spain
by Blackprint CPI, Barcelona

With a degree in mechanical engineering from Stanford University, the last thing **Melissa McClone** ever thought she would be doing was writing romance novels. But analysing engines for a major US airline just couldn't compete with her 'happily-ever-afters'. When she isn't writing, caring for her three young children or doing laundry, Melissa loves to curl up on the couch with a cup of tea, her cats and a good book. She enjoys watching home decorating shows to get ideas for her house—a 1939 cottage that is *slowly* being renovated. Melissa lives in Lake Oswego, Oregon, with her own real-life hero husband, two daughters, a son, two loveable but oh-so-spoiled indoor cats and a no-longer-stray outdoor kitty that decided to call the garage home. Melissa loves to hear from her readers. You can write to her at PO Box 63, Lake Oswego, OR 97034, USA, or contact her via her website: www.melissamcclone.com.

For everyone at cascadeclimbers.com

Without the forum Hood Hamlet wouldn't exist, and
I wouldn't have learned to climb!

Special thanks to: Karyn Barr, Kellie McBee,
Fran Sharp, Terri Reed, Daniel Smith, Jennifer Rollins,
Steve Rollins, Kevin McClone, Kurt Fickeisen,
Jon Bell, Paul Soboleski, John Frieh, Mike Leming
and all who helped out in my thread on the Climber's
Board. Any mistakes and/or discrepancies are
entirely my fault.

CHAPTER ONE

CHRISTIAN WELTON shoved his ski pole up the snow cave's air vent. He'd spent much of the night clearing snow from the shaft. Not that he was complaining. This cramped shelter on Mount Hood had saved his and his cousin's lives.

He glanced at Owen Slayter, who lay inside a sleeping bag. A foam pad kept the bottom of the bag dry from the snow beneath. The right side of Owen's face was swollen, bruised and cut. Dried blood coated his mouth. Superficial injuries.

Owen needed to be in the hospital with his multiple fractures. A helicopter rescue would be the fastest way off the mountain, but that hadn't been possible due to the weather.

Until help arrived, Christian would do whatever it took to keep them alive. That meant making sure Owen didn't go into shock or become hypothermic.

The inside temperature was approximately thirty-two degrees, practically balmy compared to the biting late-November cold. Christian listened, but couldn't hear anything outside the snow cave. He preferred the eerie quiet to the roar of wind as the storm unleashed its wrath yesterday.

For all he knew, Mother Nature had taken pity upon them, and the storm had passed overnight. A break in the weather would allow a rescue mission to be launched.

Time to find out if their luck had changed.

Christian slid off the raised sleeping platform. He wanted to see blue sky. He'd settle for gray as long as the wind and snowfall had died down.

At the entrance, he removed one of the backpacks covering the opening. Hope vanished in an instant.

Talk about an arctic hell. Seventy miles per hour winds, freezing temperature and zero visibility. He pushed aside the other backpack and peeked out. Each breath stung his lungs.

Disappointment shot straight to his cold toes. Helicopters wouldn't be flying today. No one would dare risk these conditions in the air or on foot.

Dammit. Christian's blood pressure rose to match his anxiety level.

Stupid dead cell phone battery. The thing was worthless. Useless. He hated not knowing what was going on down below or when help might arrive. If only...

Don't go there.

He had to concentrate on what was in his control. Anything else would only aggravate him more. Maybe upset him enough to make a bad decision.

Outside the cave, he struggled against the wind. He wiped snow from his neon-orange based skis—crossed in an X to mark the snow cave—so they would be visible to rescuers either from the air or ground should the weather suddenly improve.

Christian ducked inside the cave. He covered the entrance with the backpacks.

A chill shivered through him. His legs shook. He slapped his thighs with gloved hands.

What he wouldn't give for a steaming cup of hot cocoa right now. No whipped cream, but little marshmallows floating on the top.

Owen moaned.

Christian glanced at his cousin. Fantasizing wasn't going to get it done.

Time to melt some snow. Both he and Owen needed water to drink. Eating snow decreased body temperature and would allow hypothermia to set in quicker.

Carbon monoxide poisoning from using Owen's stove inside

the snow cave wasn't a big concern to Christian. Space between the packs, the vent and the wind outside allowed enough air movement and ventilation inside. But he still cleared the vent a couple times while the snow melted to make sure. He didn't want to take any chances.

With enough snow melted, he turned off the fuel then filled a water bottle. He climbed to where his cousin lay, careful not to sit too tall or he'd hit his head. Christian had been in such a rush to carve out the cave and get Owen out of the storm that he hadn't made the cave that big.

"Thirsty?" he asked.

As Owen blinked open his eyes, a grimace formed on his face. "Storm pass?"

His cousin's voice sounded hoarse, raw, like a wild animal. An injured, dying animal.

Christian's insides twisted.

Not dying. Owen was hurting. That was all. He'd groaned in pain through the night. Given his injuries a normal response. Both of them would get off this mountain and be climbing again. Not this season for Owen, but eventually he'd be back at it with Christian at his side. Or rather on his rope.

"The weather still sucks." Christian was a firefighter, used to running into burning buildings and saving people, not having to wait for someone to rescue him. He hated not being able to do more than keep his cousin warm and give him water to drink and energy bars to eat. "But people know where we are."

Owen cleared his throat. "OMSAR will find us."

He sounded stronger, confident they would be rescued.

Christian respected what OMSAR—Oregon Mountain Search and Rescue—did. Helping others when things went wrong appealed to him at a gut level. It was one reason he became a firefighter. He also loved being on a team where everyone watched each other's back and were equals.

Christian wasn't an equal of OMSAR. The mountain rescuer volunteers' skills far surpassed his own. He couldn't wait for them to arrive and get Owen out of here. But this storm would stop even the hardest of the hard men.

Still Christian knew Paulson and Thomas would get here when they could. They weren't only mountain rescuers, but firefighters. Part of the brotherhood. As soon as it was safe, they'd be here. No doubt Thomas would give Christian an earful, as usual. This time, however, he would gladly listen.

"Yes, they will," he said finally. Once the weather improved, OMSAR would know exactly where to locate them. Christian had given the 911 operator their GPS coordinates before his cell phone died. "Even if OMSAR doesn't make it up here today, we have all we need. Sleeping bag, bivy sacks, food, fuel for the stove and my wonderful bedside manner."

One side of Owen's dry and cut lips lifted in something that half resembled a smile. "You sound more like a mountaineer than a rock climber."

Christian straightened. His head brushed the ceiling. "That was the point of this climb."

"Then we succeeded." Owen had been climbing mountains since high school. Christian preferred rock climbing, but Owen thought it stupid to live on Mount Hood and not be able to climb it. Since spring, the two had climbed together throughout the Cascades. "I've always learned more from my failures."

"Then I should be an expert alpinist when we get down."

Owen laughed. Coughed.

Christian wished he could do more to help his cousin. Maybe there was something. When the rescuers arrived, they would need room to work. He reached for the shovel. "I'm going to make this place bigger. It's claustrophobic in here."

"Most snow caves are," Owen said. "Don't bother. You soaked through your clothes digging this out. You can't get your spare ones wet, too."

"If the snow settles—"

"We won't be here that long."

Christian wanted Owen to be right. At least he was more

alert. Talkative. Both were good signs after a restless and fit-ful night.

A little tension released from Christian's tight shoulders. "No worries. Remember, I'm one of Hood Hamlet Fire and Rescue's finest. Strong. Brave."

"Full of it." Owen winced. He squeezed his eyes closed then opened them slowly. "Save the firefighter shtick for the pretty ladies. I got one word. Hypothermia."

"That would suck."

"Damn straight," Owen agreed. "If something happens to you, there won't be anyone to brew water and feed me."

"Yeah, letting you go thirsty and starve wouldn't endear me to your parents."

"Grandpa would be really mad at you, too."

Their grandfather, the patriarch of the Welton clan, would never forgive him. Christian was persona non grata anyway and would remain so until he moved home and embraced his role at Welton Wineries. That wasn't going to happen because of the terms his grandfather attached to whatever carrot he dangled. If Christian ever returned, he wanted it to be on his terms, no one else's.

He forced a smile. "Grandma wouldn't be too happy, either."

"And my sisters. And yours."

Owen's teasing was another good sign, but Christian couldn't deny the truth in the words. He dropped the shovel. "Okay, I'll wait."

Taking care of Owen was the most important thing Christian could do. His family, especially his grandfather, might even see that becoming a firefighter had been a smart decision. Not simply a way to put off working at the winery.

"Thanks." Owen closed his eyes again. "Welton Winery will go on now."

"Yeah." Their grandfather claimed the future of Welton Winery rested in Christian's and Owen's hands. Never mind Christian had other goals that didn't include just the winery and living in the Willamette Valley. But family—make that his grandfather's—expectations overruled individual dreams. Or so they were taught to believe. "Whether we want it or not."

Owen took a slow, deep breath.

Christian cleared the air vent again.

"Sorry for getting you into this." Owen sounded weaker once again.

"Hey, we're in this together." Christian had suggested they climb. His cousin had picked the objective. "No cutting the rope. No blaming each other. No losing it."

No matter how long they were stuck or how bad things got up here.

Things were bad up here. Driving winds limited visibility. The temperature remained in the low teens. The conditions weren't fit for man or beast.

Yet here she was.

Leanne Thomas sniffled, her nose runny from the cold temperature. Her breath sounded against the ski mask covering her face. A layer of ice covered her goggles and clothing. Ice probably covered her pack, filled with forty-odd pounds of gear and medical equipment.

But the only other place she wanted to be right now was higher on the mountain. At 10,500 feet to be exact. The approximate location of the two missing subjects. If only the rest of the six person OMSAR team would pick up the pace...

She gritted her teeth. This slower-than-snails pace up the south side of Mount Hood was killing her. Leanne wanted to climb faster, as part of a two-or-three-person hasty team, but Sean Hughes, the team leader, didn't want anyone to break a sweat and risk hypothermia. He could be such a mother hen during missions. The trait was both endearing and annoying.

The scent of sulfur from the Devil's Kitchen hung in the air. Not as bad as some days due to the wind. The hot fumes from the mountain kept the rocks free from snow, but she could barely see them today due to the conditions.

Okay, Leanne shouldn't diss Hughes. She understood his

concerns. Hypothermia and frostbite were real threats even with better conditions than yesterday. The lack of visibility meant they had to be especially cautious. No one wanted to lose a member of the team in this weather. But she hated having to move so darn slow knowing two climbers needed their help.

Worry gripped Leanne. Something she wasn't used to feeling on a mission. But this one was different than the others.

Focus, Thomas. Maintain objectivity.

Leanne jammed her ski pole into the snow. She'd been a mountain rescuer volunteer and a paramedic with Hood Hamlet Fire and Rescue long enough to know emotion didn't belong in the field. But staying detached wasn't so easy this time.

One of their own was missing.

Not an OMSAR member, but a Hood Hamlet firefighter. The station's rookie, even though he'd been working there for over a year now. The guy was the youngest among the professional firefighters at the station.

Christian Welton.

Leanne pictured his easy smile. Tall with brown hair and an athletic build, Welton defined the phrase babe-magnet with model-worthy good looks and striking blue eyes.

Not that she wanted to date him, or vice versa. Oh, he'd flirted with her at the beginning. His interest had surprised her. She discouraged the men she worked with so they would see her as one of them, not a woman. With Christian, that had been harder to do. But then he'd backed off, acting professional and treating her like the other guys. A good thing since the fire department frowned upon workplace romances.

But Welton was too hot for her not to notice him. She might not date anyone she worked with, but that didn't mean she couldn't look and appreciate a nice piece of eye candy on occasion. One who cooked a delicious Chicken Marsala and climbed, too.

He'd told her about learning to mountain climb, but rock

seemed to be more Welton's thing. Unless a bluebird powder day appeared. Then she'd bump into him skiing.

But the North Side of Mount Hood had some challenging, technical climbs. Not something a newbie should undertake. She'd never seen Christian act rashly before. She would be surprised to find out he had with this climb.

The temperature dropped. She ignored the biting cold and took another step. A gust of wind nearly knocked her over. She clutched her ski poles and regained her balance.

"Slow down, Thomas," Hughes shouted. "You're not on your own out here."

Leanne barely heard him over the wind. She slowed her pace. She was getting ahead of the others, but she hadn't felt this anxious since last Thanksgiving when a broken snowboard binding made Sean fall, injure himself and need rescue. One of the longest Thanksgiving days of her life.

Going after strangers was one thing, but someone she knew and worked with was a completely different situation. Over a year ago, Welton had strutted into the station full of confidence. He'd shown a sense of humor with the hazing and bad duty assignments. He'd also shown surprising competence and composure for a rookie. Though he could be annoying at times, Welton was dedicated. Hardworking. Too bad he didn't put as much effort into the women in his life.

Last night at the lodge, Leanne had gone up to a beautiful, but distraught young woman named Alexa and given her a candy bar. Alexa said she'd gone out with Welton a few times and was "a little" worried about him. Alexa seemed a bit more into him than she let on. Poor girl. Welton kept things light and casual with members of the opposite sex.

Leanne cleared her goggles with her gloved hand.

She knew more about the dating habits and marriages of the men she worked with than she wanted to know. But that knowledge helped her figure out what she wanted—and didn't want—in a relationship. She'd watched male friends, both firefighters and mountain rescuers, break women's hearts as if it were a hobby or game. She'd suffered too much heartbreak in her life to ever put herself in that position again.

The rescue team's slog up the mountain continued toward the Hogsback then east. She focused on each step.

Ice clung to her exterior clothing and accessories, but Leanne's base layer remained dry. She might be cold, but she wasn't freezing. Hughes deserved kudos for that.

He gathered the team together. "We're in range of the GPS coordinates. Look for markers. Anything to tell us where they might be."

As they searched, Hughes blew a whistle in hopes the missing men would hear it and make their whereabouts known. The sound carried better than a voice in this kind of weather.

If Welton and his cousin were inside a snow cave—which Leanne prayed they were—they might not be able to hear anything. The snow muted sounds. That made for peace and quiet during a storm, but could hamper rescue efforts if subjects didn't hear rescuers looking for them.

"X marks the spot," Paulson yelled, pointing to a pair of neon-orange bottomed skis marking a snow cave.

Relief washed over Leanne. Building a shelter was key to surviving out here in this kind of weather. She hurried over to the entrance. Backpacks covered the opening from the inside.

Paulson stood behind her. "Looks like the rookie knew what to do."

Leanne removed her pack and pulled out the medical kit. "Let's find out."

"Dude!"

Christian bolted upright from a sound sleep. He hit his head. The roof had settled more overnight. Soon the ceiling would be at their noses. "What?"

"They're here." Owen laughed as best he could. "They're finally here."

Adrenaline surged through Christian. Hallucinating was a symptom of shock and hypothermia. So not good.

Owen had been getting weaker and weaker, making Christian's anxiety level spiral upward. He did the only thing he could. He checked Owen's vitals. "Can you feel your feet?"

"I heard—"

One of the backpacks fell away from the snow cave entrance. The other followed. A red helmet poked inside. OMSAR.

Relief flowed through Christian's cold, sore body. Time to get Owen out of here.

"Yes," Owen whispered.

The rescuer crawled into the snow cave. He held a red duffel bag with a white cross on it. Ice covered his helmet, ski mask, goggles and black parka. The word RESCUE was written in white down one sleeve. He removed his goggles and pulled down his ski mask to expose his mouth.

Not a he. Christian's dry lips curved upward. "Thomas."

Leanne Thomas was a paramedic at the station. Pretty with an athletic, hot body. He'd wanted to ask her out when he first started working at the station, but she hadn't seemed as into him. He'd decided not to pursue her. A good thing, he'd learned. She wasn't his normal type.

Tough as nails and all business, Thomas was like a drill sergeant on steroids when it came to being out on a call or breaking in a rookie. She took her job seriously, expected others to do the same and never let her hair down. Christian wouldn't mind being around if she ever loosened that tight ponytail or those braids she wore.

Her face was pale except for her cheeks, flushed from the cold. She acknowledged him with a nod and sniffled. "Welton."

Surprising warmth flowed through him. His smile widened. "It's so good to see you."

"Good to see you, too, rookie." She removed her climbing gloves. "Paulson's outside. The chief's been letting us switch shifts so we could bring you home. No one wants to go back to eating Frank's Turkey Meatloaf Surprise for dinner."

Christian laughed. Something he hadn't done since yesterday. It really was good to see her. "I'll cook you whatever you want when we get down."

A smile tugged on the corners of her mouth. "Be careful, I might hold you to that."

She'd saved lives as a paramedic. She would help Owen. "Do."

Thomas pulled on exam gloves. "Injured? Feet?"

"Fine. Feet are cold, but I can feel my toes," he said quickly. "My partner—cousin—Owen fell skiing the face. He's twenty-six. No preexisting medical conditions. Looks like a broken ankle and arm. Some sort of knee injury."

"Hey, I'm right here." Owen sounded annoyed. That was much better than weak. "Conscious, in pain."

"I followed the NEXUS procedure to assess his spine before moving him in here," Christian added. "The threat of hypothermia and surviving the night outweighed spinal injury concerns."

"Good job, Welton," she said.

That was high praise coming from Thomas. He would gloat about it back at the station, but right now, he was relieved she hadn't spotted any problems with his care of his cousin.

As Thomas moved toward Owen, Christian tried to get out of her way. Not an easy feat in the cramped space.

She glanced around. "Did a hobbit design this place?"

"I was in a hurry," Christian admitted. "After two nights, the snow's settled a bit."

"Well, this cave kept you safe and warm. And you know what they say, size doesn't really matter." She winked at Christian, which caught him totally off guard, then she slid beside Owen. "Hello, Owen. Your cousin's been taking good care of you."

"You have such pretty brown eyes." Owen stared up at her as if she were Aphrodite. "Milk-chocolate with a hint of cream."

Christian stiffened. Owen must be in shock if he thought compliments would have an effect on Thomas. She wasn't interested in her looks. Not the way other women were. Sweet words wouldn't sway Thomas, either. She wasn't the flirty type. Christian had never met a more challenging or unapproachable woman in his entire life.

But she was strong and capable and here. That made her the most important person in the world at this moment. "My cousin is a chocolatier wannabe."

"I couldn't live without chocolate. Thank you, Owen." Thomas smiled softly, but her gaze focused in on his cuts and bruises. "I'm with OMSAR and a paramedic with Hood Hamlet Fire and Rescue. May I examine you?"

"Yeah." Owen glanced at Christian. "You never told me you worked with any women."

Christian tried hard not to think of her as a woman. "Thomas is one of the guys."

Owen scrunched his face. "You need your eyes examined, dude."

Thomas unzipped the sleeping bag, but kept Owen covered. "What your cousin means is all the men at the station consider me one of the guys. It's the same with the rescue unit."

Appreciation twinkled in Owen's eyes. "Idiots."

Thomas shrugged. "It's easier that way."

Christian found himself nodding, but he wondered if she meant easier on her or the men she worked with. He'd never given any thought to how being one of the guys might make Thomas feel. But then again, he'd never once seen her attempt to show her feminine side. She didn't fuss with makeup or jewelry.

As she examined his ankle, Owen winced. "Still idiots."

Christian stared at his cousin. "You realize you just called me an idiot."

"Yep," Owen said through clenched teeth. "Gotta side with the pretty paramedic in hopes she has pain meds in her bag."

Thomas's eyes twinkled, making her look prettier. "Oh, I have lots of good stuff in here."

"Knew it." Anticipation laced Owen's words.

Okay, so his cousin was flirting to get pain meds. Except…

Owen didn't need to charm medication out of Thomas. He would receive pain meds no matter what. He was flirting to flirt. Thomas didn't seem to mind, either. That was…strange.

Not that what his cousin did was any of his business. Thomas, either. But if anyone was going to get to flirt with her, it should be the guy still on his feet.

"Were you wearing climbing boots during your ski descent?" she asked Owen.

"Yeah," his cousin admitted. "Should have worn alpine touring boots. Should have done a few things differently."

"Failing upward was the right decision," Christian said.

Owen nodded, as Thomas continued her examination of him. "That domed cloud hovering like a UFO over the mountain didn't leave us a lot of choices."

Thomas looked at Owen. "Tough position to be in."

Owen raised one shoulder, the one attached to his good arm. "Climbing to the summit ridge and making a fast ski descent down the south side before visibility and conditions deteriorated completely would have worked if I hadn't fallen."

"Making ski turns in AT boots might have been easier, but you still could have fallen and broken your ankle." Thomas looked at Christian. "There's not enough room in here. Put your ski mask on, stick your head out and tell them to set up the tent if they aren't already doing it."

The cave felt too cramped and a little warm with three of them inside. He was definitely the odd man out.

"Welton."

What the hell was he doing just sitting here? Christian grabbed his ski mask. "On it."

CHAPTER TWO

WITH his face covered, Christian crawled out of the snow cave. The wind wasn't as strong as yesterday, but the visibility was still limited and the temperature freezing.

Bill Paulson, another firefighter from the station, stood next to the entrance with a large pack at his feet.

"Good to see you in one piece, Welton. Didn't want to have to break in another rookie. Doubt we'd find one who cooks as well as you." Paulson unscrewed the lid to a thermos bottle and handed it to him. "Drink this."

Christian pulled his ski mask below his mouth and sipped. Hot. Sweet. He'd been expecting plain water. "What is it?"

"The unit's special brew," Paulson said. "Jell-O mix and hot water. An odd combination, but what your body needs right now."

Speaking of needs... "Thomas wants the tent set up."

Paulson pointed to a group of rescuers struggling against the wind to erect the tent. "Hughes didn't think the snow cave would be big enough."

He must mean Sean Hughes, who owned a snowboard company and had married the gorgeous socialite Zoe Carrington this summer.

Christian didn't recognize the other men. The least he would do was lend a hand. "I can help."

"Yeah, you could, but warm up instead." Paulson motioned for him to drink more. "We might need your help getting the litter down the mountain if you're up for it."

Christian straightened. "Whatever you need."

"That's what I told Hughes you'd say," Paulson said. "Now get back in the snow cave until we're ready for you."

Christian crawled back inside with the thermos in hand. The interior was more claustrophobic after being outside for a few minutes. He pulled off his ski mask. His gaze went straight to where Thomas worked on Owen. An IV bag hung from the side of the snow cave alongside a headlamp.

"You've been busy," Christian said.

Thomas didn't glance his way, but concentrated on his cousin's splinted wrist. "Just doing my job."

A damn good job, too.

Thomas annoyed Christian by needing to cross every *T* and dot each *I*, but even then she impressed him. She didn't boast about her mountain rescue or climbing or paramedic skills. She did what was required and did it very well. For that he was grateful and now in her debt. He was going to owe the entire rescue team for getting him and Owen out of this mess.

Christian didn't like owing anyone. It rankled like a blister about to pop during the crux of a rock climb. He would have to think of something special to do for each one of them when they were off the mountain.

"I know it hurts." She spoke to Owen in a quiet, soothing voice. "But you'll start feeling better soon."

Owen basked in the attention and sweet bedside manner. Christian liked her soft tone better than the curt way she usually spoke at the station. He wouldn't be opposed to a little tender loving care from her.

Oh, wait. This was Thomas. Not going to happen unless he was a patient.

Paulson kneeled in the entrance. "Need anything, Thomas?"

She didn't look away from Owen. "Only the tent."

"It's going up." Paulson shifted his attention to Christian. "Your family's been at Timberline. Waiting. Praying. Nice folks."

A burst of emotion clogged Christian's throat. He might not

see eye to eye with his family, but he loved them. He swallowed. "Do they know you found us?"

"Hughes called it in," Paulson said. "Your family will be told then the media notified."

Christian's muscles tensed. "Media?"

"The mission call out brought a wave of press rushing to the mountain. The story went national yesterday afternoon. Headline news on all the cable channels and local newspapers," Paulson explained. "Two Oregon wine heirs missing on Mount Hood. Makes quite the public interest story."

Damn. Christian hadn't told anyone in Hood Hamlet about his family's successful winery in the Willamette Valley, three hours away. He wanted to be his own person, make his own way without his family's influence and interference. He'd learned at an early age help never came without strings attached.

"I don't blame you for not telling anyone about your family's winery," Thomas said. He was surprised she'd been paying attention since she seemed so focused on Owen. "I wouldn't have told anyone. Everyone would expect you to bring the wine to parties."

Once they were down, Christian would supply the entire rescue team with bottles of wine from his own winemaking hobby.

Paulson laughed. "Just like Porter and his beer."

Jake Porter owned the Wy'East Brewing Company and the Hood Hamlet Brew Pub. He was also a member of OMSAR and an all-around good guy. Christian enjoyed going to the brewpub. The entire town seemed to hang out there. "Is he with you?"

"He and Tim Moreno are on another rescue team. They'll meet us above Palmer where the Sno-Cat will be waiting," Paulson said. "Guys from the station have been stopping by the lodge. Bringing us food and coffee. Sitting with your family."

Christian appreciated the support. But that's what firefighters did for each other. A brotherhood of trust, loyalty and respect. He couldn't imagine not being a part of that. But after a year of being the rookie he knew exactly what would happen when he was back at the station. "They're never going to let me live this down."

"Nope," Paulson admitted. "At least not until someone else screws up bigger."

Christian grimaced.

"It's not that bad, Welton," Thomas said.

"Yeah," Paulson agreed. "It's not like you're a finalist for a Darwin Award."

Christian shuddered. So not something he wanted. The Darwin Award was given to people who killed themselves in stupid ways thus removing their DNA from the human gene pool.

Thomas laughed. The melodic sound filled the snow cave.

Christian had heard her laugh before, but he didn't remember it sounding like that.

"Oh, yeah, one of the guys with such a sweet laugh," Owen said with a big smile. The pain meds must be working.

But his words echoed Christian's thoughts. He liked the way her laugh sounded. Relaxed. Softer. Feminine. Maybe she wasn't as much a hard-ass as he thought.

He shook the crazy thought from his head. Nothing about Thomas was sugar and spice. Or remotely soft.

She joked with the guys at the station and could hold her own with the pranks that went on. He liked that about her.

"Don't let that laugh fool you. I've known Thomas since we were nine. She could kick all the boys' butts back then, too." Paulson grinned at Christian. "Meant to tell you, your girlfriend is at the lodge waiting for you, too."

Christian flinched. Girlfriend was a four-letter word. "I don't have a girlfriend."

"Alexa," Paulson clarified. "That girl is smokin'."

Oh, her. "Definitely, hot, but we just date. Nothing serious." Alexa was a great girl. Fun to be with. More fun to mess around with. Perfect because that was all he wanted right now. "She won't be around much longer with Christmas coming up."

"Is she going out of town?" Thomas asked.

"Come on, Thomas," Paulson teased. "You should know how it works by now. Holidays are the time for us good-looking guys to be footloose and fancy-free."

"Oh, no, Welton." Thomas sounded aghast. "Please don't tell me you're one of those guys who breaks up with women before Christmas."

"Okay, I won't tell you." Christian grinned. "But Paulson's right. The holidays only complicate relationships."

"Not to mention the hassle and expense of buying presents." Paulson had taken over as the resident heartbreaker in Hood Hamlet after the marriage bug bit Sean Hughes and Jake Porter. "Remember to break up with them before the second Monday in December or you're stuck."

Thomas's mouth gaped. "There's a December breakup deadline?"

Both Christian and Paulson nodded.

"That's so wrong." Thomas continued to work on Owen. "I've got to side with the women here."

"Idiots," Owen said in a singsong voice.

"I hope a woman never treats you guys like this," she said.

Christian usually ignored Thomas's disapproval, but this time it bothered him a little. Weird. "The women don't seem to mind when I swing back around a few days after the twenty-fifth."

She glanced up. "You go back to them afterward?"

Christian was surprised by her sympathy for the women he dated. Thomas kept her personal life private, but he'd seen her around town with guys. Just no one from the fire station. He'd thought she might be like him—only dating casually. He never thought she could be seriously involved with someone or looking to get involved.

None of his business, he reminded himself.

"Hey, I need someone to kiss when the clock strikes midnight on New Years," Christian said.

"Damn straight," Paulson agreed.

Christian wondered what it would be like to kiss Thomas. He'd bet she kissed as well as she did everything else.

"And sometimes," Paulson continued. "If you're lucky, you get a belated Christmas gift, too."

"I thought Hughes and Porter were players." Thomas checked Owen's vitals. "They had nothing on the two of you."

Paulson beamed like a kid with straight A's on his report card. "Thanks, Thomas."

"Yeah, thanks," Christian said.

Her eyes narrowed. The color resembled dark chocolate now. Her eyes looked prettier than usual, sexier.

She sighed. "That wasn't a compliment, boys."

Interesting. Why hadn't he noticed her eyes got very sexy when annoyed?

The rescue team brought Owen down the mountain in the litter. Leanne couldn't do anything more for him out in the elements so she assisted with the descent.

Snow swirled, but the temperature remained steady. That would make things easier on Welton.

Leanne glanced his way. He moved slowly, cautiously, as if he didn't want to make a mistake. A picture of perfect mountaineering technique.

"Almost there," she said.

Welton had to be exhausted, and even a little hypothermic.

She couldn't make out his features or see his eyes with all his winter gear and goggles on, but his shoulders hunched slightly. That couldn't be from the weight of his pack. The gear had been distributed among the rescue team.

A signal his condition had changed? Better find out. Welton would never complain. "You doing okay?"

"No different from when you asked five minutes ago," he answered. "My condition hasn't changed."

"If it had, would you tell me?"

"No."

The guy had the never-say-die attitude down pat. His willingness to want to assist in the descent after two nights in a snow cave impressed her. He showed strength and courage not found in a lot of people these days.

Whoa. She was sounding like a total Welton fangirl. That wasn't like her to go on and on about a guy. Time to get back to business. "We should see the Sno-Cat and the other rescue team any minute."

"Is that them?" His ski mask muffled his voice.

Jake Porter and Tim Moreno led the way with three other OMSAR members behind them. "Yes. That's Rescue Team 2. Fresh arms and legs will speed up the descent."

The sooner they arrived at the Sno-Cat, parked above the Palmer ski lift, the sooner they could get down to Timberline and out of the cold.

Welton moved closer to the litter. "If you'd let me help more—"

"You've done enough, Welton." She understood his frustration. Firefighters were trained to help. "In a few minutes, you'll be inside the Sno-Cat and riding down the hill. An ambulance will take you to the hospital."

"I don't need—"

"If you aren't checked out and cleared by a doctor, the chief will keep you off line duty." No one at the station wanted to be forced to sit out calls. "You've got to go."

Christian grumbled. "Are you going down in the 'Cat?"

"One of our unit members is a doc. He'll be with you. I'm skiing down with the team." As Welton's pace slowed more, her concern and unease rose. "You cold?"

"Just a little down." He exhaled on a sigh. The condensation from his breath hung on the air. "Wish I could ski with you guys."

His wistful tone tugged at her heart. She would much rather

ski than ride the loud, uncomfortable Sno-Cat. Skiing was faster, too. "Another day."

He straightened. "I might hold you to that."

Leanne grinned at the way he'd mimicked her words back at the snow cave. "Do."

"When?"

The guy had been through so much. She might not be able to see his smile, but she wanted to hear it in his voice. "Whenever you want to go."

The newest member of OMSAR, Dr. Cullen Gray, charged in front of Porter and Moreno.

"Thomas." He studied Owen, bundled up in the litter like a swaddled newborn, then looked at her. "That was a fast decent."

"Seemed a little slow to me. I hope you and the rest of the team kept warm." Gray had moved to Hood Hamlet this past summer. "Patient is twenty-six. Good health. Stable vitals. Multiple fractures of his left wrist and ankle. Possible ligament tear on the right knee. Facial lacerations."

"Morphine?" Gray asked.

She nodded. "All he'd had until we arrived was a couple ibuprofen."

The second team joined the others in lowering the litter.

"We gave him an initial five milligrams and another five due to his pain level and needing to get him down the mountain," Leanne continued. "His vitals remained stable after the meds."

"We'll get him into the Sno-Cat," Gray said. "What about the other subject?"

Leanne motioned to Welton. "Twenty-eight. Excellent health. A little hypothermic. Slight dehydration. Annoying at times."

She waited for Gray to respond. He didn't. And people called her too serious and intense.

"I'm fine, Thomas," Welton said.

Gray motioned to the Sno-Cat. "We'll make sure."

Welton glanced her way. She imagined a frown on his handsome face.

"Take it easy, Welton." She wanted to cheer him up. "Follow doctors orders. Don't break any nurses' hearts."

"I'll do my best." He sounded as if he might be smiling a little. "Anything else?"

"Yeah. Feel better."

"I never knew you cared, Thomas."

The tenderness in his voice made her heart bump. Leanne must be more tired than she realized if Welton could affect her that way. She squared her shoulders. "I don't. But my stomach appreciates your cooking."

With a laugh, he climbed into the Sno-Cat. The door slammed closed.

Another mission almost ready for the logbook. She stared at the Sno-Cat with a satisfied smile.

"Race you down," Paulson challenged, the way he had since they were nine and had met her first day at elementary school.

"You're so going to lose," Leanne said as usual.

"Yeah," Paulson admitted. "But I'll still be kicking back in the lodge way before the Sno-Cat arrives."

The Sno-Cat's engine revved. She wished Welton could be with them racing down the hill instead of riding in that thing. The guy deserved a break for taking such good care of his cousin. Maybe she should invite him...

"Before you hotshots head down," Sean Hughes said. "Don't forget the media will be waiting for us."

Leanne groaned. So did a couple other members on the team. Dealing with the press was her second-least favorite part of mountain rescue. Body recoveries were the first.

"Come on, now." Hughes looked at each one of them. "The press has a job to do. You know reporters won't go home without a story. They'll make up stuff and get it wrong if we don't answer their questions. Who'll talk to them with me?"

Apprehension coursed through Leanne's veins. The media circus got out of hand fast. She didn't want or need any attention for helping others in need. If she gained some good karma for her own climbing endeavors, okay. But if not, no biggie. "I pass."

Paulson gave her a nod. "I'll do it so Thomas can put her feet up and eat some bonbons before the debriefing."

Yeah, right. She smiled. "Have at it, boys. While you're showing the cameras your good side, I'll be sure to have a bonbon or two for each of you."

Leanne skied down the mountain. With the wind and snow on her, the cold seeped into her bones the way it had farther up the mountain. She couldn't wait to park herself in front of the day lodge's fireplace and warm up.

Fortunately skiing down didn't take much time at all.

The press stood waiting like hungry piranhas ready for a meal. Reporters jockeyed for the perfect position. Camera lights blared. People shouted questions. Others took photographs.

Leanne moved quickly past them in silence. She dumped her skis and poles in OMSAR's storage/catchall room. She also removed her rescue jacket. She didn't want any press who wandered inside bothering her.

She sat at one of the day lodge's tables and removed her ski mask, helmet and gloves. The scent of fresh-brewed coffee made her mouth water, but first things first.

Leanne removed her boots. Freedom! Her feet would have shrieked in delight if they could. She wiggled her cold toes.

A cup of steaming coffee appeared in front of her. "Nice work up there."

She looked up to see a former roommate. "Thanks, Zoe."

Zoe Hughes, Sean's wife, was an associate member of OMSAR. She was also the most beautiful woman in Hood Hamlet. Straight brown hair hung past her shoulders. She'd decide to give up her tabloid trademarked blond locks and go au naturel with her hair color. "Tired, Lee?"

"A little." Leanne sipped the coffee. The hot liquid tasted so good. "Sean's out with the press."

"Figured that's where he'd be." Zoe glanced toward the double doors. "My mother thinks he has a future in politics."

"What does Sean think?"

"I don't really want to repeat it."

Leanne laughed. She took another drink. "If I fall asleep, make sure someone wakes me for the debriefing."

"I will." With that Zoe floated away. Ever since marrying Sean her feet never seemed to touch the ground.

That blissful state was something Leanne had never experienced. She'd dated, a couple of times seriously, but she'd never felt that way about any man. Someday, Leanne hoped she would.

Her heavy eyelids drooped. Fatigue from the climb and rescue overtook her need to stay awake until the rest of the team came inside. She closed her eyes.

An unexpected image of Welton appeared, smiling at her the way he had in the snow cave. Up on the moutain, he'd made her feel like the most important person in the world. His word, at least. She yawned. Too bad that feeling had to end.

Exhaustion kept her eyes from springing open. The guy smiled a lot, but she couldn't remember the last time one had been directed at her. She'd liked how it felt then. She might as well enjoy his smile now.

Two days later, Leanne arrived at the Hood Hamlet Fire Station craving a sense of normalcy. No matter where she went in town yesterday on her day off, the rescue had been the topic of conversation. That annoyed her.

She entered the dining area. The scent of fresh-brewed coffee greeted her. Paulson handed her a cup that she accepted gladly. The perfect way to start her shift. Both B and C shifts crowded around the table. A few volunteers, too.

"Finally," Marc O'Ryan, her medic partner, said. "We want to hear all about Welton's rescue."

Oh, no. Leanne swallowed a sigh. She looked at each of the faces in the room. Only Welton was missing.

Bummer. She'd wanted to hear how Owen was doing. But she also wanted to see how Welton was faring. She'd thought about him lots yesterday. More than she would have expected.

"Before we hear about the rescue," the lieutenant announced, "let's get the morning briefing over with."

The exchange of information took less than five minutes. A new record.

"Now it's Paulson and Thomas's turn," the lieutenant said.

Leanne wanted no part of this. "I'm going to let Paulson tell you what happened. I've got some stuff to do with the toy drive."

Every year the fire station put on a toy drive to help local families in the area who were in need. Leanne usually ended up in charge. Not that she minded. It was a great cause.

"Go on," Paulson said. "I don't mind telling the tale."

Leanne left him to entertain the captive audience. She preferred putting missions behind her, no matter the outcome, not dwelling on them. Nothing good came from rehashing things over and over again. Life didn't give do-overs. No matter how much a person might want to change what happened, they couldn't. Learn whatever lessons there were and move on.

She grabbed a pair of scissors and the fire station's toy drive supply box. She rolled out two large barrels from the back room into one of the apparatus bays. Additional drop-off bins around town might increase the number of donations. Right now things weren't looking so good. Only two new toys had been dropped off. One was from her.

She measured the barrels with the roll of red-and-white striped wrapping paper. If she worked fast, she could have these decorated before the rest of the station came out to check the vehicles. She kneeled on the cement.

"Thomas."

Leanne recognized the voice immediately. Welton. She turned.

With an easy smile and bright eyes, Welton strode toward her in his uniform—a navy T-shirt and pants. His steel-toed shoes sounded against the pavement with a rhythmic clip. He moved with the grace of an athlete. Not bad for a guy who'd spent two nights in a snow cave. He'd shaved the stubble from his face. His light brown hair with an above the collar cut had been neatly styled. Quite a difference from his bad-boy look a couple days ago on the mountain.

Her heart went pitter-pat, a totally unexpected, unwelcome reaction. Okay, Welton was tough. He'd survived on the mountain and saved his cousin. That explained why her insides suddenly felt like goo. "You're the last person I expected to see today, rookie."

He stopped next to her. "Good morning, Thomas."

"Bet it feels like a great morning to you."

"Nothing like a comfy bed and a hot shower to make a person realize how good they have it."

"You're right about that." She lowered her gaze from his face. Uh-oh. She was eye level with his, um, pant's zipper. Heat rose up her neck. She faced the bins. "You missed the morning briefing."

"Chief put me on light duty and told me not to rush in."

Leanne bet it would be hard for Welton to watch the engine go out without him.

"He wants me to do some interviews here today," Welton continued. "Chief thought it might give the station and town a little PR."

She cut two large pieces from the wrapping paper. "Smart thinking. Hood Hamlet's been hurting with the drop in tourism. I've never seen so few donations to the toy drive."

"It's only the second of December."

"True, but usually we receive a lot of toys when the drive kicks off. If donations don't improve significantly, we won't have enough toys to match the number of requests we've received. There are a lot more needy families around here this year."

"No worries," Welton said. "All you need is a little Christmas magic."

Most of the old-timers around Hood Hamlet, and some of the not so old ones believed in Christmas magic. Leanne, not so much. Okay, not at all. She knew better than to put her faith in legends and fairy tales. Hard work and perseverance were the only things a person could count on. Even then life could change in an instant.

She returned the scissors to the supply box. "Oh, yeah, those barrels will be filled up with toys by the end of the week faster than I can say abracadabra."

"I never knew you were so cynical, Thomas."

"Not cynical," she countered. "Realistic."

"Being realistic isn't all that fun."

Welton's words didn't surprise her. She'd met his family at Timberline Lodge. Nice folks. Caring. Wealthy. He probably had never dealt with real disappointment his entire life. That was why he acted so carefree.

"Maybe not, but being realistic keeps you from crashing to earth as often." She positioned the wrapping paper around the first bin. "What the toy drive really needs is free publicity."

He held the paper against the barrel with his large hands. The hands of a climber with several small white scars and a larger one, as if he'd scraped off skin jamming his hand into a crack. "Let me help."

Welton moved closer. He smelled nothing like the mountain today. His fresh-soap-and-water scent surrounded Leanne with intoxicating maleness.

"Thanks." As she taped the bright paper around the bin, warmth emanated from him like a space heater set on high. "Any word on Owen this morning?"

"He's with the doctors at the moment," Welton said. "My aunt's going to text me when he's out."

"Keep me posted on his condition, okay?"

"Uh, sure."

He turned the barrel, making it easier for her to tape. As she scooted closer, her left shoulder brushed his right leg.

Heat burst through her at the point of contact. Leanne tensed and moved away from him.

What was going on? They'd worked closely before out on calls, but she seemed hypersensitive this morning. Concern over his well-being from the rescue hadn't gone away yet.

She added another piece of tape. "Finished with this one."

"It looks like a giant peppermint stick."

Leanne nodded. "All I need is ribbon and a boy."

"A boy?" The humor in Welton's eyes echoed in his voice. "Is that what you want Santa to bring you, Thomas?"

Her cheeks warmed. Being around him made her feel self-conscious, tongue-tied. So unlike herself. "I meant a bow."

"Boys are more fun," he teased.

She reached for the other piece of wrapping paper to cover the second barrel. "Except those who don't want a girlfriend for Christmas."

"Hey, I'm lots of fun."

"Not from where I'm standing."

"You're kneeling."

"Go bother someone else."

"You get that honor this morning, Thomas." He took the sheet out of her hands. "You tape. I hold."

Leanne preferred doing things on her own. Well, not climbing. A partner came in handy then. Still, having an extra set of hands to wrap these barrels was…helpful. "Be careful, if you keep this up, you may find yourself on the committee."

He positioned the paper. "Committee?"

Leanne tore off a piece of tape. "The toy drive committee."

"There's a committee?"

"Me, myself and I." She taped the paper in place. "But I have lots of helpers."

"I'm more of a helper type than a committee person."

"Most guys are." Leanne placed the tape in the supply box. "If donations come in, I'll need a few strong men with trucks."

"Now it's men with trucks." An irresistibly charming grin lit up his face. "Santa's got his work cut out with you."

Leanne picked up the roll of red ribbon and wrapped it around the first barrel. "I'm actually pretty easy…"

Welton's eyebrows shot up.

"…where Santa is concerned," she finished.

CHAPTER THREE

LEANNE tied a neat bow around the first barrel then decorated the second one. "All done."

Christian nodded. "Now it's my turn."

The blue of his uniform deepened the color of his eyes. She wished she hadn't noticed that. "What do you mean?"

Her voice came out harsher than she intended, but something about Welton was messing with her senses. Her brain. Her hormones. She didn't like it.

"Things were so crazy yesterday when we arrived at the Sno-Cat, I never said thank you," he said. "I appreciate all you did up there, Thomas. The rest of the team, too."

"You're welcome. Next time—"

"There isn't going to be a next time," he interrupted. "Not if I can help it."

"Right answer, rookie."

He smiled at her.

She smiled back.

Time seemed to stop. Something passed between them.

Gratitude. That was all it was. On both their parts.

Yet his gaze lingered, as if there was something more.

Leanne looked at the wrapping paper lying on the ground.

This was Welton for goodness' sake. Sure, he was a capable, sexy guy, reliable even for a rookie, but not when it came to romance. If she were dating him, she wouldn't be satisfied with just a date, just fun. She'd want all of him.

Not that she was in the market for a romance, Leanne reminded herself. She was taking a break from the dating scene.

She placed the red ribbon into the supply box. "I need to clean up before the news crew shows up."

"Yeah, I don't want anything to get in the way of my fifteen minutes of fame," Welton teased.

"I'm sure you'll have a legion of fans by the time the fifteen minutes are over."

"A compliment?"

"Maybe."

His smile widened. "I'll take it."

Quite the charmer. She didn't know whether to envy the women he dated or feel sorry for them.

"I'm going to pay you back for everything you did yesterday," Christian said.

"Not necessary."

He shrugged, looking unconvinced. "The least I can do is share the spotlight today."

Her stomach clenched. "Really not necessary."

"It is," Welton admitted. "Chief wants you and Paulson to be part of the interviews if you're not out on calls."

Oh, no. Her heart sank to the tip of her steel-toed zip-up boots. "Interviews aren't my thing."

"Come on," Welton encouraged. "Someone like you can't be camera shy."

Someone like her. One of the guys. But the guys didn't know everything about her. She wanted to keep it that way.

Leanne shrugged, but she didn't feel indifferent. She'd put the past behind her, but she hadn't forgotten everything. She couldn't. Her life had been changed in an instant, but the media hadn't cared. They'd only wanted the story, the inside scoop. No matter what it had taken to get the information.

She shivered at the memory.

Christian touched her shoulder. "Cold?"

Leanne shrugged away from his hand. Straightened. She didn't like appearing weak. To others or herself. "I'm fine."

"You don't look fine."

She pressed her lips together. "I am."

Welton didn't look convinced.

Odd. Most of the guys around here took Leanne at her word. "Really."

His assessing gaze suggested Welton didn't believe her. His perceptiveness over her uneasiness and his seeming to care how she felt disconcerted her.

"Hello." A beautiful blond woman entered the station. Her high-heeled boots clicked against the floor. Two men, carrying bags and camera equipment, followed. The scent of her jasmine perfume wafted through the air. "I'm Rachel Murray with the Portland Evening News."

Leanne stood. She wiped her sweaty palms on the thighs of her pants then shook the woman's hand. "Leanne Thomas."

Rachel's straight teeth gleamed as if they'd been recently whitened. "I just interviewed your rescue team leader, Sean Hughes. He had wonderful things to say about you. Not only as a paramedic, but one of the best and fastest climbers with OMSAR."

Leanne shifted her weight. "Thanks."

Rachel turned her attention to Welton. "And you're Christian Welton. I'd recognize you anywhere."

He shook her hand. "Nice to meet you, Rachel. Thanks for coming all the way from Portland."

She didn't release his hand. "It's our pleasure. I'm sure you've been inundated with interview requests."

Christian pulled his arm away. "A few."

"I was told another member of the rescue team works here, too," Rachel said.

He nodded. "Bill Paulson. He's around here somewhere."

"Why don't you get set up," Rachel told her crew, who went to work. As she looked around, her gaze zeroed in on the red-and-white toy barrels. "Those look Christmassy. What are they for?"

"Drop-off bins. The fire station runs an annual toy drive for

needy children in Hood Hamlet and the surrounding areas."
Leanne didn't like talking to the media, but she would for the
toy drive's sake. "Unfortunately donations are down this year."

"That's too bad," Rachel said.

Leanne nodded. "I'm hoping more toys come in soon."

As Rachel shrugged off her wool coat, Welton lent a hand.
Interesting. Leanne had never noticed his manners before.
Or maybe he wanted to hook up with the pretty reporter. He
had a little time left until the December breakup deadline.

"Hey, I have an idea." The slow, seductive smile spreading
across Welton's face told Leanne she'd nailed the motivation
behind his gentlemanly behavior. "Any chance you could mention the toy drive on camera, Rachel?"

Okay, that was unexpected. Leanne hadn't thought he'd been
paying attention to what she'd said, or cared.

Rachel wet her glossed lips. "Are you involved in the toy
drive, Christian?"

"He's been a big help," Leanne answered for him. She wasn't
about to blow this opportunity.

"I helped decorate the barrels," he said.

"Really?" Rachel sounded intrigued.

Welton gazed into the reporter's eyes as if she were the only
woman in the world. And he the only man.

A lump formed in Leanne's throat. Not one man had ever
looked at her that way. She imagined it would feel pretty terrific.

"Every kid should have a present to open on Christmas."
Welton's gaze remained on Rachel. "I'd appreciate anything
you could say about it. So would Leanne. She heads the committee."

"Oh, you're on the committee, Christian," Rachel assumed
wrongly. "That's wonderful."

He looked uncomfortable. "Anything for the kids."

Rachel leaned toward him. A combination of eagerness and
attraction gleamed in her eyes. "I'd be happy to say something.
Publicity could spur donations and help your committee."

His committee. Leanne bit back a smile. She would make Welton an honorary member so he wouldn't be stretching the truth too much.

"That would be great." He pushed a stray strand of hair off Rachel's face. "There now I can see your pretty eyes better."

The reporter released a swoon-worthy sigh. "Thanks."

"Thank you," he said.

Leanne watched the exchange with interest. Welton impressed her. Being a player had its advantages.

"You know what," Rachel said to Welton as if Leanne wasn't there. "I'll talk to a friend at the newspaper and a couple of Portland bloggers about the toy drive, too."

He grinned. "The more the merrier."

Oh, he was good. Highly skilled in the art of seduction, no doubt. If that was what it took to fill the drop-off bins with toys, so be it. Still Leanne felt sorry for Rachel Murray.

The poor reporter had just fallen for Welton. Hard. But what woman wouldn't with him pouring on the charm like that. Rachel would be disappointed if she expected a holiday romance to develop. Though maybe she would be the one Christian kissed on New Year's Eve.

The thought left Leanne a little unsettled. She shook it off.

"We're ready," the cameraman said.

Rachel smoothed her skirt. "Why don't one of you grab Bill Paulson, and we can get started with the interview?"

"You up for it, Thomas?" Christian asked.

Leanne knew he wasn't talking about getting Paulson. The Portland Evening News broadcasted across Oregon and Southwest Washington. If Rachel Murray was willing to give the toy drive a plug and up the chances of children in need getting a present for Christmas, an interview was the least Leanne could do. Even if it was the last thing she wanted to do.

She took a resigned breath. "Yeah, Welton. I'm up for it. I'll get Paulson and be right back."

* * *

Rachel Murray was hot. Exactly Christian's type.

Her perfectly-applied makeup accentuated pretty, elegant features. His hands itched to run through her mane of blond hair. Her killer body would look better naked. She'd also asked reasonably intelligent questions these past five minutes. Beauty, brains and breasts—a perfect combination.

So why was he more interested in how nervous Thomas looked right now than the sexy reporter?

Christian always tried to pretend Thomas wasn't a woman, but today, he couldn't. She seemed almost vulnerable, spurring his protective instincts.

"Anything you wish you would have had with you in the snow cave, Christian?" Rachel asked.

"A better first aid kit and a charged cell phone would have come in handy. More food, too." He felt a little embarrassed about having to be rescued. "Otherwise, we were good."

Rachel turned her attention to Thomas. "Rescues in this time of year don't always turn out this well, do they, Leanne?"

"No, they don't," Thomas agreed. "Three climbers lost their lives in December 2009. Three more back in 2006."

She might be nervous, but she was hanging in there. Christian respected that, respected her.

"Wasn't there an OMSAR member who also died in a winter climbing accident?" Rachel asked.

Thomas's features tightened. She nodded once.

"Yes." Bill Paulson took over without missing a beat, but his tone sounded strained. "Nick Bishop, a member of OMSAR, and Iain Garfield, a talented, young alpinist, died a few days before Christmas eight years ago."

Christian hadn't heard about these two climbers before, but they'd obviously impacted both Thomas and Paulson.

"Very sad," Rachel empathized. "How does knowing others died while you and your cousin, Owen, survived make you feel?"

"Thankful," Christian said truthfully. "Grateful. Lucky."

"Do you think anything other than luck was involved in the rescue, Leanne?" Rachel asked.

"Christian and Owen had the skills to build a shelter to protect them from the environment and the proper gear to keep them warm, hydrated and fed until help could arrive," Thomas said. "Those things go a long way to ensuring a good outcome."

She'd never ever used Christian's first name before. It sounded…strange. He was used to her calling him Welton, as the other guys at the station did.

"Even with right equipment and proper training, nothing is ever guaranteed," Bill added. "A little luck and good karma always come in handy on the mountain."

"What about Christmas magic?" Rachel asked.

Thomas inhaled sharply. A sideways glance passed between her and Paulson.

"Sean Hughes said a little Christmas magic could have contributed to the rescue's happy ending," Rachel continued. "What do you think about that, Leanne?"

Christian straightened. She wasn't the person to answer this question.

"Everyone in Hood Hamlet seems to have an opinion about Christmas magic," Thomas stated without any emotion in her voice. "Whatever the reasons behind the mission's success, we're all happy Christian and his cousin are safe."

"Your opinion, Bill?" Rachel asked.

"A lot of things that could have easily gone wrong up there didn't," Paulson said. "Owen had no spinal or head injuries. The cell phone battery didn't die until the GPS coordinates had been given to the 911 operator. The weather broke long enough so we could head up the mountain and bring them down. Seems a bit more was involved than simply dumb luck."

Thomas pressed her lips together. Her eyes darkened, but not to that deep, sexy chocolate color from yesterday.

Something was bringing her down. She looked sad, as if she were hurting. Christian didn't understand why, and he fought the urge to reach out to her.

"You were the one stuck in the snow cave for two nights, Christian," Rachel said. "Do you think Christmas magic helped you and Owen get off the mountain alive?"

He shifted his gaze from Thomas to the reporter. "Finding yourself in a situation with everything out of your control, you get religious fast. Making deals and promises you know you can't keep," he admitted. "I have to agree with Sean and Bill. It seems like something more was going on up there. I've only lived in Hood Hamlet a little over a year. But if the dedicated members of OMSAR want to call it Christmas magic, so will I."

"There you have it. Christmas Magic on the Mountain." Rachel beamed. "Christian and Leanne are members of the Hood Hamlet Fire Department's Christmas Toy Drive committee. Why don't you help them drum up some magic of their own by donating a new, unwrapped toy and make a needy child's Christmas morning a little brighter? Drop-off barrels are located here at the fire station. This is Rachel Murray for the Portland Evening News in the quaint Alpine village of Hood Hamlet."

The light on the camera went off. The news crew put away their gear.

Damn. Christian had been called out on camera as a member of the toy drive committee. No way of getting out of that now.

"Great interview," Rachel said.

"I appreciate the plug about the toy drive," Leanne said, then walked away.

"Yeah, thanks," he agreed. "Very nice of you."

"My pleasure." Rachel smiled at him. "I'm happy to help."

He heard a familiar laugh. Thomas spoke with the cameraman—a tall guy with a beard. She laughed again. He did, too.

Christian rocked back on his heels. The cameraman was definitely interested in Thomas. Flirting. The guy's gaze practically devoured her.

First Owen. Now this guy. What was going on?

"I'll give you my number in case you need anything," Rachel said.

Christian turned his attention to the reporter. The way she batted her eyelashes emphasized the amount of mascara she wore. So different from…

He glanced at Thomas. She'd stopped talking to the cameraman. Had the guy asked her out? Christian hoped not. She could do better.

"Christian?" Rachel asked.

"I'd like your number." He would take her out for plugging the toy drive even though she'd landed him a spot on Thomas's committee. "Let me see your phone."

Rachel handed him a fancy smart phone protected in a silver-and-turquoise hard case.

He texted himself and handed her back the phone. "Now you have my number. And I have yours."

"Use it, okay?" She and her crew left the fire station.

"That went well," Christian said to his coworkers.

"She's hot." Paulson raised a brow. "Did you get her number?"

As Christian nodded, Thomas shot Welton an aggravated look. Interesting. Maybe she was jealous.

"Come on, guys." Frustration laced her words. "Christmas magic?"

Okay, not jealous, Welton realized with a twinge of regret.

"Hughes said it," Paulson countered.

She grimaced. "Hughes is infamous for his sound bites."

"Well, I wasn't about to disagree with our team leader on camera," Paulson said. "Besides, I believe it."

Thomas sighed loudly. "Christmas magic isn't real. If it existed, bad things wouldn't happen up here on Christmas."

"I'm bowing out of this conversation." As Paulson walked toward the station's living area, he glanced back. "If you're smart, Welton, you'll do the same."

Christian brushed aside the words. He wasn't about to let

this drop. "I thought Sean Hughes had the reputation of being a Grinch in this town, not you."

"Sean gave the appearance of being a Grinch before he met Zoe, but he would do anything for anybody," Thomas said. "And I never said anything about not liking Christmas. I just don't believe in magic."

Yesterday, her red cheeks, runny nose and sweet laughter had made her seem a little more...human. The vulnerability he'd glimpsed during the interview only added to that. Now she was back to being the same old hard-nosed Thomas. He preferred the other one. "What do you believe in?"

She raised her chin. "Being prepared, having the right skills and equipment, never getting in over your head."

"Sounds like something from an OMSAR training manual."

"It is."

"Then it's what OMSAR believes, not you."

"Wrong, rookie," she said. "I wrote the manual."

He shouldn't have been surprised. She probably approached being a mountain rescuer the same way as she did being a paramedic—by the book. "Well, if Christmas magic fills up those toy bins, you'll be changing your tune soon enough."

"Publicity and generosity will fill the bins. Nothing else."

"How will you know the difference?" he asked.

She picked up the supply box. "How will you?"

A beat passed. And another.

Stalemate. But he'd always known how tough Thomas was. The woman must have ice running through her veins. No matter how ugly it got on a call, she showed no emotion.

His gaze fell to her mouth. No lipstick. Not even a hint of lip gloss.

Christian wondered how she'd react if he kissed her.

Whoa. Thomas would deck him if he did that. He would deserve it for kissing her at the station. He needed to focus. "When's the next toy drive committee meeting?"

"I know that's not what you want," Thomas said. "You can be an honorary member of the committee."

"Thanks, but you heard Rachel. She said I'm on the committee. I need to be on it."

"No one will know."

"I will."

Lines creased Thomas's forehead. "You haven't shown any interest in the toy drive before."

"True." Christian never got too involved. He wanted only responsibilities he'd chosen for himself. "This is different."

Helping with the toy drive would be a great way to do something nice for Thomas. He'd teased her about what she wanted for Christmas, but he knew—a present for every child on the toy drive's list. She wouldn't stop working until she had enough donations. He could take some of that burden from her.

"I want to be on the committee this year," he said firmly.

Panic flashed in her eyes. "You can't be serious."

The überconfidence she usually exuded seemed to have disappeared. She seemed a little…disturbed. Good, because she was making him feel the same way.

"I'm very serious." Being on the committee wasn't only about repaying her for what she'd done on the mountain. Ever since the rescue, being around Thomas left him feeling unsettled. He didn't like that. Working with her on the toy drive would allow him to take control of the situation and conquer that feeling. "You'd better get used to the idea because you're stuck with me."

CHAPTER FOUR

Two days later, Christian parked at the curb in front of Thomas's three-story town house. The Craftsman-style architecture with wood beams and paned windows gave the neighborhood a quaint, mountain village feel. Towering, snow-laden Douglas fir trees stood behind the row of homes, but the neighborhood was walking distance to Main Street.

Snowflakes landed on his windshield. He turned off the ignition.

The single-car garage door of Thomas's house was open. Inside, three large green rubber bins with red lids sat in front of an all-wheel-drive Subaru wagon. An extension ladder rested against the front of the house. Near the top rung stood Thomas, stringing Christmas lights along the edge of the peaked roofline.

A single brown braid hung out the back of her red fleece hat. Her oversize navy jacket fell past her hips. Her black waterproof pants were tucked into a pair of snow boots. Her clothing suggested extreme weather, not a light snowfall. A storm hadn't been predicted, but the sky darkened.

He laughed.

Leave it to Thomas to predict the weather better than the meteorologists. Paulson had told him many local climbers talked to her before heading up the mountain, especially in the winter. Next time Christian would talk to her himself. Accidents happened, but he didn't want to put himself in another situation needing rescue. Once was more than enough.

Larger snowflakes accumulated on the hood of Christian's truck. He stayed in the cab, but not because of the weather.

Thirty minutes ago coming to talk to Thomas about the toy drive had seemed like a great idea. Now that he was here…

He tapped his thumbs against the leather-covered steering wheel. She might not want to be disturbed on a day off.

But leaving didn't appeal to him. Christian didn't want to wait another day until they were back at the station to talk to her. He'd been thinking about Thomas a lot since the end of their shift yesterday. He wanted to see her now.

Christian craned his neck to get a better look at her.

With one foot on the ladder and the other on the roof, she adjusted a portion of the lights. She showed no hesitation or the slightest wobble in her seamless movements. She returned her foot to the ladder as if she were standing on the ground and not a couple stories up.

Fearless. That was Thomas.

What the hell was he doing sitting here?

That *was* Thomas up there.

This wasn't a man-woman thing. He'd given up flirting with her over a year ago after seeing how gung-ho-by-the-book she was at the station. She wouldn't care if he dropped by unannounced. Christian needed to stop fooling around and get it done.

He slid out of his truck then shut the driver's door. If she agreed his plan was a good one—and how could she not?— he could pay back the entire rescue team members and all of OMSAR. Maybe he'd even put a smile back on Thomas's face.

As he walked up the driveway, his boots sunk into the snow. "Hey, Thomas."

She glanced down. Her brown eyes widened with surprise, then clouded with concern. Her mouth tightened. "Is Owen—?"

"He's recovering."

Thomas blew out a breath. The condensation hung on the cold air like a puff of smoke. "Good, for a moment I thought he'd taken a turn for the worse."

Christian appreciated her concern and was a little relieved she hadn't been keeping track of his cousin's progress herself. "Nope, Owen should be released from the hospital tomorrow."

"Good news."

"Yes." Christian studied her. Flushed cheeks. Runny nose. Stray tendrils peeked out the brim of her hat. Not primped, but fresh-faced and natural. Pretty.

"So what brings you by on your day off?" she asked.

"I have an idea about the toy drive."

Thomas adjusted a vertical strand of white icicle lights. "You want to talk about the toy drive now?"

"I can wait until you're finished hanging the lights."

"Okay," she said after a long moment. "This shouldn't take me more than a few minutes."

"Want help?" he offered.

She attached the cord to another hook. "Thanks, but I've got it."

Christian wondered how long she'd been decorating. He walked toward the front door. She'd gone all out.

Lights surrounded a large window on the second story, two smaller windows on the third level, the single-car garage door on the ground floor and the front door where a pine wreath with holly berries, pinecones and a big red bow hung. A single candle lamp sat on the inside pane of each window. A plastic snowman holding a broom stood on the porch, ready to greet visitors.

Thomas must like Christmas to go to this much trouble. Good. She would like his idea. Christian smiled.

A noise drew his attention. She stretched to the left to reach the last hook. The ladder shifted, the top scraping across the house.

Adrenaline surged through Christian. He reached for the ladder but missed it by mere inches. "No!"

"Oh," she cried.

Everything happened in slow motion. The ladder fell like a

tree, careening down until it crashed against the covered porch of the town house next door.

Christian positioned himself below Thomas, ready to break her fall. He braced himself. Except...

She didn't fall. Her feet dangled in the air while she hung from the roof.

His heart pounded. He struggled to breathe. She hadn't hit the ground, but she still could be hurt. "Leanne, you okay?"

"Yeah." She sounded disappointed, not frightened. "I only had one hook to go. I hope the ladder didn't hit you on the way down."

"It didn't." He hadn't thought about the ladder hitting him, only her taking a header and going splat on the driveway. The image still left him shaken. Partners had taken screamers—long falls—rock climbing. He'd fallen himself. Not a pleasant experience.

He stared up at her. "You anchored?"

"Of course. I installed bolts for this very reason." Thomas sounded annoyed he'd questioned her. "A fall from up here would break a lot of bones or kill me."

No kidding. Christian tried to calm the shallow breathing. A strange reaction considering the horrors he saw daily in his job. "I know."

She should have let him help her finish putting up the lights when he offered.

"You look a little pale, Welton." Concern laced each of her words. "Are you okay?"

Says the woman swinging almost three stories in the air. Most of the girls he knew would be screaming and crying, not worried about him. Talk about nerves of steel. His jaw tensed. "Come down now."

"Get the ladder."

Christian didn't move. She always seemed so in control and capable. He liked having the upper hand with her. "What would you do if I wasn't here?"

She pursed her lips. "I have my cell phone."

Of course she did. Thomas was prepared for anything whether at home or in the mountains.

"I'd call a neighbor or friend to come over," she continued.

"A good thing I'm here."

"Not if you leave me hanging up here much longer."

Point taken. Christian placed the ladder against the house and held on to it. "Come down."

"After I hook this last one."

"Leave it," he said.

"I want the lights to look nice."

"They're good."

"I want them to look great."

As she stretched to reach the final hook, he tightened his grip on the ladder. He wasn't taking any chances of her falling again.

She straightened. "There."

"I've got hold of the ladder."

"Not necessary, rookie."

"Humor me."

Thomas unclipped from the bolt. She climbed down as if the ladder were part of a bunk bed set. Both feet hit the ground. Now he could relax.

She removed her harness.

He studied her. "Sure you're okay?"

"I'm fine. Glad the fall wasn't any longer." With a smile, she folded up her harness. "That might have hurt a little."

A little? A smile tugged at Christian's lips. Okay, he liked her attitude. She would kick his butt climbing in the mountains, but he could hold his own on rock. "You rock climb?"

Thomas nodded. "I lead 5.10 and follow 5.11."

Awesome. They'd be able to hit a lot of fun routes in those grades. "Let's go to Smith Rock sometime."

Her mouth quirked. "You want to climb with me?"

"Yeah." Christian loved climbing with women. Not only were they prettier and smelled better than male partners, but nothing was sexier than a woman dancing up a wall of rock with amazing technique. He wanted to see how Thomas moved. Plus she seemed as if she would be a low-maintenance partner, one who carried her own weight, literally and figuratively, and wouldn't complain. "If you're up for it," he added, not wanting to appear too eager.

"I'm up for it." She tilted her chin. "Paulson told me you're quite the rope gun."

Christian tended to lead more routes than he followed, but he didn't mind switching off the sharp end of the rope. "Don't worry. I'll let you have a turn."

She gave him a long, hard look, making him feel as if he were on display. Thomas had never done that before. It made him feel good.

"That's generous of you." She motioned him toward the garage. "Let's get a coffee and talk about the toy drive."

Oh, yeah. The toy drive. That was the reason he'd come to see her.

Christian followed her into the garage. A minigym had been set up in the back with a pull-up bar, free weights and rowing machine. They entered the town house and went up a staircase.

He appreciated the earth tones and casual decor in the living area. The large couch, coffee table and chair looked comfortable. A purple throw lay across the back of the chair.

A river rock fireplace drew his attention. A large photograph of Mount Hood sat on the wood mantel. "Nice place."

"I like it," she said. "Some people rent to tourists, but enough of us live here full-time to give the development a sense of community."

Her words surprised Christian. She was so outdoorsy and independent. A secluded cabin built on land leased from the Forest Service seemed more her style than a town house that shared common walls and had a neighborly feel.

"All your decorations are up outside, but where's your Christmas tree?" he asked.

"I plan to get one today."

Christian studied the photographs on the walls. Mountain

landscapes. One black-and-white picture had a lone climber walking along a ridgeline. "Amazing photos."

"Thanks." She passed another staircase leading up to the third floor and a black wood dining table with a cherry top surrounded by six coordinating chairs. "I love being able to capture shots like that."

He looked at the picture then back at her. "You're a photographer?"

"A photographer wannabe." In the kitchen, she removed two coffee mugs from a cupboard, filled them with coffee from a pot on the counter then placed them on the breakfast bar. "I'm still learning, but I needed something to put on the walls. My former roommate used to display her snowboard designs. Those added a lot of color."

That roommate, a total snowboarding babe, had moved away right after he'd started working at the station. Paulson had been upset when she left for Vermont.

Christian sat on a stool at the breakfast bar. "Cocoa Marsh, right?"

"Yes, but she's Cocoa Billings now."

A wistful expression crossed Thomas's face. A look he wasn't used to seeing on her. She always seemed so…practical. In control. But she was lonely. A way he never expected her to feel. "You miss Cocoa."

Thomas nodded. "We lived together for over three. Way more good times, than bad."

"Hard to replace a friend like that."

"Yes." Thomas opened another cupboard, took out a bag and placed muffins on a plate. "Though, I didn't do too badly replacing Cocoa as a roommate. Zoe Carrington moved in last January and lived here until she married Sean in June."

That had been six months ago. Christian didn't see another car or tire tracks on the snow, but that didn't mean she lived alone. Or with another female. He leaned toward her. "Who's your roommate now?"

"No one." She placed the plate of muffins on the bar and

sat on the stool next to him. "I should try to find somebody. Hood Hamlet is a safe town, but I like knowing someone is here when I'm at the station."

Hood Hamlet's career firefighters and paramedics worked rotating shifts. Twenty-four hours on, forty-eight hours off. Volunteer firefighters had their own schedules.

He sipped the coffee. Strong and hot. "It must be nice to have the place to yourself when you're off."

She nodded. "But I don't mind having a roommate. Sure helps with the mortgage payment and utility bills."

Christian wouldn't know about a mortgage payment. Renting a room in a house with two guys from the fire station suited him fine right now.

He looked at the plate of muffins. Lots of choices. Blueberry, chocolate chip, cranberry and banana-nut.

"Help yourself," Thomas said.

He took a blueberry muffin and bit into it. Delicious.

Thomas took a chocolate chip one. "So what about the toy drive?"

Christian washed down the muffin with a sip of coffee. "I had dinner with Rachel Murray last night."

"You went out with the reporter?"

He nodded. "It was the least I could do after the plug she gave the toy drive."

"So the December deadline..."

Interesting. She remembered his dating ritual. Not that last night had been anything other than dinner. Unusual, but he hadn't felt like taking Rachel up on her offer to come in when he drove her home.

"Still in effect." He already had Alexa to cut loose. Getting involved with another woman didn't make a lot of sense. That must be the reason he'd left Rachel with only a good-night kiss. "Last night was a thank-you dinner. Nothing more."

"Really?" Thomas sounded surprised. Okay, doubtful.

Christian didn't blame her. Thank-you dinners weren't his usual MO. But even though Rachel was more his type, he couldn't stop comparing her to Thomas last night. The reporter had come up way short. "Yeah, really."

Thomas raised her mug in salute. "That was nice of you."

"Simply repaying a favor." As he wanted to do with her. He took another sip of coffee. "Rachel said there's been a lot of buzz surrounding our interview. I started thinking—"

"A dangerous thing."

He smiled. "I thought of a way to capitalize on the interest to not only help the toy drive, but OMSAR and the entire town."

"Wow, that sounds great. I can't wait to hear more."

"Picture this." As she sipped her coffee, Christian spread his hands like he was reading from a marquee. "Christmas Magic in Hood Hamlet."

Coffee spewed from her mouth and covered the breakfast bar.

Uh-oh. Not the reaction he expected.

She reached for a paper towel. "Please, Welton, tell me you're kidding."

"Seriously?" Leanne looked at each one of her friends sitting around the table at the brewpub that night. She'd known Sean Hughes, Jake Porter, Bill Paulson and Tim Moreno for more years than she wanted to count. She'd grown up with them. They were her climbing partners and her friends. The closet thing to family she had. But right now she couldn't believe they were buying into Welton's insane idea.

"Christmas Magic in Hood Hamlet?" she asked them. "A day long celebration with sleigh rides, sledding, caroling and a dinner with a silent auction where attendees not only have to purchase a ticket but also donate a new toy to attend?"

"The rookie's hit this one out of the park," Bill said.

The rookie had excused himself from the table to use the restroom. She wished he'd stay there.

Okay, she appreciated Welton being there to get the ladder for her this morning. The concern in his voice when he'd called her Leanne while she was hangdogging from the roof was pretty darn sweet. But this idea of his?

It had messed up her entire day. She'd even put off getting a Christmas tree in order to tell him all the reasons this wouldn't work. Nothing she'd said dampened his enthusiasm. She'd been forced to bring in reinforcements tonight. She thought her friends would convince Welton his idea would never work. Unfortunately that hadn't happened.

"This is not hitting it out of the park. More like a pop fly to the infield," she said. "We'd have to do this the weekend before Christmas. Two weeks isn't enough time to pull it off."

"It's an ambitious idea," Sean said. "But a Christmas celebration is a perfect way to entice visitors and shoppers to Hood Hamlet, increase donations to the fire station's toy drive and raise some much needed money for OMSAR."

Tim nodded. "This is a very good idea, Leanne. The snowboard shop could use some new customers."

She stared at her mug sitting on the table. A drop of condensation ran down the side of the glass. "And here I thought you guys would be the voices of reason."

"With the economy the way it is, this is reasonable. We could all use some more business," Jake said.

Okay, the brewpub wasn't as crowded as it normally was this time of year. OMSAR was funded by donations and grants. And the toy drive… "But Christmas magic?"

Simply saying the words left a bitter taste in her mouth.

"I can't think of anything better," Tim said. "The celebration could become a yearly tradition in Hood Hamlet."

The others nodded. The enthusiasm seemed contagious.

Unbelievable. Leanne took a sip of the hand-crafted root beer the brewpub made. She was outnumbered.

Welton returned to the table. He sat across from her. "Did she try to talk you out of going along with my idea?"

Jake laughed. "Yes, but she's been trying to talk us out of doing things since she met us."

"So far it hasn't work," Sean said.

"Yeah, we just end up dragging her along with us," Bill said.

"But we always give her points for trying to be the voice of reason." Tim grinned. "I can still hear Nick saying, 'Come on, LeLe, you gotta go. Who else will save our sorry butts when we get in over our heads?'"

Amusement danced in Welton's eyes. "LeLe?"

She narrowed hers. "Don't even think about it."

"I won't," he said quickly.

"Only Nick ever called her that," Jake warned good-naturedly. "And only when he was trying to convince her to do something she knew better than to do."

"Something we usually knew better than to do, too," Bill added.

Those were the days, Leanne thought with a twinge of sadness. She sipped her root beer.

"Nick?" Christian asked.

She realized he probably didn't know who they were talking about. "Nick Bishop. Paulson mentioned him in the interview with Rachel."

"I remember now," Christian said.

"Nick was my wife's brother and my best friend since kindergarten." Jake's gaze met hers. "Leanne, you know Nick would be behind this Christmas celebration a hundred and ten percent."

Darn him. She frowned. Pulling the Nick card wasn't fair. Nick had been the first boy she kissed. A secret. An experiment. A mistake. A good thing they were smart enough to realize, even as teens, they were better as friends. Nick and Jake had taught her and Paulson how to climb. When he'd married his wife, Hannah, Leanne had thrown the bachelorette party and been a bridesmaid.

"Yeah, I suppose he would," she admitted. "But it's going to take a lot of work."

"Everybody is going to want to be involved." Sean took a chip from the basket in the center of the table. "Think total community effort. Zoe will be all over this."

Jake nodded. "Carly, too."

"Rita will want to be involved," Tim said.

Leanne looked each of the three married men in the eyes. "Don't you dare put this on your wives."

"Of course not."

"Never."

"You know us better that that."

"Yeah, I do." She eyed them warily. "That's why each of you will be as involved as they are."

Bill raised his beer. "So glad I don't have a wife."

"Me, too," Welton agreed.

"You single guys aren't getting out of this, either." An idea formed in her head, a wonderful way to get back at the rookie for suggesting the event in the first place. "This is going to be a team effort. And I know exactly who should be in charge."

"You," Welton said, as if it were a done deal.

She grinned. "No. You."

He drew back. "Me?"

Her friends nodded with wicked smiles. About time they agreed with her. "Yes, you're the perfect chairperson."

Welton frowned. "Why me?"

"Because this event is your idea." She smiled. "And because if you're in charge all the single women in town will want to help you pull it off."

He looked shell-shocked.

Serves him right. Satisfaction flowed through her. She leaned back against her chair.

"You know," Sean said. "Something like this might be too big for one chairperson."

"Especially with only two weeks to plan it," Jake agreed. "I think cochairs would be better."

"Fairer," Tim said. "Someone with ties to OMSAR."

"Don't look at me," Bill said.

Sean laughed. "We know better than that, Paulson."

"Then who?" Leanne asked.

Everyone looked at her.

She stiffened. Her tummy did a little flip. "Wait a minute. This whole celebration thing is Welton's idea."

"True, but you're the brainchild behind the fire station's toy drive," Bill said.

Welton nodded, his eyes alight with mischief. "You're also a member of OMSAR. Since they'll receive the money raised from the dinner and silent auction, it makes perfect sense for you to cochair the event with me."

"This makes no sense at all." She couldn't understand why he and the others looked so pleased with themselves. "Guys, you have to know I'm the wrong person for this. I don't believe in Christmas magic."

Jake grinned wryly. "Then maybe this will help you have a change of heart."

A change of heart? That was so not going to happen.

Her gaze collided with Welton's.

He flashed her a devastating grin.

Leanne glared at him. The pretty boy better think twice about trying to make her feel good about this. She was immune to his charm. It was his fault she'd been dragged into this Christmas magic nightmare.

And she wasn't about to let him forget it.

CHAPTER FIVE

SHIFT change the next morning reminded Christian of his first day at the station. Excitement balled in his gut. Anticipation made him sit on the front of his chair around the dining table.

Cleared for full duty.

The four sweetest words the chief had said to Christian since hiring him. No more interviews. No more watching the engine head out to a call without him. He could do what he was paid to do, what he wanted to do—help people.

He couldn't wait.

"Good call on the doughnuts, Welton." One of his roommates, Riley Hansen from B shift, snagged a maple bar out of the almost-empty pink box. The other box sat in the recycle bin after its doughnuts had disappeared faster than crab legs at a buffet. "But next time bring three dozen."

Paulson set his coffee cup on the table. "Yeah, and get a couple of the sprinkle ones, too."

Christian had brought in a bag of Stumptown Coffee beans and two dozen doughnuts this morning. He appreciated his firefighter brothers' support of him and his family during and after the rescue, even though they would chide him about his experience for days, possibly weeks to come. But after a year of being treated like the family cat or the shift's glorified maid, he was used to it. A rite of passage for the crew. He wouldn't want to work anywhere else or with any other guys. Or girl.

Make that woman.

He glanced at Thomas standing at the far end of the room. She wore her hair in a tight ponytail. She leaned against the wall with a coffee cup in her hand. No doughnut in sight. Strange. She usually dug right in. Unless he'd bought the wrong type.

"Sprinkles, huh?" Christian knew he'd purchased the right coffee beans. She'd always said the popular coffee roaster in Portland was her favorite, which was why he'd picked up a bag. "I didn't think those were Thomas's style."

"They're not." Paulson's mouth quirked. "She's plain old-fashioned all the way."

"Better than being iced with nuts like you." She grinned wryly. "I mean, yours."

A looked passed between the two, a sort of unspoken understanding. As Paulson bit into his chocolate iced doughnut with nuts on top, Christian's gaze bounced between the two. He knew they'd grown up and climbed together, but he'd never noticed how close they were. Was there more to their friendship?

The officers entered the room. Each morning the off-going officer met with the incoming one to discuss the events and calls of the previous day, apparatus problems or equipment issues and any other pertinent information the new shift needed to know. After that the crews would be briefed.

The lieutenant stood. "The apparatus maintenance was completed by B shift. That leaves C shift the station maintenance."

Christian's gaze drifted to Thomas, who listened intently. The way she pursed her lips was kind of cute. She'd done the same thing at the brewpub. A habit or effort in self-control?

As the lieutenant talked about the maintenance needing to be completed today, Christian studied her. He'd guess the latter.

Thomas held her temper in check most of the time, but Christian had glimpsed the fire in her eyes last night. The dancing flames had made her look angry and sexy at the same time. Very…intriguing.

As the lieutenant sat, the chief stood. "We're implementing a new training workout. With Christmas coming up, we'll see lots of baked goods being dropped off from patients. Be prepared to sweat, people. You need to stay in shape."

Guys muttered comments under their breaths. Not Thomas. Her eyes gleamed with excitement. She loved any form of exercise. The more brutal, the better. They would be in trouble and puking their guts out if she ever decided to take the lieutenant's exam and be in charge of physical training.

"That's all I've got for you today. Don't forget about the toy drive," the chief added. "A lot of kids are counting on us. Remind your friends about the donation barrels. Thomas dropped off one at the library and another at the General Store."

This would be the perfect time to announce the upcoming Christmas celebration. Christian glanced at Thomas, hoping to catch her attention, but she didn't glance his way. He waited for her to speak up since the toy drive was her pet project. She didn't. That meant it was up to him.

He raised his hand.

"Welton," the chief said.

Thomas glared at him from across the room. The intense sparks flaring in her brown eyes would have burned him if he'd been closer. But her lips weren't pursed like last night.

She mouthed a single word. *No.*

Her reaction amused him. He grinned.

Thomas liked things a certain way. Her way. She wasn't happy when things didn't go as she expected like at the brewpub. But he hadn't expected that same anger today. He'd riled her up...again.

"Welton," the chief repeated.

Christian needed to work with Thomas if they were going to pull off the celebration. She already didn't want to do this. Antagonizing her more wouldn't help matters. He'd wait and wrangle this out in private. "There's a sale going on at the toy store at the mall, Chief."

The irritation disappeared from Thomas's eyes. Her lips pressed together forming a thin, tight line.

She needed to smile. Lighten up. Maybe a kiss would do it.

What the hell? This was the second time he'd thought about doing that. Thomas and the word kiss didn't belong in the same sentence. Especially at work.

Christian liked challenges, but Thomas would be an impossible one. She'd never go for it. He couldn't imagine her, Ms. Perfect Paramedic, forgetting about the station's taboo and messing around with a coworker. Too bad really.

"I'll pass that along to the missus," the chief said. "Anything—"

A series of tones blared over the speaker. "Rescue 1 and Engine 3 responding to a car accident on Highway 26, five miles east of town center," the female dispatcher said.

A surge of adrenaline brought him to his feet.

"Right back into the fire, Welton," Paulson said.

Christian headed out of the dining area. "Yeah."

He was up for the physical portion of responding to a call, but he hoped this was a fender bender and not something more serious. Car accidents were rarely easy calls to deal with.

By the time he reached the engine, Thomas had jumped on her bunker gear and was climbing into the rescue rig.

Always the first one to the truck.

Christian unzipped his boots and removed them. He jumped into his bunkers and slid his socked feet into the boots. He pulled up the suspenders.

Ready to go.

He climbed into the engine, taking his usual seat behind the driver, and fastened his seat belt.

The rescue rig pulled out of the station. They were usually the first responders at a scene no matter if Thomas was on duty or not. She'd set the bar high for all the medics at the station regardless of shift.

Paulson had told Christian the crew used to bet whether one of them could beat Thomas to the truck. No one ever did. The running joke was she would be first until she retired. Or if she ever got caught naked in the shower.

He wouldn't mind seeing that.

Christian took his role and responsibilities as a firefighter seriously, but he'd never seen anyone as driven as Thomas. She might be hard-nosed and a stickler for rules, but he admired how hard she worked. He had no doubt she would put the same effort into the Christmas celebration, even though she'd shown zero enthusiasm yesterday.

He was actually looking forward to working with her. Maybe she'd annoy him enough by the time the event planning was over, he would stop thinking about kissing her. He imagined her in the shower. Then again, maybe not.

O'Ryan drove to the accident. He preferred being behind the wheel. Leanne didn't mind one bit.

The rig's studded tires crunched against the snow-covered road. The siren blared. Traffic on Highway 26 moved to the right to let them pass.

Standard procedure for any call.

Too bad this didn't feel like a normal call to her.

The knot of uneasiness in Leanne's stomach matched the pressure at her temples.

Car accident on Highway 26, five miles east of town center.

She hated responding to car accidents. But this one hit a little too close to home for her...

Don't think about it.

"You up for the new workout?" she asked.

"No."

"I am." She massaged her throbbing forehead. A headache threatened to erupt. "It'll be good for all of us."

"You know what they say, Thomas, all work and no play."

"Oh, I play."

"I haven't heard about you playing with any guys in a long time." O'Ryan passed a school bus. "Still getting over that physical therapist from Hood River?"

"Long over him. Just taking a break from dating right now."

O'Ryan winked. "You could always date a firefighter."

"I know better than to get involved with one of you guys."

"Yeah, the chief wouldn't like that."

A sheriff's deputy's flashing blue-and-red lights shone in the distance.

Her throat tightened. "It's a small station in an even smaller town. Why borrow trouble?"

"I hear you on that." O'Ryan tapped the brakes of the medic rig. The studded tires bit into the layer of snow and ice. "Damn. This is a bad one."

Leanne stared out the medic rig's windshield as they approached the accident scene.

Flashing lights. Cars. People. Falling snow. Glass. Blood. A blanket covered a body on the road.

She glimpsed what might have once been a minivan. Air bags had deployed. The front was smashed all the way into the driver's seat. The side windows had shattered. The left side had buckled. She couldn't see the other side.

A few feet away rested an SUV spun at a weird angle with its front end and right side crushed. A police officer leaned over a passenger in the SUV, someone covered in red. In blood.

Images flashed through her mind like a movie on fast forward. Bursts of colors. Explosions of sounds. Tears of pain.

Hang on. They'll be here soon.

She closed her eyes. It didn't help stop the pictures or the memories.

The metallic taste of blood filled her mouth. Her stomach clenched. She wanted to throw up. Leanne clutched the arm handle until her knuckles turned white.

"Thomas."

She opened her eyes. She couldn't let anyone see how much this was affecting her.

Focus. She had a job to do, people to help, possibly lives to save. "I'll take the minivan. You take the SUV. Let me know what you have so we can see if we need more help out here."

The rig stopped.

She opened the door and jumped out. The frigid air made her suck in a sharp breath, one that hurt her lungs.

Screams and cries filled the air. A child wanted his mommy. Familiar sounds. Smells. Emotions.

Bile rose in her throat.

Focus, Thomas. Leanne grabbed equipment from the rig. People were counting on her to be able to hold herself together. She'd done it more times than she could count. She could do it again.

Hang on. They'll be here soon.

Not soon. Now.

With the trauma kit in her hands, she ran to the minivan.

The chatter over the radio told Christian this accident was more serious than the fender bender they'd responded to last week. At least one casualty.

The engine approached the scene.

Two vehicles. One minivan. One SUV. Police cars blocked traffic. A stuffed pink elephant lay on the snow-covered road.

Damn. His jaw tensed.

On the ground, Thomas performed CPR on a patient. A sheriff's deputy, Will Townsend, assisted her. At the mangled SUV, O'Ryan leaned halfway inside.

"This doesn't look good," Paulson muttered.

"Nope," Christian agreed.

"Welton," the lieutenant said through his headset. "Jaws of life."

"Got it," he said.

The engine stopped. Christian unfastened his seat belt and opened the door.

Time to get back into the game. He was ready.

After dinner that night, Christian emptied the dishwasher. He felt as if he'd worked a double shift, but still had half of his single one to go. Outside the kitchen window, an overcast sky hid the moon, but he wondered if the big, round ball of light was hanging up there somewhere. A full moon could explain the craziness of today. Since this morning's car accident, they'd barely had time to restock supplies after each call before being sent out again. The entire crew seemed wiped out, especially the medics.

The din of the television in the other room could barely be heard over O'Ryan's snores. The EMT had fallen asleep in one of the lounge chairs as soon as dinner was over. Thomas was nowhere to be seen. She'd been quiet, almost distracted, during the meal. She'd barely touched her dinner—one Christian had offered to cook in Paulson's place—before disappearing. Upstairs in the bunk room, perhaps?

Christian wouldn't blame her for calling it an early night. He understood why she might be upset. The car accident's three fatalities would have been enough for one day. But also losing a heart-attack patient on the way to the hospital, a teen with a traumatic brain injury following a sledding accident and a baby bitten by a dog didn't make for the easiest of days. The medical reports alone had to be daunting. Not that easy was part of the job description.

Paulson entered the kitchen. He made a beeline for the brownies the lieutenant's wife and kids had dropped off during dinner. He placed one on a napkin and wrapped it up.

"Midnight snack?" Christian asked.

"For Thomas," Paulson said. "She'll be hungry later."

His comment piqued Christian's curiosity. Paulson had a reputation around town with the ladies. Unless that was a smoke screen for his so-called "friendship" with Thomas.

"I haven't seen her since dinner," Christian said.

"She's up in the bunk room." Paulson wrapped another brownie in a napkin. "Calls with kids are the worst. She takes them pretty hard."

Christian nodded. He would never forget one of his first. A crying father had placed his nonbreathing two-year-old in Christian's arms. That had shaken him up for days. He'd learned fast to focus on the calls they could help and forget about the ones they couldn't. Easier said than done.

"Maybe it'll be a slow night," Christian said.

"Maybe." Paulson scribbled Thomas's name on the napkin.

Familiar tones sounded over the loudspeaker. "Rescue 1 and Engine 3 to RV fire."

"And then, maybe not," Paulson said.

Christian exited the kitchen. Before he reached the truck, Thomas had jumped into her bunkers.

Damn. He climbed into his gear. How did she get down here so fast? She looked sleep rumpled with her crooked ponytail. Dark circles ringed her eyes. Christian's stomach knotted. Upset didn't begin to describe the sadness he saw in her eyes or the uneasy expression on her face.

Leanne didn't need a brownie. She needed a hug.

He took his seat in the engine.

As the engine followed the rescue rig out of the station, Christian couldn't stop thinking about her. He wondered who would be the one hugging her when she finished her shift tomorrow morning. Some guy here at the station like Paulson or…someone else?

Christian wished it could be…him.

At one o'clock in the morning, Leanne restocked medical equipment on the rig. She needed to have the necessary supplies in case they received another call. Given the day so far, they most likely would.

A shiver inched down her spine. Not in anticipation of what might happen, but dread.

Ridiculous.

The car accident this morning was to blame for the way she felt, not the other calls. But she'd held herself together, done her duty and transported a critical patient to one of the best trauma centers in the Pacific Northwest. She hadn't had this kind of reaction in a couple of years. Maybe this would be the last time.

She knew the routine.

Never show weakness. Never admit you care. Empathy would only lead to a nervous breakdown.

As Leanne added additional IV supplies to the trauma kit, images from the car accident flashed through her mind. Not even a shower could get rid of the smells. Not that they were real. Just her imagination now.

She closed the kit and latched it. The rig was ready to go the next time a call came in. The rest of the crew had called it a night after the long day. But she wasn't ready for bed. A much needed nap after dinner had given her a second wind. Maybe she'd…

Leanne sensed a presence behind her. The familiar soap scent filled her nostrils. She wanted another sniff.

Bad idea. The guy was trouble with a capital *T*. "What do you want, Welton?"

"You're still awake."

"Wow." She didn't turn around. "They really teach amazing powers of observation at OSU."

"How do you know I went to Oregon State?"

She heard the surprise in his voice. "The Portland paper published your entire biography in the paper. Owen's, too."

He swore under his breath.

"You didn't know," she said.

"No."

The one word spoke volumes. Leanne shouldn't take the way she felt out on Welton.

She turned. The moment her gaze met his, unexpected warmth surged through her veins.

"I've tried not to pay attention to the press coverage or the comments that must have followed," he said.

Smart man. "A few details were mixed up in the articles, but that happens when you have reporters, who aren't climbers, trying to write stories."

"The comments…"

She didn't want him to worry about something out of his

control. Not that he seemed like the anxious type. "Typical rants about taxpayers having to pay for rescues, climbing Hood in the winter, the need for Mountain Locator Units. You've probably read the same comments every time something goes wrong up there."

"Yeah." His gaze grew serious. "Even if we'd had a MLU, you wouldn't have reached us any sooner because of the storm."

"Exactly. An MLU would have made no difference. You gave us what we needed to find you, but try telling that to the Monday morning quarterbacks," she said. "They always think they know best even if they wouldn't know a biner from a key ring."

Christian's easy smile crinkled the corners of his blue eyes. Those eyes hinted at a secret hidden in their depths, captivating her.

Leanne didn't want to look away. She couldn't.

Something between them had changed since the rescue. Leanne wished she knew what. Sure, she'd always found Welton attractive, but she'd never been so…aware and affected by him before.

He didn't seem to be in any hurry to break the contact, either. "It was a rough day. You okay?"

Her pulse quickened. "Why wouldn't I be okay?"

"You seemed a little uneasy, distracted at dinner. You're up now."

Her heart pounded against her ribs. Forget that he was a hottie, she didn't like that Welton could read her so well. "I've had a few things on my mind. Your dinner was good."

"I didn't see you eat much."

"You're not turning into some watch-my-every move stalker type, are you?"

He smiled. "Nope, just concerned about a fellow firefighter."

His words wrapped around her heart like a fleece blanket. Exactly what she needed right now. She really didn't like that. "Uh, thanks. But I'm fine."

"Hungry?"

Not hungry. Starving. Nodding, she lowered her gaze to his lips. Her mouth went dry.

"Paulson saved you a brownie," Welton said.

Leanne would rather have a taste of him. Uh-oh. Where had that come from? Okay, she'd been staring at his lips, but she shouldn't be thinking of Welton *that* way. Look, don't touch or taste. She nearly groaned as the sharp desire to do just that gripped her in a tight vise. "A brownie sounds good."

The words came out in a rush like water spewing from a broken fire hydrant. So unlike her. Maybe she should forget the chocolate and call it a night before she did or said something stupid.

"It's on the counter in the kitchen," he said. "Paulson wrapped it up in a napkin and wrote your name on it."

For all of Paulson's lack of maturity and womanizing ways, the guy was such a great friend. Always had been. "Thanks."

Eager to put some distance between her and Welton, Leanne walked toward the kitchen.

He fell in step next to her. "You and Paulson are close."

She wished the guy would leave her alone. "We've known each other for almost twenty-five years. He's one of my best friends."

"Close friends are hard to find."

"They are." She entered the kitchen and saw the wrapped brownie. "Especially ones who know the importance of chocolate."

"You climb with Paulson."

"I let him climb with me."

Christian laughed.

The rich sound filled the kitchen and made her a little dizzy. He had a great laugh. Not that it mattered. She bit into her brownie.

"So are you just friends or…?"

Welton's suggestive tone made Leanne choke on the brownie. She swallowed. "Friends. Period. Why would you think—?"

"He saved you a brownie."

She pointed to another wrapped brownie on the counter. "He saved one for O'Ryan, too."

"I didn't know that."

"Why do you care anyway?" Leanne eyed him warily. "You've never seemed interested in station gossip before."

"We're going to be working together on the Christmas event," Welton said. "I thought it might be good to get to know you better. You know my dating situation. I figured fair is fair."

"I'm not dating Paulson," she admitted. "Love the guy like a brother, but that's as far as it will ever go."

"But you are dating someone…"

She raised an eyebrow. "Is this really relative to us being cochairs?"

"Do you always answer a question with a question?" Welton countered.

"I'm not dating anyone at the moment."

Even the most macho, secure guys seemed intimidated by her job, her hobbies and especially her male friends and coworkers. She took another bite of the brownie. At least she had chocolate.

"So you were dating someone," Christian prompted.

She'd really liked Blake. Thought it might go somewhere. "It was a while ago. Summer."

"What happened?"

Most of the crew, with the exception of O'Ryan and Paulson, only cared about their own love life, not hers. "You really want to know?"

"Yes."

Welton sounded genuine. He really seemed to care. She kind of liked that. "Blake was a physical therapist from Hood River. A decent guy. We had fun, but he had issues with me working on an all male twenty-four hour shift. He didn't want me spending any time with my mountain rescue friends, either." Leanne stared at her bare ring finger. The one thing she'd dreamed of was having a family of her own. But that didn't seem likely of happening anytime soon. "Blake resented my job at the station and my volunteering with OMSAR. He told me he wanted a woman who needed to be taken care of by him not one who worked in a team surrounded by other men."

"That sure isn't you."

"Those were almost his exact words." She'd heard from a mutual friend, who worked in the nearest Emergency Department, that Blake had gotten engaged to a real-estate agent. Leanne raised the brownie to her mouth. "No big loss."

She took a bite. Chocolate always made things better.

"A guy like that would never be able to make you happy," Christian said. "So tomorrow…"

She wiped her mouth with the napkin. "What about tomorrow?"

"You and me. A little Christmas magic."

Seriously? Leanne gave him a look that should have sent him scurrying back and ducking for cover. He didn't flinch. She would try another tact. "Please tell me you've never actually used that line on a woman."

His grin could charm the underpants off an avowed spinster. "You have to admit, it's a pretty good line. Might have to add that to the arsenal."

A reluctant smile tugged at her lips. The guy was something else. She had to admit he was making her feel a little better. "You have weapons?"

"WMDs, baby." Mischief gleamed in his eyes. "Want to inspect them?"

Leanne laughed. Welton was good for lightening the mood around here. She appreciated that about him. "I'll pass, but I'm sure you won't have any trouble finding someone who wants to give them a close examination."

"So tomorrow—"

"I'm hitting the backcountry." Maybe that would remove the weight pressing against the center of her chest from this morning's accident. Fresh air and snow were the perfect combination to make her forget everything else. "All that powder is calling to me."

Maybe now he'd leave her alone.

Christian rocked back on his heels. "I'd be up for making a few laps if you want some company."

Anticipation shot through her. She hadn't expected him to want to go. "Do you have the gear?"

"If by gear you mean skins, shovel, probe and beacon. Yeah, I've got them." He set his chin. "I know how to use them, too."

Leanne really shouldn't. But she had offered to go skiing with him when they'd been at the Sno-Cat. Maybe she should get it over with tomorrow. She wanted things to go back to the way they'd been before the rescue when she was satisfied looking at Welton, but not wanting to touch him. Kiss him.

His charming smile spread all the way to his eyes and took her breath away. "Wondering if you can keep up with me?"

"No." Welton might be hot stuff down here, but up on the mountain was another story. That was one place she could hold her own against any guy without even trying. "Wondering if you can keep up with me."

"I'm always up for a challenge," he said. "In fact, we can put a little wager on it."

She raised brow. "Such as."

"Dinner."

Her heart leaped. Oh, no. Wrong reaction. "I hope you don't mean a date, Welton."

"I know better than that, Thomas. I meant the loser has to take the winner's turn cooking dinner at the station."

Leanne should have known he wasn't talking about a date. She ignored the twinge of disappointment. Welton was a coworker. Nothing else. As long as she kept remembering that, she would be fine. And this outing was going to be good. Fun. Exactly what she needed. "You're on."

"You're going down, Thomas."

She fought the urge to laugh at her impending victory. Welton would be begging for oxygen by the time she finished with him. She would stop thinking about him as anything more than a showboating rookie who she had rightly put back in his place. Yeah, this was exactly what she needed to put the rescue and all these weird feelings behind her. "We'll see about that."

CHAPTER SIX

A PERFECT day for backcountry skiing on the northeast side of Mount Hood. The sun shone bright. No goggles, only sunglasses required. A breeze blew over the snow and through the trees. The temperature was comfortable.

Christian wore a thermal top over his ski pants. He'd shoved his jacket in his backpack before leaving the parking lot. The uphill climb would make him sweat if he wore too much. Layering clothes was key to comfort out here.

The trail from the Cooper Spur Ski Area was well traveled. With skins on the bottom of his skis to grip the snow, Christian led the way following the path of skiers and climbers who'd come before him that morning.

He glanced back at Thomas.

Two braids dangled from beneath the brim of her wool beanie. She also wore a thermal top that stretched across her chest. Her breasts bounced as she moved.

His smiled widened. A nice view. Too bad he couldn't skin backward. "Thanks for letting me tag along."

Sunglasses hid her eyes, but nothing could disguise the huge grin on her face. She looked like he felt. Carefree and loving life. "It's more fun to have company out here."

"Do you ski here a lot?"

"It depends on the weather and conditions. I try to get in as many turns in a year as I can," she explained. "There are lots of places to ski around here."

No kidding. Christian faced forward and continued up. Two

hours ago he'd been getting off his shift at the fire station. Now he was skinning his way toward the Tilly Jane Cabin with Thomas. There was nowhere else he'd rather be right now. "I want to try them all."

A party of three skied down through the charred toothpicks that used to be trees until the Gnarl Ridge fire ravaged the area in 2008. The fire came close to taking out both the cabin and the historic Cloud Cap Inn, but was contained in time.

Snow flew from the tips of the men's skis. Some pockets of powder seemed deeper than others. The descent looked a little tricky with narrow passages between trees, lots of turns and steep, uneven trails, but still fun.

The three men whooped and hollered. Two waved in Christian's direction. He didn't recognize them and glanced back at Thomas. "Know them?"

"Yes."

Not enough information. "OMSAR."

"No."

His mouth twisted in frustration. Most women wanted Christian to ask questions about their lives. Once they started talking, they didn't stop. Not Thomas.

Most females found him attractive. A fun time. A catch.

The fact Thomas acted as if he had an infectious disease intrigued him as much as it annoyed him.

A dog barked. Around the Pacific Northwest animals frequented the trails right alongside their owners.

Christian looked toward the burnt trees. A black lab bounded through the snow, practically riding on the tails of his owners' skis.

Leanne laughed. "Now that's a ski dog."

"I wonder how he'd do on a lift."

"Mount Bachelor's K-9 Avalanche Dogs ride the lifts with their handlers." She watched the pair descend and disappear in the trees. "You'd be surprised how well dogs do. Often better than people."

Some people had problems with chairlifts. The station had

responded to calls at local ski areas. A few situations defied logic. She was probably right about dogs doing better.

Thomas usually was right. He, along with the rest of the crew, had finally resigned themselves to the fact. But one of these days she'd be wrong about something. Maybe that something would be him. Christian grinned at the thought.

The Tilly Jane Cabin came into view. Outdoor enthusiasts made the most of the A-frame structure with glass windows, a woodstove and a fireplace. A local group kept the building maintained. Overnight stays were available in the sleeping loft via a reservation system, but anyone could stop in during the day to warm up and use one of the picnic tables inside. Nothing fancy, but a good place to get out of the cold, relax and eat.

Outside the cabin, he removed his skis. "I brought hot chocolate."

"One of my favorite things." Leanne stepped out of her bindings. "I've got blueberry scones."

They chatted about climbing and ate quickly.

Fifteen minutes later with skis on, they set out again. The snowfall from yesterday had covered the previous ski tracks heading up the mountain. That would mean fresh powder runs on the way down, but breaking trail on the way up. They wouldn't have a path to follow as on their way to the cabin, but would have to make their own. That meant more work.

"I'll go first," Leanne offered.

Christian let her pass him. "We can switch off."

"Sure."

She skinned up toward the Stone Hut, another shelter like the cabin built in the 1930s for people using the Timberline Trail. After they reached the hut, they would see what the conditions were like and decide whether to continue on up to Tie-in Rock.

He followed, not minding one bit about being behind her. He enjoyed this view of her backside almost as much as he had her front.

Right away Christian knew this wasn't going to be a leisurely trek up the mountain. Thomas's skinning was more like sprinting. They gained elevation fast. He felt every vertical foot. Worse, they were still below the tree line.

A couple days in a snow cave shouldn't affect him this much. But he struggled to keep up with Thomas as she skinned higher.

The climb didn't seem to bother Leanne at all. She chatted about the Civilian Conservation Corps without sounding the slightest bit winded or tired. But as she explained how the CCC had built the Tilly Jane Cabin and several of the stone huts around Mount Hood, Christian's lungs hurt.

Was Thomas some kind of mutant? A real-life Amazon? Or a robot?

No, a robot's butt wouldn't look that nice. When she wore tank tops around the station her skin looked really soft, too. Thomas must be human, but he didn't understand why she hadn't slowed her pace up the mountain.

Maybe she wanted to win the cooking dinner bet. Maybe she wanted to show off. Maybe she wanted to show him that he wasn't as excellent a skier, athlete, insert-another-noun-here as he thought he was. Probably the last one.

"Is the pace okay?" she yelled back.

No. But he wasn't about to admit that. He could hold his own. "Fine."

Rays of light sparkled off the foot of fresh powder covering the morning. A pretty setting, but he needed to focus on moving higher.

Christian forced himself forward. One step. And another.

He couldn't breathe. Okay, he could. Or he'd be flat on his back unconscious. He just couldn't breathe very well.

Damn. If Thomas saw him like this, she wouldn't slow down. She'd turn around.

No way. Christian didn't want to be the reason they didn't make it to Tie-in Rock. He sure wasn't going to concede their bet, either.

Time to remedy the situation. Or at least hide it.

He breathed through his nose and exhaled through his

mouth. It didn't help. He tried the other way around. Still nothing.

His lungs burned like a three-alarm fire.

The distance between him and Thomas increased. She skinned uphill as if a pack of wolves chased after her. An exhausting pace, one that left him gasping for breath. But she looked like poetry in motion, her skis and her poles in perfect coordination.

Christian wanted to know her secret.

She glanced back. "Such a gorgeous day."

"Uh-huh." He couldn't talk with his breathing so ragged.

Facing forward, she broke trail as if she were walking across wet sand, not twelve inches of new snow.

The woman amazed him. Christian thought he was in shape. Not even close when it came to Thomas. She had the lungs of a world-class athlete. The legs, too. She would easily lap him if they decided to do more than one run today.

Christian winced at his words of challenge from last night. So much for trying to impress her. All he'd done was prove he was an idiot, just as Owen had said. And she'd known it as soon as Christian opened his mouth.

A few minutes later, Thomas stopped. She removed her sunglasses.

It took him longer than he liked to catch up. His heart beat like a snare drum roll.

"Let's take a break," she said.

His ego wanted him to say he didn't want one, didn't need one. They had a bet riding on today. Appearing weak wouldn't get it done. But self-preservation made him nod. A little rest and maybe he'd be good to go.

Who was he kidding? Christian was still going to lose.

Thomas shrugged off her backpack. She pulled out a water bottle, thermos and her puffy jacket. She put on her coat and sat on her pack.

All he wanted to do was sit, but he removed his pack and

took out his jacket. He sat on top of his backpack and took off his sunglasses.

She took a sip of water then passed the bottle to him. "It's going to get cold fast if we're not moving."

Christian knew that. He put on his jacket.

"I've got tea," she said.

He should have added a bottle of oxygen to his first aid kit. "Thanks."

"The breeze is stronger up here. The snow will be wind-blown near Tie-in Rock. It might be iffy around the Stone Hut, too. We might not want to go much higher."

Relief washed over him. They wouldn't be going all the way up. He hated being a wimp, but right now all he wanted to do was slow down and breathe. He drew in much needed air and willed his heart rate to slow.

She dug in the snow with her gloved hand. The casualness of the gesture made him wonder if she was even aware of doing it. She fit so well out here.

Guilt coated the inside of his mouth. She might be disappointed about not skinning all the way to Tie-in Rock. "If you want to go up and check conditions—"

"Not today."

Christian should leave it, but he couldn't. "Earlier, you sounded excited to go up."

"I changed my mind."

"But—"

Her gaze met his in unspoken understanding. Not pity, but empathy. The tender expression in her eyes reached all the way to his heart.

She was giving him a way out without having to admit he was tired, winded and not in as good of shape as her. A way to save face even though they both knew he wasn't up to it. His respect for her increased exponentially. His admiration, too. But she didn't need to spare his ego.

"You don't have to pretend," he said.

She pulled out a plastic baggie full of trail mix. "What are you talking about?"

"I'm man enough to admit when I'm beat."

Her eyes widened. "You're conceding?"

"Only the ascent." He wanted to take a shot at beating her down. "I'm man enough to let you lead on your own turf."

"No one's ever said that to me." She sounded surprised, pleased.

"I'm not just any guy."

"You sure aren't."

Her words made Christian sit taller. "Wait until we're on my turf. Smith Rock. It'll be a different story then."

"I'm looking forward to it." Her voice held a hint of anticipation. She held up the bag of trail mix. "Hungry?"

"Yes." Thomas handed him the bag, and he took some. "Thanks."

She leaned back and gazed off into the distance. "I love it out here."

Christian followed her line of sight—a beautiful view of the Eliot Glacier. Snow, rock and blue sky greeted him. "Wow."

"*Wow* sums it up perfectly. I couldn't imagine living anywhere else in the world. I wouldn't want to."

He looked back at her. His breath caught in his throat.

Joy radiated from Thomas.

Beautiful. Serene. Two adjectives he'd never used with Thomas before fit her now.

Thomas inhaled deeply. She leaned her head back farther. Her jacket opened. Her thermal shirt tightened across her breasts.

Hot. Christian's pulse skyrocketed. If not for every muscle aching and his gasping for breath...

No, he still couldn't make a move on her. But he could enjoy the view. Christian shouldn't, but he sneaked a peek for a few extra—

"Up here," she said. "I feel as if I'm that much closer to heaven."

Jerk. He was leering at her breasts like a randy teenager while she was opening up to him. Christian wanted to redeem himself. "A good feeling."

She glanced his way. Her gaze locked on his.

His heartbeat stumbled.

"The best," she said.

Thomas removed another plastic baggie from her backpack. She broke off a small piece of a half-eaten scone and held it in the air.

A gray bird with a white forehead appeared out of nowhere and landed on Thomas's hand. The small beak picked at the scone. "Gray jays love people food."

"I've heard about them, but never seen one up close." He studied the bird. "So tame eating right off your palm like that."

"They don't migrate." She added more food to her hand. The bird helped itself. "They hoard food so they have enough to last through winter."

"Or steal yours."

Her gaze softened, making his heart beat in double time. She was attractive, sexy, dangerous. He bet she would want to call the shots when it came to romance. She might even be too much for him to handle. He definitely couldn't keep up with her out here, but she was still oh-so-tempting.

"Not stealing," she said. "I'm giving the food to him."

"It could be a her."

"They do look alike." She handed him the baggie. "Try it."

"I don't want to take your little bird away."

She smiled. "Gray jays travel in pairs."

"Everyone needs a wingman," he teased.

"Gray jays are monogamous."

He made a face.

"Let me guess," she said. "You hate that word as much as you dislike relationship, girlfriend, commitment."

"Yeah, but how do you know that?"

"Jake, Sean and Bill." She watched the bird eat. "A few other guys in the unit. And the station."

"You have a lot of guy friends."

"Occupational hazard in my line of work, but I have a few girlfriends."

Christian remembered what she'd said at her town house. "Zoe Hughes."

Leanne placed a little of the scone on her hand. "Carly Porter and Hannah Willingham, too."

Two more gray jays flew down from the trees and landed on his arm. "Monogamous, huh? I'd like to know how the third one gets to come along. Never knew birds could be so kinky."

She released a drawn out sigh. "Get you're mind out of the gutter, Welton. Sometimes a younger bird stays with the parents or an older couple for a while. Nothing kinky."

"Sticking around your family is boring." He put out more of the scone for the birds. "Kinky is lots more fun."

"Family is wonderful."

"Not when they want you to leave the place you love and move home."

Christian's shoulder muscle stiffened. He'd said more than he intended.

"Your family doesn't like you living in Hood Hamlet."

It wasn't a question. But he didn't want to leave her hanging the way she'd left him. "No, but I love it here. I'm not about to be pressured into moving back to the Willamette Valley, no matter what they offer me."

"But they're family." The passion in her voice surprised him. Her eyes deepened to that sexy dark chocolate color. She touched his arm. "Family is so important, Welton. You have no idea how lucky you are to have people who love you so much. Find a way to work things out. Compromise."

Christian had never seen Thomas act this way. He liked her hand on his, the pressure firm but comfortable. "My grandfather doesn't know the meaning of the word compromise. He'll do whatever it takes to force me to do what he wants."

Her fingers squeezed his hand. "Force you?"

"Bribe me is probably a better way to describe it, but I've

held my ground," Christian said. "When I was younger I needed to figure out what I wanted out of life. He didn't want me to leave, even though I needed to figure out what was important to me and what wasn't."

She pulled her hand away. "What did you do?"

"I packed my car and left home for eighteen months."

Her mouth gaped. "A year and a half? What did you do for all that time?"

"Rock climbed," he said. "All over the United States. Tuolumne, Eastern Sierras, Tetons, Boulder Canyon, City of Rocks, Devil's Tower, Vedauwoo. The list goes on. I lived like a dirtbag. Slept in my car or tent. Washed in bathrooms. Avoided private investigators my grandfather sent after me. Had the time of my life."

"Why'd you stop?" she asked.

"Got tired of living like a dirtbag. The investigator caught up with me. I missed my family. I realized they were important to me, after all."

But he hadn't been important to one of them, to his ex-fiancée. Christian didn't want to think about her and what she'd wanted him to do.

Thomas's gaze never left his. "It had to be better when you went home."

He nodded. "Until I became a volunteer firefighter. I was working at the winery, too, but that wasn't enough for my grandfather. He offered me one hundred thousand dollars. Handed me a check with my name on it. A year's salary up-front. I just had to quit firefighting and only work at the winery."

"That's a lot of money to turn down."

Christian stared off into the distant. "I liked working at the winery, but I loved firefighting. I wanted to do both. I knew I could do both. No way could I accept the money. My dad always took whatever carrot my grandfather dangled. Giving into that pressure cost my dad his marriage to my mother and his life. He died of a heart attack from all the stress when he was in his forties."

"I'm so sorry, Christian."

"Thanks," he said. "My dad made his own choices, and I'm making mine. If I choose to do something, it's going to be on my terms, not someone else's."

"Makes sense," she agreed. "Have you explained this to your family?"

"I've tried, but…"

"Maybe it's time to try again," she encouraged.

Christian stared at the three birds—a family. He hadn't felt like part of his family until the rescue on the mountain. "Maybe I should. The rescue seems to have changed things. My grandfather wants the family Christmas celebration to be in Hood Hamlet even though he's never visited me before. He's rented a huge house for all of us."

"That sounds wonderful."

"We'll see. Nothing has ever come without strings attached," he admitted. "We might end up having a very blue Christmas."

"I'm sure it'll be great." She sounded sincere and a bit wistful. "Families should be together on Christmas."

"Is your family around here?" he asked.

"Not too far away location wise, but in a completely different place."

"I know that feeling."

Her eyes clouded, but she didn't say anything.

The three birds flew away.

She watched them go then placed her baggie inside her pack. "Ready to ski?"

"I could skin up a little farther."

Leanne eyed him cautiously.

"If I'm the one breaking trail." And setting the pace. Otherwise, he'd be doomed.

"Go for it." She winked. "I want to see what you've got."

Her playfulness pleased him. All of her did. Being with

Thomas out here was cool even though she'd kicked his butt skinning. "Great."

"Yeah." Her grin seemed a constant up here on the mountain. "I'll have more energy to beat you down."

Her eyes sparkled and matched the beaming smile on her face. A fresh pink colored her cheeks. He'd never seen a woman so full of life, healthy and vibrant.

Christian stared at her mouth. He wanted to know what her lips tasted like. "I knew there had to be a catch."

"There's always a catch, Welton. Sometimes you get lucky and other times you don't."

He flashed his most devilishly charming smile. Most women appreciated it. Maybe Thomas would. "I like getting lucky."

"Feeling lucky today?"

Her flirty tone sent his temperature up ten degrees. "Yeah."

She brushed the crumbs off her lap and stood. "Then let's get going. I have a bet to win."

"I still have a chance."

Not with skiing, but with her.

She gave him the once-over. "I never knew you were such an optimist, Welton."

"I always knew you were so cynical," he teased.

Amusement twinkled in her eyes. "Try it, you might like it."

He'd like to try something, all right. He was pretty sure he'd like it. Her.

She drank a sip of water. The tip of her tongue darted out and ran over her lips.

Christian liked flirting with her. He liked being with her. The more he learned about Thomas, the more intrigued he became. His usual tricks weren't going to work with someone like her. She was so confident, so comfortable with men.

A challenge, yes. But not as impossible a one as Christian had first believed. He saw signs that he was cracking that hard shell of hers. She came out skiing. She flirted. He was finally getting to her. He wasn't about to give up now.

* * *

With a potent mix of excitement and adrenaline pounding through her veins, Leanne skied through the trees and the knee-deep powder. The one good thing to come from the Gnarl Ridge fire was additional ski terrain. She made the most of it today.

With Welton.

Watching him get winded on the ascent and trying to pretend as though nothing was wrong made her want to laugh. But he'd impressed her by stopping the charade and admitting defeat. She respected that. Not many men were as sure of themselves as he was.

She would love spending more time with him. He was easy to talk with, easy to hang with and easy on the eyes. He was probably easy when it came to other things.

Nope. Better not let her lonely mind to go there with the handsome firefighter. For all she knew, he might not be ready to settle in Hood Hamlet. He had things to work out with his family. He could decide to take off on another extended road trip to figure out what was important in his life now.

Leanne stopped. The edges of her skis sent snow flying into the air. She turned uphill to watch Welton ski.

Pretty impressive. She had to give him credit. Even after she'd lapped him doing extra runs—two in her case—he hadn't cursed, shot her dagger-worthy stares or puked. Definitely a different kind of guy.

Welton stopped next to her, spraying her with powder. "You're one badass, Thomas. I can't believe you lapped me and still beat me down another time."

"You sure know how to sweet-talk a lady."

"You're no lady. Not the way you just booked down the mountain. Not to mention up it."

"I'll take that as a compliment."

"Go right ahead. It is one."

That meant a lot to her. "I'm up for one more run."

Christian stared at her in disbelief. Shock, really.

She tried not to laugh. "But we can call it a day."

"You're a total ringer." He sounded amused, not upset. "You wore me out on purpose."

"Guilty as charged," she admitted. "But you deserved it for being so cocky and arrogant."

He flashed her a lopsided smile. "What if I was only trying to impress you?"

Was he serious? That would be so sweet. No, he had to be joking. "Yeah, right."

Christian didn't say anything. But that didn't mean he hadn't been teasing her.

"You did better than I thought you would. Better than a lot of guys have in the past," she admitted. "And that's a compliment, in case you were wondering."

"I'll take it." He drank water. "Can anybody keep up with you?"

"Sean Hughes. Well, before his accident last Thanksgiving, but he's getting back to where he used to be," she said. "But it's not as if I always try to ski people into the ground."

"So the bet—"

"I really like your Chicken Marsala."

Welton laughed. "I never stood a chance."

"There's always a chance," she said. "Do you want to go double or nothing?"

His smile crinkled the corners of his eyes and made Leanne's heart want to sigh. "I may be younger than you, Thomas. But I'm not stupid. No sucker bets for me anymore."

"You pick up quick, Welton."

Wicked laughter lit his eyes. "You should see what else I can pick up."

"I can imagine."

"I'd be happy to show you for real…"

The invitation hung in the air. Joking again or flirting this time? Maybe a combination?

Temptation drew her closer to him. She forced her legs to stop moving.

Silly. This was Welton. He knew better. So did she. He had to be joking. Just like at the station. Yet a part of her wished…

No, that was loneliness talking. Leanne couldn't cross that line with Welton. She couldn't take that chance even if he made her feel like…a woman. So not good. All she'd ever wanted was to fit in. She'd done that in spades both at the fire station and with OMSAR. She didn't need Welton—okay, her attraction to him—to mess that up for her.

Today had been fun. Much better than skiing solo. She enjoyed his company. But being anything other than skiing or climbing partners didn't make sense. They were at different places. Not so much age-wise, but in life. Welton liked playing the field. When she started dating again, she wanted to find Mr. Right. Best not to get too attached to him. Too close.

Leanne raised her chin. "Thanks, but I'll pass. Call Rachel or Alexa. I'm sure one of them would be happy to oblige. You've still got a few days until the breakup deadline."

Welton laughed. Definitely joking. Good.

Disappointment squeezed her chest. She adjusted her grip on her poles.

Confusion knotted Leanne's stomach. Her reaction made no sense. She wasn't looking for fun or a fling. She wanted forever.

No matter how handsome or charming or entertaining, Welton wasn't a forever kind of guy. Leanne gave him a long, hard look. Not even close.

CHAPTER SEVEN

THREE days later, Leanne stood outside Mr. Freeman's General Store on Main Street. She'd come straight from her shift. Only a few skiers, snowboarders and people heading to their jobs were out, but she noticed a change in Hood Hamlet.

Excitement buzzed in the air. So did optimism. Possibility. Hope. It was all due to one person. Welton.

She stared at the flyer she'd hung in the window.

Leanne had to laugh. She'd been wrong. Not about Christmas magic. That didn't exist. But she'd been wrong about the celebration he'd proposed.

Believe it or not, his pipe dream was becoming a reality.

The adage many hands made light work had never been truer. Adults and children, merchants and stay-at-home moms were helping to make the event happen. The downturn in the economy had hurt all of them. Now they saw a chance to change things, if they worked together.

The community effort warmed her heart.

Leanne loved Hood Hamlet. She had since the first time she visited her grandparents when she was a little girl, but seeing everyone work on the celebration made the small town feel that much more special.

Amid the snow-covered street and icicles hanging from the buildings, the sounds and sights of Christmas increased by the day. White lights and garland were a Hood Hamlet tradition, but not the lighted figurines and festive trees that had been added. The charming window displays in storefronts were new, too.

So much work. So much effort. So much love for this town and each other. She hugged the stack of flyers in her hands against her chest, careful not to wrinkle them.

Footsteps crunched on the sidewalk. Chains on tourists' cars rattled against the snow-covered road. "It's Beginning to Look a Lot Like Christmas" played from a speaker outside Muffy Steven's coffee shop. The sound of someone whistling along with the tune carried on the cold air.

Recognition blasted through her. Welton whistled at the station, too. Leanne glanced left. A family of five with a dog barreled down the street. The Norwegian elkhound pulled against the leash. She looked right, past two snowboarders.

There he was.

Taller than the others, Welton strode in her direction. He wore a striped beanie on his head. He'd changed out of the station's navy colored uniform into jeans, a blue jacket and winter boots.

His gaze met hers.

Leanne's pulse kicked up a notch. The casual style of clothing looked so great on him, almost as if he'd stepped off the pages of an outdoor magazine spread. But his killer smile made her breath catch in her throat.

Wowza. She liked seeing his smile directed straight at her. Liked it a lot. Leanne swallowed. Probably too much.

He stopped in front of her. Amusement gleamed in his eyes. "Didn't we just spend the night together?"

Heat rose up her neck. Had her face just given her away? "You, me and seven others."

"With all this time we're spending together, people are going to talk."

"It's the fifth day in row."

His gaze sharpened with interest. "You've been counting."

Uh-oh. Leanne liked being with him, but she didn't want him to get the wrong idea. "I'm only counting so I'll know when I can go back to doing what I want on my days off."

"Ski."

"And climb." Her words sounded lame. "I still haven't decorated my Christmas tree yet."

"Eight more days. That's all we have left."

She thought he liked working and spending time with her. The fact he didn't bristled. "You've been counting, too."

He glanced across the street at a family of skiers loading their gear into a minivan. "Not for the same reason as you."

What did he mean by that?

"Too bad we're not skiing this morning," he continued.

Leanne would rather be skiing with him today. Not him specifically, she corrected. Any one of her ski partners.

She straightened. The top of her head came close to the tip of his nose. Welton redefined the expression tall, dark and handsome. "Well, your event isn't going to happen without some work. You had to realize that would mean our days off."

A sheepish expression crossed his face. "I didn't really think that part through."

She laughed. "Figured as much."

He motioned to the store window. "So that's the flyer."

"Tim Moreno had them for me at the snowboard shop. Mr. Freeman waved me down to get his." She read the colorful flyer hanging on the front window of the store. "Come celebrate Christmas Magic in Hood Hamlet with a day of small town holiday fun and old-fashioned good cheer."

"Zoe did an amazing job designing it," Welton said. "I like the photograph of Main Street she used. Is it one of yours?"

Leanne was pleased he remembered her photography. "I took the picture at the tree lighting ceremony the day after Thanksgiving. The fresh snow, white lights and giant decorated Douglas fir screamed Christmastime to me."

He cocked an eyebrow. "You really aren't a Grinch except when it comes to…"

"Let's leave Christmas magic out of this, 'kay?" She handed him half the stack of papers. "We need to get these passed out."

He waved his flyers. "The list of activities has grown."

"More people stepped up after the meeting. Carly asked if we minded. I told her to do what she felt would be best for Hood Hamlet. That's what she did."

"Caroling, concerts, dogsled rides, horse drawn sleigh rides, a snowboarding demo, a snow-sculpture contest."

Leanne nodded. "Don't forget the craft bazaar, cookie decorating, card making, beer and wine tasting and the dinner and silent auction to benefit Hood Hamlet Fire and Rescue's Christmas Toy Drive and OMSAR."

"Not bad with only a few days planning."

"Not bad at all," she agreed. "People might show up."

Christian grinned wryly. "Admit it. You're impressed."

Grudging respect grew, too. "I...am."

"Knew it."

She hoped that was all he knew. Her attraction intensified each time she saw him. Better get away from him now. "You canvas that side of the street. I'll do this one."

Leanne took two steps toward Wickett's Pharmacy that served the best chocolate malts at an old-fashioned soda counter.

Welton touched her shoulder. "Wait."

She stopped, conscious of his hand on her even though she wore a camisole, a turtleneck, a fleece pullover and a soft-shell jacket. His light touch made her feel tingly. "What?"

"What's the rush? We have all day. Let's grab a cup of coffee. Do this together." He lowered his arm to his side. "I want to discuss a few things about the dinner."

Tempting, but she couldn't give in to it. She had to fight her attraction. "We have a lot to accomplish today. The flyers need to be taken to all the surrounding towns, too. And I have plans this afternoon."

"A date."

The guy needed to stop jumping to conclusions. "Babysitting."

His brows furrowed. "Babysitting?"

"Watching other people's children."

"I know what babysitting is." Christian sounded annoyed. Good. That was how he made her feel. "Whose kids?"

Austin and Kendall were biologically Nick's kids, but Garrett had adopted them. "Hannah and Garrett Willingham's."

"Okay," Christian said after a long moment. "Let's split up so we can get the flyers passed out faster. Call Hannah when you can and ask if she minds if I come over to babysit with you."

Leanne laughed. "Yeah, right."

But Christian wasn't smiling.

"Come on." Perplexed, she stared. "You can't be serious."

His eyes darkened to a midnight-blue. "Why not?"

"You don't look like the babysitting type."

"There's a babysitter profile?"

"Mary Poppins. Nanny McPhee."

He made a face. "We need to talk about the dinner. It's important."

"Yes, but—"

"I've watched kids before."

"What kids?"

"My niece." He sounded offended she'd question him. "My cousins have kids, too."

Okay, the guy was an adult, but she'd seen Paulson around kids. She gave Welton a dubious look.

"Kids like me. Ask Owen. Not that you need to call him or anything." A vein throbbed at Christian's jaw. "After the kids go to bed, you and I can work on the event."

"I don't know."

"Only eight more days to go. The longer we procrastinate—"

"I'm not procrastinating," she interrupted. "It's all happening so quickly."

"Quick is good."

"If you're climbing light and fast, yes," she said. "But if not, it's better to take your time and think things through carefully."

"There's not time for that."

Unfortunately, she knew he was right. That made this… harder.

"Ask Hannah," he said.

The papers in Leanne's hands crinkled. She loosened her grip on them. "The kids will expect you to play with them."

"Call her."

He sounded earnest, but… "Don't say I didn't warn you."

"I stand duly warned," he said. "It'll be fun."

Maybe for him. Not for her.

She was having too many odd and inappropriate thoughts involving Welton. Playing house with the hot firefighter was a recipe for disaster. One she couldn't afford. Time to take charge of the situation and stop spending so much time with him. The solution didn't appeal to her, but she didn't have a choice. She had to put an end to this now.

"You know, I'm sure you've got lots to do, Welton. Women-to-woo. Hearts to break before your second Monday in December deadline." She moistened her dry lips. "Forget about being cochair on the event. You've kicked it off. Turned it into reality. That's enough. I'll take care of the rest myself."

His eyes darkened, narrowed. "You're already in charge of the toy drive."

"I don't mind." For her self-preservation, she needed to convince him this was the best, the only. "So many of the jobs have been delegated already."

He studied her.

"Really," she said, in case he had any doubts.

Christian was thinking about it. She could tell. This was going to work.

"Sorry, Thomas," he said finally. "I can't dump all this on you in addition to the toy drive. That wouldn't be fair."

"Fair?" Her voice rose. She lowered it. "I've seen you play Ultimate Frisbee and darts. Fair isn't part of your vocabulary."

"Those things involve winning. I don't like to lose. But this is different. We're going to be cochairs and I'm babysitting with you, too."

The sincerity in his voice threw her for a loop.

Maybe he wanted to work with her, spend time with her.

Her pulse skittered. She was flattered. Interested. What was she going to do?

"After you talk to Hannah, text me her address and the time you want me there," he continued.

Leanne wanted to know what was going on. "Is there any other reason you're going to so much trouble?"

"What do you mean?" he asked.

"Ever since the mountain rescue, you've been acting different. Not that you weren't nice before, but you've been going out of your way for the toy drive and OMSAR."

And me.

He shifted his weight. "You and OMSAR did something nice for me. I'm returning the favor."

Irritation revved. "I told you that isn't necessary."

"It is to me."

Leanne ignored the unexpected twinge of disappointment. Pathetic.

She was one of the guys in his eyes. That was the way Leanne wanted it to be, but...

Being one of the guys all the time was getting really old. For the first time, she wished she knew how she could change that. Especially with...Welton.

That afternoon, Christian parked behind Thomas's car in the Willinghams' driveway. White icicle lights hung from the roof of the log cabin. A snowman wearing a rainbow-striped scarf stood in the front yard. A lone electric candle sat on a windowpane, flickering as if it were a real flame. Light glowed from the other windows. With the tall fir trees surrounding the cabin, the scene looked like something from a Christmas card.

Quaint. Homey. Inviting. He liked it.

Christian exited the truck. His boots sunk into the snow as he made his way toward the porch.

Babysitting gave him the perfect excuse not to see Alexa or Rachel tonight. He really needed to tell them it was over. At least until after Christmas. But he would probably find someone else to go out with after that.

Too bad it couldn't be Thomas, but she wanted nothing to do with him that way. She'd laughed off his asking her out when they were skiing. She'd thought he was joking, but he'd been serious. Not that he blamed her. The fire station romance taboo complicated things.

Still he preferred working with her on the Christmas celebration than going out with either of the other women. Thomas acted so serious, yet she was quick with a smile or a laugh. Genuine ones. Not fake ones to appear more interested in him. She was more comfortable to be around, didn't probe into his feelings or make him feel as if she wanted…more. She wanted nothing from him. That was so different than most everyone else in his life.

Christian climbed the porch steps.

A green wreath with a red velvet bow hung from a brass holder on the front door. The same wreath Thomas had on her door. Someone's kid must sell them.

He stood on the landing.

The sharp scent of pine filled the air. He inhaled. The smell of Christmas. Well, Christmas in Hood Hamlet.

At the winery, some holidays were less traditional than others. The year before last everything had smelled like eucalyptus around the house, even the tree. The Norman Rockwell and Thomas Kincaid versions of Christmas complete with evergreens, holly and snow appealed to Christian more than whatever current decorating trend happened to be hot. At least the family decorated, even if everything had been handpicked ahead of time by an interior designer.

He knocked on the door.

A stampede of feet sounded from inside the house. Someone yelled. Another giggled.

The door swung open. Two kids greeted him with wide grins. One was a girl around eleven or twelve. The other a boy, maybe nine or ten.

"We've been waiting for you. Leanne saw your truck out the window and told us we could open the door." The girl opened the door wider. "Come in."

"Thanks." Christian entered and closed the door behind him. Heat from the fireplace blanketed him. So did the smell of chocolate baking. He extended his arm toward her. "I'm Christian."

The girl shook his hand. "I'm Kendall."

"I'm Austin." The boy also shook Christian's hand. "You had to be rescued off the mountain."

Out of the cold and into the fire. The kid had no idea how that statement made Christian feel. No matter where he went in town someone brought it up. Maybe if the event were successful, everyone would forget what happened up on the mountain. He shrugged off his jacket and hung it on a rack by the door. "Yes. OMSAR rescued me and my cousin."

Kendall beamed. "OMSAR rocks."

"They do," Christian agreed.

Austin studied him. "It's good what happened."

The kid was the first one who had said what happened was good. "You think so, dude?"

He nodded. "Better to be rescued than be dead."

That was one way to look at it. "I'm very happy to be alive."

"Our daddy was a member of OMSAR, but he died climbing the Reid Headwall," Kendall said. "It was an accident."

Nick Bishop. Christian should have put two and two together before this. "Accidents happen sometimes."

Both kids nodded. They stared at him as if they expected him to do a magic trick or something.

"Where's Leanne?" he asked.

Austin scrunched his face. "She's upstairs changing Tyler's poopy diaper."

"So you're a firefighter like Bill and Leanne," Kendall said.

"Yes, I am."

Kendall studied Christian as if he were a science experiment. "Bill's not married. Are you?"

"Nope."

"Do you date as many girls as him?" Austin asked.

"Not quite as many." But pretty darn close.

"Good." The boy sounded relieved. "Sammy Ross says if you kiss too many girls you'll wind up with some horrible disease."

Christian stifled a laugh. His gaze bounced between the two kids who waited expectedly for a response. What could he say? He wasn't versed in having a conversation about the birds and the bees with preteens. "I, uh—"

"Sammy Ross has three older sisters," Austin added sagely.

"That explains it," Christian said. "I have an older sister, too."

"Do you want to get married?" Kendall asked.

Christian had been imagining playing a couple of games of Twister with a certain female paramedic and OMSAR member tonight, not being examined at an inquisition by two precocious kids.

"Maybe someday?" He glanced toward the stairs. How long did a diaper change take? "If I met the right person."

Two lines formed above Kendall's nose. "Leanne's nice. She's not married."

A twelve-year-old playing matchmaker. He shifted his weight between his feet. "Yeah, but we work together."

Both kids looked at him as if he'd grown a third eye and horns.

"Leanne and I are just friends," he clarified.

Austin sighed. "That's what Uncle Jake and Aunt Carly used to say, but the next thing you know, they're kissing."

Kendall nodded. "Then I got to be a flower girl at their wedding. And now we have a new cousin. Nicole is so cute."

That was okay if you wanted to be on the family plan; Christian preferred being single. Women always wanted something in return for loving you. They also wanted you to be someone you weren't.

Christian's gaze strayed to the front door. Okay, Thomas had warned him. But he hadn't expected all these personal questions. He needed to find a way to distract the kids. And fast.

The Christmas tree with twinkling multicolored lights, popcorn-and-cranberry strung garland, silver bells, gold balls and all sorts of one-of-a-kind ornaments caught his attention. "Nice tree."

"We cut it down ourselves," Austin announced.

"With help from our dad and Uncle Jake," Kendall added.

The house where Christian lived had no decorations. No tree. No wreath. No lights. But he and his roommates would put something up eventually.

Last year, Riley had found a Charlie Brown worthy tree two days before Christmas. They'd decorated it with chili pepper shaped lights, poker chips and playing cards. The angel on top had wings, but wasn't quite angelic looking with her ample hourglass figure.

Christian liked the Willinghams' tree better. "Who wants to tell me about the special ornaments on the tree?"

The kids rushed for the tree nearly knocking each other over in the rush to pick out an ornament.

He followed, a smile warming his heart.

Austin pointed to a teddy bear on a rocking horse. "This one is from when I was a baby. It was my first Christmas. But I don't remember it."

"What was all that noise?" a familiar feminine voice asked. "Did a herd of elephants stop by looking for some peanuts?"

Christian turned and sucked in a sharp breath.

Leanne stood on the bottom stair with a toddler in her arms. The boy sucked his right thumb and twirled the hair at the end of her braid with his left hand. A smudge of flour was on her cheek. More covered the front of her red-and-green apron, including two distinct kid-size handprints.

The little boy glanced up at her with total adoration. A wide smile broke across Thomas's face.

Christian's heart lurched. She looked like a...mom.

"I see you've met Kendall and Austin." Her tender gaze went to each one of the kids. "This is Tyler. He'll be two on December 23."

Tyler rested his head against Thomas's shoulder. He looked perfectly content cradled in her arms.

Lucky kid. Christian's stomach felt funny. Might have been the grande burrito from lunch.

Austin wrinkled his nose. "Does he still stink?"

"Nope," Thomas said. "He's all clean with a new diaper."

Austin exhaled loudly. "Thank goodness. Was it green?"

"Not this time," she said.

Thomas joined them in the living room. She wore no shoes, only socks. Colorful ones with stripes and polka dots. "So what's going on?"

"We're telling Christian about some of the ornaments." Kendall pointed to a pink-and-purple snowboard hanging from one of the branches. "This one is from Sean. He gave me the ornament and a matching board last Christmas."

"Me, too." Austin pointed out his blue-and-red snowboard ornament. "But Uncle Jake says we still have to keep skiing."

"Your uncle Jake is a smart man," Thomas said.

That sounded more like her. Good. Christian wasn't sure what to make of the motherly version when she always seemed so hard-nosed and detached at the station. This new side of her made him a little light-headed.

"It's easier to learn how to skin with skis," she continued. "You can always switch to a split board when you're older and know how to snowboard really well."

"The kids go into the back country?" Christian asked.

"They've gone a couple of times when the conditions were right," she said.

Kendall sighed. "I can't wait until I'm old enough to climb the mountain."

"A few more years, sweetie, then we will." Affection filled Thomas's voice. "I can't wait to see you standing on that summit. Just like your dad used to."

Dad equaled Nick. The guy must have been something special based on how everyone in OMSAR talked about him. But Thomas's sincerity and love for these kids left Christian feeling a little off balance. He sat on a nearby rocking chair.

Kendall beamed.

Tyler wiggled in her arms. "Dow-dow."

Thomas laughed. "Okay, big man, I'll put you down."

Amazing. Christian stared captivated. He'd watched her be sweet and gentle with Owen, but Christian never thought he would hear Thomas sound so nurturing. He didn't need mothering, but he wouldn't mind her caring for him like that.

As the kids pointed out special ornaments, he tried to reconcile the woman in front of him with the strong, athletic, badass he knew from the station, mountain rescue and back country skiing. Tried and failed.

He liked paramedic, mountain rescuer Thomas, but something about this Mother Earth Thomas appealed to him at a gut level. He didn't want a wife, but a fling sounded good.

She placed the boy on his feet, but didn't let go of him until she knew he was stable. "There you go, Tyler."

The kid toddled toward the tree. "Bah."

Christian watched Leanne follow after the kid. Not quite hovering, but close enough to catch if he fell. His sister, Brianna, did the same thing with his niece. Brianna was pregnant again, due on January 2. Her husband, Jeff, kept joking he wanted the baby to be born by the 31st for the tax write-off.

"Bah means box," Kendall translated. "Tyler likes boxes."

Austin nodded. "All of his *B* words sound the same."

"Just wait," Leanne said. "This time next year, Tyler will have a much bigger vocabulary."

A buzzer sounded from another room. It reminded him of an oven timer.

The kids cheered. Even little Tyler joined in.

Christian's gaze locked with Thomas's brown eyes. Something jolted inside him. Must be his lunch. "What's cooking?"

"A Yule Log," Kendall answered.

"What's that?" Christian asked.

Austin jumped up and down. "A special Christmas cake."

"It's also known as *Bûche de Noël*," Leanne explained.

Austin placed his palms together then spread them apart. "Imagine a giant Ho-Ho. Only better."

Christian laughed. "Better than a Ho-Ho, huh? That has to be a really special cake."

Enthusiastic nods answered him.

"Come on. We don't want the cake to overcook." Thomas motioned to Tyler. "Can you grab him for me, Welton?"

The toddler climbed over an upholstered ottoman as if it were a boulder project. A devilish grin lit up the kid's face.

"No problem," Christian said. "I've got the size advantage."

With that, she hurried to the kitchen. Austin and Kendall followed as if Leanne were the Pied Piper.

"Come on, bud." Christian swooped the kid into his arms. "Let's go."

Tyler twisted, kicked his legs and tried to get away.

"Sorry, little dude." Two sad hazel-green eyes met Christian's. The kid looked ready to cry or scream. "Failure is not an option. Don't even think about making me look bad in front of Thomas. Leanne. Got it?"

Tyler stared at Christian as if he were crazy.

Yeah, rationalizing with a two-year-old wasn't the smartest thing he'd ever done, but the kid wasn't struggling or crying.

"Let's go see the cake," he said.

"Cake."

Christian laughed. "Hey, you said that word perfectly."

"Cake," Tyler repeated.

"Everything okay out there?" Thomas yelled.

"Fine." Christian lowered his voice. He looked at Tyler. "Come on. We'd better get in there before she sends out a search party."

CHAPTER EIGHT

LAUGHTER drowned out the Christmas music playing on the kitchen's iPod docking stereo. Leanne whipped more cream. She loved babysitting these three kids. The older two reminded her so much of her friend Nick. Kendall had inherited his have-no-fear personality. Austin looked like a mini version of his dad and had the same sense of humor.

Christian sat at the kitchen table and held Tyler on his lap. The two seemed so natural together, as if they did this every day. Unexpected, but so appealing.

Leanne could imagine Christian as a father, something she'd never thought of him as before. It took every ounce of strength not to pull out her cell phone to take a picture.

He met her gaze. "Now I see why you like babysitting."

Leanne's heart squeezed tight. "Fun times."

Austin showed off his latest hip-hop moves holding a spatula in his hand that he used as a microphone to sing "Rocking Around the Christmas Tree." Kendall sat at the table and concentrated on spreading the filling over the chocolate cake. Tyler licked a spoon covered with whipped cream.

A warm and fuzzy feeling enveloped Leanne, as comforting as a cup of hot chocolate after a day on the hill. She'd expected chaos with Welton here, but instead it almost felt as if they were a…

Family.

"You're doing great, Kendall." Christian acted like a big kid at the station, sometimes giving Paulson a run at the most immature title, but he knew how to interact with kids. Even little Tyler, who was a handful under the best of circumstances, seemed enchanted by the playful firefighter. "Remember what Leanne said. Spread the filling to a half inch of the edge."

Falling under Welton's spell would be so easy to do. Easy, Leanne reminded herself, but stupid. They worked the same shift at the only fire station in town. He dated more than one woman at once. Commitment was so clearly not his thing. But she couldn't deny her attraction.

Any woman with a pulse wouldn't be able to do that. Especially after seeing him interact with the kids. Her heart sighed.

Kendall added more whipped-cream filling to her spatula and layered it on the cake. "Like this, Christian?"

"Exactly," he said with a tender smile that could melt the thickest glacier.

Leanne swallowed and looked away.

Austin licked the homemade whipped cream off a spoon like Tyler.

Christian laughed. "Austin, dude, make sure you leave some for the cake."

"Is the chocolate frosting ready?" Kendall asked with an expectant look on her face.

"We'll make that after we roll the cake and are waiting for it to chill in the refrigerator," Leanne explained. "Don't forget we still have to eat dinner."

Tyler used his spoon to feed whipped cream to Christian. "Din-din."

None made it into Christian's mouth, but was smeared over his face instead.

Leanne chuckled.

He grinned, his straight white teeth surrounded by the whipped cream on his lips and mouth. "Thanks, little dude."

"Mo," Tyler said.

Christian laughed. "No more."

Austin scrunched his nose. "You look like a snowman."

"Or Santa Claus," Kendall offered. "The whipped cream looks like a white beard."

Leanne appreciated Christian being such a good sport about it. She grabbed a handful of napkins and handed them to him.

"Can we tell you what we want for Christmas, Santa?" Austin teased.

"Sure," Christian said. "If Santa can get a few more napkins first."

Tyler wanted to help make an even better mess. His little hands grabbed at the napkins.

"This isn't working," Christian said.

Austin giggled. "No, it's not. But you sure look funny."

"That's not nice," Kendall scolded.

"But he does," Austin countered.

Kendall nodded.

Leanne grabbed a roll of paper towels. "You hold Tyler so he can't help. And I'll wipe."

Christian's gaze met her. "Thanks."

Her mouth went dry. "I haven't done anything yet."

"It's the thought that counts."

He gave Tyler his car keys to keep the toddler's hands occupied during the cleanup. Smart man.

She ripped off several sheets. "This won't take long."

"I don't mind," Christian said in a husky tone that sent a shiver down her spine.

"You're a good sport."

As she brought the paper towel to his face, her pulse sped up like an out-of-control semitruck that lost its brakes coming down Highway 26. An odd reaction. This wasn't the first time she'd cleaned up one of the guys from the station or rescue team. This was no different than helping a climbing or ski partner, either. Well, except blood wasn't involved. Whipped cream was.

Leanne ran the paper towel over his face. Smooth. No razor stubble. She preferred the clean-cut look that most of the firefighters, including Welton, sported. The only time she'd seen him unshaven was when she found him in the snow cave or when he first woke up on their shift. The early-morning stubble did look sexy and bad boyish.

His gaze met hers again.

"Almost finished," she said.

"You missed under his chin and by his nose," Austin said.

"Yes, I did." She broke eye contact with Christian, tossed the first paper towels then grabbed more. "There's a lot of whipped cream here."

"Such a waste." Christian raised a brow. "I can think of some much better uses for it."

So could Leanne.

Fluffy, yummy, sexy. Lots of different uses for whipped cream popped into her mind. None of them rated G.

She fought the urge to fan herself. When had it gotten so hot in here?

Too bad Welton wasn't interested in dating past Monday.

Wait a sec. She wasn't looking to date him.

"The whipped cream should be on the cake," Kendall said.

Thank you, Kendall. Leanne's mind had been going elsewhere. Time to focus. The sooner she finished, the better.

Wiping Welton's face felt different than cleaning up a co-worker, team member or climbing partner. Intimate. Even with three pint-size chaperones.

Worse, she liked it. Liked cleaning him up. Liked being close enough to smell the scent of his soap and shampoo.

Uh-oh. Better get some distance. Fast.

"There." Leanne wiped off the last bit from Christian's face. She balled the napkin so the whipped cream was trapped inside. As she tossed the paper towels into the garbage can, her hands shook. She pressed them against her sides. "All done."

"Yep," Austin agreed. "You got it all."

Kendall nodded.

Christian's gaze remained on Leanne. "You're going to have to let me return the favor."

Her stomach tingled. The look he gave her. His saying her

name… She couldn't have responded even if she'd known what to say.

Kendall scraped the bowl of whipped cream with her spatula. "No worries. There's enough to finish the cake."

Leanne forced herself to look away. She wiped her hands. "You're right, Kendall. Spread the rest of the filling while I take Tyler upstairs to change his clothes."

Christian stood with a whipped-cream-covered Tyler in his arms. "Do you want me to take him up?"

Leanne met them in the doorway. She held out her arms. Tyler went to her without any fuss. "Thanks, but I know where everything is."

"I'll supervise these two."

The older kids cheered.

"You have a fan club," Leanne said.

Amusement gleamed in Christian's eyes. "The more members the merrier."

Very charming. She would give him that. "We'll be back."

"Wait." Austin pointed at the kitchen doorway. "You're standing under the mistletoe."

Leanne glanced up. Sprigs of mistletoe with holly berries hung from a red ribbon attached to the top of the doorway with a thumbtack. She kissed Tyler's forehead. "A mistletoe kiss for my favorite almost two-year-old."

"Don't forget Christian," Kendall said.

"Yeah." His eyes filled with mischief. "Your favorite firefighter needs a kiss under the mistletoe."

Leanne inhaled sharply. A kiss sounded like a bad idea. If only because the thought of kissing him appealed to her.

"You have to kiss," Austin urged. "It's tradition."

"I'm all for tradition." Christian looked at Leanne. "What about you?"

"Oh, she's all for tradition, too," Kendall said with certainty. "Isn't that right?"

"Yes." Leanne lowered her voice to a mere whisper. "This is only for the kids. Got it?"

Christian nodded once.

She rose up on her tiptoes to kiss his cheek. As she neared his face, Christian turned his head. Her mouth landed right on his lips.

Something sparked. Static electricity? Leanne had no idea. She only knew his kiss was hot, oh-so-very hot. It burned, but in a very good way.

His lips moved over hers as if they'd done it a million times, but she'd never been kissed so thoroughly in her entire life. Heat rushed through her veins. Her heart rate quadrupled.

Something touched her face. Sweet, sticky.

Her eyelids flew open.

Tyler.

Oh, no. No. She jerked away from Christian. Welton. What had she done?

The surprise in his eyes matched the way she felt inside. She looked at the kids at the table. Big grins lit up their faces. "Satisfied?"

They both nodded.

"Well, I'm not," Christian whispered.

"Too bad," she whispered back. "You were only supposed to get a peck on the cheek."

"I knew you were going to say that." Amusement laced each word. He would think this was funny. Darn him. "But a kiss on the cheek isn't in the spirit of the mistletoe tradition. It's more like sticking your tongue out at it."

All three kids stuck out their tongues.

Leanne laughed, a mix of nerves and wanting to pretend what happened hadn't meant anything when her lips still throbbed. She fought the urge to touch her mouth.

The older two kids were distracted as a new song came on. They sang along at the top of their lungs. Tyler clapped along.

"Well," she whispered to Christian. "Sticking my tongue out is better than sticking it down your throat."

"Sure about that?" His warm breath fanned her neck. "Maybe we should find out?"

Anticipation hummed through Leanne.

Heaven help her, but her lips wanted more of Welton's kisses. Worse, she was tempted to see if it was better or not.

She swallowed around the lump in her throat.

So not good.

Hours later, the kids were nestled in their beds. Christmas carols continued to play. Logs crackled in the fire. Two cups of hot chocolate sat on the coffee table.

A great night. Especially with Leanne setting next to him on the couch. She'd long since removed the apron and washed off the flour smudges.

But all he wanted to think about was her rock-his-world kiss.

Leanne kissed as well as she did everything else. She tasted so sweet and warm. Sugar and spice and everything nice. A way he hadn't expected. He wanted another taste. Without three kids watching them.

But she wanted only to work on the event.

Fine. But once they finished he wanted to get back to what they'd started in the kitchen. Even if it meant bringing the mistletoe into the living room.

"Donations for the toy drive are still low." Her laptop rested on top of her jean-covered thighs. He preferred her in well-worn jeans that accentuated the curve of her hips and a sweater that fit tight across her chest to the unisex fire station uniform.

She stared at the monitor. "But even with these conservative estimates for the dinner and silent auction, it looks like this should bring in much needed funds for OMSAR."

"You sound surprised every time it looks like the Christmas Magic celebration might be a success."

"That's to offset you," she said. "Your confidence never wavers."

"Not about this."

Curiosity shone in her eyes. "About what then?"

Damn. Christian had left that door wide-open. He searched for a noncommittal way to answer. "A few things."

"That many, huh?"

He shrugged, half laughed, wondered how he could change the subject.

"What are they?" she asked.

Christian hesitated. He wasn't one to admit weakness, but this wasn't just any woman. If he wanted to get to know her better—he did—and kiss her again—he really wanted to—he needed to talk to her. Openly. Honestly. Not something he was used to doing. He dragged his hand through his hair. "Remember when I told you about my climbing road trip?"

"Eighteen months climbing and living like a dirtbag to figure out what was important to you."

He nodded. "At the beginning of that trip my confidence wavered big-time. My family didn't want me to go. Neither did my girlfriend."

"You didn't want her to go with you?"

His collar tightened around his throat. "She didn't want to come."

"That had to be tough."

"I kept wondering if I'd made the right decision to go. If I should have stayed at the winery and got engaged instead."

"Engaged." Leanne sounded surprised. "It must have been serious."

"The most serious I've ever been." He hadn't thought of Kelly in a couple of years. "We met at OSU. We were both taking Enology and Viticulture courses. Fell in love over wine-making."

"Was the road trip the right decision?" Leanne asked.

"Definitely," he said without any hesitation. "I met amazing people and learned a lot about myself. I'd do it again in a heartbeat."

"Sounds like a trip of a lifetime."

"It was."

"What about the girlfriend? Regrets?"

"None. She didn't really love me," Christian explained. "She wanted the lifestyle being a Welton could give her and her winemaking. When I wasn't sure that was the future I wanted, she didn't want me."

"Ouch."

Kelly wanted to trade her love for a life that wasn't right for him. She was one more in a line of women who always wanted something from him that he couldn't give. The same as his family. "I got over it."

"And the other time…"

"You really want to know?" he asked.

"I do," she said. "We haven't spent a lot of time together outside of the station except for working on the celebration."

"We've backcountry skied together and babysat." And kissed.

His gazed lowered to her lips. He really wanted to kiss her again.

"Please," she said.

If only she was asking for another kiss… Christian took a deep breath. "It was on the mountain with Owen. He had more experience. All the experience. I wasn't sure I could build the snow cave right and fast enough with the storm on top of us. I'd only practiced once before. It was like starting all over as a rookie again. I was out of my element up there. I knew if I failed we would die."

There. He'd said it. Christian expected to see pity, even disgust from Thomas.

Instead her eyes softened, full of compassion. She touched his arm. "You didn't fail. You'd practiced. Many people don't even do that. You knew what you had to do and did it. You saved both your and your cousin's lives. You did well, Christian. I'd tie-in with you anytime."

Warmth flowed through him. Her hand remained on his arm, but it wasn't enough. He wanted to reach out to her, to draw her closer to him, but he hesitated.

She'd said the kiss under the mistletoe had been for the kids. Yet she'd kissed him back. Hard. That couldn't have been for the kids' sake. But for hers. And his.

Still he didn't want to make a move only to be shut down. Not with so much event planning they still had to do. Best to stop thinking about kissing her.

"Anyone would have had doubts in a situation like that," she added.

"You?"

"Heck, yeah," she admitted. "Having a lot of experience doesn't mean you know everything. Or aren't afraid."

"I never thought I'd hear you say that."

"Well, if you tell anyone I'll deny I said it." She winked. "I have a reputation to uphold."

"One of the guys."

Thomas nodded once, but she looked uncomfortable. "So…"

"So I told you mine, you tell me yours."

Her brows furrowed. "Mine?"

"When your confidence wavered or when you were afraid."

"We'd be here all night."

Christian liked spending time with Leanne, more so than any woman he'd dated in a long time. Maybe…ever. "I wouldn't mind."

"Hannah and Garrett might."

"They aren't home yet."

Leanne took a deep breath and exhaled slowly. "There was this one time on Stuart."

"Mount Stuart in Washington?" Christian asked.

She nodded. "It was sunny. Only a few clouds in the sky. Good conditions for a day climb on the West Ridge. About half-way up the weather pattern changed. It was so strange. Rain, hail, snow, sun again. We should have turned around, but we were young with one goal, the summit, so kept climbing."

"We?"

"Paulson and I." She remembered the climb as if it was yesterday, not twelve years ago. "We reached the summit and started our descent, but daylight disappeared so fast. I couldn't see the route. Neither of us was really sure where we were. Turns out we'd gotten into Ulrich's Coulior instead of the Cascadian. We ended up stuck on this narrow ledge. It downsloped so much I kept thinking I was going to slide off. We had belay jackets, but no sleeping bags or bivy sacks. The "ten essentials" were more like "ten suggestions" to us back then. I sat on my pack and my feet dangled over the edge. They were so cold, but there was really no place for them. I tried curling up in the fetal position. Paulson cuddled against me. It took a real effort to stay like that, but at least one side of us was warmer."

She tried to sound lighthearted, but Christian had done enough climbing to know being stuck out in the elements overnight was not a situation anyone wanted to be in. At least he and Owen had had a snow cave to take shelter in. "How did the night go?"

"Uncomfortable doesn't begin to describe what we went through. We kept our harnesses on and anchored ourselves as best we could. It was freezing cold. The temperature kept dropping. I shivered so badly my helmet sounded like a jackhammer against the rock behind me. We shared one of those space blankets. Neither of us wanted to fall asleep. We kept slapping each other and ourselves to stay awake and warm. Paulson and I both knew if it snowed or rained again, we would be dead. But neither of us said a word to the other. I know I didn't. I was afraid of jinxing us."

Christian placed his arm around the back of the sofa, careful to avoid her shoulders. It was the only way to get closer to her without physically touching her. "You're here, so you made it down."

She nodded. "The night seemed to last forever, but finally the sun peeked over the ridgeline. It was so beautiful to see the dawn break. As soon as there was enough light, we started our descent and figured out where we'd gone wrong. An hour later, snow started falling, but we were moving and warmer by then."

"You were lucky."

Another nod. "Learning when to turn around greatly reduced my future unplanned bivvies. Paulson's still working on that one. He and Cocoa ended up stuck in a snow cave on Hood. Though part of me thinks Paulson did that on purpose."

Christian laughed. "I wouldn't put it past him."

"Cocoa didn't seem to mind much, either."

"What about you? Did you mind them bivying?"

Leanne's forehead wrinkled. "Why would I mind?"

"You and Paulson must have gotten friendly on that ledge."

"What happens on bivy ledges stays there. Paulson and I only did what we had to do to stay warm," she explained. "If anything, our unplanned bivies over the years made it clear we should be only friends if that's what you were getting at."

"It was."

"You're sure curious about me and Paulson."

Christian shrugged. "It's hard to believe you're just friends."

"Believe it. Paulson sees me like his little sister. We can't take each other seriously most of the time." She sounded irritated. Christian didn't blame her. He shouldn't care. It's not like he wanted anything more than a fling with her. Who she dated didn't matter.

"Did we get to everything about the celebration you wanted to cover?" she asked.

"Yes."

She closed the laptop. "Thanks for coming over here tonight."

"That sounds like a good-night."

"We're finished talking business."

"We could talk about other stuff," he offered.

"It's your night off. Tomorrow we have to meet with the others about the dinner and auction," she said. "It's kind of late, but you could still hit the brewpub."

He didn't want to go anywhere. "I don't mind keeping you company."

"Hannah and Garrett should be finished Christmas shopping soon."

"We still have a little time to head back into the kitchen and stand under the mistletoe," he half joked.

She laughed, but wouldn't meet his eyes. "We could, but we both know why we can't."

He recognized that serious, all-business tone. "It's not official fire-and-rescue policy that employees can't date."

"No, but it's my policy." Her eyes darkened. "And be real, Welton, you don't want to date me."

"Okay, I don't," he admitted. "I don't want to date anybody right now, but I want to kiss you."

"I appreciate your honesty. But I told you the only reason we kissed. Tradition is very important to the kids," she explained. "The kiss was…nice. Let's leave it as that."

"The kiss was hot. And I don't want to leave it."

The song "All I Want for Christmas" played on the radio. Christian knew what he wanted.

Leanne turned to face him. "The truth is, Christian, even if you weren't a firefighter, I wouldn't kiss you again. You and I are very different."

"I'm younger."

"It's more than an age thing. I haven't dated in a while, but when I do I know exactly what I want."

"What's that?" he asked.

"Not a casual date or a fling. I want a real relationship. A serious one. Something that will last a very long time."

"I appreciate your honesty." That kind of relationship was the last thing he wanted. Still Christian couldn't forget how her kisses made him feel, how much he enjoyed being with her and talking to her. He leaned toward Leanne. "We could always share a few kisses until you're ready to find what you're looking for."

"That wouldn't be a good idea."

She backed away, but not before he glimpsed the longing in her dark chocolate eyes.

A-ha. "You want me to kiss you."

Leanne stared at the Christmas tree. "Don't complicate things, Welton."

She hadn't said no. That meant yes. A smug smile settled on his lips. "Kisses won't complicate anything."

"We don't want the same things."

"True, but that doesn't mean we can't have a little fun in the meantime."

She wouldn't meet his eyes.

"I am going to kiss you again, Leanne Thomas," he said. "Even if it means I have to buy all the mistletoe in Hood Hamlet to do it."

"Please…"

"Kiss you," he offered.

"Don't do anything embarrassing." Her gaze implored him. "I'd rather keep this between you and me."

"And the kids?"

She ignored his quip. "You might not care about your reputation, but I care about mine."

Her words felt like a slap to his face. "I would never do anything to hurt you."

Doubt filled her eyes.

His insides twisted. He wanted her to believe him. "I wouldn't."

"Then stop talking about kissing me again, okay?"

"Okay." The last thing he wanted to do was upset her. "I won't bring it up again."

And he wouldn't.

But if she gave him any indication she wanted another kiss, he was going to be all over it. All over her.

CHAPTER NINE

SUNDAY morning, Leanne entered the station ready to work. She wanted something to do other than sit around her house thinking about kissing Christian. She'd been so preoccupied by him she hadn't done more than string the lights on her Christmas tree.

Pathetic.

I am going to kiss you again, Leanne Thomas. Even if it means I have to buy all the mistletoe in Hood Hamlet to do it.

Romantic, no doubt. No wonder so many women wanted to date Welton. He said the words they wanted to hear. Not even she was as immune as she'd like to be. Her lips tingled with anticipation thinking about more kisses.

But all Christian wanted was kisses. Strike that. He probably wanted more, whatever he could get in the moment. But nothing…else.

No relationship. No commitment. No love. No thank you!

When she got involved again, Leanne knew what she wanted—everything he didn't. She should be relieved.

Leanne walked into the garage. Besides, a relationship with someone at the station, someone who worked her same shift, wasn't a smart idea. It wasn't against the rules, but highly discouraged. Still, a part of her was disappointed she'd scared him off so easily by saying she wanted a serious relationship.

Her gaze landed on Christian. She pulled up short.

He leaned against the back wall of the station bays, looking gorgeous in his blue uniform and neatly-styled hair.

Her pulse rocketed.

Okay, she had a crush on him. On a younger man. Did that make her a cougar?

His intense blue eyes studied her. "Good morning, Thomas."

Not Leanne. She reminded herself that was how she wanted it. "Welton."

"How's the toy drive looking?" he asked.

Yesterday, he'd sent a text message telling her not to come to the meeting. She could work on the toy drive while he handled the event planning. She'd appreciated that. Though she'd missed being a part of the get-together. All her friends were attending. Many of the town's business owners.

Who was she kidding? She'd missed Christian. Stupid.

"The library barrel had a few toys," she said. "Donations are still way down."

"We'll get plenty of toys at the dinner."

"Hope so." His confidence appealed to her. "The morning briefing…"

"We have a couple of minutes." He straightened. "I have good news about the dinner."

They wanted to attract sponsors to offset some of the expenses. "Did someone buy a table?"

"Better than that." He grinned. "My grandfather called. Welton Winery is going to underwrite the entire dinner and silent auction. My family is going to attend, too."

Her mouth gaped. "That means…"

"No expenses," Christian finished for her. "Whatever money we raise goes directly to OMSAR."

This was exactly what the unit needed to pay for new equipment and training, except…

His brows furrowed. "I thought you'd be happy."

"I am, but I don't want you to be pressured into doing something you don't want to do in order to help OMSAR. If there are strings attached to your grandfather's offer…?"

Christian's eyes softened. "No strings. I made sure. But I appreciate you…"

Something passed between them again. A look. A connection. Leanne held her breath.

"...asking," he said finally.

"Thank-you." Her voice sounded husky. "And your grandfather."

"This is because of what you, the rescue team and all of OMSAR did for me and Owen. Thank yourselves."

Excitement rocketed through her. This was going to make such a big difference for the unit. Part of her felt like twirling around. But one thought kept her from wanting to celebrate. "This is going to sound bad, probably really bad, but given how things are turning out, I'm kind of glad you and Owen needed to be rescued."

Christian gave a laugh. "You know, Thomas, I feel the same way."

At least she wasn't the only one. Leanne motioned to the doorway. "Morning briefing."

"Ladies, first."

"One of the guys, remember?" she teased.

"Yeah, I remember." Christian didn't sound too happy about it, but he walked in front of her. "But you should remember there's nothing wrong with being one of the girls."

Leanne stood in the doorway a bit stunned. No one at the station had ever said that to her. No one at OMSAR, either.

This was a man's world. She wanted—needed—to fit in. Didn't Christian understand that?

Of course not. He was a guy.

Leanne entered the briefing room. Her gaze shot to Christian. He was a guy who would be kissing someone on New Year's Eve. Alexa or Rachel or another woman. Maybe Leanne should be one of the girls and find a man to kiss, too. But the thought of kissing a guy who wasn't Christian seemed annoyingly unappealing...unsatisfying. She plopped into the closest chair.

The lieutenant cleared his throat and ran through the briefing. Nothing too out of the ordinary, except more physical training. Leanne liked the new workout, but not everyone agreed.

"Before I forget," the lieutenant added. "There's a full moon tonight so you know what that means."

"The crazies will be out," Paulson said.

She forced herself not to look at Christian. "And anything can happen."

At two o'clock in the morning, on fire attack, Christian headed toward the house fire with a hose line. He wore his full turn-outs and a SCBA—Self-Contained Breathing Apparatus. The smoke wasn't dark or breathing around the doors and windows. No sign of a possible backdraft situation.

He entered through the front door and remembered something from fire academy.

Right wall in. Left wall out.

Dark. He couldn't see a thing. No dim orange glow.

He listened. That was when he heard it. The familiar crackling of fire and burning.

Paulson, Baer, a longtime volunteer firefighter, and Keller followed Christian.

Smoke billowed, filling the doorway out of the living room. He couldn't see out of his mask very well.

As Christian moved to the doorway, the noise and heat increased. Orange. He opened the hose nozzle.

Flames licked the ceiling. With Keller behind him, Christian aimed the hose to douse them and other hot spots. They needed to get to the stairs.

One adult and child were outside being treated for smoke inhalation by Thomas and O'Ryan. Another adult and child were unaccounted for. Still in the house. Somewhere.

Paulson carried an ax. He'd searched the downstairs with Baer. "They have to be upstairs."

They attacked the fire on the way up. The higher they went, the thicker the smoke. Visibility decreased more.

Christian aimed the nozzle at the flames, but the fire didn't want to die.

"Help!" Coughs followed the cry.

Water from the hose cleared the path toward the sound.

"We've lost the garage," a voice said over the radio. "Find them and get out."

A door was ajar. No flames. No heat. But smoke filled the room.

Christian readied the hose. Paulson opened the door. The four of them entered.

In the darkness, figures lay on the floor. A man. A child. Gasping for breath, coughing, alive.

Paulson scooped up a little girl wearing a pink nightgown. She struggled against him with frightened eyes. "Kitty."

Baer helped the man.

He coughed. "Can't find Tinkerbell. Kitten. In here some-where."

"Do you have everyone?" the lieutenant asked.

"Yes," Keller replied.

Not everybody. Christian thought about the little girl's kit-ten.

"We're starting to lose the house. Evacuate the structure."

As Christian stepped out of the bedroom, he remembered the fear in the little girl's eyes and voice. This family was going to lose everything right before Christmas. He didn't want them to lose the kitten, too.

"Welton," Keller called.

"Take the hose," Christian said. "I'll be right behind you."

A firefighter never went into a fire or stayed in alone. But orders and regulations wouldn't mean anything to that family, especially the little girl. All Christian needed was sixty more seconds to find the cat.

Animals got scared and usually hid in situations like this. The room wasn't that big. He checked under the bed, behind the dresser and in the closet.

The smoke thickened. The heat intensified.

Thirty more seconds. He pushed aside a toy box. The kitten wasn't underneath.

"Welton."

He ignored the call over the radio. Fifteen seconds.

Leanne's smiling face appeared front and center in his mind. But she was outside. Safe. Christian didn't need to worry about her. He had to find the little girl's kitten. Tinkerbell.

"Get out, Welton," the lieutenant ordered. "Now."

A two-story dollhouse sat a few inches away from the wall. He pulled it out. Inside one of the rooms lay a small, gray kitten. Unconscious.

Damn.

Flames covered the doorway and spread to the ceiling. He slipped the kitten into his pocket.

"Welton." The lieutenant did not sound happy. "Retreat. That's an order."

"Got the cat," Christian replied. "Unconscious."

Heat surrounded him. Flames, too. Noise roared.

Something in the hallway collapsed. They weren't losing the house. They'd lost it. The structure was failing. And he was trapped.

He thought about Leanne, about wanting to hold her one more time, gaze into her brown eyes and kiss her. Time to get the hell out of here so he could do that.

Christian opened the window and pushed out the screen. Lights from the engine flashed. Firefighters aimed hoses and sprayed water. Not for the house, the structure was a lost cause, but for him.

"Bailing out the window," he said into the radio.

He grabbed his escape kit, one of the newer pieces of gear they'd started carrying for self-rescue, and anchored the rope to the window frame. As the flames danced toward him, he climbed out and rappelled down the rope. He ran from the burning house.

Leanne met him halfway across the yard. Worry filled her pretty brown eyes. "Christian…"

He pulled the kitten out of his pocket and placed the limp animal onto her hands.

She checked the cat. "It's not breathing."

He hadn't been able to tell with his mask and all the smoke. As she began mouth-to-mouth, he ripped off his mask.

Leanne hurried to the medical gear. Christian followed.

"Tinkerbell," the little girl cried. Thankfully the mother held her back.

"Come on, Tinkerbell," he said. "Breathe, kitty."

Leanne kept working on the kitten. Finally she looked at him. "Tinkerbell's breathing."

Relief washed over him.

Leanne placed an oxygen mask near the kitten's face. "You could have been killed."

She sounded tense, scared. "I knew I could find the cat."

She continued giving the kitten some blow by oxygen. "You were ordered to retreat."

"I'm sure I'll be reprimanded."

"And rightly so. That was an incredibly reckless thing to do." The kitten perked up. "An incredibly brave thing, too."

He smiled at her compliment. "For the record, I wasn't trying to impress you this time."

Leanne's gaze met his. She looked at him the way he'd pictured her when he was inside the burning house. Smiling. Beautiful. His. "Well, you did."

Christian's heart thudded. He wanted nothing more than to kiss her right now.

The kitten squirmed. *"Mew."*

She placed the cat in Christian's gloved hands. "Take Tinkerbell over to the little girl."

"Me?"

"You found the cat. That makes you the hero."

"I'm not—"

"Go." Pride filled Leanne's eyes. "You earned this."

Christian handed the wiggly kitten to the little girl now wrapped in a blanket. Someone snapped a picture.

She hugged him. "Thank you, Mr. Fireman."

Another flash lit up the night sky.

Neighbors surrounded the family. Someone clapped. Others cheered. Everyone joined in.

He nodded his appreciation then made his way back to the engine.

A muscle throbbed on the lieutenant's jaw. "We'll talk about this at the station."

"Yes, sir."

With that the lieutenant walked away.

Paulson slapped Christian on the back. "Well done, Welton."

"Thomas got the cat breathing."

"She couldn't have done that if you hadn't found Tinkerbell," Paulson said. "Don't mind the lieutenant. It's his job to make sure we all make it out safely. I'm sure you gave him a few gray hairs tonight."

"Not the intention."

"He knows that, rookie. Even if he won't admit it."

Christian glanced over at Leanne. He'd never seen that kind of worry in her eyes. Had it been for him?

A smile tugged at the corners of his lips thinking it might have been. Maybe he would get more kisses, after all.

"She's upset, too," Paulson said. "You know Thomas. Always a stickler for rules."

Christian's gaze remained on her as she packed up her equipment. "Yeah, but that's what makes her who she is."

"You're right about that." Paulson stared at Leanne, too. "She's tough and strong and totally self-reliant. I pity the fool who falls in love with her."

Christian nodded, but had a sinking feeling in the pit of his stomach. "Me, too."

Later that afternoon, Leanne glanced at the clock on her microwave. Christian was supposed to stop by to help her with the dinner program and auction catalogs. They hadn't set a firm time. She wished they had.

Ever since the house fire, she'd been on edge. She'd always been able to detach from what was going on with her coworkers on a call. Not this morning. Fear had gripped her heart when Christian hadn't exited the house with the others. She'd thought he was lost until he rappelled from the second story window like a superhero. Her relief had been palpable. And that's when she knew...

She cared about him.

Not like Paulson or Hughes or Porter or Moreno. Not like any of her fellow firefighters or OMSAR team.

Leanne had feelings, deep feelings, for Christian. Ones that couldn't go anywhere. Ones she would have to ignore. For the sake of the fire station. For the safety of her heart.

Once the Christmas celebration was over, it would be easier. Until then, she would...survive.

The doorbell rang.

She ran down the staircase and opened the door.

Christian stood on her porch. He held a red poinsettia plant. Behind him snow fell from the sky. "This is for you. I know all our work on the event has kept you from decorating."

Leanne's heart melted. If only... Nope. She knew better than to fantasize over something that wasn't going to happen. She took the plant. "Thanks."

He went upstairs.

She followed and set the plant on the breakfast bar. "I've got everything ready to collate."

"Let's hit it."

Time flew by. Leanne sat on her living room floor with Christian across from. They inserted the programs into each of the catalogs and clipped a bid number to the front. "This is my last one."

"Two more to go for me." A minute later, he placed his stack of catalogs in a box. "That's it."

"I can't believe how many catalogs there are."

"Carly said tickets sales have been brisk," Christian said.

"We should be set for the toy drive. We might even have enough donations to pass on to other organizations."

"Don't get ahead of yourself just yet." She placed lids on the boxes. "Let's wait to see how many toys are donated first."

His gaze racked over her. "So cautious for someone who takes risks every day?"

He was one to talk after this morning. "This is a different kind of risk."

"How so?" he asked.

"On the mountain skiing or climbing, it's an individual risk. Or you and your partner taking the risks together."

"Not if you're on a rescue."

"Then the team leader assesses the risk, too. The same way the lieutenant or the chief does on a call. But this celebration…" The weight of the boxes seemed to press down on her shoulders. "It feels as if all of Hood Hamlet is counting on this to save Christmas. If the event fails…"

"Christmas will survive no matter what happens. But I have a feeling it's going to be a huge success," he said. "What's left on the To Do list?"

She scanned the list. "Nothing. We get the rest of the night off. Now I can finally decorate my tree."

"Want some help?" he offered.

Temptation flared. She would love him to help her. But did she dare say yes? "I'm sure you have something better to do."

"I want to help you."

Last year she'd been alone at Christmastime for the first time in three years. Decorating the tree by herself had been a chore, not fun. She didn't relish the thought of a repeat performance this year.

"What do you say?" he pressed.

Having Christian trim the tree with her wasn't the same as kissing under the mistletoe. He wouldn't be kissing her again. He'd given his word. She would be safe having him keep her company. "Sure," she said finally. "I'd love the help."

* * *

Christmas carols played on the stereo. Flames crackled in the fireplace. Rubber boxes filled with ornaments neatly separated by cardboard sat on the living room floor. The only thing missing was…mistletoe.

Christian pushed that thought aside. Leanne wanted a boyfriend. He didn't want a girlfriend. Best to keep things platonic. No matter how sexy she looked in her tight-fitting jeans and turtleneck. Or the way she kept glancing his way.

He removed a paper star ornament. Gold-and-silver sparkles covered one side. The name LeLe was scrawled in a child's writing on the other. He remembered someone mentioning the nickname at the brewpub.

He held up the star by the attached gold ribbon. "Did you make this?"

"When I was seven." Leanne hung a red ball on the tree. "I have lots of ornaments from when I was growing up."

He placed the star on the tree. "You really do like Christmas."

She nodded.

"So Christmas magic—"

"I prefer Christmas spirit," she interrupted. "Magic implies some supernatural force that makes everything okay. Bad things happen this time of year, so does that mean that Christmas magic is only for some people? That doesn't seem fair."

He returned to the box. "I see your point, but it's still a nice thought."

Leanne shrugged.

Christian pulled out a frame made out of Popsicle sticks. The picture showed three children. Two teenage boys and a younger girl dressed head to toe in pink. The back read Cole (13), Troy (11) and LeLe (6). "Are these friends of yours?"

She took the ornament and stared at the picture. Her soft smile took Christian's breath away, but sadness filled her eyes, the way it had during the news interview with Rachel.

"My brothers." Leanne hung the frame on the tree right in the front. "I had two older brothers."

Had. Past tense. Christian didn't know what to say.

Leanne took another ornament out of the box.

"What happened?" he asked.

"A car accident." She hung a silver bell on a branch. "Black ice. Head-on collision."

No wonder the accident last week had affected her. Leanne reached for another ornament, but Christian touched her arm. "Wait a minute, okay?"

Leanne nodded.

"How old were your brothers?"

"Fourteen and sixteen." She pointed to a picture on the book-case. A family portrait. Christian hadn't noticed it before. The little girl had curly ringlets, pink ribbons in her hair and a frilly pink dress. It looked nothing like Leanne. "That was taken a few months before the accident."

Such big smiles. Happy eyes. Christian remembered when his dad died suddenly. He never thought he'd feel happy again. "You must have been young."

"Nine."

"What about your parents?"

"They were killed, too."

He winced. His mother had taken off when he was twelve. His dad passed when he was twenty. But Christian couldn't imagine losing both parents when he was nine. "I had no idea."

She shrugged. "Everyone around here knew because of the stories in the newspaper. I saw therapists and grief counselors for years. But no matter what I said, my family wasn't coming back. So I stopped talking about it."

Always so tough. On the outside at least. Christian squeezed her arm. "Leanne, I'm so sorry."

She picked up another ornament, an angel. "Thanks."

Feathers covered the wing. Gold braided thread made the halo. The sweet face reminded him of Leanne. "At least you weren't with them."

"I was in the car." Her lower lip quivered. "I was the only survivor. Everybody else died. It was…"

He recognized the faraway look in her eyes. He'd seen it in his own reflection after his father died.

Christian took the angel out of her hand and carefully placed it back in the box. He led her to the couch and pulled her down to sit next to him. "Sit for a minute. You don't have to tell me anything."

"I want to." She stared at the photograph in the bookcase. "We were on our way home from my grandparents' house. It was late afternoon. We'd had an early supper. I was in the back-seat. My brothers were on either side of me. I was playing with a new doll I'd just gotten."

She closed her eyes. Willing herself to remember or wanting to forget? Christian stroked her hand with his thumb.

"My mother screamed. She sounded so scared. Headlights were coming straight at us. My dad yelled. My brothers leaned over me. Covering me. Protecting me like they always did." Leanne grimaced. "And then that sound. The crunching. Jerking. Glass breaking. Spinning. It went on forever."

She trembled.

Christian let go of Leanne's hand, wrapped his arm around her and pulled her against him. "You're safe now."

She opened her eyes.

The vulnerability he saw made it difficult for him to breathe. He wanted to kiss her until all the hurt disappeared and a smile returned to her face.

"I'm…okay," she said, her voice a mere whisper. "When the car stopped, the sounds did, too. I hurt all over. I tried to move, but couldn't. My brothers were on top of me. Cole told me to stay still, to hold on because someone would be coming to help us. I called for my mom and dad and Troy. But no one answered. Cole tried to keep me calm, but his voice faded in and out. When it would come back, he kept telling me some-one would be there soon. That someone was a paramedic. By then Cole had stopped talking. Breathing."

Tears gleamed. She wiped her eyes. "Once I recovered and

was out of the hospital, I came to live with my grandparents here in Hood Hamlet. End of story."

Not even close. "And you became a paramedic."

"I wanted to help others the way I'd been helped."

"You are an amazing, brave woman, Leanne Thomas." Christian's admiration and respect grew exponentially. He rubbed her back. "Does the paramedic who helped know you followed in his footsteps?"

"Yes, we've kept in touch." She blinked. "Sorry, I'm usually not like this in front of others."

He brushed the hair off her face. "It's okay."

"Maybe for you." She tried to sound lighthearted and almost succeeded except for her red eyes. "It's my reputation at stake."

"Don't worry," he said. "Your tough-as-nails-never-let-anything-get-to-you reputation is safe with me. I promise I won't say a word."

"Thanks." She peered up at him, looking more shy than tough. "You're only the second person I've ever told exactly what happened during the accident."

"Was Paulson the other?"

"Nick Bishop."

"You were more than friends."

"For like five minutes. We were so young, but figured out really fast we were much better as friends."

"He and Hannah—"

"Were perfect for each other. Two people couldn't have been more different. Hannah's terrified of heights and hates camping and the outdoors. But she made Nick happy in a way no one else could."

"Not even you."

She half laughed. "I wouldn't have wanted to try."

"Thanks for telling me about the accident."

Leanne stared up at Christian. Holding her felt so natural, so right. Her face was so close to his. He wanted to kiss her. But he couldn't.

She needed a friend tonight, not a lover. Plus, he'd told her he wouldn't bring up kissing again.

Leanne's eyes darkened to that sexy dark chocolate color. They mesmerized him. Her lips parted. She brushed her mouth against his.

Magic. Fireworks. Heaven.

She jerked back. Her cheeks reddened. "I'm so sorry."

"It's okay."

She stood and stared at the carpet. "But I told you no more kisses then I..."

Christian rose. He raised her chin with his fingertips. "No worries. I won't hold it against you."

The corners of her mouth curved upward. That was the response he was hoping for. Christian wanted nothing more than to kiss her again. His gaze wanted to linger on her lips. His tongue wanted to taste her again. But kisses weren't what she needed from him.

Leanne wasn't some random woman he'd met at a bar or the ski resort. She worked with him. She'd rescued him. She deserved more than he was willing to give.

Christian lowered his hand. "What do you say we get this place looking like Christmas?"

CHAPTER TEN

LEANNE stood on a step stool and placed the star on the top of the Christmas tree. The scent of pine filled her nostrils. The multicolored lights blinked. Her vision blurred. She toyed with an ornament. Not because the candy cane needed fixing, but she needed a few minutes to herself.

She couldn't believe she'd told Christian about her family. Nick had pried the information out her during a moment of weakness, but she'd spilled to Christian like a fire hose with its nozzle wide-open. Worse, she couldn't believe she'd kissed him.

Okay, Leanne could believe it. Christian had been here to listen and to hold her. He'd also made her smile and laugh as they decorated the tree and the house. She'd fallen for him. Hard. Just like Alexa had. And Rachel. And probably every other single woman in town. After Christmas, he would start dating again.

Leanne grimaced. What was she going to do? Pretend nothing had changed? Switch shifts?

Paulson and O'Ryan would want to know why. So would the chief. He'd been the paramedic who saved her. She didn't want to disappoint him.

"The tree looks great," Christian said from behind her.

She climbed down and folded up the step stool. "Thanks to you."

"It was a team effort."

If only... Leanne took a deep breath. She forced herself to smile and turned around.

Christian held a stuffed reindeer. "Where does Rudolph go?"

She touched its ear. The reindeer's red nose lit up, filling the dark room with its glowing light. His mouth moved and the song "Rudolph the Red-Nosed Reindeer" played.

"He deserves a special place of honor," Christian said.

She'd received Rudolph during a white-elephant gift exchange. Cocoa wouldn't let Leanne regift him the next year. "I usually stick him in the bathroom."

"Come on, buddy," Christian said to the toy. "Let's put you where you belong."

Leanne placed the lids on the now-empty ornament boxes. Christmas carols continued to play. Flames danced in the fireplace. With all the decorations up, the atmosphere was cozy and romantic.

Christian returned. "It's getting late. I should head home."

Of course he wanted no part of romance. "I'll get your coat."

Christian followed her downstairs. She removed his coat from the closet and watched him shrug the jacket on. "Thanks for helping with the catalogs, listening and decorating."

"That's what friends are for."

Friends. Leanne tried out the word, let it swirl around her mind. Hated it. Maybe once the event was over with she'd look back and laugh at falling for Christian.

She opened the door. Wind howled. A sheet of white fell from the sky.

"The storm moved in early," he said.

A sense of dread filled her. "The roads might be bad."

He took a step toward the door. "I've driven in worse."

"I'm sure you have."

As he moved past her, a knot formed in the pit of her stomach. The thought of him out on the road sent a shiver of foreboding down her spine. "Stay."

Christian stopped. His eyes widened. "You want me to stay?"

Leanne heard the surprise and the confusion in his voice. She was confused herself. He probably could make it home. Still… Not trusting her voice, she nodded.

"Spend the night here," he clarified.

Bad idea. Really bad idea, except… "The visibility and the roads will be horrible. If something happened to you…"

A beat passed. And another. He closed the door. "No sense taking chances. I'll stay."

Relief washed over her. Then she tensed. Oh, no. She'd invited him to spend the night. "I have a guest bedroom."

Leanne said the words so quickly they all ran together.

Christian flashed her a charming smile. "A bed will be better than the couch."

Tension filled the air. Leanne wouldn't mind him sleeping in her bed. Her mouth went dry at the thought.

His gaze met hers. "We should probably call it a night. I have a bag in the truck."

She raised a brow. "That's handy."

"It's for the gym." He sounded slightly annoyed. "I'll be right back."

When he returned, snow clung to his hair. But he looked hot, not cold. The way he stared made Leanne feel like the last chocolate cookie on the plate, and he wanted it. Her. She swallowed. "Need a toothbrush?"

It was his turn to raise a brow. "You have spares for overnight guests?"

"I was at a warehouse store. They only sell packages of six."

"I'd love a toothbrush."

What was going on? This shouldn't be so awkward. She'd slept in the same bunk room with him for over a year. It wasn't as if they were strangers. And this sure wasn't a date. Still nerves threatened to get the best of her. "Help yourself to whatever you need."

"Does that include you if I have a nightmare?" he asked.

"Uh, I…" Leanne needed to get out of here, away from him.

Christian was short-circuiting her brain. She didn't like it. "I'll show you where the bathroom and bedroom are upstairs."

"I'll be right behind you."

And he was. She kept moving to stay ahead of him.

Leanne stood in the hallway, full of uncertainty. She pointed out where Christian could wash and sleep. Now all she needed to do was say good-night. "Thanks again for tonight."

"I'm glad you told me about your family. You're the strongest woman I've ever met." His gaze grew serious. "I'm not talking about how much you can bench press or the number of one-arm pull-ups you can do, either."

Emotion clogged her throat. "Thanks."

Desire filled his eyes. Leanne's heart thundered against her ribs.

The corners of his mouth curved. He tilted his head. His warm breath caressed her cheek.

Leanne wanted him to kiss her. She moistened her lips.

Reality hit her hard and fast like rime ice. No more kissing. "We'd better get to bed. Sleep, I mean. Lots to do tomorrow."

Laughter lit his eyes. "If this nasty weather keeps up, we'll be stuck inside."

That wouldn't be bad. No, she corrected. That would be very bad. She took a step backward and bumped into the hall wall. "Let's hope the storm blows over."

"Do the same rules apply for inside bivvies as ones on ledges?" he asked with a hint of mischief in his voice.

"Rules?"

"What happens on bivy stays there." Christian winked. "Sounds a little like Vegas."

Desire flared. No one would know if anything happened between them. Tempting, yes. But she would know something happened. Leanne had to get away from him before she did or said something she might regret. "Good night, Christian. See you in the morning."

She said the words for as much her benefit as his.

* * *

A phone rang. Christian reached for his nightstand then realized the sound wasn't coming from his cell phone.

He blinked open his eyes. It took his eyes a moment to adjust to the darkness in the room. Not his room. Leanne's guest room.

Wind howled through the trees, but he was warm and comfy in the queen-size bed. The only thing that would make it better was if he weren't alone. Thoughts of Leanne filled his mind, making it difficult to fall back asleep.

What was going on? Christian had spent over a year sleeping in the same bunk room with Leanne. Sure he'd noticed her. Especially during the summer when she wore a tank top and shorts to bed. What guy wouldn't? She had a killer body. Of course, every guy at the station pretended not to notice.

He rolled over, trying to get comfortable.

But he couldn't stop thinking about her. He wanted to know if she was thinking about him. Maybe if he peeked into her room and she was awake

"Christian," a familiar feminine voice called.

Oh, yeah. He wouldn't have to sleep alone, after all. Christian raised himself up on his elbows. He'd hoped to see her standing next to his bed in a sexy nightie or nothing. She was dressed for the storm outside. "What's going on?"

"Sorry to wake you so early," she said. "I received a call-out for a mission. Two teenagers were skiing, but never made it home. Their car is still in the parking lot."

He brushed his hand through his hair. "It sounds nasty out there. You won't be able to do much in this weather."

"They're just kids, Christian. We have to do something."

"I'll come with you."

"There's no room. Hughes is picking a few of us up. He's got a plow on the front of his truck." She smiled softly. "Get some sleep. Make yourself at home. Eat whatever you want."

The thought of her outside in this weather chilled him to the bone. He didn't want her to go, but he couldn't ask her to stay. Not when she had a job to do and people to help. "When will you be home?"

She inhaled deeply. "I have no idea. Just lock the door behind you when you leave."

He wasn't going anywhere. Not until he knew she was back, safe and sound. "I may stick around."

"Whatever you want."

Christian knew exactly what he wanted—her. But that wouldn't take Christmas magic. That would take a Christmas miracle.

Leanne ran outside. She tossed her backpack inside the shell on the back of Hughes's truck and shut the hatch.

Snow swirled around her, pricking her face and sending a chill down her spine. She hoped those two kids found shelter for the night.

She climbed into the pickup truck and slammed the door. Bill Paulson and Jake Porter sat in the back of the dually. "Hey, guys. Where's Moreno?"

"Stomach flu," Hughes said.

Paulson motioned to her driveway. "What's Welton's truck doing here?"

She fastened her seat belt. "It was safer for him to stay the night than drive home in this storm."

Paulson's nostrils flared. "That's the excuse Welton used so he could sleepover?"

"Come on, Paulson." Hughes drove out of the town house development toward the main road. The plow attached to the front of the truck pushed snow out of the way. "I'm sure you've used that one yourself."

"Not with Thomas, I haven't," he said.

"Welton didn't ask to spend the night," she clarified. "I invited him. I do have a spare bedroom."

"So what happened?" Porter asked.

"Not that it's any of your business, but nothing happened." She didn't appreciate his assumption something would. "We're only spending time together because of the Christmas celebration. Thanks to all of you, in case you've forgotten."

"Stop protecting the guy." Paulson's jaw thrust forward. "Knowing Welton, I'm sure he tried something. Pretty much anything in a skirt is fair game with him."

"I don't wear skirts," she reminded. "I told you nothing happened."

Hughes glanced her way with a grin. "You must have shut him down real good when he made his move."

Leanne sighed. "Welton didn't make a move. Why would he when I'm just one of the guys?"

The traction tires sounded against the snow. The wipers continued to sweep back and forth.

"Be careful around him, Leanne," Hughes said finally.

"Real careful," Porter said.

"There's nothing going on." She leaned back against the truck's headrest. "I don't understand why you guys are acting like this."

"We care about you," Porter said.

Hughes nodded. "None of us want to see you get hurt."

Again was left unspoken, but the word hung on the air.

Paulson nodded. "You can do better than someone like Welton."

Leanne knew Christian wasn't the right man for her. He couldn't give her what she wanted—a commitment—and no way could she give him what he wanted—a no-strings relationship. Though that hadn't stopped her from kissing him. Last night and under the mistletoe were the most action she'd had in six months. Okay, her choice. But still…

Christmas wasn't all that far away. New Year's Eve a week after that. She didn't want to be alone. Truth was, right or wrong, she wanted to spend the holidays with Christian. More than she'd wanted anything in a very long time.

Christian couldn't go back to sleep. He understood why Leanne had to go. Helping others, making a difference, was why he'd become a firefighter. But that didn't lessen his concerns about her.

What the hell was wrong with him? All this time he'd worked with Leanne, and seen all the rescues she'd gone out on, he'd never worried about her. He shouldn't be acting and feeling this way over a woman who'd seen more danger on the mountain than he ever had. A woman he wasn't even dating. Or fooling around with. Or kissing.

He showered then headed down to the kitchen where he scrambled a couple of eggs and toasted two slices of wheat bread. Sitting at the breakfast bar in her kitchen, he stared out the window.

Snow continued to fall. Not quite a blizzard, but close. Low visibility. Big, fat, wet snowflakes. Freezing temperatures.

Christian was inside and warm while Leanne was probably out in the middle of it. The thought brought a chill. Yes, she was capable and strong. He didn't doubt her abilities or skill, but anyone was susceptible to hypothermia and frostbite. Even someone as experienced as her.

What little appetite he'd had disappeared. He moved the eggs around his plate with his fork.

Wait a minute. Christian straightened. Rescuer safety was always the priority. Every news station always reported that whenever anything happened on the mountain. OMSAR wouldn't head out in weather like this. Leanne was safe.

Except he couldn't forget the concern in her voice.

They're just kids, Christian. We have to do something.

When kids were involved, emotions ran high and the stakes changed. But Leanne played by the rules. He hoped she was a stickler for them today.

His gaze strayed to the window again. He wished he knew what was going on. Maybe he could find some information…

The radio had no reports. Neither did the Northwest Cable News channel, nor the internet.

Christian released a frustrated sigh. Being on this side of a rescue—the waiting side—sucked big-time.

A blanket of white continued to fall from the sky.

The not knowing grated on his nerves.

This must be how his family had felt when he and Owen had been on the mountain. Maybe even with his firefighting.

Family is so important, Welton. You need to work things out. Compromise.

Christian knew why family meant so much to Leanne now. She didn't have one. But he did. He pulled out his cell phone and pressed the button for his grandparents' house. The voice mail announcement clicked on after the fourth ring.

"You've reached the Weltons," his grandma's pleasant voice said. "We're out and about at the moment. Leave your name and number. We'll call you back when we get home."

Beep.

"It's Christian." Uncertainty coursed through him. This was his family even if he hadn't felt like a part of it for a while. "I wanted to say hi. See what you and Grandpa were up to. It's snowing up here on the mountain. I'm looking forward to seeing you at the Christmas Magic dinner. Talk to you later."

He pressed the end call button on his phone.

Okay, that had taken less than a minute. Leanne would be happy he called. Now what?

Christian needed something to do to distract him from thinking about Leanne out there. He washed his dishes and cleaned the kitchen. He stripped the sheets from his bed and gathered them up with the towel from the bathroom to take to the laundry room.

The door to Leanne's room was ajar.

Christian wondered if she had anything that needed to be washed. He pushed open the door with his foot.

What the…

The flowery, frilly feminine decor of Leanne's bedroom was completely different than the rest of the house. Completely opposite to Leanne herself. Lace, flowers and pink. Not just one shade, but many shades. So…girly.

What was going on? She was one of the guys at the station

and on the mountain. Even in town. Kickass tough and unemotional. That Leanne wouldn't be caught dead sleeping in a room decorated like this.

Christian remembered how tender and nurturing she was babysitting. The emotional woman he'd held in his arms last night, the one who'd kissed him so gently before thinking better of it. This decor fit that Leanne better.

But he still didn't get it. Her. The woman was a total contradiction. Which one was the real her?

Christian wasn't sure he wanted to know. He liked the softer side of Leanne more than he thought possible. But he didn't want to find himself in a relationship, pushed into a corner having to live up to the demands of someone else. For both their sakes, it would be better to think of her only as Thomas again, one of the guys, a total badass and hardnose, not the attractive, sexy, desirable woman he wanted to kiss again.

And he would. Once she got home from her mission.

Hours later, Leanne arrived home tired, wet and cold. Welton's truck was still parked in her driveway. That surprised her. But pleased her, too.

She pressed the keypad on her garage. The door opened automatically. She dumped her gear inside. A shower and food were her first priorities. She'd unpack and dry things later.

With her boots off, she entered the house.

Christmas carols played on the stereo. The scents of basil and tomato lingered in the air. Oh, man, it smelled so good. Her stomach growled. She climbed the stairs.

Christian stood at the stove stirring something in a pot. Leanne's heart jolted.

He smiled at her. "You're home."

She studied him, feeling much warmer than a minute ago. Home had never felt so good. "The kids found shelter last night. They made their way to Highway 35 once the sun came up."

"Hungry?"

"Starving."

"I raided your fridge and cupboards. Found enough for spaghetti and meatballs."

Her chest tightened. Cocoa used to always make something for her to eat when she returned from a mission. Zoe, too. And now Christian…

"Thanks," Leanne mumbled, not wanting to give in to the emotions swirling through her. "This is exactly what I need."

He poured and handed a cup of coffee to her. "You're wet."

She nodded. Sipped. The hot liquid tasted so good, but she would have preferred a kiss.

"Grab a shower," he said. "After you warm up, we can eat."

A few of his kisses would take the chill right away. But a few of his kisses would never be enough. Leanne wanted so much more. Too bad "more" would never happen with a commitment-phobe like Christian.

CHAPTER ELEVEN

THE next few days passed by in a blur between work at the fire station and in town on Christmas celebration. Ever since the lunch at her town house, something had changed between her and Christian. Something good.

They didn't kiss, but accidental touches and brushes of the hands happened more frequently. Phone calls and texts were exchanged when they weren't together. Which wasn't often. They didn't discuss only the upcoming event, either.

It was…nice.

Leanne was willing to leave it at that. For now. She wanted to ask Christian if he wanted to go on the annual snowshoeing excursion on Christmas Day with her and her friends. All she needed was the opportunity and the nerve.

On Thursday, two days before the big celebration, Leanne went down the mountain to go shopping with her friends at the closest mall.

"I love girls' nights, I mean, days, out." Zoe Hughes stared at the glittery Christmas decorations and lights hanging from the mall's ceiling. She spun around to take in all the sights. The bottom of her skirt flared, showing the tops of her brown leather boots. The woman knew how to take a plain skirt and blouse and turn it into high fashion with a couple of choice accessories. "Especially when it involves shopping with my girlfriends."

"Here, here." Carly Porter wore a purple sweater, faded jeans and a big smile on her face. Life and love with Jake and their nine-month-old baby girl sure agreed with her. "I love being a mom, but I have no time for myself."

Hannah laughed. "You won't until Nicole goes to college."

Zoe smiled at Leanne as if they were partners in crime. "At least we don't have to worry about that."

"I know I don't." But a longing deep inside Leanne ached. She forced a smile. "I doubt it'll be long for you."

Carly raised a finely-arched brow. "You and that hottie firefighter seem pretty close."

Zoe nodded. "He's gorgeous."

"Total eye candy," Hannah said.

Leanne looked at each one of them. "You're married women."

Hannah laughed. "True, but we can still look."

"Looking is all I'm doing myself," Leanne admitted. "I wish we weren't just working on the celebration together."

"Tell Christian that," Zoe encouraged. "He looks like he'd rather be working on you."

Carly laughed.

"The kids love him." Hannah glanced at a group of high school students performing Christmas carols. "They want to know when you two are going to babysit again."

Zoe looked at her. "You and Christian babysat together?"

"We had work to do and thought after the kids went to bed would be a good time," Leanne explained.

"He's totally into you," Carly said.

Leanne was afraid to hope. "You think?"

"Come on," Zoe said. "You know these guys better than anyone. A man doesn't offer to babysit unless he's got ulterior motives."

"Jake did with Carly," Leanne countered.

"Jake was still crazy about Carly even after she'd been gone for six years," Hannah said. "The kids told me you and Christian kissed."

Leanne's cheeks burned.

Zoe tapped her foot. "Spill. Now."

Thinking about Christian's lips against hers made Leanne's temperature rise. "A mistletoe kiss. That's all."

"I remember when Sean first kissed me under the mistletoe." Zoe sighed. "Mistletoe should be mandatory all year long."

"I kissed him."

The three women stared at her. "You?"

"I wanted to get it over with. I was going to give him a peck on the cheek, but he turned his head and I ended up kissing him on the lips."

Zoe pursed her glossed lips. "And?"

"So where did you want to go to look for dresses?" Leanne asked.

Mischief gleamed in Zoe's eyes. "Somewhere where we can find you a dress so sexy the firefighter will be dragging you under the mistletoe all night long."

Heat rose up Leanne's cheeks.

Carly and Hannah laughed.

"You like him," Carly said.

"Of course I like him," Leanne said. "He's a good firefighter."

"Is he a good kisser?" Zoe asked.

Yes. Leanne got chills thinking about his kiss. But she wasn't ready to tell her friends that. She noticed the North Pole Village right in front of them. "Oh, look, it's Santa."

"This is the best mall Santa ever," Carly said. "There isn't a long line. Let's tell him what we want for Christmas."

Leanne would do anything to keep the subject off her and Christian. "I'm game."

"Sure," Zoe said.

"Lead the way, Carly," Hannah said.

Leanne took up the rear. The other women seemed to know exactly what they wanted for Christmas. All she could think about was Christian.

Her turn.

Santa's blue eyes twinkled as she approached his chair. His

cheeks were rosy. He even had dimples. "Do you want to sit on my knee?"

"Uh, no thanks, Santa."

"So what would you like for Christmas?" he asked.

Christian popped into her mind. As if she could ask to find him under her tree on Christmas morning tied with a pretty red ribbon. "I'd like new skins."

The lines on Santa's face deepened. "Skins?"

"For my skis." Leanne thought about skiing with Christian. That had been such a fun day. "I climb and backcountry ski."

"Oh, that would be a practical gift." Santa's blue eyes twinkled behind his gold wire-rimmed glasses. "But I know what you really want."

"You do?" What she really wanted was a family.

Santa nodded. "To get that, you're going to have to believe."

Okay, this Santa was a little weird, but he'd piqued her curiosity. "Believe in what?"

"Christmas magic, Leanne."

"How do you know—" a six-foot-tall elf escorted her away before she could finish "—my name?"

She glanced back, but Santa was already talking to a child dressed in a fancy party dress with matching bows in her hair.

"Ready to shop until we drop?" Zoe said.

The exchange with Santa left Leanne feeling strange, unsettled. Maybe shopping would make her feel a little less off balance. "Sure. Where do you want to start?"

Leanne stepped out of the changing room wearing the perfect dress for the Christmas Magic in Hood Hamlet dinner and silent auction. She wanted to look nice. Christian's family would be there. "What do you think?"

Three pairs of eyes stared at her.

Her heart sunk. "What? Do I look fat?"

"Not at all," Hannah said. "It shows off your figure nicely."

Two little lines formed above Carly's nose. "It's just—"

"You're going to a Christmas party, not a funeral, Leanne," Zoe interrupted.

"Black is versatile," Leanne countered.

"Black is boring." Zoe motioned with her hand. "Turn around."

Leanne did.

"I'll be right back." With that, Zoe disappeared from the dressing room.

Leanne stared at her reflection in the three-part mirror. "A funeral, huh?"

Carly shrugged. "Maybe if it didn't have long sleeves."

"Or a just-below-the-knee hem," Hannah added.

Leanne sighed. "I'm so not good at this."

"No worries." Zoe appeared with a handful of colorful, sparkly dresses. "Because you have me, and I'm great at this."

Leanne gulped.

Zoe held up a yellow dress in front of Leanne. "Washes you out."

Next came a red one with a deep V-neckline. "The color is good. But the design screams nightclub, not community dinner."

Carly and Hannah nodded.

"This purple one might work." Zoe scrunched her nose. "No, too prim and proper. We want Christian's eyes to bug out when he sees you."

"No man's eyes are going to bug out around me," Leanne said, resolved to her fate. "I'm one of the guys. Well, minus the hot-pink toenail polish."

Carly laughed. "You are not one of the guys."

"They only pretend not to notice you," Hannah added.

Leanne made a face. "That's not true."

"All you have to do is crook your little finger and they'd come running," Carly said. "Trust me."

Leanne shook her head. "No way."

"You'll see." Zoe placed a shimmery blue dress in front of

Leanne. Satisfaction filled the former socialite's eyes. "This one."

The little girl inside Leanne, the one who used to live in princess dresses and play with makeup from the time she could open a container of eyeshadow, stared at the dress with a longing so intense she couldn't breathe. But that girly girl had died along with her family. "Isn't it a bit too…sparkly?"

"It's perfect." Zoe shoved the dress into Leanne's hands. "What's your shoe size?"

"Eight."

Leanne stared at the dress. It was so beautiful. Her fingertips itched to feel the fabric, but self-preservation held her back. "If I wear something like this, I'm never going to hear the end of it."

Carly's eyes softened. "You're stronger than most men I know. You can take it."

"But—"

"Put it on." Zoe waved her into the dressing room. She looked at Hannah and Carly. "Keep her in the dress. I'll be back with shoes and accessories. I love makeovers."

"This isn't necessary," Leanne said.

Zoe closed the door. "No, but it sure is fun."

Inside the dressing room, Leanne slipped on the blue dress. The fabric floated over her body, clinging to her hips in a flattering way.

"Do you have the dress on?" Hannah asked.

Leanne glimpsed at her reflection in the mirror. She felt feminine and pretty, the way she'd always dreamed of feeling. But the dress was so not her. She would never be able to pull it off. "Yes."

"Let us see," Carly said.

With a slight hesitation, Leanne opened the dressing room door. Both Carly's and Hannah's mouths gaped.

Leanne stiffened. "I look silly."

"Beautiful." Carly grinned. "You're buying the dress. And whatever accessories Zoe thinks you need to go with it."

"You're not walking out of here without that dress." Hannah said. "Men aren't going to be able to take their eyes off you, Leanne."

She didn't care about men looking at her. Only one man. Christian. She didn't check the price tag, a first for her. "Okay, I'll buy it."

On Saturday, Christian stepped outside the station after shift change. Not a cloud or a snow flurry in sight. Only clear-blue skies overhead for the big event today.

"Perfect weather." He glanced at Leanne, who walked toward her car. "It's got to be Christmas magic."

"You know how fast things can change up here." She tossed a duffel bag into her car. She wore jeans and a red sweater. A candy-cane-striped scarf and Santa hat finished off her outfit. "I hope the weather holds."

Leanne could be so stubborn. He should have known she wouldn't play along even today.

"Ready?" she asked.

Christian was ready to spend another twenty-four hours with her. He'd spent the past twenty-four hours with her. Minus the time driving to calls, responding to calls and sleeping. He didn't want to think about what would happen after today. At least they still had to climb at Smith Rock. "Let's go."

They walked the short distance to Main Street.

"Lots of traffic this morning," Leanne noted.

As they rounded the corner, she gasped. People crowded the sidewalks of Main Street. A group of carolers dressed in Victorian costumes sang. The Hood Hamlet city manager roasted chestnuts on the corner of Main and First. The scent lingered in the cool, mountain air.

"Yes." Christian pumped his fist. "This is awesome."

Lines creased Leanne's forehead. "It's not supposed to start until ten."

"Nobody's going to complain. Come on." He took her gloved

hand in his. The gesture felt so natural to him. "Let's get to the information booth."

Hood Hamlet merchants and business owners smiled. A line of people stood outside the coffee shop. More waited in a line outside the café. The brewpub, serving a special breakfast buffet this morning, also had a wait.

Leanne squeezed Christian's hand. "I can't believe it."

"Believe."

A funny look crossed her face. "You're the second person who's said that to me recently."

"Who was the first?" he asked.

"Santa Claus."

Christian laughed. "Well, Santa knows best."

As they approached the information booth, she slipped her hand out of his hand.

"Here they are," Sean Hughes announced. "The cochairs extraordinaire."

"Hold your applause," Leanne teased. "We have work to do."

Bells jingled.

Christian glanced down Main Street. A beautiful, black horse pulled a red-and-green sleigh decorated with fresh, green garland. Two lanterns, tied with red ribbon, bobbed. The driver looked like something from a Dickens's novel in his stovepipe hat and cap.

Christmas magic. Christian had no doubt. If only Leanne could see it. Feel it. Maybe by the end of the day, she would.

That night, Leanne entered the foyer of the community center where the dinner and silent auction were being held. White lights outlined the doorways. She felt like a fairy princess in her sparkling blue dress, silver shoes and makeup. She wore her hair down at Zoe's urging, something Leanne never did, as well as makeup and jewelry.

The day had been an overwhelming success. The toy drive donation barrels overflowed. Cash registers continued to ring up sales. Not even a traffic jam into town dampened people's enthusiasm. She hoped tonight went as well.

She glided into the multipurpose room, decorated with more white lights, flocked trees, white tulle and shining silver stars. It looked…magical. Compliments of the dinner's sponsor, Welton Winery, and Hood Hamlet Flowers.

"Whoa, Thomas." Her partner, O'Ryan's gaze filled with male appreciation. "You look…nice."

Nice hadn't been the adjective Zoe was after, but Leanne would take it. She'd dressed up for weddings, but never like this. "Um, thanks."

O'Ryan kept staring at her. Okay, her breasts. "You should wear dresses more often."

Everywhere she turned people made similar comments. A few people didn't recognize her. Handsome Johnny Gearhart, the owner of the Hood Hamlet Snowboarding Camp and Academy asked if she had plans for New Year's Eve. The compliments gave her a boost of confidence. Maybe Christian would want to spend the holidays with her.

Leanne saw him on the other side of the room. Christian looked so handsome in his navy suit, dress shirt and tie. She wove her way through the crowd toward him.

When he saw her, his eyes widened. A smile spread across his face. He met her halfway. "You look hot."

Zoe had been right. Leanne shivered with delight. "Thank-you."

"No, thank you." His gaze practically caressed. "So you got plans for New Year's Eve?"

She flashed a flirty smile. "Maybe."

"I'm only half joking," he whispered.

"Me, too."

"Come with me." He led her ten feet to the right. "Oh, look. We're standing under the mistletoe."

"Christian."

"Come on," he urged. "It's tradition."

People stared at them. Apprehension coursed through her.

She didn't like being the center of attention, but she longed to feel Christian's lips against hers again. Even if that meant kissing in public. No one would say anything if it was just a mistletoe kiss. "Make it fast."

As she parted her lips, he lowered his mouth to capture hers.

Sparks. Again. She nearly gasped at the intensity of them. Forget the fireworks a local ski resort shot off on New Year's Eve. Nothing could compare to the pleasurable sensations Christian's kiss brought.

His lips pressed against hers with desire and longing. Matching the pressure, she leaned into him, eager to get closer.

Hot. But no fire extinguisher needed. She wouldn't mind cranking up the heat. She wanted more of his kiss, more of him.

The kiss went on, and on, and on.

Someone cleared his throat. She recognized the sound. The fire chief.

Leanne backed away from Christian, her lips on fire, her cheeks burning and her heart pounding. The kiss left her shaken and wanting more. She took a deep breath to calm herself. It didn't help. "Th-thanks."

Desire shone in his eyes. "We'll take this up where we left off later when not so many people are around."

With her lips tingling, all Leanne wanted to do was kiss Christian again. But that would have to wait until later. She nodded.

He straightened his tie. "We'd better attend to our duties."

During the meal, Leanne didn't have time to eat. She closed two of the silent auction tables and urged people to place bids at the final ones. Not that she was hungry for anything but Christian's kisses.

A giggle welled up inside of her. She felt as if were… floating. Her sling-back heels didn't seem to touch the floor.

She liked feeling special, desired and most especially feminine, a side she'd neglected way too long in order to fit in, a side Christian didn't seem to mind at all.

Maybe he would say yes when she invited him snowshoeing. Maybe she would even have someone to ring in the New Year with.

Leanne touched her lips that still throbbed.

"That was some kiss earlier," Paulson said.

Her cheeks heated. She lowered her hand. A kiss couldn't change everything, but every relationship had to start somewhere. "You know Welton."

"I do." A muscle throbbed at Paulson's jaw. "He's a player, Leanne."

"I've told him what I want." She raised her chin. "He wouldn't have kissed me like that unless he'd changed his mind and wanted that, too."

"You've fallen for him."

"Yeah, I have." No one had ever made her feel the way Christian did. "My heart is still pounding from his kiss."

Paulson grimaced. "Lee—"

"I appreciate the concern, Bill. I really do, but it'll be okay. I know what I'm doing."

He didn't look convinced. "I hope so for your sake."

Her heart brimmed with anticipation at seeing Christian again. This was the perfect time to invite him snowshoeing. "I need to close the final tables. We'll talk later."

Christian stood with his sister and brother-in-law. His grandparents had left with Owen. His cousin had wanted to call it an early night due to his injuries and still using a walker.

"Who were you kissing earlier?" His thirty-eight weeks pregnant sister, Brianna, asked.

"Leanne Thomas." Christian looked for her in the crowd. He couldn't wait to get her under the mistletoe again later. "She's one of the members of the rescue team who found Owen and me."

His brother-in-law, Jeff, gasped. "That's her? We met during the rescue. She cleans up well."

She kissed even better. Christian grinned.

"I thought Kelly turned you off ever getting serious again,"

Brianna said. "Good to know I was wrong. Will Leanne be joining us for Christmas?"

Only people in relationships spent Christmas together. Christian put up his hands. "Whoa, sis. You're way off base. There's nothing serious going on here."

Just the thought made his collar shrink two sizes.

Curiosity filled his big sister's eyes. "But that kiss…"

"Mistletoe and holiday cheer," he explained. "Leanne knows exactly where I stand when it comes to relationships."

Still, Christian hoped Leanne took him up on his New Year's Eve offer. Maybe she'd be willing to settle for something casual, hanging out and having fun. No one would need to know.

Brianna frowned. "You know, just because you don't want to live your life like Dad did, doesn't mean you have to run away from being with anyone."

"I'm not running away from anything."

She looked doubtful. "If you say so, but do you want to end up alone?"

"If I'm alone, it's because I choose to be alone."

"Tying yourself to others, whether it's a woman or your family, won't turn you into Dad. Being with those you care about is a choice. Your choice, Christian."

"That choice still means giving things up." He glanced at his watch. "I'll find you later. I have a couple more things to do."

Christian headed toward the silent auction tables.

"Welton." Paulson cornered him by one of the tall, flocked trees decorated with white lights and red bows. "What the hell are you doing with Leanne?"

Leanne, not Thomas. "If you're talking about that kiss—"

"Everybody is talking about that kiss. Including the chief." Paulson's eyes darkened. "Leave her alone. Leanne deserves better than to have her heart broken by someone who isn't good enough to polish her shoes."

Christian put up his hands as he'd done with his sister. "No hearts are involved, dude. It was just a kiss."

"You might think so." Paulson lowered his voice. "But not Leanne. She's all starry-eyed, and it's because of you. Fix it. Before she's hurt even more."

"Fine. I'll fix it." Christian didn't buy for a minute what Paulson said was true. "But you're overreacting."

Fifteen minutes later, Leanne approached him. She looked radiant and beautiful. Her eyes sparkled, too. But that didn't mean anything.

"Hi." She sounded breathless. "You were right. We've exceeded our toy donation quota!"

"Great." Christian fought the urge to touch her long hair. He liked seeing her finally wear it down. The strands looked silky soft. "Everything's turned out better than I imagined."

"I know." She beamed. "I feel all Christmassy. Speaking of which, I was wondering if you wanted to go snowshoeing on Christmas Day. A group of us go every year."

An invitation for Christmas meant one thing. Leanne wanted a relationship even though Christian told her that wasn't what he wanted. His heart dropped to the toes of his tight dress shoes. Paulson had been right. Brianna, too.

His muscles tensed. Disappointment washed over him.

Leanne Thomas wasn't different. She wanted him to give himself up and live his life a certain way. Be a certain way. Her way.

No way. He'd been honest with her. It wasn't his fault if she chose not to listen. "I'm spending Christmas Day with my family."

"It's only for a couple hours," she explained. "We're never out long so people can get back to their families."

He wasn't about to be pressured into saying yes. Into anything. She'd proven nothing, not even kisses, came without strings. "No, thanks."

"Th-that's okay." Leanne wouldn't meet his eyes. "I saw you with your family. It looks like everything is going well."

"Yeah, the bridge is being mended." He had her to thank for that, but if he said anything she might get the wrong idea.

"I showed my grandfather an empty storefront on Main Street. Told him he should open a tasting room and store up here."

"I'm happy for you, Christian."

Leanne didn't sound happy. She looked a little sad. Not his problem. Better to disappoint her a little now rather than hurt her more later. "Thanks for all your hard work on everything."

Her face brightened. "It was a team effort. Cochairs extraordinaire."

"Yeah, about that." He shifted his weight between his feet. "I only did this to repay you and the rescue team for saving me and Owen. Now you have enough donations for the toy drive and OMSAR has money for gear and training. We're even."

Confusion clouded her eyes. "All this was your way of paying us back?"

Christian nodded.

"We didn't rescue you in order to get something from you."

"You admitted you were happy it happened."

"So did you." Leanne stared into his eyes. "Where did the kisses under the mistletoe fit into this?"

"They were fun." As he said the words he knew that wasn't the whole truth. "You knew I wasn't looking for a girlfriend or anything serious."

No emotion showed on her face. "You made it quite clear."

Rachel waved mistletoe in the air. She motioned him over.

Leanne's lips thinned. "Guess the reporter didn't get the memo about you not wanting a girlfriend for Christmas."

The hurt in Leanne's voice rang clear. He felt like a jerk, but it was better this way. Might as well finish it. "Kissing doesn't make a woman my girlfriend."

Something inside her seemed to turn off. Her eyes dimmed. Christian didn't like it. He touched her arm.

She jerked away as if burned. "Don't."

Her reaction bothered him. "Hey, we're friends."

"No, rookie. We were never friends. A friend doesn't need to pay back another friend for helping them." She spoke with a curt tone that made him feel like slime. "You'd better go see to Rachel. If you blow her off, she'll never go out with you on New Year's Eve."

He opened his mouth to speak, but Leanne was walking away.

Christian's chest felt like it might explode as he watched her go, but what else could he do? Say? They wanted different things in life. She deserved someone who could give her what she wanted. But thinking about Leanne with another guy left a surprisingly bitter taste in his mouth.

"Christian." Rachel saddled up against him in a low-cut sparkly red dress. She held mistletoe over her head. "It's my turn to kiss the firefighter under the mistletoe."

Habit kept Leanne from showing any emotion on her way out of the room. She stopped by the coat check to retrieve her jacket and purse.

Hannah exited the ladies' room and rushed over. "Where are you going?"

"Home."

"The night's still young."

"I'm…" Her voice cracked.

Hannah grabbed her arm. "What's wrong?"

"Nothing. Everything. I feel so stupid." Leanne sniffled. "Christian isn't interested in me. He was only trying to pay OMSAR back for rescuing him and Owen."

"I saw the way he kissed you."

"He's under the mistletoe kissing a news reporter the same way right now." Leanne's throat tightened. "I'm nothing… special."

Her heart shattered. Which made matters a hundred times worse. She had known better.

"Lee—"

"I don't know why I'm so upset. I'm blowing this all out of proportion." She shrugged on her coat. "We aren't involved. We only kissed a couple of times."

"You have feelings for him."

"Had. Past tense." Loneliness allowed her feelings to get carried away. She wouldn't make that mistake again. "Welton's a coworker. Nothing more."

Concern clouded Hannah's eyes. "Want a ride home?"

Leanne had ridden with Zoe and Sean to the dinner, but she could walk home. "Thanks, but I've got it under control."

Hannah hugged her. "Call me if you need anything."

Leanne left without a glance back. After six feet in her high heels on snow-covered sidewalks, she realized walking home wasn't possible. She needed a ride, but the only transportation she saw was the horse-drawn sleigh. She pulled out her wallet and climbed aboard. The driver handed her a wool blanket.

As the sleigh headed down Main Street, the jingling bells irritated her. This ride would be so romantic if she weren't alone. But she was always alone. Probably always would be. Tears welled in her eyes, but she didn't cry.

When she arrived at her town house, half the Christmas lights on her house were out. Just her luck. Inside, petals from the poinsettia plant Christian had given her lay on the floor.

Leanne felt as if she was withering inside, but she didn't know how to make things better. Friends weren't enough anymore. Her job, either. She wanted more. She wanted…

The telephone rang. She ignored it. She didn't check caller ID. Someone was either going to ask why she'd cut out early or tell her how successful the celebration today had been.

If that kind of magic existed, she wouldn't feel so awful and alone.

Christmas magic. She kicked off her high heels. What a joke.

CHAPTER TWELVE

By Tuesday morning, Leanne had resolved not to let Welton get to her. She was a big girl. It was time she acted like one.

She dried the tears from her eyes, put on her uniform and arrived fifteen minutes early for her shift. Not bad considering she hadn't showered on Sunday and Monday.

But she'd realized something important. Welton couldn't give her what she wanted. It was all about being in control with him. Yes, she was hurting, but he could never love her the way she wanted to be loved. He wasn't the kind of man she wanted to be with. Not now. Certainly not long-term or…forever.

The realization didn't ease the ache in her heart, but it helped work through the swirling emotions.

That afternoon, she watched pickup trucks loaded with toy donations leave the station to deliver gifts to local families and other charities.

"You did it, Thomas," Christian said.

Her chest tightened. Time to toughen up. Not be affected by him.

"You were on the committee, too." Then she remembered. He was repaying a debt. The toy drive and Christmas celebration hadn't mattered to him. "Never mind."

An older couple entered the fire station. The man and woman moved slowly as if trying to protect their fragile bones. She carried a round tin in one hand and held the man's hand with her other. They looked familiar. Leanne remembered why. The woman had been a patient.

Grateful for the distraction, she walked over to them. "Hello, I'm Leanne Thomas. How can I help you?"

"I'm Mabel Nichols. This is my husband, Earl. These are for you." The woman's hand trembled as she gave the tin to Leanne. "Snickerdoodles and chocolate chip cookies. I baked them fresh this morning."

Leanne smiled at the couple. "Two of my favorites."

"It's a small way of saying a big thank-you for saving my Mabel's life after her heart attack," Earl said.

"You look well," Leanne said to Mabel. "How are you feeling?"

Mabel's green eyes twinkled. "Much better these days."

Paulson, O'Ryan and Welton greeted the couple. Everyone tasted one of the delicious cookies.

"I remember you," Christian said. "Heart attack. Code save."

A "code save" was someone who wasn't breathing or didn't have a pulse when the rigs arrived, but was alive by the time they arrived at the hospital.

The man kissed his wife's hand with such adoration and tenderness it took Leanne's breath away. She fought the urge to look at Christian. She wouldn't give in to that temptation.

"Today is our sixty-fourth wedding anniversary," Earl said. "We are blessed to have six children, thirteen grandchildren and five great-grandchildren. I'm so grateful to have the love of my life with us this Christmas. She wouldn't be here without all of you."

The love in his voice brought tears to Leanne's eyes. She blinked them away.

After a few more thanks and cookies, the couple left, holding hands like teenagers experiencing the first blush of love.

Hope blossomed in Leanne's heart. Maybe she could find that.

"See," Christian said.

"What?" she asked.

"They wanted to pay us back for saving Mabel's life. The

same way I did with the toy drive and Christmas celebration," Christian explained. "It's no different from me."

Leanne faced him. "There's a big difference, rookie. Mabel said thank you out of gratitude from the very heart that had stopped beating. Earl thanked us from a heart that isn't mourning the loss of his beloved wife this Christmas. But you wouldn't understand that, because you just don't want to feel indebted. Your heart isn't involved because you protect it too much. You're so afraid of being pressured and losing control you can't even let someone do something nice for you. I have only one thing to say to you. Get over yourself, rookie."

With that, she walked away. This was the last shift she had to work with him until after Christmas. Maybe she'd switch a few more shifts so she wouldn't have to see him until the New Year.

Thursday night, customers filled every single table at the brewbub. The smell of beer and grease wafted in the air. The din of conversations drowned out the Christmas carols playing from overhead speakers. A pine swag decorated with miniature lights, holly and pinecones hung around the bar.

Christian sat next to his cousin Kaitlyn. Owen sat opposite them so he had room to rest his broken ankle. A pitcher of beer and a plateful of pretzels sat on the table.

Owen glanced around. "Business is booming."

Christian nodded. "It's been this way since Saturday."

Kaitlyn dipped a piece of pretzel into the brewpub's special mustard sauce. "I've got to hand it to you, Christian. You knew what you were doing with that celebration thing."

Owen nodded. "Imagine what you could do at the winery."

"I had help." Christian took a long swig of Mistletoe Ale, the brewery's special winter ale. The beer tasted good going down his throat. He didn't want to think about Leanne.

"Grandpa said you showed him a storefront," Kaitlyn continued.

Christian stared into his glass. "I did."

Owen leaned forward. "Thinking of moonlighting?"

"My life is here."

Owen's gaze pinned his. "Your family isn't."

Family is so important, Welton. You have no idea how lucky you are to have people who love you so much. Find a way to work things out. Compromise.

Leanne's words echoed in Christian's head. He was trying. "You're all here for Christmas.

"You only work about ten days a month." Owen wasn't being swayed. "That leaves you plenty of time to work at the winery."

Christian took another drink of his beer. "You have it all figured out."

Kaitlyn covered his hand with hers. "We know what Hood Hamlet means to you. But we miss you. Grandma and Grandpa aren't getting any younger."

"We'll have plenty of time to talk about things over Christmas." Christian had lucked out with the shift rotation this year. "I've got Christmas Eve and Christmas Day off."

A familiar laugh floated across the room. The sweet sound wrapped itself around Christian's heart and squeezed tight. Leanne. He glanced across the crowded dining room. She sat with Bill Paulson, Dr. Cullen Gray and Johnny Gearhart.

"Hey," Kaitlyn said. "Isn't that your mountain rescuer? The one you kissed under the mistletoe much to the chagrin of every single man there. Lee-something?"

"The beautiful Leanne." Owen glanced around. "Where?"

"At a table with the three hotties," Kaitlyn said. "Rough life being surrounded by gorgeous men at work and at play."

Owen shifted to get a better view. "The one in the plaid shirt is Bill Paulson. The guy in the black thermal top is Dr. Gray. Not sure about the other one."

Christian stared over his beer. "Johnny Gearhart."

"He's as gorgeous as the other two." Kaitlyn fluffed the ends of her hair. "I'd like an introduction to all three, please. They look totally into Leanne, but there's only one of her. I'm happy to take whoever's left."

Each of Christian's muscles tensed. He rolled his shoulders. *Get over yourself, rookie.*

She didn't know what she was talking about. Not that it mattered. He didn't want a girlfriend. Thomas was free to date whoever she wanted. It was absolutely none of his business what she did or who she spent her nights with.

Owen slid from the booth. He grabbed his crutches. "I'm going over there."

"Sit down," Christian said.

"She saved my life." Owen adjusted the crutches under his arms. "The least I can do is say hello. Coming?"

Christian refilled his glass. "I see her at the station."

That was plenty. More than enough actually.

Outside the Willinghams' log cabin, on December 23, familiar sounding sirens wailed.

Leanne's pulse quickened. She gripped the back of a kitchen chair.

Hannah Willingham placed colorful birthday plates next to the Thomas the Tank Engine cake. "Wish you were with them?"

Leanne pictured Christian in the engine with his helmet strapped under his chin. His eyes would be dark. His lips pressed together in thoughtful contemplation. So serious. So handsome. Such a jerk.

She needed to stop thinking about him.

Leanne released the chair. "And miss my godson's second birthday? No way. I'm so happy Stan traded shifts with me."

Hannah placed two blue candles into the cake. "You'll have to work Christmas Eve and Christmas morning again."

"Stan needs to be with his family." Leanne didn't want to wake up alone on Christmas morning. That was why she always traded shifts over the holidays. The station was the only family she had. She'd rather be there than home. "I'm off in time to go to church and snowshoeing."

"Austin and Kendall can't wait for the snowshoeing."

"They missed Sean and Denali last year."

"Yes, but this year they get Zoe, too."

"Our little group keeps getting bigger."

Hannah wiped her hands on the towel. "Will anyone else be joining in the fun?"

"Not that I know of."

"What about Christian?" Hannah asked.

Leanne stiffened.

"Nothing's going on. I got carried away. Caught up in the holiday spirit and success of the event, that's all."

"And the kiss under the mistletoe?"

"No big deal."

Hannah took a picture of the cake. "You sure about that?"

Leanne thought about the elderly couple at the station. "Positive. I know what I want now."

"What?"

"I want to meet a man, fall in love, get married and have a family."

But that wasn't going to happen until she made some changes in her life. Being one of the guys had served its purpose while she was growing up and finding her way as a paramedic. But she needed to move beyond that if she was ever going to find a man who would love *her,* not who he thought she was.

"That man isn't Welton," she admitted with a pang. "I only wish I knew who he was."

"You'll figure it out," Hannah said. "There are lots of men out there besides those who live in Hood Hamlet. Garrett lived in Portland when we met."

"Jake introduced you to him."

Hannah nodded. "I just had to let myself be open to possibilities."

"I'm open."

Now more than ever. Leanne liked feeling part of a…team wasn't the right word. She was a team at work and at OMSAR. She could only do so much with friends. She wanted to be one half of a couple. Laughing, helping, sharing. With Christian—

Not him, she corrected. Someone else. A man who would enchant her and be enchanted by her, too. One who wasn't afraid to commit his heart, not out of duty or sense of obligation, but out of love.

She sighed. "I wish it would happen soon."

A child squealed from the living room.

Hannah reached for the matches. "It will happen when the time's right. You're just going to have to be patient."

"That's never been a strong point of mine, but I'll try." Leanne stared at the birthday cake, somehow seeing it as three layers with pretty white roses and a bride and groom standing on top. "And hope it's worth the wait."

Christmas Eve arrived with a winter storm warning. Snow fell in the morning and continued into the evening. A few A shift families braved the weather to share a ham dinner at the station with their loved ones. Leanne didn't feel much like celebrating, but being surrounded by so much holiday cheer and joy made it easier to smile.

At ten o'clock that night, right in the middle of a classic Christmas movie, familiar tones sounded. "Rescue 1 and Engine 3 responding to woman in labor, Hamlet Heights, number five."

Leanne jumped into her bunkers and boots. She slid into the medic truck's passenger seat. She glanced at Tucker, her partner for this shift. "Two hours until the twenty-fifth. You think we'll have a Christmas baby?"

Tucker pulled out of the station. Chains had been installed on the rig earlier in the day. "For the kid's sake, I hope he comes before midnight."

"Lots of people are born on Christmas."

He concentrated on the road. Not easy driving with white-out conditions. "I'd bet most of them wished they'd been born another day."

Getting up the hill to the Hamlet Heights development, eight huge custom-built lodges, wasn't easy. The rig made it to the fifth house and stopped in what they hoped was the driveway, in front of two large double doors.

"Want the OB kit or do you want to see what we have first?" Tucker asked.

Leanne would rather transport, but with this weather it was best to be prepared. "Bring it in."

One of the front doors opened. A man walked outside.

Tucker grabbed the kit. "Isn't that Welton?"

Her stomach clenched. He was the last person she wanted to see.

"Glad you guys are here. My sister, Brianna, is in heavy labor. Thirty-nine weeks. She didn't want to spoil Christmas Eve and thought she had more time since she was in labor for seventeen hours with her first. Her water broke and things are moving fast." Christian spoke fast. Nerves. "I thought I was going to have to deliver the baby."

Leanne followed him into the house. Vaulted ceilings gave the modern lodge an airy feel and allowed a twenty-foot Christmas tree to take center stage in the massive living room full of expensive furniture. She'd never seen so many presents in her entire life. "How far apart are the contractions?"

"She wants to push."

So much for transport. Leanne's pulse rate increased. "Where is she?"

"Upstairs."

Leanne entered the large bedroom. She recognized the woman in her early thirties laying on a queen-size bed and the man holding her hand. Both looked stressed and panicked.

"Hi, Brianna. Jeff. I'm Leanne Thomas. We've met before." She wanted to put them at ease. "I'm a paramedic with Hood Hamlet Fire and Rescue. This is my partner, Derek Tucker. Looks like you're getting an early Christmas gift."

Brianna panted. Sweat beaded on her forehead. "I need to push."

Leanne put on gloves. "Let me do a quick exam first, okay?" Depending on what she saw would determine whether to go to the hospital or deliver here. Brianna wore a dress so that would make the exam easier.

Christian stood on the other side of Brianna. "You're in good hands, sis."

Brianna moaned.

Leanne saw the top of the baby crowning. Oh, boy. Her muscles tensed. This was something she'd done before, but nothing she did regularly. Her anxiety level rose, but she forced a smile. "Looks like we're going to do this here, okay?"

Brianna nodded.

Tucker got everything out that they needed and prepared the bed for delivery.

"Give us a minute, Brianna." Leanne draped the expectant mother's lower half with sheets and put on the necessary gear herself—gown, new gloves and safety glasses.

Tucker readied the clips, scalpel and bulb syringe. A blanket and hat for the baby were within arms reach. He also had the emergency airway equipment available just in case.

"Okay, Brianna." Leanne ignored everybody else in the room. Nothing else mattered but the mother and baby. "At the next contraction, I want you to push."

Brianna screamed.

"Push."

"Come on, Bri," Jeff said.

The head moved more. So far so good. But until Leanne could see the cord wasn't around the baby's neck, her nerves weren't going to settle down.

Another contraction hit. Brianna pushed. Jeff and Christian encouraged her through it.

The head came out. No cord.

Leanne breathed a sigh of relief. "The shoulders are next."

The delivery went smoothly after that. Before she knew it she held on to a perfect little baby boy. Tears stung her eyes. "It's a boy."

She suctioned the baby's mouth. She stimulated and dried the baby, who wailed at the top of his lungs. A good sign.

The cord was cut and clipped.

She placed the baby on top of Brianna's chest, skin to skin for warmth, and covered him with a blanket. While everyone fussed over the new member of the family, Leanne doubled-checked to make sure Brianna wasn't bleeding excessively. The placenta sill needed to come out.

"We're going to prepare her for transport," Leanne announced.

Christian's eyes gleamed. "Thank you."

She nodded, afraid of sounding too emotional after bringing a new life into the world.

"Yes, thank you." Brianna stared at the baby with love. "I think Thomas sounds like a good name. Don't you, Jeff?"

"A perfect name," he agreed.

Emotion clogged Leanne's throat. She blinked back tears. "Th-thanks."

With help from the engine crew, they made fast work of getting baby and mother to the rig.

Christian followed her out. "Leanne. Wait."

She didn't have time for this. Him. "What?"

"You were amazing."

"It was all Brianna."

"When you get off work tomorrow, spend Christmas with me."

Leanne drew back. "You're spending it with your family."

"I want to spend the day with you, too."

"Yeah, right." She couldn't believe him. "You don't owe me anything for delivering your nephew. It's what I'm paid to do."

"I'm not—"

"I do have to thank you, Welton." She didn't care what he had to say. "Because of you, I figured out I want what that older couple Mabel and Earl have. I thought for a brief second I could have it with you. But we both know I was fooling myself. Wishing for something that wasn't there. The guy I want, the guy who wants to be with me not because he thinks he owes me but because he loves me, that guy is out there. Somewhere. And one of these days I'll find him."

Heart pounding in her chest, she climbed into the back of the rig with Brianna and the baby. Leanne's hands shook as she closed the door. She looked at Christian's sister. "We're going to get you to the hospital as soon as we can."

The rescue rig drove away with its lights flashing. The engine followed without any lights or siren. Christian was cold and covered in snow, but that didn't bother him as much as the way Leanne had spoken.

He wanted to spend time with her, not pay her back. Watching her deliver his nephew had touched Christian's heart. Leanne was so confident, even if he saw a hint of uncertainty in her eyes at the beginning. Brianna had been scared, but Leanne's strength had given his sister courage. And when Thomas arrived...

Tears welled in Christian's eyes. He brushed off the snow, stepped inside and removed his wet shoes. He wanted to share more moments like that with Leanne.

In the entryway, Owen leaned on his crutches. "What's going on with you and Leanne?"

Christian cleared his throat. "Nothing."

"I'm going to ask her out then," Owen said.

"Over my dead body."

Owen raised a brow. "Then why'd you say nothing?"

Christian was the one who'd drawn the line in the sand about no relationship. Leanne was merely reacting to it. "It doesn't matter."

But he couldn't stop thinking about her, wanting to be with her. Maybe he'd been too rash. Maybe he needed to rethink things. No, she'd made it clear tonight.

He'd had his shot at being the guy she wanted, but he'd blown it. She was going to find someone else. "Leanne doesn't want me."

Owen raised a brow. "If you're going to let her go that easily, you don't deserve her."

"Leanne's not the kind of woman you can catch, unless she wants to be caught."

Right now she didn't. Unfortunately Christian only had himself to blame.

The smell of coffee filled the air. Leanne opened her eyes. Half the beds in the bunk room were occupied, the other half empty. Someone snored. And then she realized…

Christmas morning had arrived.

Leanne preferred the buildup to Christmas more than the day itself. She crawled out of bed.

Last night after the baby delivery, they'd only had one other call. A quiet night.

Downstairs, presents filled the stockings hanging on the wall. Everyone on duty got a little something to put in the stockings. This year, she'd put a mini flashlight—a practical gift—and yo-yo—a not so practical one—in each stocking.

Paulson stood with a cup of coffee in his hands. "Merry Christmas, Thomas."

"Same to you." She poured herself a cup of coffee. "Why are you here on your day off?"

"My mom made breakfast for you all."

"That was sweet of her."

He motioned to the window. "It's dumping snow."

Darn. She sipped her coffee. "That'll make for great skiing tomorrow, but not so great snowshoeing today."

"When has a little snow ever stopped us?"

"That was before Kendall, Austin and Wyatt joined the crew," Leanne reminded.

"They're tough kids."

"True, but we still might want to shorten the distance." She hated suggesting that. Snowshoeing with everyone was one of her favorite things about Christmas day. "We have to think about the kids."

Bill thought for a moment. "Yeah, you're probably right."

The tones sounded throughout the station.

"So much for an easy Christmas," he said.

She placed her cup on the counter. "Christmas is never easy."

Whether calls came in or not.

Wrapping paper and ribbons covered every inch of the floor of the rented lodge. Christian's nieces and nephews, dressed in brand-new pajamas they'd received last night, tore through presents as if their lives depended on how fast they could open each gift. Even little Emma, with her parents at the hospital with her new brother, shred through presents.

One of the kids handed his grandfather a box. As Grandpa read the tag, Christian fought the urge to hold his breath. "It's from Christian." Slowly his grandfather unwrapped the paper. He lifted the lid off the box and raised the bottle of wine out of the box. Tears glistened in his eyes. "You've been making your own wine."

Christian nodded. "I needed something to do in my time off, Grandpa."

"Besides chasing hot women," Owen said.

Christian ignored his cousin. "The flavor would have been a little deeper if I'd had better barrels."

His grandfather stared at the label. "I'm sure it's fine. We'll try it as soon as we're done here."

"You'll wait until a reasonable hour." His grandmother patted his grandfather's hand. "But I think it's time for Christian's present."

His grandfather carefully placed the bottle back in the box. "I agree."

Emma handed Christian a small box wrapped in holly-covered paper and tied with a red ribbon. "This is for you, Uncle Christian from Grandma and Grandpa."

Based on the size, Christian guessed what might be inside— a key ring or money holder. Possibly a gift card. A practical gift everyone always said. He removed the ribbon.

"Rip it, Uncle Christian," Emma urged.

"Rip it. Rip it," another cheered.

He didn't want to disappoint the kids, so he did as told. The little ones cheered.

"It's a box," Emma shouted.

Christian removed the lid. He opened the white tissue paper. A gold key.

"What is it?" Kaitlyn asked.

"A key." He looked at his grandparents. "What does it open?"

"The future," Grandpa said.

"Whose future?" Christian asked.

"Yours."

The gold key gleamed as bright as a star. His gut clenched.

"I really should say ours. The key is to the empty shop on Main Street you showed me," Grandpa continued. "It'll make a perfect retail and tasting store for Welton Winery. We could even put in a winemaking section. I hadn't realized you were still interested… Since this is your neck of the woods, I thought you might want to be a part of it."

"You're opening a branch of the winery here?"

Grandpa nodded. "I don't think I'm going to be able to take the mountain or the firefighter out of you, so I figured I might as well bring the winery to you."

"What do you want in return?" Christian asked.

"Nothing," Grandpa said. "I butted heads with your father and forced his hand more times than I care to remember. I don't want to do that anymore. I trust you, Christian. Whatever you want to do with the store, we'll work it out. I don't want a grandson who can't bear to talk to me."

Christian stared at the key. Emotion welled up inside him. His grandpa wasn't pressuring him. His family loved him. He wanted to do this. He'd missed being part of the winery. That was why he made wine as a hobby. He'd missed being a part of the family.

"Thanks, Grandpa. It's great." And it was. Christian would be able to do things his way. He was still honoring what his dad told him about not being pressured. But he didn't need to hold everyone at arm's length. Not only his family, but Leanne. "I'll do my best to make you proud."

"You've already made me proud," Grandpa said to Christian's surprise. "I'm sure you'll continue to do so."

He couldn't stop thinking about Leanne. "I will."

As the present opening continued, Owen joined Christian on the couch. "Nice gift."

He looked at the key. "Yeah."

"Maybe you can carry some of my chocolates," Owen said. "Grandpa told me I could make some for the winery."

"Great."

"You don't sound all that excited about any of this."

Christian didn't want to appear ungrateful. "I have a lot on my mind."

"It can't be Brianna and the baby. All reports from the hospital have been good. That leaves…the pretty paramedic."

Leanne was pretty, smart, sexy. "I messed up."

"Apologize."

"She wants a relationship. A commitment. I can't—"

"Better rethink not wanting to make any commitments," Owen said. "You just made a huge one with Grandpa and the wine store."

Christian stared at the key. He had committed to something huge. Yet, it felt good. Right. The same way being with Leanne had felt. He'd worked things out with his family. Maybe he could do the same thing with her. "She still might not want me."

"You'll never know unless you try."

What did Christian have to lose? His pride. His heart. Both, he realized, were worth risking for Leanne. She had told him to get over himself. He had. But he couldn't get over her. She didn't need him, but he needed her. Maybe, just maybe, that would be enough. The least he could do was apologize for being such a jerk to her.

He rose.

So did Owen.

"Where do you think you're going?" Christian asked.

"If she says no to you, she might say yes to me." Owen hobbled on his crutches. "Otherwise we can drown our sorrows together."

Leanne walked out of the Christmas service at church. Singing carols and hearing the message about this special day should have made her feel better. But seeing all the families together, the loving couples and the excited children, only made her feel worse. She trudged through the snow in the parking lot.

A quick dash home to change her clothes then time for snowshoeing. Too bad Leanne didn't feel like going. Unusual for her.

But the kids were counting on all of them being there. She couldn't let them down even if she wanted to spend the rest of her Christmas by herself.

Christmas Day at the fire station was a happy time. Families showed up with presents and joined the crew for meals. Christian didn't see Leanne's car in the parking lot. Maybe she'd caught a ride with someone else. He left Owen in the car and went inside. Two of the B shift wives stood in the kitchen cooking lunch.

"What are you doing here, Welton?" the chief asked.

"Looking for Thomas."

"She left for church a couple of hours ago."

Damn. She might already be somewhere else. "I need to track her down."

"Joining Thomas and Paulson on their annual Christmas snowshoeing trek?" the chief asked.

Leanne had invited Christian to go snowshoeing on Christmas Day. "I can't remember where we're supposed to meet."

"She's probably with Paulson, but Jake Porter, Sean Hughes or Hannah Willingham would know."

"Thanks." Christian headed out the door, ran to his car and slid inside. "She's going snowshoeing."

Owen sighed. "Do you know how many trails there are on this mountain?"

"A lot, but I know who to ask."

Paulson didn't answer his cell phone. Christian drove to Sean and Zoe Hughes's house. No one, not even their Siberian husky, Denali, was home. Next stop was Jake and Carly Porter's house. No one was there, either. Finally he pulled into Hannah and Garrett Willingham's driveway.

Christian stared at the cabin. "I'll be right back."

He exited the car. A single candle burned in the window. Snow angels decorated the front yard, but were being covered by falling snow. He hurried up the snow-covered path and rang the doorbell.

The door opened. Hannah wore the red-and-green apron Leanne had worn when they babysat. "Christian?"

"I need to know where everyone is going snowshoeing today."

She wiped her hands on the apron. "Everyone or Leanne?"

"Please, Hannah," he urged. "I need to talk with her."

"You've already ruined her Christmas."

"I need to apologize. See if she'll give me another chance."

Hannah straightened.

At least he had her attention now. "Please tell me where she is?"

"It'll be easier if I show you." She untied her apron. "Kendall and Austin are there with Jake and Carly. Garrett and I have Tyler and Nicole."

Garrett came to the door. "What's going on?"

Hannah handed him her apron. "I'm going with Christian. I'll be back in a little while."

Garrett looked stunned. "O-kay."

Large snowflakes fell from the sky. Hannah headed to Christian's truck. "We'd better hurry in case they cut their snowshoeing short due to the weather."

She climbed into the truck's backseat, introducing herself to his cousin. "I'm Hannah."

"Owen Welton Slayter."

"She knows where Leanne is," Christian said.

Owen grinned. "I'm glad someone does."

"Take 26 to the snow park," Hannah directed. "The road before the parking lot leads to another small lot and the trail head."

Christian shifted the car into gear. "Thanks, Hannah."

"Don't thank me yet." Concern filled her eyes. "Do you know what you're going to say to Leanne?"

"I thought I'd start with I'm sorry."

"After that?" Hannah asked.

"That I'm lower than pond scum." Christian gripped the steering wheel. "I...I don't know what to say after that."

"You really shouldn't wing this," Owen said.

"Tell Leanne whatever's in your heart of hearts," Hannah suggested.

"This is never going to work," Owen said. "My cousin doesn't have a heart of hearts."

"Well, he'd better find it quick," Hannah said. "And hope a little Christmas magic helps him out."

"You're so screwed," Owen said.

"Thanks, dude." As Christian turned onto the road, he thought about his ex-girlfriend, Kelly. He'd blamed the breakup entirely on her, but he was just as guilty. She'd wanted one thing. He'd wanted another. Neither of them had been willing to compromise. Leanne was different. She didn't want to take. She wanted to give. Even though she'd lost everything, that didn't stop her from giving her all, her heart, to whoever might need it. The crew at the fire station. Their patients. OMSAR. Friends. She wasn't trying to pressure him. She didn't want payment. She wanted nothing in return.

No, Leanne did. She wanted love.

He'd been wrong about her. Oh-so-wrong.

Christian no longer cared about what he wanted. It was all

about her. "I'm going to tell Leanne the truth. And hope it's enough."

"Anything is possible if you believe," Hannah said with sincerity.

He believed, but what about Leanne? Could she believe... in him?

The snowshoeing trip had been a success. Denali, Sean's dog, ran from person to person trying to snag marshmallows. The kids entertained everyone with Christmas carols.

Leanne forced herself to sing along. This was their tradition every December 25. Everyone was here this year. No injuries like last year. She should be having fun.

Leanne stared at her friends. Little Wyatt had fallen asleep in Tim's arms. Rita, Tim's wife, was home cooking, as she did every year because she didn't like the cold. Jake and Carly stood close together, the love for each other apparent with every glance. Zoe leaned against Sean, a picture-perfect couple.

Leanne's heart tightened. She wanted to find that kind of love. But she wasn't like Zoe or Carly or Rita.

Men like Sean, Jake and Tim were hard to find. Not that Leanne would have ever dated any of them when they were single. But love had made the men realize what was really important in life. And what wasn't.

All Christian wanted was to be free. Free of commitment and obligations, to be able to do what he wanted with no pressure. Maybe when he finally fell in love he would realize he didn't have to be so scared of trusting and losing control. It would take a special woman to make that happen. Leanne hoped for his sake, Christian found her someday.

CHAPTER THIRTEEN

PAULSON'S SUV and Sean Hughes's pickup were parked in the lot. Fresh powder covered the hoods and windshields.

Relief washed over Christian. He pulled into an empty space. "They're still here."

"Do you see Leanne's car?" Owen asked.

Christian didn't see Leanne's red Subaru there. The muscles in his shoulders tensed. "No, but she could have ridden with someone."

He put the truck in Park and set the emergency brake. "Stay inside where it's warm."

Hannah unbuckled her seat belt. "I'm going with you."

"Me, too." Owen opened the door. "Turn off the engine."

Christian didn't think that was a good idea. Owen's face was pale. "You look tired."

"I'm fine."

Christian turned off the engine and exited the truck.

Hannah pointed to a group of people bundled up in hats and coats sitting by a fire. "They're over there."

Christian fought the urge to run. As he walked, snow drenched the hem of his pants. He couldn't wait to see Leanne.

Paulson noticed him first. "What are you doing here, Welton?"

A glance passed between the men. Zoe and Carly shared one, too.

Christian studied each person's face. Leanne wasn't with them. His heart plummeted to his feet.

"Christian!" Kendall and Austin had red, runny noses and pink cheeks. Their eyes sparkled and smiles lit up their faces. "Merry Christmas."

"Merry Christmas to you," Christian said.

Hannah caught up to him. "Merry Christmas everybody."

"Mommy!" the kids shouted.

"I'm looking for Leanne," Christian said.

Another look passed between the snowshoers. Okay, he got it. They were friends of Leanne's. He'd hurt her.

"She left," Kendall announced.

Hannah placed her hand on Christian's shoulder. "Does anyone know where Leanne went?"

Paulson stood. "She had someplace to go, but didn't say where."

"It's a small town." Compassion filled Hannah's voice. "You'll find her."

Christian nodded. He wasn't going to give up now.

"I'm sorry, dude. I don't think I'm going to make it out here much longer," Owen said with a yawn.

"I'll drive you back," Sean Hughes offered.

Tim Moreno held a sleeping child. "I can, too."

"Take Wyatt home for his nap," Sean said. "I've got it covered."

Tim walked to the parking lot with the snowshoes and poles tucked under one arm.

"I'll ride with Carly, Jake and the kids," Hannah said.

Sympathy filled Zoe's eyes. "I hope you find her, Christian." Him, too.

The others walked to their cars. Jake and Sean glared back.

"They don't like me," Christian said.

"You hurt Leanne," Paulson answered.

Regret lay heavy on Christian's heart. "I did."

"You have to understand, we might treat her like one of the guys, but she's more like a sister to us. Always there. Always ready to help out or take off on some adventure to make sure we don't hurt ourselves."

"I didn't mean to hurt her."

"You still did."

"I want to make it up to her."

Paulson didn't say anything.

"I care about her." No, that wasn't right. "I love her."

He eyed Christian warily. "You love Leanne?"

"Yes." There was no doubt. No hesitation. She'd been right. Again. He'd been too scared to admit how he felt, too scared about a lot of things. But no longer. He'd give her his heart, his life if that was what she wanted. "I love her."

"I swear. If you make her cry again, Welton, I'm going to hurt you. Bad."

"Go ahead," Christian said. "I'll deserve it."

Paulson stared at him with respect in his eyes. "You want some company trying to find her?"

"Thanks, but it's Christmas," Christian said. "Go be with your family."

"I should really know where she is today," Paulson said. "But I have no idea. Let me know when you find her."

When, not if. Paulson's confidence bolstered Christian's own. "Sure."

But he had no idea where to start. He thought about what she'd said last night.

I want what that older couple Mabel and Earl have.

They had a long marriage. Kids. Grandkids. Great-grandkids.

Family.

A barrage of images flashed through Christian's mind. The homemade ornaments on the tree. The name LeLe written on the back of the star. The family portrait. The way she reacted whenever someone mentioned Christmas magic.

There isn't such a thing as Christmas magic. If there were, bad things wouldn't happen on Christmas.

Christmas. Not December.

He'd thought she was talking about Nick and Iain, but the two climbers hadn't died on Christmas.

We were on our way home from my grandparents' house. I was playing with a new doll I'd just gotten.

Family. Her family. Christmas Day.

Is your family around here?

Not too far away location wise, but in a completely different place.

The pieces of the puzzle clicked. Christian ran to his car. He knew exactly where she'd gone. It was the one place she shouldn't have to be alone.

He climbed into the truck and turned on the ignition.

Christian didn't want to show up empty-handed. He backed out of his parking spot. The general store might be open. If not, he'd figure something else out.

He turned onto the road. The tires spun on the snow.

Not now. He let up on the gas. He didn't have time to get stuck. If ever some Christmas magic was needed, it was now.

Christian pressed down on the accelerator. The car jerked forward onto the highway.

All he had to do was get to Leanne. He loved her. Even if she didn't need him or want him, maybe she'd still let him spend Christmas with her. Because he really didn't want to spend today without her. He didn't want to spend another day without her.

He only hoped he could convince her to give him another chance.

"Merry Christmas." Leanne placed an evergreen wreath with pinecones, holly and a weatherproof red bow in front her family's headstone. She looked at each name with a pang in her heart.

"I love you." Tears stung her eyes, but she didn't blink them away. She touched the headstone with her gloved hand. "I miss you."

But it wasn't the same heart-wrenching emotion the first few Christmases had brought with them. When she was younger, she used to come here all the time. To think. To talk. But she didn't need to do that now. She came only once a year. On the anniversary of the accident. The one day—okay, a few hours— she allowed herself to be...herself. A few hours weren't enough anymore.

"I wonder if you'd be surprised by the person I've become. I'm not sure I can keep it up much longer. I need...more. A family like we had."

She had friends. Good friends, but she wasn't with them today except for snowshoeing. She wanted to be celebrating the holiday with family, not standing in a cemetery alone.

"I hope it's not too late."

A gust of wind came out of nowhere. Snow blew from tree branches. It sounded almost like a whisper.

LeLe.

She froze. The hair on the back of her neck stood up. Only her family and Nick had ever called her that. All of them were buried in this cemetery.

She glanced around. No one was there.

Relief washed over her. For a second she thought she might see the Spirit of Christmases Past. Okay, now she was being really silly. She laughed.

Maybe it was a sign she wasn't supposed to ignore her LeLe side anymore. And she wouldn't. No matter what people thought.

"LeLe."

The sound of her name was clearer this time and hung on the air. She turned.

Christian strode through the snow with a box full of poinsettia plants in his gloved hands. A puff of condensation accentuated each breath. He wore a green jacket, khaki slacks, boots and a wool beanie on his head.

Gorgeous. Not that she wanted him. Still, regret clawed at her heart.

He stopped in front of her.

She raised her chin. "How did you know I was here?"

"Christmas magic."

"Yeah, right, so—"

"Let's put these down first. Then we'll talk."

Christian placed two poinsettia plants on each side of the wreath. Red foil covered the plant pots, the effect very pretty and Christmassy.

Four plants remained in the box. She stared, confused. "Who are those for?"

"Your grandparents, Nick Bishop and Iain Garfield."

Her mouth gaped. "How…"

"Show me where they are."

She led him to her grandparents' grave. She'd already placed a wreath there. "They were in their seventies when I came to live with them. They died within two weeks of each other, right after I turned eighteen. I think they tried to hang on until I was old enough to be on my own."

"Eighteen is still young."

She was about to shrug. She was so used to acting tough and appearing as if nothing bothered her. The truth was she had been young. Too young to be on her own. "Yeah. I still hadn't graduated high school."

"They would be proud of the woman you've become."

"I hope so." Her grandparents had done the best they could. But they hadn't been prepared to raise another child at their age. She'd had few rules except to make good grades and be home by bedtime. She could have gotten into a lot more trouble if she'd fallen in with a different crowd. "I tried to stay out of their way and be good. It mostly worked."

"Mostly?"

"Except when I went against my better judgment and took off with the guys."

"They became your family."

Her first instinct was to say yes. Jake and Nick were the ones who attended her high school graduation, but they probably would have come anyway since Bill was graduating, too.

"The closest I've had in a very long time." But she wanted more. "They say I'm one of the guys, but I'm not always treated that way. Whenever something big went down, like when Nick was missing or Sean wanted to get Zoe back, I was the one left to stay with the wives, girlfriends and kids. Even though I tried hard to be one of the guys, when push came to shove I'm still a girl."

"I'm glad you're a girl."

She straightened. "Me, too."

"So who are you planning to spend Christmas with today?" Christian asked.

"No one," she admitted.

"You prefer being alone."

"No."

"Why aren't you spending Christmas with anyone?"

"I'm spending it alone."

"No one invited you."

"You did last night." She took a deep breath. "I could have asked—"

"Not your style."

No, it wasn't. She couldn't believe he knew her so well. "It's okay. Nick used to always invite me over, so it's not like I've been alone since my grandparents died."

"Only since Nick died. Eight years."

"Cocoa was here for three of those Christmases."

Accusation filled Christian's eyes. "That doesn't make it right."

"It's no one's fault. Things changed when Nick died," Leanne explained. "People had their own grief and pain to deal with. Carly and her parents moved away. Jake was so busy helping Hannah and the kids. Tim had just met his future wife and was head over heels in love. Bill was…well, Bill."

Christian started to speak then stopped himself. He handed her one of the poinsettia plants. "This is for Nick."

She walked to his gravestone. She placed the plant on the ground. "Nick loved Christmas. He wore a Santa hat the entire month of December. Even when we were in high school. He was a lot like my oldest brother, Cole."

"Which is why he called you LeLe."

She nodded. "He was a good guy. He knew exactly when I needed a friend or a big brother. Or when he needed to push me out of my comfort level to try something new."

Christian held the remaining plant in his hand. "Where's Iain?"

"His parents didn't want him buried here on the mountain."

Christian placed the poinsettia next to Nick's. "They're probably together."

The gesture touched her. She shoved her gloved hands in her pockets. "Thanks for bringing these by. But I'm not really sure why you did or why you're even here. You don't owe me anything."

"I know, but I wanted to see you."

Her pulse quickened. "On Christmas?"

He nodded. "I went by the station, but you'd already left. I ended up at the snowshoe trailhead."

"No one knew where I was going."

"I know," he said. "I was feeling pretty lost and a little desperate."

"Desperate?"

"Yes, until I figured out where you would be." He motioned to the poinsettias. "I didn't want to show up empty-handed so I stopped by the General Store."

"It's not open on Christmas Day."

"I called Mr. Freeman."

She didn't get it. "You went to a lot of trouble."

"You're worth it," he said. "As you said, it was time to get over myself."

The air rushed from her lungs. Her mouth gaped. That was what she'd said to him at the station.

He took her gloved hand in his. "Come with me."

A million questions filled her mind, but she kept quiet.

Christian led her to a trail at the far side of the cemetery. Her boots crunched on the snow as they headed up. Tall trees flanked the path. She had no idea where they were going. She also knew they weren't prepared for a hike in this kind of weather without any gear or water.

But she kept her mouth shut.

He stopped in a clearing, surrounded by snow-covered pine trees. A perfect Winter Wonderland setting. Snow flurries fell down on them as if they were standing in the middle of a snow globe.

Christian took a deep breath. "I'm sorry I've been such a jerk."

Her heart stuttered. He wanted to apologize. That was why they were here and he'd brought the flowers. Disappointment shot through her.

"Apology accepted." She looked at a snow-laden branch, then at an intricate snowflake spinning and twirling its way to the ground. She would stare at anything if it meant not having to meet his gaze again. "Thanks for bringing the poinsettias, too. We're more than even now."

"I'm not trying to repay you, Leanne. You have to understand. In my life, strings were attached to everything. There was always pressure to do what others wanted. Because of that I wanted everything to be my choice, be under my control." He took her hand. "You made me see I went too far. Caring for someone is not an obligation or pressure. It's mutual giving. Can you forgive me?"

Her throat tightened. She blinked back the tears in her eyes.

"I forgive you," she said. "I'm sorry for being so emotional. I've kept that side hidden for so long, when it comes out it's hard to control."

"Please don't feel the need to control it around me. You're the most capable, self-reliant woman I've ever met. You don't need anyone. I thought I didn't need anyone, either. I tried to be entirely independent, but that isn't the best way to live. It's not what I want anymore. I need you. I want to be part of your life."

"As a friend."

"More than a friend."

"Oh, you want someone to kiss on New Year's Eve."

"You know me well," he admitted, to her regret. "But I don't just want to kiss anyone. I want to kiss you."

Her heart wouldn't survive. Even if her lips wanted to kiss him again.

"I also want to kiss you on Valentine's Day, St. Patrick's Day, Easter, Fourth of July, Halloween, Thanksgiving and Christmas," Christian continued. "For the next, say…sixty-four years. I love you, LeLe."

Her heart skipped a beat. Maybe three. "You love me?"

He nodded. "I think I may have fallen in love with you the minute you appeared in the snow cave. I'd never been happier to see someone. Granted, I was slightly hypothermic at the time. But I should have known it the second I kissed you under the mistletoe in the kitchen."

She listened in disbelief. "I…"

"I may be younger than you and an idiot at times, but I learn from my mistakes. If there's one person in this world who I can trust, it's you. I'll never have that with anyone else because no one else gives so much of herself for so little in return." The sincerity in his words rang true. "I don't want to lose you. I don't care what anyone says or thinks, not even the chief. If you want me, just say the word. I'm yours."

She struggled to breathe. Her heart raced, matching her pulse rate. This was more than she imagined, more than she'd ever dreamed.

"Word." Leanne rose on her tiptoes and kissed him hard on the lips. No one was watching. She didn't have to hold back. She poured all her emotion, all her heart into the kiss. Nothing had ever felt so right. "I want you. I need you. I love you."

"I love a woman who knows what she wants and isn't afraid to say it." He grinned. "Marry me."

Leanne sucked in a cold breath. She opened her mouth to speak, but nothing came out. He had to be joking, right? She was afraid to ask.

"Oops. Forgot something." Christian took her hand and

kneeled in the snow. From his pocket he pulled out a plastic container, the kind found in a gumball machine. Inside was a toy ring. "Will you marry me, LeLe?"

This couldn't be happening. At any moment she would wake up at the station. Except she felt the snow hitting her face and the cold air as she inhaled. "You're serious."

"Very." He showed her the plastic ring. "I hope this will do until after Christmas. No jewelry stores are open today. It was either this or a mood ring."

Her mind reeled. "But you didn't want a girlfriend for Christmas."

"No, but a fiancée for New Year's sounds perfect."

Her heart slammed against her chest. He was serious.

"If I don't rope you into marrying me, you might take off up the mountain, and I'll never catch you. Just like when we went backcountry skiing. We've both shut ourselves off, Leanne, and now we need to take the same sort of risk we take every day on the job, and trust each other, not waste more time. Let's not be afraid to live the life we both want."

His gaze captured hers. She couldn't have looked away if she wanted to. The love in his eyes sent a burst of tingles shooting through her. Joy overflowed. "Oh, Christian…"

"I'm a firefighter. I'm trained to put out fires." He touched his chest, right where his heart would be. "The one right here. You ignited. I want it to keep burning. What do you say, LeLe? Marry me?"

She'd never imagined feeling so cherished before. This was the fairy tale. At least as close as one got these days. Leanne grinned. "Using my name doesn't always guarantee a yes."

Hoped gleamed in his eyes. "But I'm sure it can't hurt."

"You realize I'm not just one of the guys."

"You like pink, frilly things. Flowers and lace, too."

"How did you know?"

"I saw your bedroom, though it confused me."

"I'm sure it did." She laughed. "I used to be a little princess-type girl. But after my family died and I came to live in Hood

Hamlet, I needed to fit in somewhere. Anywhere. I missed my brothers so much. When I met Bill and Jake and Nick, they reminded me of Cole and Troy so much. I wanted to be friends with them so I did everything I could to be one of the guys. It carried on to the station."

"I get it." Christian caressed her cheek with the side if his fingertips. "But all that matters now is you're my girl. Whether you're kicking my butt skiing or dressed from head-to-toe in pink sparkly stuff or in your bunkers."

"I am your girl. I think somehow I always knew even when I tried to talk myself out of it." Full of love, contentment flowed through her veins. "My answer is yes, Christian. I'll marry you."

He kissed her on the lips. "Merry Christmas, LeLe."

She stared at the snow falling and clinging to his hair. So handsome. So strong. And hers.

"Merry Christmas, Christian." She placed her palm on his chest and felt the beating of his heart. "Maybe there is a little Christmas magic in Hood Hamlet, after all."

*****

A MARINE FOR CHRISTMAS

BY
BETH ANDREWS

First published in Great Britain 2011
by Mills & Boon, an imprint of Harlequin (UK) Limited,
Eton House, 18-24 Paradise Road, Richmond, Surrey TW9 1SR

© Beth Burgoon 2010

ISBN: 978 0 263 88929 1

23-1211

Harlequin (UK) policy is to use papers that are natural, renewable and
recyclable products and made from wood grown in sustainable forests. The
logging and manufacturing processes conform to the legal environmental
regulations of the country of origin.

Printed and bound in Spain
by Blackprint CPI, Barcelona

Dear Reader,

"Life is what happens to you while you're busy making other plans." —*John Lennon*

As we're all well aware, life does not follow a set road map—no matter how much we'd like it to. There are bumps that leave you flat and broken down. Turns that lead to wonderful new destinations. You may find yourself at the top of a high hill, joyous and certain that if you reach up, you'll touch the stars. Or in a valley so low you wonder how you'll ever climb out.

Ex-marine Brady Sheppard is in one of those valleys. The woman he loves has married another man. He's drinking too much and is also suffering post-traumatic stress disorder from his time served in Afghanistan. Too full of pride and anger to ask for help, he spends his days bitter and alone. Until he finds out he's going to be a father. Too bad the mother of his child, Jane Cleo (JC) Montgomery, is his ex's kid sister.

Let me just confess right here and now that Brady was no walk in the park to write. He was harsh and angry and dealing with some very big, very real issues. But as I wrote him, I fell for him in a huge way, because somehow he finds a way to deal with those issues. To overcome his anger and ease his bitterness. He learns that life goes on. I love to hear from readers. Please visit my website, www.bethandrews.net, or write to me at PO Box 714, Bradford, PA 16701, USA.

Beth Andrews

Beth Andrews loves Christmas, wine and chocolate—though not necessarily in that order. During the writing of this book she listened to hours of Christmas carols, visited a local winery (several times) and made many, *many* homemade chocolate truffles. All for research purposes, of course. Beth is a Romance Writers of America RITA® Award finalist and Golden Heart winner. She lives in northwestern Pennsylvania with her husband and three teenagers, who claim they are her children but are a far cry from the sweet, quiet babies she gave birth to. Learn more about Beth and her books by visiting her website, www.BethAndrews.net.

For my fabulous critique partner Tawny Weber.
Thanks for always finding something to love in my
stories and for being such a wonderful friend.

Acknowledgments

My sincere gratitude to Mitzi Batterson of James River
Cellars Winery in Glen Allen, Virginia, for taking
the time to answer my questions about running a
family-owned winery in Virginia.

CHAPTER ONE

IT MIGHT HAVE BEEN the numerous shots of whiskey and the goading of his fellow drinkers down at The Empire Bar, but Brady Sheppard thought crashing his ex-fiancée's wedding was the best idea he'd had in years.

Too bad he wasn't drunk enough to believe he'd gone through the side entrance of the First Presbyterian Church undetected because of his stealth and military training. He'd caught a break, that was all. It'd been bound to happen eventually.

The sounds of a string quartet masked the soft click of him pulling the door shut. Bracing his weight on his crutches, he slanted forward. To his left, waning sunlight filtered through two stained-glass windows, breaking up the shadows of a long hallway. Glancing around the corner, he spied five women in identical dark purple gowns lined up in a haphazard row, flowers clasped loosely in their hands as they chatted in hushed whispers while waiting for their cue to walk down the aisle.

The door at the end of the hall opened and Brady's heart rate picked up. Backing against the wall, he stayed hidden in the shadows as Jane Cleo Montgomery stepped into the hall. She, too, had on a purple dress and held flowers, her brown, corkscrew curls piled on top of her head. As she passed him unaware, she said something over her shoulder and laughed.

And that was when he saw her. Liz. *His* Liz.

He didn't move, barely breathed as the woman he was supposed to marry glided toward him, a serene smile on her beautiful face. His hands tightened on the crutches. Of course she was happy. She was getting what she'd always wanted. A fancy, summer wedding in her hometown, surrounded by family and friends. Except he wasn't the groom.

Ignoring the throbbing pain in his knee, he hobbled out into her path. "Hello, Lizzie."

The color drained from her face as she pulled up short, stumbling over her long train. "Brady."

That was it. After everything they'd meant to each other, the years they'd been together, all she could give him was his name. He wanted to shake her. Demand that she take back everything in that goddamn letter she'd sent him over a year ago when she'd blown his life apart. Wanted to see more in her eyes than nerves. Something that told him she regretted what she'd lost. That she was hurting, even just a little.

And how pathetic was he that he'd take whatever scraps she tossed his way?

"I'll get Dad," J.C. said from behind him.

Swinging his crutches forward, he backed Liz down the hallway. Her familiar floral scent confused his already muddled brain. Her gown had a fitted, beaded bodice and puffy skirt that accentuated her hourglass figure. She'd swept her glossy, dark hair up and wore one of those tiara things attached to a veil that ended below her small waist.

She was the most beautiful thing he'd ever seen.

"Glad I'm not too late," he murmured.

She swallowed, her hazel eyes wide. "Too...too late?"

"For the ceremony."

"Brady, please..." She held out her hand only to curl her fingers into her palm and lower it back to her side. "Please don't do this."

He went hot, then cold, trembling with the effort to contain his anger. Those were the exact same words he'd said to her after he'd read that damn letter. He'd called her from his base in Afghanistan, begged her to give him another chance.

He moved even closer, crowding her. She gasped, her warm breath washing over his face. "What do you think I'm going to do, Lizzie?" he asked quietly.

"I...I'm not sure." Her voice was as quiet as his. And when she met his eyes, the strange intimacy of their conversation reminded him of how he used to hold her after they'd made love. How it seemed as if they were the only two people in the world. "Make a scene or... or interrupt the ceremony..."

He shook his head to clear it. The ceremony. Right. He stepped back, grimacing with the pressure on his left leg.

"Are you all right?" she asked. As if she cared about him. Dr. Elizabeth Montgomery, trying to heal the poor Jarhead's injuries.

He glared at her. "Afraid I'm going to stand up when the minister asks if anyone objects?"

Someone laid a heavy hand on Brady's shoulder. "Son, you need to leave."

Brady glanced at Liz's father. Don Montgomery, tall and pudgy with intelligent brown eyes and thinning dark hair threaded heavily with gray. The physician's round face was red above his starched collar.

"I'm not your son," was all Brady said. Though, until recently, he'd considered Don to be like a second father.

Jane Cleo brushed past them to stand next to her sister, looking from him to Liz and back again.

"Go home," Don said, not unkindly. "Don't make this harder than it has to be." When Brady didn't so much as blink, the older man sighed and reached into the inside pocket of his dark suit jacket. "I'm afraid if you won't leave on your own, I'll have to call the police."

"No," J.C. and Liz said at the same time.

Liz pushed between them, facing her father. "Brady would never do anything to hurt me." Then she turned to him, pleading with her eyes. It just about cut him off at the knees. "Would you?"

Damn it. *Damn it!* She was right. No matter how much he'd had to drink, no matter how pissed he was, he'd rather die than hurt her.

He was as big of a fool for her as he'd always been.

"Goodbye, Brady," she said softly before linking her arm through her father's and tugging him down the hall, J.C. following.

He stood in that dark hallway while the music changed to a classical song he'd heard before but never in a million years would be able to name. All he knew was that as that song played, Liz was walking down the aisle toward the man she was going to marry.

He wiped a hand over his mouth. He wanted a drink. Needed it to dull his mind.

Instead, he found an empty spot in the back where he could stand unnoticed. And torture himself by watching the woman he'd loved for half of his life become someone else's wife.

"I NEED A FAVOR."

J.C. licked sweet buttercream icing off her fork. "I'm not holding your dress while you pee again," she told Liz quietly, hoping the other members of the bridal party seated next to her at the head table couldn't hear. "Once in a lifetime is one time too many."

An elderly couple walked past, congratulating Liz. She thanked them before turning back to J.C. "This is serious," she said in a harsh whisper.

"More serious than wedding cake?"

Liz had detached her veil but kept the tiara firmly in place. She always had liked to pretend she was a princess. Which left J.C. to play the role of lady-in-waiting.

Liz picked up J.C.'s plate and carried it with her as she pulled her sister to her feet. "Come on."

They made their way across the large room, weaving around the tables and chairs tied with wide, purple taffeta. The tables were topped with narrow glass jars of varying heights filled with water, lavender rose petals and lit, floating white candles.

Liz stepped behind a large column. "Get him to leave."

J.C. didn't need to be told who *him* was. Brady Sheppard. She peeked around the column. Yep. There he sat at the end of the bar, all scruffy and brooding in his rumpled T-shirt and faded jeans, his dark blond hair still military-short. He stared at the spot where she and Liz stood. No surprise, given he hadn't taken his eyes off the bride ever since he'd hobbled into Pine Hills Country Club a few hours ago.

Poor Brady. She should be ticked at him for crashing her sister's wedding—and she was. A little. But after everything he'd gone through, everything Liz had put him through, it was tough to work up a good mad. Especially when he seemed so...lost. So alone.

Taking her plate back from Liz, J.C. scooped up a small bite though she could no longer taste the delicious vanilla cake and milk chocolate ganache filling. "Ignore him. Don't let him ruin your special day."

It was a refrain she, the other bridesmaids and the mothers of both bride and groom had repeated numerous times already.

"I have ignored him and he's already ruined my day. And now it's time for him to leave." She nodded toward the other side of the room. "Before Carter's frat brothers talk him into doing something stupid."

J.C. looked over to where her new brother-in-law stood by the presents table. Pale blond hair, green eyes, chiseled features...Carter Messler—make that *Dr.* Carter Messler—was not only handsome, funny and smart, he was also the most easygoing guy J.C. had ever met. Usually. Surrounded by his groomsmen, though, they had one thing in common: they were all scowling at Brady. Carter's scowl was the darkest.

"But...Carter's a pediatrician," J.C. said. "Pediatricians don't go around getting into fistfights."

"I've never seen him so angry." Glancing nervously at her new husband, she lowered her voice. "Brady could get hurt."

J.C. smashed the remaining cake crumbs under her fork. Brady had never backed down from a fight. Which was probably what had made him such a good Marine. And she doubted he'd let a bum knee and crutches stop him from taking a swing or two.

Liz was right. He had to go. And not just because J.C. didn't want to see him get his stubborn head bashed in. The disheveled, ex-Marine partaking in the open bar was preventing Liz and Carter from enjoying their day.

"What do you want me to do?"

Liz squeezed J.C.'s hand. "Whatever you have to. He'll listen to you," she said desperately, as if willing it to be true. "He's always liked you. He used to tell me you were like the little sister he never had."

And wasn't that enough to make her ego take a serious nosedive.

"I'm not making any promises" she said, handing her plate to Liz. "But I'll do my best."

J.C. resolutely kept her gaze forward instead of glancing at her reflection as she passed the mirror behind the polished bar. She didn't need visual confirmation that her hair was rebelling against the dozens of bobby pins the stylist had used. Unlike Liz, ignoring problems usually worked pretty well for J.C.

She stopped in front of him. "Hello, Brady."

"Janie." He sipped from a squat glass of amber liquid. "You look different."

She'd heard a variation of that statement all day from numerous friends and relatives who hadn't seen her in the past two years. And while it usually pleased her to have people notice the sixty-five pounds she'd dropped, she could've sworn she'd run into Brady since then. "I lost some weight."

His narrowed eyes roamed from her head to her feet

and back up again. "I was talking about the dress." Her skin prickled.

"Oh," she said breathlessly as she wiped a damp palm down the front of the simple, halter-style gown. "Is there someone I can call to come get you?"

Resting one arm against the bar, he leaned back. "Am I going somewhere?"

"I think it's for the best if you did."

His light blue eyes sharpened. "You do? Or Lizzie does?"

"Me. Liz. Carter. My parents. The other brides-maids… I'd say it's unanimous."

"What if I'm not ready to leave?"

She fisted her hands around the material of her skirt. She felt for him. Honest, she did. But just because Liz had moved on with her life didn't give Brady the right to act like an ass. It wasn't as if he was the only person in the world to be in love with someone who didn't love him back.

Moving to his side, she was careful not to touch him. "I get it. You're upset and you want to hurt her back. Well, congratulations, you succeeded. But enough's enough."

Other than a momentary twitch of his left eye, he remained expressionless.

After a moment, he raised his glass to her, downed the remaining drink, then set the glass on the bar. "Don't bother calling anyone on my account. I'll see myself home."

Positioning the crutches under his arms, he stood, gazing somewhere over her left shoulder. She glanced back to see Liz and Carter, arms around each other as they swayed to the band's version of "Unchained

Melody." When she turned back, Brady was already halfway to the door.

What she wouldn't give to have Brady look at her with even a fraction of the longing she'd seen in his eyes when he stared at Liz. To have him see her as Jane Cleo instead of just Liz's little sister.

Lips pressed together, she watched him until he went out the side door of the clubhouse. Could he drive with his injured knee? Would he? No. The Brady she'd known most of her life would never drink and then get behind the wheel. She pushed a loose bobby pin into her hair, jabbing her scalp in the process. Of course, the old Brady didn't have a permanent glower, would never crash a wedding or suck back whiskey as if it were the only thing getting him from one minute to the next.

She headed to the rear of the bar where the bridal party had stashed their personal items. No one would miss her if she slipped away for a little bit. Long enough to make sure Brady got home safely.

Twenty minutes later, J.C. wondered which of them of them was the bigger idiot. Him for thinking he could walk the ten miles home on crutches. Or her for leaving her sister's wedding to give him a ride, all because she still hadn't gotten over her stupid, childhood crush.

Her. Definitely her. She'd not only driven him, but helped him inside and onto the couch and even made coffee.

She frowned as it dripped into the pot. Well, wasn't that what people did when they cared about someone?

Carrying a cup of coffee, she made her way to the living room where Brady was slumped on the couch, his head resting against the back of it, his left leg out straight.

"I thought you could use this," she said, holding the mug out as she sat next to him. When he made no move to take it, she put it on the coffee table and then clasped her hands together in her lap.

Other than to tell her he was staying at the cottage on The Diamond Dust, the historic plantation the Sheppards called home, he'd remained silent on the drive over. So there she was, in the middle of the woods in a sparsely furnished living room with her sister's stoic, drunk ex.

Finally she cleared her throat and made a move to leave. "I'd better get going."

Nothing. No "Thanks for getting me home." The man didn't even blink. She'd taken one step toward the front door when his gravelly voice stopped her.

"I didn't want to hurt her."

"Excuse me?"

He finally sat up and took a long gulp of coffee. Stared down at the mug. "I didn't go there to hurt her."

Her heart racing, she retook her seat. "Why did you do it then?"

"I had to see."

"Had to see what?"

He set his coffee down then rolled his head from side to side. "I had to see it happen. Had to watch her marry someone else. So I'd know it was real. And that it really is over between us."

She laid her hand on his forearm. "Brady, I...I'm so sorry."

He looked down at her hand then up at her face, his gaze hooded. "You're still as sweet as you always were, aren't you, Jane?" he murmured.

His tone was low and dark. Dangerous. Gooseflesh rose on her bare arms. "I…I hate that you're…" In pain. Broken. Unable to see beyond Liz. "That you have to go through this."

He shifted, his knee bumping hers. She slid over several inches. But…was it her imagination, or did he keep getting closer?

"Like I said, sweet." He skimmed the tip of his forefinger down her cheek.

She sat motionless, her mouth dry as he cupped the back of her head. Then he tugged her head down and kissed her, his lips brushing hers once. Then again. The third time, he slowly deepened the kiss, his lips warm and firm, the rough pad of his thumb caressing her jaw. His tongue slipped between her lips, coaxing a response.

He eased back, his eyes searching hers. "Okay?" he asked softly.

She exhaled shakily. Was it okay? She'd dreamt of this, of him touching her, kissing her…wanting her… her entire life. Almost as long as she'd loved him.

Ignoring all the reasons why they couldn't do this, she pressed her mouth to his.

Brady groaned and speared his fingers into her hair, scattering bobby pins across the couch. When his other hand cupped her breast through the silk of her gown, she almost jumped out of her skin. But then he lightly pinched her nipple and she arched her back, fitting herself more fully into his palm.

Willing herself to relax, she tentatively smoothed her palms over the hard contours of his chest up to his shoulders. He lifted his head long enough to strip his shirt off, tossing it behind him before kissing her again.

She couldn't stop touching him. Couldn't believe she really was touching him. He was so beautiful, his body lean but muscular. His skin soft. And hot.

Still kissing her, he grabbed hold of her underneath her thighs, tugging her down until she lay flat on her back. Lifting her dress, he swept his hand up to her hipbone, leaving trails of warmth in his wake. He parted her legs and lightly stroked her through her panties. She squirmed. Her thigh muscles clenched.

Before she could raise her hips in a silent demand for him to touch her harder, he pulled her panties down, leaving them around her ankles. Then he lifted his mouth from hers so he could unfasten and shove down his jeans. Her head was still spinning as Brady thrust her dress up around her waist. Cool air washed over her.

Slow down. She brought her legs together. And for the first time, she noticed Brady's features etched in pain.

"Your knee," she said. "Are you—"

He kissed her again. Settled on top of her, spreading her legs insistently, keeping most of his weight on his right side. And then he was at her entrance. Hot. Hard.

He didn't return her feelings. But she couldn't refuse him.

He pushed into her, his thickness stretching her. He gave her a moment to adjust to his size. His hardness. Then he took her hips in a viselike grip and began to move.

Unlike her fantasies, there were no tender words. No lingering looks. None of the fireworks she'd imagined. There was no connection between them other than the joining of their bodies.

Oh, God. She'd made a huge mistake.

Her throat burning, she stared up into his handsome face, her hands clutching the cushion beneath her. His mouth was a thin line, the hair at his temples damp with sweat. And no matter how hard she silently willed him to, he never once opened his eyes.

Finally, after what seemed like an eternity, his pace quickened and his body grew taut. Emptying himself inside her, he gave a guttural growl.

And called out her sister's name.

CHAPTER TWO

Three months later

SEVEN O'CLOCK in the morning—on Thanksgiving, no less—was way too early to start throwing up.

Bent over the porch rail, J.C. wiped a shaky, gloved hand over her mouth. Wrinkling her nose at the bushes below her, she straightened. At least she hadn't thrown up in her car. Again.

Her stomach still churning, she crossed Brady's porch and pounded on the door before digging into the pocket of her bulky coat for a mint. She would not freak out. She could handle this. And once Brady knew, he'd help her. He'd figure out what to do.

But first he had to answer the damn door.

Wrapping her arms around herself, she scanned the surrounding woods. A blanket of damp leaves covered the forest floor and not even the sun shining in a gorgeous blue sky could pierce the darkness of the trees. She'd parked behind Brady's silver pickup, so it stood to reason that if his truck was here, he was here.

She rattled the doorknob—only to have it turn easily in her hand. She blinked, then slipped inside and shut the door. "Hello? Brady? It's me. J.C."

The living-room blinds were drawn, but she had no trouble making out the shape of the cream sofa. The sofa where what should've been her dream come true had turned into her greatest nightmare.

The blinds to her right were drawn, but sunlight shone through the tiny window above the kitchen sink. She crept through the small foyer toward it but stopped at the doorway.

The cottage had seemed sterile, just-moved-into, when she'd last been there three months ago. But now the kitchen was a mess. And not your ordinary, didn't-do-the-dishes-last-night-and-left-the-empty-milk-carton-on-the-counter mess she often made in her own apartment. Dirty dishes were piled high in both sides of the sink and took up half the counter space. Garbage overflowed from the bin in the corner and crumbs littered the hardwood floor. Cupboard doors hung open as if someone had ransacked the place. And it would take a jackhammer to chisel through the food on the stovetop.

And she didn't even want to know what that awful smell was. Covering her nose and mouth with her arm, she ducked her head and rushed down the hallway, careful not to brush up against anything lest she risk some sort of infectious disease.

"Brady," she called again as she passed the small bathroom, her eyes straight ahead. After the horror of that kitchen, you couldn't pay her to look in the man's bathroom. At least, not without some sort of Hazmat suit on. She stopped at the closed door to his bedroom and knocked. "Brady, are you up?"

No answer. She twisted the silver stud in her left earlobe. She'd already let herself into the house, no sense stopping now. She opened the door but couldn't see a thing. Did he have something against mornings?

Or just sunlight in general? She found the light switch and flipped it on.

The bedroom was as messy as the kitchen, minus any decaying food or garbage. Clothes were tossed on top of and all around the three-drawer dresser. A sock hung from a hardback chair in the corner and a lamp lay on its side on the carpet next to the bed, where a large lump snuffled softly and then began to snore.

She stepped hesitantly into the room. "Brady," she whispered. He continued snoring. With the toe of her sneaker, she nudged a white T-shirt out of her way, then stepped over a pair of dark boxer briefs to the head of the bed.

She picked up an open bottle of whiskey from the nightstand and wasn't sure if she should be relieved it was still half-full. Finding the cap behind a digital clock that blinked twelve, she screwed it on.

Brady slept on his stomach, his long body stretched diagonally across the bed. A sheet covered him from the waist down, leaving his naked back and one bent leg exposed. His shoulders were broad, the lean muscles clearly defined. He had a black vine tattoo that started at his right hip, wound its way over his back and up to his shoulder before curling out of sight. His right arm hung limply off the side of the bed, his left held a pillow over his head.

Too bad or she might have poured the rest of the whiskey over his face.

"Brady." Nothing. If not for his soft snores, she'd think he was comatose. "Wake up."

Other than a twitch of his toes, he didn't move. Holding the whiskey bottle by the neck, she nudged his shoulder with the bottom of it. "Wake—"

Brady's hand shot out and grabbed the bottle, tossing it onto the bed at the same time he wrenched her forward. Before she could so much as open her mouth to scream, he flipped her onto her back and pinned her to the mattress, his muscular thighs straddling her hips.

His large, strong hand was around her throat.

Panic shot through her as his fingers tightened, cutting off her airway. She bucked wildly underneath him, clawing at his wrists, but she may as well have been fighting a statue. The wild tangle of his shaggy, wheat-colored hair and the darker stubble on his cheeks and chin sharpened the already sharp lines of his handsome face. His blue eyes were like ice chips, cold and empty.

"Brady…stop…it's me," she managed to spit out, though it hurt to talk. To breathe. "Jane Cleo. Please…"

He blinked, and his hold on her loosened. Realization flashed across his face and he leapt off her to the other side of the room. She rolled onto her side as she gasped for breath.

"Damn it, J.C.! What the hell are you doing?" Brady demanded, the hint of Southern accent doing nothing to soften his harsh, sleep-roughened voice. "I could've killed you."

"I…I was trying to wake you," she rasped.

He pressed the heels of his hands against his eyes. "How did you even get in here?"

Her arms shaking, she pushed herself up into a sitting position, keeping her gaze off his naked body. "The door was unlocked."

"That didn't give you the right to come in."

"No. Of course not. But I wanted…"

"What? A repeat of the last time you were here?"

he asked, then gave one quick shake of his head. "Not interested."

Tears stung her eyes, made her already sore throat burn. "I didn't come here for a repeat of anything, you bastard," she said fiercely, her hands gripping the crumpled sheet. "I came to tell you I'm pregnant."

BRADY REARED BACK, hitting his already spinning head against the wall behind him with a dull thud and jolt of pain. "What?"

"I'm pregnant."

Oh, shit. He swallowed, but his tongue felt as if it were wearing a fur coat. "How?"

"The usual way."

"Who?"

She struggled to her feet, her arms crossed against a coat bright enough to burn his retinas. "A traveling salesman," she snapped. "Who do you think?"

That was the problem. He couldn't think. Not with his head pounding. And a panic unlike he'd ever felt crawling up his spine.

He stared at her stomach, but her coat was too bulky to discern any changes in her body. "Are you sure?"

She threw a sandwich bag at him, hitting him in the chest. "See for yourself."

Shoving his hand through his hair, he frowned down at the bag where it'd landed by his feet. "What are those?"

"The pregnancy test I took last night, along with the two I took this morning. You'll notice every last one of them has a stupid plus sign."

He dropped his hand, hitting his bare thigh. And realized she'd literally caught him with his pants down.

Searching for and finding a pair of gym shorts, he jerked them on, ignoring the throbbing in his bad knee. He took a deep breath and held it for the count of five.

"No," he growled. "Are you sure it's mine?"

She bristled, reminding him of some mortally offended, overgrown Shirley Temple impersonator with her round face and her frizzy curls smooshed down by an ugly, piss-colored hat. "Of course I am."

And with those words, any hope he might've had that he hadn't royally screwed up yet again flew out the window. Just proved how useless and cruel hope could be.

Instead of kicking a hole in the wall like he wanted to, he shrugged. With his bad leg, he probably couldn't do much damage anyway. "Can't blame me for asking."

But the look she gave him said she not only could blame him, but likely would for a hellishly long time.

He worked to not limp as he crossed to the bed. Told himself it didn't bother him when she darted away like a rabbit. His stomach roiled from not having anything in it other than the Jim Beam he'd downed last night.

The idea of having a kid should make him feel something besides disappointment. Even the angry red marks on J.C.'s slender throat, the marks he'd put there, should make him feel something. Guilt, at least. But to feel guilty about any of it would mean he'd have to have some semblance of conscience, of humanity, left.

Sitting on the bed, he reached back for the Jim Beam before picking up a spotted water glass with smudged lipstick on the rim from the floor.

"Do you think that's going to help?" J.C. asked, disgusted.

He flicked her a glance, then poured two healthy shots into the glass. "Can't hurt."

She made a sound, sort of like his mother's teakettle right before it starting whistling. But thankfully, she kept her mouth shut. He gulped his drink, savoring the burn as it hit the back of his tongue.

He carefully stretched his left leg out in front of him. And noticed J.C.'s eyes lock on the webbing of scars. The raised, white welts were from the shrapnel when the roadside bomb had gone off. The thinner lines were from the two surgeries he'd endured only to be told his leg would never be one hundred percent.

His fingers tensed on his glass and he debated risking another death glare from J.C. to get a second shot. As if the pain and stiffness could let him forget he wasn't whole anymore, the scars reminded him.

As did the pity in people's eyes.

Wiping the back of his hand over his mouth, he worked to keep his expression bland.

She blew out an exasperated breath. "Well?"

"Well what?"

"Don't you have anything to say?"

He scratched the side of his head. Realized he never did make it to that barber appointment his mother had set up for him last week. Or had it been two weeks ago? "Can't think of anything."

Her mouth popped open. "You can't think of anything?" she repeated, her voice rising. "Don't you think we should discuss this?"

"Seems a little late for that."

"But what are we going to do?"

"That's up to you."

She stepped back, her hand to her heart. "Me? Don't you have an opinion?"

He turned his attention to pouring more whiskey into his glass. "Your body. Your decision."

"I am not having an abortion, if that's what you're getting at." Underneath the slight tremble in her voice was a determination that he'd never before heard from Jane Cleo.

"Like I said, your decision."

Whipping her hat off, she crushed it in her hand, her hair poofing out around her head as if it had a life of its own. "But what are we going to do now?"

He drained his glass as he stood. "I'm not sure about you, but I'm going to hit the head and then go back to sleep."

She blocked his exit. "That's it? You don't have any reaction to the fact that you're going to be a father?"

His skin grew clammy. "I'm not going to be a father."

"I told you," she said, speaking through her teeth, "I'm sure it's yours."

"I don't doubt that." His memory of what had happened between them was blurry at best, but he knew she was telling the truth. Even if he'd spent the past few months pretending that night had never happened. That he hadn't taken advantage of J.C. That he hadn't slept with Liz's sister.

That Liz hadn't married someone else.

But that didn't mean he was going to saddle some poor kid with him as a father. And he sure as hell didn't need the added responsibility of a child. Especially when Liz wasn't the mother.

"What I mean is," he continued, "I don't plan on being a father. Not to your baby or any other kid."

"You want me to handle this alone?"

He slammed the bottle down on the nightstand. She flinched. "What do you want from me?" he growled. "You can't show up here, wake me up and throw something this huge in my face and expect me to take care of it. To take care of you. Because if that's what you expected, you're talking to the wrong man."

She shut her eyes. "This isn't happening. This isn't happening."

What was she doing? J.C. had always been a bit... eccentric. Which was fine when she'd been a teenager and had staged a one-person sit-in at the high-school cafeteria to protest the school's refusal to offer meat-free lunches once a week. But this was just plain weird.

And if that one word didn't sum up Jane Cleo Montgomery, nothing did.

She opened her eyes and walked away. Finally, his torment was ending. Except, she whirled back around and threw her hat. It sailed over his head and hit the wall behind him.

"Do you have any idea what I've been going through?" she asked quietly, but his headache spiked just the same. "How scared I've been? For over a month I told myself that I couldn't really be pregnant. But now, well—" she gestured to the bag of pregnancy tests "—there's no more denying it. My worst fears are confirmed and now I get to deal with the joys of an unexpected pregnancy, which includes puking every morning, no matter what I eat or even if I eat."

Brady rubbed the back of his neck. "What do you

want me to say, Jane? That I'm sorry? Okay, I'm sorry."

"I don't want an apology. I want you to get your head out of that bottle and help me. How am I going to tell my parents?" she asked, her voice breaking. "How am I supposed to face Liz?"

Grinding his back teeth together, he reached over for the whiskey bottle and added more to his glass. Ignored the unsteadiness of his hand as liquid splattered over his fingers. Damn it, did she think this was easy for him? Any of it? He wiped his hand on the sheet. He'd regretted what had happened between them the moment he'd come to. The last thing he wanted was for Liz—the woman he'd sworn to love for the rest of his life—to find out he'd slept with her kid sister.

"Your family's close," he said. And they'd coddled J.C. her entire life. They wouldn't let her go through this alone. "I'm sure once they get used to the idea, they'll help you out."

"Thank you for sharing that brilliant piece of logic," she said so coldly, so sarcastically, he raised his eyebrows. "Tell you what, when you figure out what, if any, part you want to play in this baby's life, let me know. In the meantime, you can go to hell."

He saluted her with his glass. "Already there."

With a low growl, sweet Jane Cleo Montgomery, the girl who was so bubbly and happy it was as if she'd swallowed a goddamn beam of sunshine, stormed out. A moment later, the front door slammed shut, followed by a dull thud. Which was probably one of the framed family photos his mother had hung in the living room falling.

Brady finished his drink and hung his head, his hands

between his knees. Once she thought things through, she'd agree he shouldn't have any part of this kid's life. And he sure didn't want any part of it. Yeah, he used to think about having kids, of becoming the type of father his own dad had been, but that was before. Before his knee, and his life, had gone to hell. Before Liz decided he wasn't enough.

WHO SAID SHE DIDN'T have a backbone?

So what if Brady was no help to her at all? Or that he didn't want anything to do with the baby she was carrying? Or with her, J.C. thought late that afternoon as she ignored the heated debate her mother and grand-mother were having next to her over whether to thicken the turkey gravy using cornstarch or flour. J.C. shut off the flame under the huge pot of boiling potatoes. She'd handled Brady's rejection. Not only handled it, but told him where to get off.

Too bad her backbone turned to Jell-O whenever she thought about telling her family she was pregnant. She sipped from her glass of ginger ale, but it did little to soothe her suddenly dry throat. Picking up two pot hold-ers, she hauled the heavy pan of potatoes to the sink and dumped them into the waiting colander, leaning back from the steam in an effort to keep her hair frizz-free, if even for just an hour.

Well, she just had to suck it up and tell them. It wasn't as if she could hide it much longer anyway. When she'd put on her long suede skirt earlier, she hadn't been able to button it around her rapidly expanding middle. Which had resulted in a fifteen-minute crying jag and her re-thinking her stance against elastic waistbands. A stance she'd taken up after she'd lost weight and had worn her first pair of size-six jeans.

Now she had a large safety pin holding the two edges of her skirt's waistband together and it still dug into her with every inhalation.

Would the indignities of this day ever end?

She poured the potatoes back into the pot and carried it over to the counter. Giving up this round of culinary battle, Grandma Rose carried a tray of her homemade angel biscuits to the living room, a pinched expression on her wrinkled face, her heavily shellacked blue-tinged hair bouncing with each step. J.C.'s mother, Nancy, stayed at the stove stirring the gravy. And humming.

"What did you do to Grandma?" Liz asked as she came into the room. "She's in there mumbling about the sad state of the world today and how the youth of America have no respect for the traditional way of doing things."

"Mom schooled Grandma in the art of gravy making," J.C. said.

"I didn't school anyone." Nancy adjusted the heat beneath the pan with one hand while stirring with the other. "I just pointed out that I've thickened my gravy with cornstarch for the past thirty-four years and that her son has never had any complaints about it."

"Ooh…burn," J.C. mouthed to Liz.

Liz's sleek chestnut hair swung as she nodded. "Second degree," she mouthed back. They shared an easy smile.

Until J.C. remembered what she'd done. How she'd broken the number one rule of sisterhood: no going out with your sister's ex.

J.C. wiped the back of her hand across her damp

forehead. It had to be one hundred degrees in her sister's cramped kitchen. It didn't help that she'd had to wear her heaviest turtleneck sweater today, an oversize, soft cable-knit that covered her stomach. And hid the slight bruising from her encounter with Brady. And while she sweated in clothes that added at least ten pounds to her curvy frame, her mother and sister were both cool and stylish. Nancy in trim dark pants and a V-neck top, her short, layered hair was a shade darker than Liz's with only a few strands of gray. Liz had on skinny jeans and a gorgeous billowy mauve top with a wide band at the bottom that accentuated her tiny waist.

Not that J.C. was bitter or anything.

They usually had Thanksgiving dinner at their parents' spacious house, but Liz had wanted to host her first official holiday dinner in the house she and Carter were renting while their dream home was being built. And since Carter's family was in Ohio, it was going to be him, Liz and J.C., their parents and Grandma Rose.

J.C. poured cream over the potatoes, then shook in salt and pepper. All the people she loved the most in this world, everyone she needed to tell about the baby, would soon be gathered around the table. She'd get to face them over plates filled with green bean casserole, sweet potatoes, turkey and stuffing, and then see their shock turn to disappointment when they heard about her latest screwup.

What better way to spend the holiday?

She threw a stick of butter into the pan. Then, seeing the amount of potatoes, added half of another stick before shoving her sleeves up to her elbows, picking up the masher and mixing it all together.

Her mother, obviously satisfied no lumps would dare

appear in her gravy, poured it into a gravy boat and peered over at J.C. "Honey, are you feeling all right? You look a bit flushed."

"I'm fine," J.C. said. "Just…it's hot in here." Okay, so there was a definite edge of whining in her voice. Her life was falling apart and so far she'd had a really crappy day. She deserved a pout.

Nancy laid the back of her hand against J.C.'s forehead, the gesture bringing tears to J.C.'s eyes. "I don't think you have a fever," Nancy decided. "Are you sure you're over that stomach bug?"

She averted her gaze. "Definitely. It was probably something I ate," she said, referring to the lie she'd told her mother last Sunday when she'd gotten sick after they'd had brunch.

Nancy smiled and rubbed J.C.'s arm. "Good." She glanced at the potatoes. "You need to scrape the sides down or you'll miss lumps. Here, I can finish—"

"I've got it." J.C.'s grip tightened when her mother tried to take the masher from her. "Why don't you go on out and save Dad and Carter from Grandma's lecture about the merits of thickening with flour?"

"Be careful you don't overmash them or they'll get gluey," her mother warned. "And remember, you can always add a little milk if they're too thick."

"I've got it, Mom. Really."

Though she seemed conflicted about leaving the fate of the potatoes in J.C.'s hands, Nancy nodded and then walked away.

Her mother's back disappeared around the corner and J.C. let go of the masher as if it had caught fire. God. As if she needed an advanced degree to mash potatoes. And considering it was the one task her family entrusted her to handle for family dinners, you'd think they could give her more credit. Picking up a large spoon, she scraped down the sides and then began pounding away in earnest.

By the time Liz came back into the kitchen, J.C.'s arms were aching from the effort and sweat was trickling between her shoulder blades.

"You can stop now," Liz said as she attempted to work a few potato pieces out of J.C.'s curls. "Those vicious potatoes are dead."

"Just making sure I got them all."

"I think that's a safe bet. Here," she added, handing J.C. a large blue serving bowl. "Put them in this."

"Did you have to cook the entire ten-pound bag?"

"I didn't want to run out."

"Who did you think was coming? The Jewell High School marching band?"

"If they do," Liz said, shutting off the oven, "we'll be covered."

J.C. scraped the last of the potatoes from the pan and added them to the mountain already in the bowl. "We could cover ourselves with mashed potatoes and still have enough to eat."

"Now I know what Carter and I can do with all the leftovers."

"Eww... Please. That's one visual I really don't need."

"Wait," Liz said, when J.C. picked up the heavy bowl. "I made something special for you."

J.C. set it back on the counter. "What?"

"Close your eyes."

J.C. squeezed her eyes shut. She heard the oven door being opened and then shut.

"Ta-da!" Liz said.

"Uh…" J.C. studied the brown, football-shaped loaf in the baking pan. "I repeat, what is it?"

"Tofurkey."

"Is that like a contagious disease? Because that thing looks like a breeding ground for bacteria."

"It's not a science project, it's a tofu turkey." Setting the pan down, she used a large metal spatula to transfer the loaf onto a small serving platter. "Mom and I didn't think it was fair that you got left out of the biggest tradition of Thanksgiving, so we decided to make you a vegetarian turkey. I found the recipe online. It's basically tofu wrapped around stuffing—Mom made a special version of her bread stuffing using vegetable broth instead of chicken broth."

J.C. blinked and for some reason, the blob of browned tofu didn't look half as bad as she'd first thought. At that moment, it looked downright delicious. "You made that for me?"

"Well, I'm sure not going to eat it and I doubt anyone else here is, either."

"I think it's beautiful," J.C. managed, unshed tears thickening her voice.

There were times, more than a few, when they were growing up when J.C. thought she hated her sister. Times when she'd wanted to hate her, if only to try to ease the jealousy that came with having an older sister who was smarter, prettier and more popular than J.C. could ever hope to be.

But the truth was, J.C. loved Liz. There was no way she could harbor any animosity toward the person who was not only her sister but also her best friend.

She threw herself at Liz, knocking her sister back a full step as she clung to her.

"Hey," Liz said, returning the hug, "what's this?"

And Liz's concern made J.C. feel even worse. "You made me a tofu turkey."

Liz smoothed J.C.'s curls away from her face. "It's tofu and stuffing, not a cure for cancer. Now come on, what's wrong? It's not like you to get emotional over a meat substitute."

God, how she wanted to tell Liz everything. And maybe if she told Liz about the baby, then Liz could break the news to their parents.

But while that had worked when J.C. had been fifteen and had gotten her belly button pierced, she doubted she could get Liz to bail her out of this situation.

J.C. stepped back. "I always get emotional at the holidays."

"Yes, but usually you reserve it for sappy commercials."

"That one where the college kid comes home to surprise his family and makes coffee to wake them gets me every time," she said lightly, picking up the potatoes again. "Now come on. Let's get these real potatoes and that fake turkey on the table."

And the sooner they all sat down, the sooner she could admit she'd had a one-night stand with her sister's ex-fiancé and was now pregnant. Pregnant and scared out of her mind.

CHAPTER THREE

J.C. PUT THE POTATOES on the table and sat next to her mother. Even though they were eating at the picnic table Carter had brought inside, it somehow still looked like one of those fancy layouts in a home and garden magazine. Liz had covered it with a red tablecloth and then added a white runner down the middle. On the runner, gourds and a few pinecones were scattered around glass bowls filled with bright red and green apples, cranberries and minipumpkins.

J.C. unfolded her red-and-white cloth napkin onto her lap and tried not to think about how the last time she'd hosted a family dinner, they ate off paper plates. And her mother had provided most of the food.

Ten minutes later, grace had been said, dishes had been passed and her plate was piled high with food. J.C. nibbled at a flaky, buttery biscuit but couldn't seem to swallow properly. If she didn't come clean to her family right now, she'd never be able to eat her meal. And she was starving.

Setting her biscuit down, she brushed the crumbs off her fingers. "I have an announcement," she said but her voice was so reedy, no one heard her over their laughter and conversation. "I have some news," she yelled, blushing when everyone quieted and stared at her.

To her left, Grandma Rose peered at J.C. over her glasses. "Did you get fired again?"

Jeez. You get fired a few times—okay, five times, but that third time was *not* her fault—and suddenly it's, what, a habit?

"No. I'm still employed." J.C. drank some water. "I…"

"Come on, sweetie," her dad said, giving her a wink as he scooped sweet potatoes onto his fork. "Whatever it is, it can't be as bad as when you stopped going to college but didn't officially drop out, leaving me to foot the bill for a year's worth of classes you didn't take."

"Daddy," Liz admonished while Carter ducked his head and coughed—the sound suspiciously close to a laugh. "We all promised not to talk about that again, remember?"

J.C. twisted the napkin around her fingers. "I told you I'd pay you back."

"We've been through this," Nancy said, shooting her husband a loaded look. "You can worry about paying us back once you're on your feet." She sipped her wine. "Now, what is it you want to tell us?"

"You…you and Daddy…" Her voice shook so she took another drink, and then, staring at the table, said, "You're going to be grandparents."

When no one spoke, J.C. raised her head.

A huge, proud smile broke out across her dad's face. He pumped Carter's hand, not noticing his son-in-law was too flabbergasted to return his handshake. "Congratulations. When are you due?" Don asked Liz.

"Due?" Carter repeated, his gorgeous face devoid of color, his green eyes panicked as he gaped at his wife. "What's due? Who's due?"

BETH ANDREWS   39

"I thought you wanted to wait a few years before having children," Nancy said to Liz.

"Yeah," Carter choked out, his hand still being pumped by his father-in-law, "me, too. Why didn't you tell me?"

"I didn't tell you," Liz said slowly, "because I'm not pregnant."

Frowning, Don let go of Carter's hand and sat back. "What? But Janie said…"

Staring at her plate again, J.C. felt five expectant gazes turn on her.

"Jane," her mother said sharply, "are you pregnant?"

Biting down on her lower lip, she nodded.

"Oh, dear Lord," Grandma Rose murmured.

"But…but I didn't realize you were seeing someone," Don said, sounding lost and hurt. J.C. winced.

"I'm not." Raising her head, she sent Liz a beseeching look. "It was a…a mistake."

"Oh, Lord Almighty," her grandma cried, throwing her hands up as if she were at a tent revival meeting.

Her mom shook her head, her disappointment palpable. "Didn't we teach you to have more self-respect than that?"

J.C.'s throat constricted. "It wasn't like that," she whispered.

No, it was worse. Because even though she'd known Brady was using her as a substitute for Liz, J.C. had gone along with it.

Liz rushed around the table and, crouching next to J.C., put her arm around her sister and squeezed. "Now, let's all calm down. This can't be easy for J.C."

Don stood. "What's his name?" he asked in a low,

deadly tone J.C. had never heard before. Not even when she'd sold the car they'd bought her as a high-school graduation present to pay for a trip to Europe.

"It doesn't matter. He doesn't want anything to do with me or the baby."

He slammed his palm down on the table, and they all jumped.

"Don!" Nancy admonished, catching her wineglass before it fell. "Calm down."

"I want his name, Jane Cleo, and I want it now," her father said.

J.C. wound the napkin around her finger so tightly, her fingertip went numb. "I… It…" Her stomach burning, she forced herself to meet Liz's eyes. "It was Brady."

Liz jerked as if she'd been slapped. "Brady? You… you and…" She shook her head slowly. "You slept with Brady? With *my* Brady?"

"Your Brady?" Carter asked, his eyebrows shooting up.

And with that, all hell officially broke loose. Don wanted to force Brady to "do the right thing" while Nancy tried to calm him down. Grandma Rose was worried what her Bunco group was going to say when this got back to them, and Liz and Carter were having a heated argument off to the side over Liz's lingering feelings for her ex-fiancé.

J.C. slouched down in her chair so far, her chin was level with the tabletop. For half her life all she'd wanted was Brady Sheppard to notice her. To want her. And now that he'd slept with her—albeit he hadn't exactly wanted *her*—this was what she got.

Her mother had always warned her to be careful what she wished for. As usual, she'd been right.

TWO HOURS LATER, Liz was elbow-deep in a sink of soapy water and seriously regretting not taking her mother up on her offer to stay to help her clean. But after the dinner disaster, she'd needed some peace and quiet.

Though peace seemed to be out of the question, she had more than her share of quiet.

"I've already apologized," she said, proud of how composed she sounded when all she wanted to do was hit something. Or someone. Or burst into tears. "Several times. How long are you going to continue with the silent treatment?"

Setting leftovers in the refrigerator, Carter glanced coolly at her over his shoulder. "You're the one who said you didn't want to discuss it."

Since when did he use that biting, condescending tone? She couldn't say she cared for it much. She threw the tofurkey into the sink. Shoved it down the disposal with a wooden spoon. As the whirring sound filled the air, she tapped the spoon repeatedly against the sink. And to think, she'd been so excited about hosting her first holiday as a married woman. Thrilled to be able to spend one of her precious few days off from the E.R. with her family.

Now she didn't think she'd ever be able to look at J.C. the same way again.

Liz turned off the disposal. "There's nothing to discuss. I made a mistake. A slip of the tongue." She tossed silverware into the water. "I don't see where you have any right to hold it against me."

Shutting the fridge door, he faced her, his shoulders rigid, his pale hair sticking up from where he'd run his fingers through it. "Some would say that slip of the tongue indicates your true feelings. Such as you still considering your ex as belonging to you."

"You're a pediatrician, not a psychiatrist. Don't try to analyze me. And I didn't appreciate you humiliating me in front of my parents by accusing me of still having feelings for Brady."

His expression darkened. "You were humiliated? How did you think I felt when your ex-lover crashed our wedding?"

She blew the hair off her forehead. "What did you want me to do, Carter? Let your idiot friends throw him out?"

"No, but you could've trusted me to handle it."

"I didn't want a scene."

"Right," he said, his sarcasm setting her teeth on edge. "But it didn't bother you that I was embarrassed in front of three hundred people."

Of course it'd bothered her, but how could she worry about something that happened three months ago when all she could think about was what had happened at dinner? She scrubbed the bottom of the roasting pan. No, she shouldn't have reacted that way but she'd been… shocked…hearing that J.C. and Brady had…been to-gether…she hadn't been able to censor herself.

Still, it wasn't like Carter to get so angry. To treat her so coldly.

When they'd first met while doing their residency training at George Washington University Hospital, she'd immediately been attracted to him. And guilt-stricken over that attraction since, at the time, she'd been wearing Brady's ring. For months she'd deluded herself into believing the pull between her and Carter was just physical, a result of only seeing Brady a few times a year. She'd tried to ignore the attraction, tried to think of Carter as only a friend, but after working with him day in and day out, her feelings for him became too big. Too real. She found his intelligence, sense of humor and easygoing attitude impossible to resist.

Especially after years of Brady's quiet intensity.

She wished Carter would display some of that laid-back attitude now.

"I'd think you'd be happy Brady has moved on," Carter said as he began drying dishes. "Weren't you the one who was worried he wouldn't be able to let you go?"

"I want him to move on. Just not with J.C."

"Why not?"

She gaped at him. How could he be so intelligent and still be so clueless? "Because it's not right. She's my sister."

Drying a handful of spoons, he glanced at her. "Because it would be uncomfortable—for all involved."

"Exactly," she said with a sigh. Now this was more like it, and more like the man she'd fallen for so hard for. The man she'd chosen.

Carter nodded. "I get that. But from what J.C. said, he's not going to be involved with her or the baby."

The baby. Brady's baby. With her sister.

God, why did it hurt so much?

She swallowed past the lump lodged in her throat. "Brady would never abandon his own child."

"You sound pretty convinced of that."

"I am. I know him."

Carter tossed the towel over his shoulder and stood eyes downcast, feet apart, hands braced against the edge of the sink. "Do you still love him?"

She blinked. He'd never asked her that before. Not on their wedding night when they'd argued over her not wanting him to confront Brady. Not almost two years ago when she'd gone to him in tears because she'd ended her relationship with Brady. Ended it so she could be with Carter.

"Wha-what?"

He faced her. "Do you still love him?"

"I love *you*," she said, taking his hand in her wet one.

He shook his head and stepped away from her. "That's not what I asked."

Suddenly chilled, she crossed her arms. "I…I don't understand."

"I need to know if you still have feelings for Brady."

"Of course I do," she said carefully. "I'll always… care…about him. I was with him half my life."

"But you're not with him now," Carter said quietly. "You're with me. And I can't help but wonder if with me is where you really want to be."

HEADLIGHTS CUT THROUGH the darkness as the car pulled into the short driveway. A motion-detection light above the garage came on, illuminating the bottom half of the stairway on the side of the building. Where Brady sat at the bottom of those steps. He didn't move. Wasn't sure he could so much as stand since his leg had stiffened up during the two hours he'd been waiting in the cold for J.C. to come home.

She opened her car door, grabbed something from the seat next to her and then got out of the car. She took two steps before she noticed him and stopped, a huge purse clutched to her chest. Her gaze flicked from him to her apartment above the garage, then behind her to her car.

"If you take off," he said, figuring she was thinking of doing just that, "I'll still be here waiting when you get back."

She turned back to her car anyway but didn't get in. After a moment, she mumbled to herself and started walking toward him again. "What do you want?"

Gripping the wooden railing, he put all of his weight on his right leg and stood. "Things got out of hand this morning and I wanted to make sure we're on the same page."

"As much as it may shock you, I'm not a complete idiot. You don't want anything to do with me or with this baby. See? Same page. Now, I've had a really craptastic day and all I want is for it to be over. Goodbye."

Then she brushed past him and climbed the stairs, another motion-detecting light coming on when she reached the top. As he watched, she went inside and shut the door. No slamming this time, but somehow the quiet click was just as final.

That hadn't gone quite as planned. He shoved his frozen fingers into the pockets of his jacket. After J.C. left his house earlier, he'd tried to forget she'd been there in the first place. Forget what she'd told him…and how shitty he'd treated her.

While he'd sat in his living room staring into a glass of whiskey, she'd more than likely been telling her family—telling Liz—he'd gotten her pregnant. And that he didn't want anything to do with his own child.

Oh, yeah, he'd wanted to forget all of it.

Unfortunately, his usual method of temporary amnesia hadn't worked.

He scanned the long, steep staircase. At least thirty steps.

Shit.

The railing was on the wrong side to be of any help to him but he'd have to make the best of it. Have to take it one step at a time. Literally. He debated getting his cane from his truck, but when he faced J.C. he wanted to do it on his own two feet.

Clutching the rail, he leaned on his arm to take some of the weight off his left leg while he lifted his right onto the first step. He gritted his teeth against the pain and stepped up with his left leg.

He repeated the process. Then again. And again. Halfway up, he stopped to catch his breath. To think, less than a year ago he was running top speed up mountainsides in full combat gear. With that cheery thought still in his head, he glanced toward the dark house to find J.C.'s grandmother glaring at him from a bedroom window. From what he could remember, J.C. had moved into the apartment above her grandma's garage a few years ago after her latest attempt at college had failed.

He was just thankful Mrs. Montgomery hadn't come home with J.C. It was going to be hard enough to fix things with J.C., he didn't think he could handle facing anyone else in the Montgomery family.

By the time he reached the top, his shirt clung to his sweat-soaked skin and he had an inch-long sliver imbedded in his palm from his death grip on the wooden railing. But hey, at least he'd made it. Bracing his shoulder against the door, he wiped the sweat from his face with the bottom of his T-shirt before knocking. After a minute, he knocked again. Another minute, another knock.

He'd forgotten how, underneath that sunny personality, J.C. was as stubborn as they came.

"Last winter I waited in a cave in southern Afghanistan for over fourteen hours," he said, pitching his voice so she'd be sure to hear him through the door. "Sitting out here until you go to work tomorrow won't be a problem."

A moment later, the door opened to reveal a pinched-face J.C. holding the fattest white cat he'd ever seen. She stepped aside to let him in. "Like I said, I'm tired so wh—"

"I thought you were allergic to cats."

"What?"

"I remember you wanting a cat when—" When he and Liz were together. Seemed as if his life could be defined in two ways: when he and Liz were a couple, and now. "In high school. But you couldn't get one because you were allergic."

"I couldn't get one," she said with enough frost to cause the temperature in the apartment to drop at least ten degrees, "because Liz is allergic to them." The cat gave Brady a sneering, you-are-a-dumb-ass look, then leaped to the ground and waddled off. "I didn't get a chance to finish my dinner, so I'm going to make a sandwich. Do you want one?" she asked so grudgingly that even if all he'd had to eat for the past week were MREs—meals ready to eat, the packaged, precooked meals given to military personnel out in the field—he would've said no.

"I'm good."

"I guess you might as well sit down, then. I'll be back out in a minute."

But when she would've walked away, he grabbed her by the wrist. Ignoring how she went as stiff as a new recruit at attention, he lightly tugged her forward, hooked his finger under the edge of the neck of her sweater and pulled it down. She swallowed and tried to step back but he didn't loosen his hold. All day long he'd tried to convince himself that he hadn't hurt her, that his hangover had dulled his recollection of what had happened. Of how bad it'd been.

The cat was right. He was a dumb-ass.

He brushed his thumb over the light bruises on her pale, delicate skin, his stomach turning. "I didn't mean to hurt you."

Apprehension flashed in her eyes. "I'm fine."

This time when she pulled away, he let her go. She disappeared through a doorway, and he crossed over to the white couch. He sat on the edge—the only spot available among six pillows of varying shapes, sizes and colors. Stretching his left leg out, he rubbed his knee and glanced around.

Her apartment was a good deal smaller than his house, so how did she get so much stuff in it? He remembered the squat, light blue chair he used to sit in in her parents' living room next to her sofa. But not the two red velvet ottomans on the other side of a chipped, painted coffee table. Or the two hardback chairs on either side of a round table underneath the window. A large, glass-fronted case took up an entire corner, its shelves filled with everything from ceramic animal figures and music boxes to tea cups, crystal bowls and books, both paperbacks and hardcover. As if a rummage sale had blown up.

The cat padded in and jumped onto a low stool and then up onto the blue chair. J.C. followed a minute later, one hand curled into a loose fist. In the other she carried a glass of water with a sandwich balanced on top. She set the water on the coffee table in front of him and picked up the sandwich.

"Here," she said, holding out her hand to show him the two small, white pills in her palm.

"What are those?"

"Acetaminophen. It's all I have." When he didn't move, she shrugged irritably and set them next to the water. "From the look on your face when I opened the door, I thought you could use them."

Tossing the yellow pillow from the chair to the floor, she nudged the cat onto the arm rest and then sat, curling her bare feet under her. She took a bite of her sandwich and stared straight ahead.

Brady scratched his cheek. Realized he forgot to shave again today. He supposed he appreciated her bringing him the pills—though he knew from experience a few over-the-counter pain relievers would barely take the edge off. But she was too generous. Too sweet. After everything he'd done, she shouldn't give a crap if he was in pain or not. Not to mention how humiliating it was that he'd been so easy to read.

"Thanks." He took the pills and washed them down with the water. "Did you... Have you told your parents?" She gave a terse nod. Leaning forward, he picked up an ugly ceramic duck, turned it in his hands. Cleared his throat. "And Liz?"

J.C.'s mouth flattened. "Is that why you're here?

To see how Liz reacted to finding out that we slept together?"

"No." Maybe. He rubbed his thumbnail over a chip on the duck's beak. "How did…your family…take the news?"

"About as well as you'd expect." She bit into her sandwich again. "And so you won't be wondering…Liz didn't take *the news* well."

Okay. And what the hell was that supposed to mean? Not that he dared ask. "I didn't handle things as well as I could have this morning."

"You don't say," she said dryly.

"I've done some thinking and…I'm not going to shirk my responsibility."

She set the remainder of her sandwich on her lap. "What do you mean?"

Talking about this made it hard for him to breathe. Hell, it was as if his lungs were being squeezed by a vise. "That I'm willing to support you and the baby."

Her eyebrows drew together. "Support?"

"I'll call my lawyer tomorrow. We'll figure out some sort of financial agreement." He rubbed his damp palms up and down the front of his jeans. This was for the best. For J.C. and the baby. And for him. "I'll make sure you and the child are provided for, but…I won't be in Jewell much longer."

"Where are you going?"

He had no idea. "I'd only planned on staying until I was back on my feet." Which would probably happen faster if he showed up at his physical therapy sessions. "I'll probably be doing some traveling, so it'd be best if we don't set up any type of…shared custody or visitation rights."

"This is perfect," J.C. muttered as she got to her feet, her sandwich falling to the floor. The cat pounced on it and began eating while J.C. paced on the other side of the coffee table, swerving to avoid the ottomans. "So what am I supposed to say in a few years if your child asks about its father?"

The idea of J.C. having to tell her kid—their kid—he'd essentially abandoned them... He set the duck down with a sharp crack. "You can tell it whatever you want."

She shook her head, her dark curls bouncing on her shoulders. "What happened to you?"

What happened to him? He went to hell and he didn't think he'd ever get out. His hands fisted, so he forced himself to relax. To stand with no sign of weakness—when all he felt was weak. And out of control.

She wanted him to be the man he used to be. Someone honorable. The type of guy who did the right thing no matter what the cost.

"People change," he said flatly. "Look, I'm willing to take responsibility—"

"But not too much responsibility, right?" She rubbed her temple and exhaled heavily. "You know what?" she said, dropping her hand. "Forget it. Let's just pretend I never came to you this morning."

"What the hell are you talking about?"

"Don't bother meeting with that lawyer tomorrow. I don't want your money."

He pinched the bridge of his nose as he focused on keeping his voice even. "Then why did you come to me this morning?"

"Because I...God...I'm such an idiot." Then she met his eyes and shocked him for the second time that day. "I wanted you to ask me to marry you."

CHAPTER FOUR

BRADY GRIMACED. The man actually grimaced, his face going so white, J.C. thought for sure he was about to pass out. At the thought of marrying her.

Jerk.

"I don't think marriage is the best thing," Brady said in a low rumble. "For either of us."

Yeah, no kidding. But he didn't have to act as if it were the worst thing, either.

"I wouldn't marry you even if you tied me up and threatened to force-feed me a hamburger," J.C. said. "I wouldn't marry you if we were the last two humans left and the only way to save mankind was—"

"I get it. Then why did you say you did?"

"I said I wanted you to ask me." Noticing Daisy devouring the remainder of her peanut butter and jelly sandwich, J.C. bent and picked it up, much to her cat's annoyance. She met Brady's eyes. "You should've at least asked."

She went into the kitchen, tossing the sandwich into the garbage before getting herself a glass of water from the sink. Staring at her reflection in the small window, she held her glass with two hands to steady it as she drank when what she really wanted was to put her head on the counter and weep.

God, could this day get any worse? Her grandmother

was ashamed of her, her parents disappointed. And while she'd certainly disappointed them in the past, her failings—while numerous—had never been anything of this magnitude. But the worst part had been Liz's reaction. Her sister was hurt. So hurt J.C. wondered if she'd ever forgive her.

Which was a crazy thought. No matter how badly J.C. screwed up, Liz was always there for her.

And Liz always forgave her.

Brady's reflection joined hers as he stepped into the doorway.

"Why did you sleep with me, J.C.?"

She choked and bent over the sink to spit out the water in her mouth. Coughed to clear her airway. "What?"

"Did you…" Walking into the room, he shoved a hand through his hair, causing it to stand on end. "Did you do this…on purpose?"

Her eyes widened. The glass slipped out of her fingers, but Brady caught it. Not that it mattered. What was a broken glass when her life was falling apart?

"You think I wanted to get pregnant? I'm only twenty-six. That's way too young to become a mother. I hadn't planned on kids until I was older." Her voice rose and she waved her hand in the air. "Mid-thirties, maybe. *Married*. I have plans. Dreams I need to fulfill before I get tied down with motherhood."

She bit her tongue before she told him everything. How she was unprepared to become a mother. And worse, how unhappy she was about this pregnancy. How guilty she felt over feeling the way she did.

She sure didn't need his crazy accusations adding to her stress. "Why on earth would you think I did this on purpose?"

He looked at the glass in his hands and, as if realizing he still held it, set it on the counter. "When you were a kid you seemed to have a...a crush on me—"

"You knew?" she asked weakly. "Did Liz know?"

He nodded.

Buzzing filled her ears. "I can imagine how much fun you two had laughing about it, about me. Poor chubby, silly Jane and her unrequited love for one of the beautiful people. Doesn't she have delusions of grandeur?"

"Neither one of us laughed at you," Brady said. "I was flattered."

"Flattered?" she repeated tonelessly. Groaning, she bent at the waist and covered her face with her hands, her curls falling forward to hide her face. "Oh, my God. Just kill me now. You're a Marine, you must know a hundred different ways to do it quickly and painlessly."

She heard him step forward but before she could move, he wrapped his fingers around her wrists and gently pried her hands from her face. "Did you sleep with me so we could...because you hoped we'd get together?"

Straightening quickly, the blood rushed to her head and she swayed. "You got me," she said, tugging free of his hold. "What started out as a childhood crush developed into a mad infatuation that's lasted all these years. So when you showed up at my sister's wedding, uninvited, unwanted and drunk, how could I resist? And the rumors about you drinking every night, getting into fights and sleeping your way through the females of Jewell make you all the more enticing. Now I not only get an unwanted pregnancy, but I'm also a notch on Brady Sheppard's bedpost. It's like a dream come true."

"I'm trying to understand how this happened. Didn't we use a condom?"

"What do you remember of that night?" she asked, her stomach sinking.

"You came up to me at the bar at the country club and asked me to leave, so I did." He frowned and stared off in the distance. "Then, when you found out I planned on walking home, you offered to drive me…"

She waited. And waited. "You don't even remember."

"Bits and pieces," he admitted, having the decency to look abashed.

"Let me give you the CliffsNotes version. I took you home and made you some coffee. We started talking and then you kissed me. You. Kissed. Me." She pointed her finger at him with each word. "Not the other way around."

"Janie, I—"

"It was sort of…intense. One minute we were kissing, and the next…" She shrugged. "The next we were having sex."

And she'd been so wrapped up in the fact that Brady wanted to be with her—and then so devastated by how it'd ended—she didn't even realize they hadn't used protection until she got home.

"Did I hurt you?" he asked quietly, his expression giving none of his thoughts away. "I didn't…I didn't force you, did I?"

"No. Of course not."

He shut his eyes briefly. Had he seriously thought he'd forced her?

"I knew what I was doing," she continued. And now she had to take responsibility for that decision. "But I didn't get pregnant on purpose and I have no desire to trap you into marriage. Right now I'm not even sure I want to see you again." She pushed herself upright, locked her knees so they wouldn't tremble but couldn't stop her voice from shaking. "So now would probably be a good time for you to leave." When he didn't so much as blink, she pointed to the door. "Get out."

"Not until we come up with the terms for a financial agreement."

"The terms are I'll take care of this baby and you can pretend we don't exist." Because the reality was, she didn't know if she wanted to keep this baby. The poor thing hadn't been born yet, and so far neither its mother nor father wanted anything to do with it. How messed up was that?

There was so much involved in having a baby. Diapers. Doctors' visits. Day care. And she'd never once considered being a single parent, of being solely responsible for another life. She had enough trouble taking care of herself.

"Having a child is expensive," he said as if she hadn't spoken. "How are you going to manage?"

She swallowed. Worked to keep her expression disdainful so he couldn't see the terror she was trying to hide. "Unlike you, I have a job."

Nothing. No reaction to her dig. The man really was made of stone. "I'm guessing tellers aren't the highest paid employees at the bank."

True. Another point to consider if she decided to keep the baby. She had a hard enough time making ends meet now. The only reason she could even afford this apartment was because her grandmother was her landlord. How would she support not only herself but a baby?

She clutched his arm above his elbow and pulled him toward the door. His muscles tensed under her fingers but he didn't resist.

She opened the door, and the cool rush of crisp autumn air helped settle her stomach. And her nerves. "Goodbye, Brady."

"I want to help."

"Why?"

He seemed taken aback. "Because it's my responsibility."

More exhausted than she'd ever been in her life, she shook her head. "I'm officially absolving you of any and all responsibility, then."

Yes, she usually accepted any and all help getting herself out of the many jams she managed to get into, but she didn't want him trying to assuage his guilt by tossing money her way. Bad enough he'd only slept with her because he'd been drunk…and that she'd slept with him when he'd really wanted Liz. She'd be damned if she'd take his pity, too. And that was all this was. But it wasn't enough.

Seemed she had some pride, after all.

"Damn it, Jane, you're—"

"You've done your part. If anyone asks, I'll be sure to tell them how you tried to get me to see reason. Go back to feeling sorry for yourself in your dark, dirty house. Drown yourself in Jim Beam for all I care." She nudged him outside so she could shut the door and put an end to this horrible day. "This baby doesn't need anything from you. And neither do I."

BRADY PULLED UP to the cottage and shut off the ignition. Every light in the place was on, and seeing as how they'd all been off when he'd left, that—plus the black sports car parked out front—meant one thing. He had company.

Damn, he hated company.

As he got out of the truck, his leg buckled. He tried to catch himself on the door but wasn't fast enough. He fell on his bad knee, landing hard on the cold ground. Gulping down air so he wouldn't howl with the pain, he pulled himself back up and reached into the cab for his cane. Slowly he made his way across the gravel to the front door.

He heard them as soon as he stepped inside. Seemed both his brothers had come calling. He stood there for a moment, the front door still open in case he changed his mind and decided to make a run for it anyway.

A nice dream, considering he could barely stand.

One of them—Matt, from the sound of it—laughed, the sound easily carrying throughout the small house. Brady scowled. How many times over the past few years had he wished he could be home for the holidays? Times when he would've given anything to come back to Jewell, if even for a day, to see Liz and his brothers and mother. Now he'd do anything to avoid them.

Too bad a few of them couldn't take a freaking hint.

Leaving the cane by the door, he went into the kitchen. Aidan, his older brother, leaned against the sink, his legs crossed at the ankles, not a wrinkle on his khakis or dark blue dress shirt. He didn't say a word when he noticed Brady, just raised an eyebrow over eyes the same light blue as Brady's.

"Why are the windows open?" Brady asked.

Sitting on the counter, wearing dark jeans and a

lightweight, V-neck sweater, his light brown hair pulled back into a stubby ponytail, the youngest Sheppard grinned. "Because it smells like you're hiding a dead body in here," Matt claimed.

"Not yet," Brady muttered. "But the night's young." He tossed his keys onto the cluttered table. "Why are you here?"

"Happy Thanksgiving to you, too." He slid off the counter, landing with an ease Brady hated him for. "Missed you at dinner."

Brady grabbed a bottle of pain relievers from the table. He couldn't take one of his prescriptions, not with Aidan watching, but maybe adding a few of these to the ones J.C. had given him would do the trick.

Opening an upper cupboard, he frowned. He could've sworn he had a bottle of Jack Daniel's in there. Shoving aside a box of cookies he didn't even remember buying, he shifted his weight onto his right leg. "You two ever hear of a little thing called trespassing?"

"Heard of it," Matt said with his usual freaking good cheer. "But it doesn't count when we're all equal owners in this place."

"Your leg bothering you?" Aidan asked.

"It's good."

"You sure? Because you seem—"

"I said it's good." And since he was being watched, being judged, he carefully shut the cupboard door before opening the next one to find a few mismatched plates and bowls. But no bottle. His hand shook as he moved on to cupboard number three. "I'm not in the mood for company."

"There's a news flash," Aidan murmured.

"Go away."

"Now is that any way to treat the people who brought you Thanksgiving dinner complete with half a pumpkin pie?" Matt asked.

"I don't like pumpkin pie," he said, searching the meager contents of his fridge for the six-pack of beer he'd bought the other day. Damn but he needed a drink.

"I do." Matt reached over Brady's shoulder and took out the pie. "Don't worry, Mom sent over two big slices of pecan pie, too."

"Looking for something?" Aidan asked.

It was his tone that clued Brady in. He leaned his arm against the fridge. Shit. They'd cleaned him out.

"This your idea of an intervention?"

"What do you mean?" Aidan asked, unbuttoning a sleeve and rolling it up.

Brady's eyes narrowed. The smug son of a bitch. "What's the matter?" he goaded. "You're not man enough to admit you snuck in here and hid all of my booze?"

Repeating the process with the other sleeve, Aidan stepped forward, his unhurried strides at odds with the cold, hard expression on his face. "I didn't hide it. I trashed it. Dumped it down the sink. When are you going to be man enough to admit you've got a problem?"

Hands fisted at his sides, Brady limped forward until he and Aidan were nose to nose. "Why don't you go—"

"Back it up," Matt said, stepping between them. A surreal experience considering Brady used to be the one breaking up fights between the other two. "Remember Mom and Dad always said you have to set a good example for me."

The urge to throw a punch still vibrating through him, Brady went back to the fridge. He took out several of the plastic containers his brothers had brought along with a half-empty jar of mayonnaise. "What do you want?"

"Why didn't you show up for dinner?" Aidan asked. He sounded so much like their deceased father.

Sounded like Tom Sheppard, but wasn't. No matter how hard he tried.

"I was busy."

Setting everything on the counter, he swallowed a couple of the pain relievers before shoving aside a dirty frying pan and a stack of plates. He pulled out a few slices of bread from the loaf behind the toaster, checked for mold then searched for a halfway clean knife.

"You're lucky Mom didn't come here instead of us," Matt said. "She'd kick your ass if she saw this kitchen."

Sweat broke out above his lip at the thought of his mother seeing firsthand how messed up he was. "I'm all sorts of lucky," he agreed, slathering mayo on the bread.

"Mom cried."

Brady froze, his grip tightening on the knife. "I told her I couldn't come."

"It's Thanksgiving," Aidan continued. "The first one in years where you've been on the same continent and you didn't show up."

Brady slowly, deliberately, set the knife down. Opening all the containers, he found turkey, stuffing and sweet potatoes. He piled turkey onto a slice of bread. "Don't push it," he said, his voice quiet. "I've had a really shitty day."

BETH ANDREWS 63

And he didn't need his sanctimonious brother heaping
the guilt on, he thought as he topped the turkey with
stuffing and another slice of bread. Hell, he felt so much
guilt right now, any more and he'd explode.

"Worse than watching your mother leave Thanksgiving dinner in tears because your selfish, idiot brother
didn't bother to show?" Aidan asked.

Brady sat at the table, took a bite and pretended to
think that question over as he chewed. "Yeah. Worse
than that. Besides, something came up that I had to take
care of."

"What could be so important that you skipped out
on a holiday family dinner?"

Taking his time, Brady had another bite of sandwich
before he answered. "I'd say the woman who's going to
have my baby was more important."

Blessed silence.

"You're kidding," Matt finally said.

"Serious as Aidan gets about…well…everything."

"Who?" Aidan asked.

A piece of turkey seemed to be stuck in his throat.
He cleared it. "Jane Montgomery."

Another beat of silence. Then Aidan shook his head.
"You slept with J.C.? Are you insane?"

"I'd sleep with her," Matt interjected.

Both Brady and Aidan stared at him. "What?" he
asked, offended. "I would. She's got a body like one of
those old-time movie stars. And that mouth of hers? The
combination of that sexy mouth with those big brown
eyes?" He nodded, a half smile on his face. "Oh, yeah,
I'd—"

Aidan gave him a hard smack upside the back of the
head. "Shut up."

Matt rubbed the spot. "I'm just saying..."

Sexy mouth? Brady frowned, picturing the way J.C. had looked when she'd shoved him out of her apartment. There hadn't been anything sexy about her then. He could see where some guys might find her attractive and she did have a certain...warm appeal. But compared to Liz, she was ordinary.

Aidan crossed his arms and glared at Brady. "What are you going to do?"

"Nothing."

"What do you mean, nothing?"

"J.C. said she and the baby didn't need me."

Which should be a relief, right? And what he wanted. No obligations. No ties to either J.C. or the baby.

"Doesn't matter," Aidan insisted. "You have a legal right to your child. And now is the perfect time to re-think that job offer we discussed."

Right. The job offer.

A few weeks ago, Aidan had driven Brady to the V.A. hospital for a checkup. On the way home, he'd offered Brady a position at the Diamond Dust Vineyard, the winery their father had started more than thirty years ago. Aidan had pointed out that Brady had been away from the wine business a long time. And while he'd worked at the winery as a teenager—all three brothers had—a lot had changed in the past twelve years. Change that would take Brady time to catch up on. So he'd suggested Brady ease back into the swing of things by taking over the bookkeeping of the Diamond Dust.

His brother wanted him stuck in some office behind a desk taking care of invoices and orders and adding figures. Trying to keep him away from alcohol, most likely. Sounded like hell.

"I don't need to think about it," he said. "I'm still not interested."

"You have other prospects?"

Brady snorted. He used to have prospects. He'd always planned on joining the Virginia State Police after he got out of the service. But like all his goals and dreams, that idea went up in smoke, starting when Liz decided he wasn't enough and ending with his knee getting shot up.

"I think I'll take some time to work on finishing my great American novel."

"How are you going to support a kid—"

"I'm not." He shrugged as if it didn't matter, but deep down, he knew it did. "J.C. doesn't want anything from me. Including child support payments."

Aidan's lips thinned. "So that's it? You're just going to abandon your own kid?"

"I'm thinking about leaving—"

"To go where?" Aidan asked.

Brady stretched out his leg. "North. New Hampshire, maybe. Or Maine."

Somewhere far from Jewell. Where there wouldn't be a chance of him running into Liz and her new husband. Or J.C. and the baby. So his kid wouldn't have to grow up in the same town as him, knowing his father didn't want anything to do with him. Or her.

Even he wasn't that big a prick.

He wasn't trying to hurt J.C. or the kid or make their lives more difficult. He just…couldn't be what they wanted. What they needed.

"You are some piece of work," Aidan said, staring at him as if he were a lowlife. "Why did you even come back?"

"Now that's an easy one," Brady said, working to keep his voice even. "I had nowhere else to go."

Instead of laying into him like Brady expected him to, Aidan snatched his jacket from the back of the chair so quickly, the chair toppled over.

"You need to get your head out of your ass," Matt said before following Aidan to the door.

Brady slouched in his chair. What he needed was for his family to leave him alone instead of trying to bring him back into the fold like a goddamn sheep. He had no interest in joining the winery. Having all three sons run it had been his father's dream.

But his father wasn't here anymore.

And just because Aidan had quit law school after their dad died to run the Diamond Dust Vineyard didn't mean Brady had to follow his footsteps. Matt hadn't. He'd lit out of Jewell right after graduating high school and hadn't looked back. He now made bucketfuls of money advising top wineries around the world. Brady wasn't about to cave, either.

Even if he didn't have any other options.

And he didn't. Not in Jewell, anyway.

Standing, he picked up a dirty coffee mug, rinsed it out and hobbled to his room. He grimaced as he stepped inside. His brothers hadn't bothered opening the windows in here…but he wished they had. The room smelled like his high-school gym locker. Maybe he'd do a load of laundry, he thought as he sat on the bed and picked up the almost full bottle of whiskey on the floor between the nightstand and bed.

He filled the mug halfway and drank deeply, ignoring the tremor in his hand. He concentrated on how the alcohol seemed to wash away his anxiety. Leaning back against the headboard, he took another, slower sip.

Tomorrow he'd worry about dirty laundry. About what he was going to do with his life now that his knee was useless and the woman he loved had exchanged him for some overeducated brainiac doctor. Tomorrow he'd think about what to do about J.C., with her warm brown eyes and huge expectations of him.

He finished the drink. Debated all of two seconds before pouring more into the mug. Yeah, he'd figure it all out.

Just not tonight.

CHAPTER FIVE

SHE DIDN'T USUALLY MAKE mistakes. More like…missteps. Paired the wrong shoes with an outfit. Picked up a real soda instead of sugar-free after a bad day. And when she was fourteen, there had been an unfortunate decision to perm her hair. But overall, Dr. Elizabeth Montgomery-Messler made the right choices.

Screwing up was J.C.'s department.

But as soon as the door opened, Liz knew she'd made a mistake, a huge one, in coming here.

"Good morning," she croaked, her face heating.

Linking her hands together in front of her, she tried to give Brady her professional smile—cool, calm and detached—but couldn't manage it. Not when he glowered at her, his hair tousled, his eyes red-rimmed.

Not when he stood in the doorway wearing a pair of low-slung, faded jeans. And nothing else.

"Liz," he said in his low voice.

"How…how are you?"

Widening his stance, he crossed his arms, the muscles in his arms bulging, the eagle tattoo on his left bicep shifting. "Cold."

If the goosebumps covering his arms were anything to go by, he was freezing. But he didn't shiver. Didn't give any indication he was uncomfortable at all. At least not enough to invite her inside.

"Yes…it's quite…chilly this morning," she said lamely. Though it was almost 9:00 a.m., frost still covered the ground, the sun unable to penetrate the cloudy, gray sky. "We're due for some rain…"

He raked his gaze over her. "Why are you here, Liz?"

"I…I'm running errands… I don't have to work until this afternoon and I…I came here to…"

He raised one eyebrow. She'd forgotten how much that annoyed her. "To…? To discuss the weather?"

She stuck her hand into the pocket of her brown leather jacket, her fingers closing around the velvet jeweler's box. "I wanted to see you. To see how you're doing," she amended quickly.

"Never better."

"Good. That's…good." The breeze picked up, blowing her hair into her face. She tucked the errant strands behind her ear.

"How's your knee?" she asked.

He seemed upset by the question. "It's fine."

"Are you taking physical therapy here in town or at the V.A. hosp—"

"Don't," he warned quietly.

"Don't what?"

"Don't pretend you give a damn."

Her throat constricted. "I…I wanted to visit you," she confessed, "when you were in the hospital."

"But you didn't." He leaned against the doorjamb, studying her in that way that used to make her feel like he could read her thoughts—when all she'd wanted was to keep a few of her thoughts to herself. "I guess your husband wouldn't have been too happy with you sitting by your ex's bedside."

No, Carter probably wouldn't have been happy, but he wouldn't have stopped her, either. When she'd discovered Brady had been injured, that he'd almost died, Carter had told her he understood if she needed to go to him. But she'd been too afraid to face him again.

Afraid he'd ask her to take him back. Terrified she'd say yes.

"After the way things...ended...between us," she said, staring at a point over his shoulder, "I thought a clean break would be best."

"And yet here you are."

She squeezed the box. Then pulled it out. "I wanted to give you this."

He went very still. "You've got to be kidding."

"I can't keep this, Brady. I...I want you to have it back."

"And you always get what you want, don't you? Sorry to disappoint you, but not this time." He pushed himself upright. "Toss it in the garbage. Hell, flush it down the toilet for all I care. But I'm not taking it back."

Her hand trembled. She should've returned his ring long ago but she hadn't wanted to send it overseas and risk it being lost or stolen. And she hadn't been brave enough to drop it off at his mother's house, knowing how angry his family must be with her.

But now she needed him to take it back. Things were still...tense...between her and Carter and if he discovered she still had it, he'd see it as a sign she hadn't let go of Brady. Not completely. She had to show her husband she'd moved on. That she didn't regret the choice she'd made.

"I'm not taking it back," Brady repeated. "So, if that's all..." He started to close the door.

"Did you sleep with my sister to hurt me?" she blurted, then bit the inside of her lower lip. Hard. "Never mind. Let's forget I was even here."

Shoving the ring back into her pocket, she hurried down the steps, the high heels of her suede boots sliding on the wet wood. And wouldn't landing on her rear be the perfect ending to this misadventure?

She wrenched open her car door.

"No."

Her heart pounded against her ribs. "What?"

He looked down at the porch, his hands on his hips. "No," he repeated, lifting his head. "I didn't sleep with Jane to hurt you."

She nodded, got into her car, started it and drove down the gravel road. Well, that was a relief. Brady hadn't become the kind of man who'd deliberately set out to cause pain. Who'd use J.C. as a tool to get back at Liz. He hadn't slept with her sister out of revenge.

He'd slept with her because he'd wanted to. Because he'd wanted J.C.

Her vision blurring, she wrung the steering wheel. Yes. That certainly was a relief.

BRADY'S TOES WERE NUMB. The tip of his nose tingling with cold. But he didn't move, couldn't force himself to turn from the sight of Liz driving away.

He did a few slow neck rolls. She thought he'd take it. Well, why wouldn't she want to get rid of it? She couldn't still wear it, not when she had another man's ring on her finger. Yeah, he'd noticed. Hard not to notice a rock that size. One that made the diamond he'd spent three months' salary on look like a freaking speck.

Guess better jewelry was just one of the perks of trading up from a grunt Marine to a doctor.

A car came barreling toward the house and his heart beat faster but it wasn't Liz coming back. No, it was worse than seeing the woman who was everything he'd always wanted and couldn't have.

It was his mother.

Diane pulled to a stop and got out of her big boat of a luxury car. "You're up," she said, striding toward him. "Good."

"Mom."

By choice, he'd hardly seen her since he'd moved back to Jewell. Her mouth was set in a disapproving line, and her frame was a few pounds heavier than he remembered. But with her graying blond hair cut in a new style and the remnants of the tan she'd acquired on her trip to Florida a few weeks ago, she looked good.

Ready to tear him apart limb from limb, but good.

"Shall we stand out here staring at each other all day," she asked, "or are you going to invite me in?"

He shifted his weight. Let her inside? Now? Before he'd had a chance to rent a backhoe to clean the place out? "Do I really have a choice or is that one of those trick questions?"

She went in ahead of him—straight to the kitchen.

"Oh, Brady," she called in disgust. "Look at this mess."

"I've seen it," he said as he entered the room.

Her eyes narrowed behind her glasses. "Are you sassing me?"

"No, ma'am," he responded automatically.

"Go put a shirt on while I make some coffee…you do have coffee, don't you?" He pointed toward the container next to the coffeepot on the counter. "You and I," she continued, "are going to have a little chat."

Aw, hell. This couldn't end well for him.

By the time he came back, wearing a Carolina Panthers T-shirt, Diane had the coffeepot scrubbed, a fresh pot brewing and was at the sink tackling his mountain of dirty dishes.

"I was going to get to those," he said, brushing crumbs off a chair before sitting.

She didn't even glance at him. "I could see it was high on your to-do list."

He slouched down and stretched his leg out. "I've been busy."

"You obviously have some free time this morning," she said, not mentioning that without a job, he had free time every morning. "And I could use some help."

He wasn't stupid—or brave—enough to point out that they could air dry. He got up again and found a towel at the bottom of a drawer. They worked in silence while the coffee finished brewing.

"You haven't returned any of my phone calls," Diane said, rinsing a heavy white mug.

And here they went. "I meant to—"

"No. You didn't. You're avoiding me." She scrubbed at a spot of dried ketchup on a plate. "When you first came back to Jewell and insisted on living here instead of at the house with me, I thought you just needed time and space to accept all the changes you've gone through."

"I appreciate it," he said, guessing that her giving him space was about to come to an abrupt end.

"But," she continued, stressing the word, "when you didn't show up at Thanksgiving, I realized I was wrong."

Noticing he'd twisted the towel in his hands, he smoothed it out before drying a glass. "I didn't want to do the whole celebratory dinner, that's all. Don't make more of it."

"The problem is, I haven't made enough of it. That needs to change." Her voice softened. "Let me help you."

"I'm fine."

"If you're so *fine,* then tell me why you've been avoiding your family." She tossed the dishcloth into the sink with enough force that water splashed them both. "And while you're at it, you can also explain why I had to hear from someone else that you're going to be a father."

Wincing, Brady scratched the back of his neck. This had to be some sort of gossip speed record.

"I was going to tell you…" In a few weeks. As soon as he'd figured out a few things. Like how to get J.C. to accept child support without wanting more from him. And what he was going to do with the rest of his life.

"Now you don't have to. Shirley Hanold down at the coffee shop told me, in front of my entire walking group, no less."

And so his day continued to get worse. He poured himself a cup of coffee so he wouldn't have to look at her. "Things are…complicated right now."

"Getting the sister of the woman you'd once planned to marry pregnant certainly is complicated. What are you going to do now?"

"About?"

"Don't play dense with me, Brady," she snapped. "Are you, or are you not, going to take responsibility for this baby?"

"I've offered J.C. child support."

His mother waved that away with one hard stroke

of her hand through the air. "Raising a child is about more than money. It's about being there, day in and day out. Nurturing your son or daughter. Loving them...no matter what mistakes they may make."

"Subtle," he muttered.

"You're too stubborn for subtlety." She poured herself a cup of coffee. "Your father and I raised you to be the type of man who steps up and takes responsibility for his actions."

He was willing to support the child for the next eighteen years. To make sure he...or she...was provided for. Wasn't that enough? He chugged a quick gulp of coffee and succeeded in burning his tongue.

"Does this have anything to do with Liz?" Diane asked.

And that was the last place he was going. Bad enough he still loved the woman. He wasn't about to admit it to his mother.

Besides, Liz was married now.

"Liz and I are over."

"Then why did I pass her car on my way here?"

His answer was a hard stare.

"That's it. I've had enough." Setting her cup down, Diane braced her arms against the table, getting right in her son's face. "You live like an animal. You refuse to go to physical therapy. When you're not ignoring your family, you're arguing with us. And your drinking is out of control."

He kept his expression blank. As if it didn't bother him that his mother knew how low he'd sunk. At least she didn't know about his nightmares. That he woke up in a cold sweat. He sipped his coffee.

"I'd think a winery owner would be all for drinking," he said.

"I'm disappointed in you, Brady." She cleared her throat and when she spoke again, her words were louder. Stronger. "I've never said that to any of my sons, never thought I would have reason to, but it's the truth."

What she'd said ripped him through him like a razor. He stood. "If that's all, I think I'm going to go back to bed."

"I'm not finished. You've done nothing to help yourself heal."

"The doctors at the V.A. hospital said my knee will never be a hundred percent."

"I'm not talking about your physical wounds." Hands trembling, she took her coat from the back of the chair and put it on, her movements jerky. "Every day I thank God your life was spared. That I'm not one of those mothers who's had to bury a child. You were given a gift, but instead of embracing your second chance, you'd rather dwell on the past. On what you lost. As much as I love you—and I do love you—I can no longer sit back and watch you self-destruct."

Damn it, that was not what he was doing. He may not be dealing with things how his family thought he should, but he was doing the best he could.

"Get yourself the help you need," his mother continued. "If you don't…" She swallowed.

"Don't stop there," he said softly.

The woman who raised three boys with equal doses of love and discipline stared him down. The woman who was as formidable and implacable as a drill sergeant. Who didn't make idle threats.

"If you don't, you'll have to find somewhere else to waste your life. Because you'll no longer be welcome here."

THE THIRD STREET DINER was packed with a boisterous lunch crowd, but J.C. spotted Liz seated in a small, two-person booth in the back. Hard to miss her, what with that halo highlighting her perfectly straight hair.

Okay, the halo was just the sun shining through a skylight. Still.

J.C. patted her hair. Yes, it was as big and frizzy as she feared. She made her way through the restaurant. She smiled and said hello to a few people but she didn't stop. She had to get her sister back.

"Hi," J.C. said when she got to the booth.

Even though she was sitting—and J.C. was a good three inches taller than her—Liz managed look down her nose at J.C. "You're late."

She checked her watch, then shrugged out of her coat. Bit her tongue instead of pointing out that anything under five minutes shouldn't be considered late. "Sorry. My last customer had a couple savings bonds and…"

And her sister didn't give a rat's behind about her job.

J.C. hung her coat on the metal pole next to the bench seat before sitting down. "I'm glad you came."

Liz folded her hands on the table. "I'm only here because Mom asked me to hear you out."

"Oh. Right. Well…" So she'd had to get her mother to talk to Liz for her. She didn't have a choice. Liz had ignored all of her attempts to explain. J.C. couldn't remember a time when they'd gone five days without speaking.

Couldn't remember there ever being a time when Liz was so angry with her that she didn't want to talk to her.

Their waiter, a short, stocky college kid, took their

orders. Once they were alone again, J.C. cracked her thumb knuckle. "So...how are you?" she asked awkwardly.

"Fine."

J.C. drummed her fingers on the table. This was going to be harder than she'd thought. While she had plenty of experience apologizing for her blunders, she didn't know how to be the one who smoothed things over. She'd always relied on Liz for that.

The waiter delivered their drinks and J.C. unwrapped a straw and stuck it in her ginger ale. Took a sip to calm her churning stomach. She'd had her first prenatal visit yesterday and Dr. Owens had assured her the morning sickness would end soon, it being the second trimester.

And then, after receiving that hopeful news, J.C. had been informed by the doctor's office manager that her medical insurance would barely cover sixty percent of the expenses she'd incur during this pregnancy. No wonder she still felt sick.

"How's Carter?" J.C. asked. She'd been worried about the two of them ever since that awful Thanksgiving scene. When she'd left their house, she'd overheard them arguing in the hallway about Liz's reaction to the news of J.C.'s pregnancy. And who the father was. "Is...are you two okay?"

Liz, her mouth set in a thin line, squeezed a lemon slice into her water. "Of course," she said, but wouldn't meet J.C.'s eyes.

J.C. leaned across the table and covered Liz's hand with her own. "Lizzie, I...God...I'm so sorry."

Liz eased her hand away. "I knew you had a crush on him when you were a kid." She shook her head. "What did you do? Wait all these years for your opportunity? For us to break up?"

"It wasn't like that. And it's not as if he ever would've looked at me twice—at any other woman—if you two were still together." She lined the salt and pepper shakers up with the front corners of the napkin dispenser. "It just sort of…happened."

Liz pursed her mouth. "How exactly does that work? You and my ex-fiancé were both naked and one of you tripped and fell on the other?"

"It was a mistake." She took another drink but it did little to ease the dryness of her throat. "One I'd give anything to go back and undo. It was wrong. *I* was wrong. I…I convinced myself it wouldn't matter to you because you'd broken up with him. That you didn't want him anymore."

"I don't." Her cheeks colored. "That's not what this is about."

"No. Of course not." Liz couldn't still want Brady. Not when she had Carter. Could she? "I didn't mean to hurt you."

"You never mean to do the things you do. You don't think about the consequences of your actions. You just charge forward, not caring about anything except what you want. Then, when it blows up in your face, you expect someone else to pick up the pieces."

Stunned, J.C. sat back. That wasn't fair. She could fix her own messes. She just never had to before.

That part about her only thinking about what she wanted? Total crap. Of course she'd thought of Liz, of her reaction, that night she'd slept with Brady. Had thought of her sister but hadn't let anything stop her, she realized, her queasiness now having nothing to do with being pregnant. She'd betrayed Liz because Brady had wanted her.

Because she'd wanted him.

"I thought I could do this, but I can't," Liz said, sliding out of the booth as she dug into her purse. She tossed some cash onto the table but J.C. got out and stopped her.

"What about lunch?" she asked. What about their relationship?

"I'm not hungry."

"I'm sorry," J.C. rushed to say, her throat so tight it came out as a croak. "Please…can you forgive me?"

Liz slowly looked at her. "Not today," she whispered.

Their waiter passed Liz as she walked out. "Everything all right here?" he asked, setting their food on the table.

Sitting back down, J.C. gave him a pathetic excuse for a smile. "Fine. Thanks."

He took the hint and didn't press. "Let me know if you need anything else."

This was bad. Real bad. Liz hadn't forgiven her. What if she never did? J.C. studied her cheese and mushroom quesadilla and then shoved it aside. Liz just needed more time. To…work through her hurt and anger. She'd forgive J.C.

Because J.C. couldn't get through this without her.

CHAPTER SIX

J.C. LEANED AGAINST the steering wheel and stared up at the white Colonial house that had been in the Sheppard family for five generations. It was lovely with tall, narrow windows, black shutters and wide porches on both the ground and second floors. The front door was a deep, inky shade of blue and had leaded glass windows on both sides, another one shaped like a fan on top. Listed on the Historical Register as one of the oldest structures in the county, there was nothing even remotely intimidating about it.

Right. That was why she'd been sitting there for twenty minutes.

She unbuckled her seat belt. After the week she'd had, failure was not an option.

Too bad. Failure was the one thing she excelled at.

Taking a deep, fortifying breath, she stepped out into the bright midday sun before she could change her mind. She tucked a small, white bakery box under her arm and crossed the cement drive. Once on the porch, she lifted her hand to knock only to lower it again.

Why did last-ditch efforts have to be so difficult?

Shutting her eyes, she rapped on the door. Maybe no one was home. Maybe they were all out in the vineyards doing…whatever people who had vineyards did. Pruning. Or…or fertiliz—

Someone tapped her on the shoulder.

"God!" J.C. whirled around, her heart racing.

A sleek, long-legged brunette in tight jeans and T-shirt proclaiming Conserve Water, Drink Wine smiled. "Not even close. But it's better than a lot of other things I've been called. I'm Connie."

Still trying to catch her breath, J.C. shook the woman's hand. "J.C. Montgomery."

Connie tipped her head to the side, the sunlight picking up reddish highlights in her short, choppy dark hair. "Montgomery, huh? Liz's sister?"

If she had a dollar for every time someone asked her that, she wouldn't have to look for ways to supplement her income. "Yes."

"I was a few years ahead of Liz in school. Plus, she used to come out here before…"

Before she broke Brady's heart.

Connie tucked her fingers into her jeans pockets. "So, is it J-A-Y-C-E-E or just the letters?"

"Uh…the letters."

"Well, J.C. just the letters, is there something I can do for you?"

She glanced at the door. "I'm looking for Aidan Sheppard."

"I need to see him, too. So what do you say we go in and track him down?"

Connie let herself in and J.C. followed her into a two-story foyer with elegant wainscoting, rose-colored walls and a wooden staircase leading to the second floor.

"Shouldn't we wait for someone to let us in?" she whispered.

Humor lit Connie's blue eyes. "I run the vineyards

for the Sheppards. They're used to me coming and going."

Oh. Well. That made sense, then. At least J.C. wasn't letting herself into another house belonging to the Sheppards. The one time she'd done that, things hadn't worked out so well for her.

Connie pulled out a cell phone and pressed a number. "Aidan's office is upstairs. I'll call him." She lowered her voice conspiratorially. "He gets grumpy when people barge in on him."

J.C. smiled weakly. Of course he did. "Yes. That's so rude."

Maybe she shouldn't have come without an appointment.

"He's not answering, which means he's probably on the office line. Let me text him that we're here—" she flipped her phone the other way, her fingers flying over the keys almost as quickly as the words coming out of her mouth "—and he can come down when he's finished."

Then, sticking the phone back into her pocket, she walked around a corner. J.C. switched the box to her other hand. Should she follow? Sit on the cute wooden bench against the wall and wait for Aidan to come downstairs? Take her impetuous self and this whole crazy idea and get out there?

Connie poked her head back around the corner. "You coming?"

She sighed. "Right behind you."

They went into a family room so big, J.C. could've fit her apartment in it. And still have space left over. A stone fireplace took up most of the wall to the left while sliding glass doors led to a bricked veranda at the back of the house. The room opened up into a large kitchen with ceramic tiles on the floor, oak cabinets and stainless-steel appliances—including a double wall oven and a six-burner range top like the ones J.C.'s mother had been bugging her father to get for their own kitchen. Passing a small breakfast nook with three sides of floor-to-ceiling windows, J.C. crossed to the granite-topped island in the middle of the room. After setting the box down, she lovingly ran her hands over the cool surface.

"You want me to give you two a few minutes alone?"

J.C. returned Connie's grin. And how sad was it that she couldn't remember the last time she'd smiled? "Do you have any idea how many truffles I could shape on this much counter space?"

Connie tapped a forefinger to her lips. "Quite a few?"

"Eight…maybe even ten dozen. And I wouldn't even have to set cookie sheets of them on the coffee table or washer and dryer. I can't even reach the edge," she said, stretching her arms across the width of the counter.

"It truly is an amazing structure." Connie carried a large, frosted glass jar with a silver lid over to the island. "Which is why Diane likes it so much. She doesn't make truffles, but she's big on baking."

J.C. blanched. She'd been so worried about meeting with Aidan she hadn't even considered running into Brady's mom. "She's not…she's not here, is she?"

Connie shook her head. "She and Al are spending the weekend up in D.C."

Al being Al Wallace, Mrs. Sheppard's boyfriend—if you could call a sixty-something retired senator some-one's boyfriend—and God bless him for taking Mrs.

Sheppard away for the weekend. J.C. would gladly avoid Brady's mom for...oh...forever would work.

Not that she was afraid of her or anything. Ha.

Diane Sheppard had a reputation for getting what she wanted and had no qualms about stomping on anyone who got in her way.

What if she wanted to be a part of the baby's life? What if...what if she wanted to have a say in any decision she made regarding the baby?

J.C. rubbed her temples. Mrs. Sheppard might not even know about the baby. And if she did, well, this was J.C.'s body. Her baby. And ultimately her decision whether she kept the baby or not.

"Here," Connie said, holding out a thick, pumpkin-shaped sugar cookie with orange frosting. "You look like you could use a sugar rush."

J.C. reached for the cookie only to remember how, when she'd stood on the stupid scale at Dr. Owens's Monday, the nurse had moved the little metal slide up. Then she'd moved it some more. And yet some more.

"I'm good, thanks," she managed to say, lowering her hand. She may be eating for two, but that didn't mean she had to eat everything. Besides, being this virtuous was almost as good as a giant sugar cookie.

And the day she believed that was the day she hoped she stopped breathing.

Connie shrugged, then polished off the cookie before reaching for another one.

J.C. hiked herself up onto one of the two high-backed, black stools. "Even though we just met, I already hate you. But it's nothing personal."

Connie's laugh was deep and husky—and the perfect fit for someone so sexy.

"I'm guessing you're one of those women who can eat anything she wants without gaining weight," J.C. continued. Connie grinned and went for a third cookie. "See? I have to hate you. It's the principle of the thing."

"A girl's gotta have her principles." Connie put the lid back on the cookie jar when the sliding glass door opened.

Brady stepped inside and stopped abruptly when he saw J.C. "Everything okay?"

She twisted her fingers together in her lap. Crap. She'd gone seven days without any more fun-filled run-ins with him. And she'd like to keep that streak alive for the next eighteen years or so.

"Everything's fine," she said.

His hair was mussed, the black T-shirt he wore underneath an open gray and black checked flannel shirt was wrinkled and the stubble from the last time she'd seen him had grown into a full-fledged, if scruffy, beard.

Not even glancing at Connie—who watched them intently—he crossed to the end of the island. Close enough that J.C. could smell the fresh air on his skin.

He studied her as if he were a scientist and she were some perplexing, never-before-discovered insect. "Why is your hair like that?"

"You are such a moron," Connie murmured.

J.C. couldn't agree more. She lifted a hand to her hair. "I straightened it."

"I called you a few times," he said, obviously not having anything else to say about her hair. Like how nice it looked.

Not that she cared. She certainly hadn't spent a solid hour and a half ironing her hair into submission for him. "I got the messages."

All seven of them. He'd called once a day since leaving her apartment Thanksgiving and each time he said the same thing. "It's Brady. Call me."

"You two together?" Connie asked.

J.C. snorted. "No."

"Beat it, Connie," Brady said.

"But I don't want to leave. Not when this is so fascinating."

Brady glared at her. "Goodbye."

She held her hands up in surrender. "I can take a hint." She gave J.C.'s arm a quick, reassuring squeeze as she walked past. "I'll go up and see what's taking Aidan so long."

He frowned. "Aidan? So you're not here because you've changed your mind?"

Please. Even if she wanted his money, she couldn't accept it now.

"I'm not here to see you," she said, glad to hear a touch of ice in her voice. "I'm here on business."

He raised his eyebrows. "Business?" She nodded. "With the Diamond Dust?" Another nod, this one jerky. "Is that why you're dressed like that?"

"What's wrong with how I'm dressed?"

She forced herself to remain still and not fidget or tug at her clothes while he slowly inspected her from the tips of her pointy-toed shoes, up the black, wide-legged pants and over her small baby bump currently covered by a loose white button-down shirt. When she thought he was done and she could breathe again, his gaze lingered at the black lace peeking out of the top of her shirt.

Her breasts had already gone up a cup size and since she liked being able to breathe, she'd left the top three buttons undone and worn a silk camisole underneath. Now, as her skin warmed under his scrutiny, she wished she had on a sweater. Preferably with a high neckline.

He jerked his eyes up, his jaw tight. "You don't look like yourself."

That'd been the point. The hair, the clothes, they were supposed to show Aidan she was a businesswoman. Professional. Capable. Confident.

Someone he would want to do business with.

"YOU'RE NOT HERE to see me?" Brady asked, trying to wrap his head around what she was saying. Why was she dressed like some sort of naughty librarian? With her hair straightened, there was a noticeable resemblance between her and Liz. A resemblance that was eclipsed by the way J.C. filled out that damn shirt.

"I'm really not here to see you. I was hoping to talk to Aidan."

"About doing business with the Diamond Dust?"

"Yes," she muttered.

What sort of business could J.C. have with his family's winery?

"Why don't I wait in the foyer for Aidan?" she asked. "I'm sure you have…things…to do."

He shrugged and went to the refrigerator. Out of the corner of his eye, he noticed J.C. pick up the white box from the island.

"Do you have an appointment?" he asked.

"An appointment?"

Brady took a container of some sort of leftover pasta out before closing the fridge door. "An appointment with Aidan."

She didn't. For one thing, if she had an appointment,

Aidan wouldn't have told her to come to the main house. His brother used their father's home office upstairs, but he held all meetings down the road at the converted farmhouse where the Diamond Dust's main offices were located.

And he never would've let her wait this long. Aidan was nothing if not organized. He'd be willing to bet Aidan scheduled every minute of his day, including his trips to the bathroom.

J.C. fumbled the box in her hands before setting it back on the island. "No. Do I...do you think that'll be a problem?"

"Only if you're serious about doing business with him."

She blanched. No, Aidan wasn't that big prick, to hold something like an impromptu visit against her. But the truth was, Brady didn't want her to go to his brother.

Not when she wouldn't even take his phone calls.

"Maybe I should leave," she said, biting her lower lip, her brow furrowed.

"You're already here," he pointed out. His knee began to ache so he lifted himself up to sit on the counter. "You might as well do what you came here to do."

"But if it's going to make Aidan angry—"

"You don't need Aidan." Brady took the lid off the container. Lasagna. Great. Even better. He opened the drawer between his legs and grabbed a fork. "You've got me."

She wrinkled her nose. "I've got you for what?"

He waved the fork. "To discuss your business idea."

"Have you been drinking?"

She didn't add *again,* but sure as hell implied it. "Not yet."

He would've started already but he'd been starving and all he had at the cottage was cereal…but no milk. Guess he needed to make a trip to the grocery store. The grocery store where he could limp behind a cart while everyone stared. Or asked him how he was doing, what his plans were next.

Better yet, he could have a flashback, proving to everyone how little control he had over himself.

Was it any wonder he needed the oblivion alcohol provided?

The only reason he'd come to his mom's house was because he knew she wouldn't be there. Despite her being pissed at him, she still kept him informed of her comings and goings and two days ago, she'd left him a message saying she was spending a long weekend in D.C. with Al.

"Are you working for Aidan?" J.C. asked.

He could be. If he gave in to his mother's threats and Aidan's pressure.

Brady scooped up more cold lasagna. "Tell me."

She tucked her hair behind her ear—just like Liz always did. "I've had some unexpected expenses. And I need to supplement my income."

He narrowed his eyes at her hesitant tone. "What kind of unexpected expenses?"

"It doesn't matter. But I—"

"Jane. What expenses?"

She shrugged, the movement causing her full breasts to rise and lower. He averted his gaze. "Some…doctor bills."

For the baby. *His* baby. "I'll pay them."

"No. You won't."

"I want to," he said, realizing it was true. He wanted to help her, even if all he had to offer was a few bucks.

"I told you, I don't want your money." Her hands were clenched at her sides, her shoulders rigid. "I have to do this on my own."

And that was when he saw the real reason she wouldn't accept his help.

Pride.

Hell. He knew a thing or two about that. And he wasn't about to try to injure hers.

"Go on," he said quietly.

She looked at him with such gratitude, he felt like a complete ass. Damn it, she shouldn't be willing to accept so little from him.

"When I saw that first bill," she said, "I was a bit stressed so I did what most women do when they're stressed."

"Found some poor bastard to castrate?"

"Ha-ha. No, but only because I didn't think you'd let me within ten feet of you if I happened to be carrying a machete."

He grimaced. "Ouch."

"I searched for some chocolate. But I didn't have any so I decided to make some." She took the lid off the box and carried it over to him.

He set the lasagna aside. "I didn't know you made chocolates." He inspected the candies set on waxed paper.

Then again, there was plenty he didn't know about her. Like why she'd slept with him. Or what her plans for the future were. How she would raise their baby on her own.

But being this close to her he did find out a couple of things about her. She smelled sweet, like vanilla. Her eyes weren't plain brown as he'd always thought, but a deep, rich caramel.

"I usually make them as gifts," she said, "for holidays and birthdays or if a friend needs a pick-me-up. And I made them for—" she dropped her eyes "—for Liz's wedding and they went over pretty well and I…I started to think maybe I could sell them. So, I took some down to Horizons—"

"Is that the gift shop Sandy O'Donnell owns?" he asked, remembering the one time he'd gone into the small store on Main Street. He'd been on leave from basic training and had stopped in to buy a Mother's Day gift. But being surrounded by all those chick gifts— crystal glasses, tableware, picture frames and ceramic figurines—had given him the hives.

"Yes. She carries chocolates from a candy maker in Danville during the holidays and Easter, so I thought she might be interested in selling mine, as well. But she has an exclusive contract with the other guy." J.C. rolled her eyes as if her encounter with Sandy hadn't been all that pleasant. "I tried Kent Goodwin at the Main Street Mercantile and he said he would've been interested…if I'd contacted him back in August when he was accepting inventory for the holiday season. Then he gave me the old 'if I make an exception for you, I have to make an exception for everyone' speech and—"

"The point of all this?" he asked, pinching the bridge of his nose.

"I'm getting there. Rhonda, the manager at Country Crafts, declined because she'd tried gourmet food at her store before and it hadn't sold well. Of course, she didn't tell me that until *after* she ate half a pound worth of samples. I went to Delgato's but he wouldn't even hear me out. You'd think, seeing as how I was the one he fired, *I'd* be holding the grudge and not the other way around."

Couldn't she have just said all three gift shops in town and the only gourmet grocery store within an eighty-mile radius had turned her down? "And now you're here…?"

"I'm here because when I left Delgato's, I saw the flyer for the holiday open houses the Diamond Dust is hosting and I had an epiphany."

"An epiphany on Mechanic Street. That's not something you hear every day."

"That's what makes it special," she assured him solemnly, but her eyes were lit with humor. "I think my chocolates and the Diamond Dust would be a perfect match. Sell the chocolates in the gift shop."

He carefully slid off the counter landing with his weight on his right leg, the box still in his hands. "You want to start making chocolates—"

"Gourmet chocolates." She closed the distance between them and picked out a candy. "Here. Try one." She popped it into his mouth.

The outer shell was dark chocolate, the inside a creamy milk chocolate that melted on his tongue. Damn, that was good. He looked into her eyes and found it difficult to take a full breath.

He pushed away from the counter, set the box down and took a glass from an upper cabinet. "Let me see if I've got this straight," he said as he filled it with water from the sink and took a long drink. "You couldn't find anyone in town willing to sell your chocolates so you decided the best place for them would be at the Diamond Dust?"

She crossed her arms, which drew his attention again to that damn lace covering her breasts. "You make it sound like this is my last resort."

"Is it?"

"So what if it is?" she asked irritably. "It's not like it's the end of my world if this doesn't pan out. I'm sure I can get a part-time job somewhere."

"You don't sound very convincing."

"It's just…I've had some trouble finding a job that suits me. And when some employers see my employment history they're not real anxious to give me a chance."

"How many jobs have you had?"

"Total?"

Sleeping with her was the biggest mistake of his life and she was a pain in the ass for wanting more from him than financial support with this pregnancy. For expecting more from him than he could give. So why did he find her amusing as hell? "How about you give me a rough estimate?"

She pursed her lips. "Around a dozen. Give or take one or two."

Twelve jobs in less than what…ten years? There was no way Aidan would go for any sort of deal with her no matter how good her candy tasted.

Luckily, Aidan wasn't here.

"You've got a deal," he said. "You can sell your candy at the Diamond Dust gift shop."

For a moment, she seemed confused, but then she broke into a grin. "Really?" she asked breathlessly.

"The details will still have to be ironed out." Which would be the perfect job for Aidan. His older brother loved nothing more than ironing out details. "But, yeah, really."

Her cheeks flushed with pleasure. "This is so great. You won't regret it, I promise." He ground his back teeth together when she did a little hip-shaking, shoulder-wiggling dance that brought her closer to him. "Thank you, thank you, thank you!"

Then she grabbed his face with both hands, pulled his head down and kissed him.

CHAPTER SEVEN

J.C. STOPPED DOING her victory dance when Brady's hands tightened on her hips as she pressed her mouth against his. There she went again, throwing caution aside and letting her spontaneity get the better of her. She'd meant for it to be nothing more than a celebratory kiss. Light and fun. To express her gratitude—and relief.

But as soon as her mouth touched Brady's, she knew it could never be any of those things. Not when her heart stuttered at the feel of his lips against hers. Not when warning bells were clanging in her head.

Not when fixing things with Liz meant she had to stay away from him.

She fell back on her heels.

You just charge forward, not caring about anything except what you want.

No. Not anymore.

"Don't take that the wrong way," she warned him in a raspy whisper.

His eyes hooded, he studied her. "How should I take it?"

She shivered. And realized she was touching him, still cupping his face.

She dropped her hands and stepped back. But she could still feel the scratchiness of his beard on her palms. "It's been a tough week and I'm...grateful...

and…" And she was babbling like an idiot. She held her breath for the count of five. "I'm happy. That's all."

"Do you kiss a man every time you're happy?"

"Every chance I get," she assured him soberly. "You should've seen the lip-lock I laid on Marty Boyd last month when he told me my car passed its inspection."

"That impressive, huh?"

"Well, I hate to brag, but it was enough of a kiss that I'm pretty sure he thinks we're engaged now."

And then, to her amazement, Brady smiled. Disheveled, miserable and, if she wasn't mistaken, broken Brady Sheppard smiled. At her. It didn't last long and for a moment, it seemed as if even that small bit of happiness pained him, but what else could she do but smile back?

Someone behind her cleared their throat. "I hope I'm not interrupting anything."

J.C. whirled around. Aidan stood at the other end of the kitchen, gazing shrewdly from her to Brady and back again. Her face flamed.

"Nothing that meant anything," Brady said. "Isn't that what you said, J.C.?"

"Uh…right."

"Connie said you wanted to speak with me?" Aidan asked J.C.

Like Brady, Aidan was tall with broad shoulders and blond hair, but that was where the differences ended. His eyebrows were heavier, his lips fuller, his eyes more green than blue. And though it was the end of the day, his button-down shirt and khakis were still neatly pressed, as if wrinkles dared not mess with this cool-eyed man.

Thank God she and Brady had made the deal and she

didn't have to try to convince Aidan to do with business with her. Though Aidan was polite, the way he scowled at his brother made him seem about as approachable as a wolverine. And not the Hugh Jackman kind.

"No." She cleared her throat. "I mean, yes, I did want to speak with you but now I guess I don't have to…" The tension between the brothers was palpable. And nothing she wanted to get in the middle of. "I'd better get going." She smiled at Aidan as she sidestepped him toward the family room. "I have…things. To do."

"I'll walk you out," Brady said.

"Oh. That's not necessary."

But the expressions on the brothers' faces told her it was. And far be it for her to argue.

"Bye, Aidan," she said.

He nodded. "Nice to see you, Jane."

As they walked back toward the foyer, she snuck a glance at Brady. He reached past her and opened the front door. "I'll have Aidan call you with the details."

"Thank you," she said, careful not to touch him as she passed. She stepped off the porch and into the sunshine.

"I opened a savings account. For the baby."

Shading her eyes with her hand, she looked up at him. He didn't know how important it was for her to prove she could take care of herself. And the first step was to be able to pay her own way. When the office manager at Dr. Owens's office had told her that her insurance wouldn't cover all her expenses, she hadn't been too worried. No, she'd done what Liz accused her of doing. She'd gone to her parents to take care of her.

While her parents were far from thrilled with the situation, they'd told her they'd support whatever decision she made regarding the baby. And that they'd be more than willing to cover her medical expenses.

But she wasn't going to be that person anymore, the one who let everyone else take care of her. "We've been through—"

"My attorney will send you the account information. I'll deposit money into it each month." He stood gripping the porch rail, the muscles of his arms knotted. "You can do what you want with it. Use it or not. Either way, it'll be there. And whatever's left when the kid is eighteen will be turned over to him."

"I don't want to go over—"

"Do you really hate me so much that you'd deny your baby financial security?"

She made a soft sound of surprise. Was that what he thought? That she was doing this as some way to get back at him? That couldn't be further from the truth. But really, what was it hurting if he put money into a bank? She was still trying to figure out how she was going to pay her doctor bills. Knowing she had a cushion for the future would be a huge relief. And as he pointed out, she didn't have to use it.

She could still keep her pride.

She nodded. "Okay."

"Thank you," he said, as if she were the one doing something for him.

"Listen, you said you weren't staying in Jewell and, well, in case I don't…see you again…I want to wish you good luck. With whatever you do. And I…I want you to know…I don't hate you," she blurted. "I could never hate you."

He regarded her intently, his eyes a brilliant blue. Her

cheeks warmed. Her breath clogged in her lungs as the silence stretched on.

"Not that it matters," she added feebly.

Okay, then. She gave him a half-hearted wave and walked away, hoping he couldn't tell how unsteady her legs were.

As she opened her car door, his voice carried to her, soft as the cool breeze.

"It matters."

"YOU MUST BE MAKING PROGRESS," Aidan said when Brady came back into the kitchen. Aidan popped the top of a can of cola and took a drink. "I'm glad you're stepping up and doing the right thing."

Brady grunted and rolled his head side to side so that his neck cracked. Progress? He'd agreed to a business deal he wasn't entitled to make and had told J.C. about the account he'd set up for the baby.

But he was ditching her, leaving her to raise their kid on her own. He wouldn't blame her if she did come after him with that machete.

And what had been up with that kiss? It'd taken every ounce of control he still had left not to pull her closer.

"When's everything going to happen?" Aidan asked.

Brady picked out a dark chocolate from the box next to him and tossed it in his mouth, hoping to replace the lingering taste of J.C.'s kiss. "Everything?"

"You need to tell Mom." Aidan waved his can. "It shouldn't take too long to plan the wedding—"

"Wedding?" Brady choked out.

"Stop repeating everything I say. It's pissing me off."

Aidan's lips thinned and he straightened. "Aren't you and Jane getting married?"

"No."

"No? That's it?"

Brady pretended to consider that. "How about, hell no."

Aidan tapped his fist against his thigh. "Then why did she seem so happy? Did you finalize a financial agreement about the baby?"

"We did." Brady put the lid back on the half-eaten lasagna. Since there was no food at the cottage, he might as well take it back with him. If he took enough of his mom's leftovers home, he could put off the inevitable trip to the store for another day or two. "I'm going to pay child support." Whether she ever used his money, he had no way of saying.

"We'll name you Father of the Year," Aidan said.

And Brady wasn't about to get into it again with his sanctimonious brother.

"As to the reason she seemed happy, that's probably because I told her the Diamond Dust would purchase some of her homemade candy to sell."

The silence was broken only by the soft ticking of the antique wall clock that'd belonged to their mother's great-grandmother.

"You did what?" Aidan finally asked softly, a muscle jumping in his jaw.

"I told her we'd buy her chocolates. We can sell them in the gift store, offer them at the open houses."

"We? I hadn't realized you were on the payroll."

Brady went back to the fridge to see what else he could take home to stock his own fridge. "I'm going to need you to draw up a contract—"

"No way."

"What's the problem? You wanted me to step up and do the right thing with J.C. and I am. Besides, you've been bugging me to get more involved in the Diamond Dust for months. So, I got involved."

"I wanted you to work for the company. Maybe pitch in with some paperwork. Handle some shipping issues we've been having. Not offer someone a deal behind my back."

"It wasn't behind your back," Brady muttered, irritated. "I just told you, didn't I?"

"You made a deal on behalf of the Diamond Dust without discussing it with me or Mom."

Brady grabbed a container of cheese spread, some lunch meat and a half-empty carton of eggs, shutting the door with enough force to shake the condiments. "Isn't that what you've been doing all these years? You've never once asked for my opinion on anything you wanted to do with the Diamond Dust."

"I'm the president. Mom's the owner. You don't even work for the winery. The way I remember it, both you and Matt couldn't wait to get away from Jewell and the Diamond Dust fast enough."

"Dad didn't have a problem with my decision to join the Corps," Brady said, carefully setting the egg carton on the counter instead of hurling it at his brother's head like he wanted. "Just buy the candy from J.C. It's good. Which means we're sure to make a profit. It's a win-win situation."

"Doesn't matter how good it is. Our budget for holiday spending is already set. Tell her you can't keep your end of the bargain."

"No."

Aidan shifted into what Brady recognized as his fighting stance—legs wide, hands loose at his sides, weight on the balls of his feet. "That wasn't a request. That was me not giving you a choice."

Aidan picked up his soda dismissively. As if whatever he said was the last word on the subject. Brady wanted to go after his brother and knock his fat head in. Too bad that, with his bum knee, he didn't have a chance of beating up his brother.

Aidan did whatever it took to win. Even if it meant fighting dirty.

Maybe Brady should consider going to his physical therapy sessions once in a while. The pain would be worth it if he could kick Aidan's ass.

"Just try one." He shoved the box at Aidan.

Even as Aidan chewed, his expression remained sour. Which was nuts considering how good those chocolates were. Then again, ever since their dad died and Aidan's wife left him a month later, he always looked as if someone had switched his favorite Petit Verdot with grape-flavored children's cough medicine.

"Well?" Brady asked when he couldn't stand it any longer.

"You're right. It's good. But that doesn't change anything."

"I already told J.C. we'd do this."

"And your word is your bond?" Aidan asked dryly.

"When I say I'll do something, I do it," Brady managed through gritted teeth. He may not be living up to his family's high ideals but he kept his word.

He just didn't give it very often.

"Sorry," Aidan said, not sounding sorry at all, damn

him. "But it's not going to happen. You'll have to assuage your guilt some other way."

"DO YOU HAVE any chocolates?"

J.C. blinked at Brady. Why was he at her apartment…
carrying a large pizza box, no less? When she'd left his
mother's house earlier today, she'd figured, other than
occasionally running into him while he was still in town,
she'd never see him again.

She nudged Daisy back into the apartment with her
foot before the cat could slip out into the dark. "Halloween was last month. And you're about twenty years
past the normal trick-or-treating age."

"I'm not out begging for treats," he said in his rough
voice. "Aidan didn't go for it."

So much for being able to pay her doctor bills with
the money she'd get selling her chocolates. So much for
trusting Brady Sheppard. "But you said…"

Wait a minute. What exactly had he said? She'd asked
if he worked for Aidan and he'd said… She searched
her memory. Nothing. He'd said nothing.

"You have no authority to decide anything about the
winery, do you?" she asked.

"No."

Guess she should've asked him that question earlier.
"Then why did you act as if you did? Why did you say
it was a deal?"

He glared, as if he had a right to stand on her doorstep all big and imposing and fierce. "Do you have any
chocolates made or not?"

The strap of her tank top slid down her arm and she
pulled it back up. "A few, but—"

"If you still want to sell your chocolates at the Diamond Dust, we need to do a pairing."

"I thought Aidan wasn't—"

"We're going to change his mind."

She crossed her arms. As if she'd accept his help after he lied to her about the deal in the first place. "How?"

"I thought we could discuss the particulars over dinner." He held up the pizza box, his expression unreadable. "What do you say? Can I come in, Jane Cleo?"

She felt warm, tingly. She'd never heard her name sound so...so sexy...before. Was that how Liz felt when he said her name, too?

How would Liz react if she knew Brady had come to J.C.'s apartment on a Friday night, even for reasons that were decidedly nonpersonal? Then again, Liz didn't have to find out. Not if J.C. didn't tell her. She stood on her tiptoes and peered at her grandma's house. Except for the porch light, it was dark. Grandma Rose must still be at dinner. And J.C. really had pinned her hopes on selling her chocolates.

She stepped aside.

"Bring them up," Brady called down the stairs.

Peeking around the corner, she saw a kid taking the steps two at a time, a large wooden crate in his skinny arms, a dark blue ball cap on his head.

"Where do you want it?" he asked Brady when he reached them.

Brady gestured with his chin. "On the table is fine."

The kid glanced up at J.C., then did a double take. "Hey," he squeaked, blushing. He cleared his throat. "How's it going?"

She smiled at him and his eyes seemed to cloud over.

"Uh…I'm fine. Thanks." Had his voice gotten deeper from when he'd spoken to Brady?

"Eyes straight ahead," Brady said, then nudged the kid's shoulder.

As Brady and the boy walked over to the table, J.C. bent and scooped Daisy into her arms. The sound of someone choking made her spin around and she saw the boy staring at her, his mouth hanging open.

She took a hesitant step toward him. "Are you all right?"

"Don't make eye contact. He'll see it as encouragement," Brady said under his breath as he took a hold of the kid's arm and steered him past her. At the door, he shoved some money at the boy and practically pushed him outside. "Thanks. I appreciate it."

Now standing at the top of the stairs, the teen tore his eyes away from J.C. long enough to check out the amount of cash in his hands. "Hey. Thanks a lot. If you need anything else, call me." Then he grinned sweetly at J.C. "Or I could hang around. In case you—"

Brady shut the door in his face.

"Well, that was rude." J.C. stroked Daisy's soft fur. "What was that all about anyway?"

"You really don't know?"

"Know what?"

Brady set his hands on his hips, his jaw tight. "You made his night. And gave him enough material to stoke his sexual fantasies for the next year or so."

She almost dropped her cat. She set Daisy down on all fours but the feline didn't take well to nearly landing on her head. Sticking her chin in the air, she meowed and then took off like a shot.

"First of all," J.C. said, her nose wrinkling, "ewww.

Second of all, I'm at least ten years older than he is. Why on earth would he…" She gestured vaguely with her hands. "About me?"

Brady's mouth quirked. So glad to see her confusion amused him. "Maybe he'd want to…" He repeated her hand gesture. "Because you smiled at him. Or maybe it's because when you bent over in those shorts you're barely wearing, that kid thought he'd just seen heaven."

Her face flamed. "They're pajamas," she said in a strangled voice, tugging on the hem of her purple cotton shorts.

And she had on the loose—albeit tiny—shorts and matching tank top with eyelet trim because it felt as if her internal body temperature had gone up twenty degrees since she got pregnant.

Brady shrugged, his intense gaze never veering from her face. "Doesn't matter what you call them. They don't leave much to the imagination. And believe me, teenage boys have vivid imaginations, especially when it comes to barely dressed women."

Great.

She hoped the kid wasn't scarred for life.

J.C. crossed her arms and frowned at Brady's back as he went into the kitchen. She wasn't going to apologize for putting on her pajamas after she'd taken an early shower. She was in her own apartment, after all. And she'd seen no reason not to answer the door when she was just as covered as she'd be if she had on any other pair of shorts and tank top.

She went in after him. "What are you doing?"

He opened the top cupboard to the right of her stove and took down two of her mismatched plates. Held them up to her. "Plates." Taking the roll of paper towels off the counter, he brushed past her, his movements slow, his limp slight but still noticeable. He set the items on the table, came back into the kitchen and took milk out of the fridge.

"I never said I'd eat with you," J.C. pointed out.

In the act of pouring milk into a tall glass, he glanced at her. "Not hungry?"

Hungry? She shouldn't be. She'd had dinner a few hours ago. But the rich scent of tomato sauce and melted cheese made her mouth water. "I don't want to have dinner with you, that's all."

"You're willing to lose out on a chance to make that deal with the Diamond Dust?"

Possibly. Because at the moment, it felt as if she had to decide between making the deal that would enable her to prove to her family she could take care of herself, and loyalty to her sister.

"Will any of this even make a difference?" she asked. "And can I trust what you say?"

He flinched. Well, well. What a shock. Maybe he wasn't completely dead inside after all.

"I messed up," he said, putting the milk back in the fridge. "I never should've let you believe I had the authority to make a deal on behalf of the winery."

"Why did you?"

He tugged on his ear. "I wanted to help you."

He seemed sincere. As sincere as a hard-eyed, hard-drinking man could get.

"Fine. You can tell me about this idea you have while we eat. But," she stressed, "then you have to go."

Before Grandma Rose came home. If she found out he was here, it was sure to get back to Liz.

He didn't look relieved or particularly happy about

her acquiescence. "I appreciate you hearing me out." Then his hooded gaze raked over her, from the tips of her brightly polished toes to the top of her still-damp hair. "Before we eat," he said gruffly, "could you put something...else...on?"

CHAPTER EIGHT

BRADY WATCHED J.C. walk away, his gaze locked on the sway of her hips, the curve of her ass in those damn shorts.

Pregnant women weren't supposed to be so…sexy… were they? He even found the slight roundness of her belly alluring.

He scrubbed a hand over his face. Alluring. J.C. Montgomery. Sweet God, but he needed a drink.

He set the milk on the table when she came back out. She'd put her damp, curly hair up into a knot on top of her head but a few spirals had already come loose. She wore a boxy sweatshirt and loose black sweatpants.

Too bad he was still imagining her in those pajamas.

He cleared his throat and handed her the glass of milk. "Here."

She looked at it suspiciously. "What's this for?"

"I thought maybe you'd want some." He felt like an idiot. Weren't pregnant women supposed to drink a lot of milk?

"Oh. Sure. Thanks."

His neck warm with embarrassment, he put a slice of cheese pizza onto a plate before handing it to her. "I got half plain cheese in case you were still doing the vegetarian thing."

"I can't believe you remembered that."

He sat and helped himself to two pepperoni slices. "Hard to forget you with that duct tape over your mouth at Easter dinner."

"I'd forgotten about that. As a protest against my mom's baked ham." She tore off a piece of crust. "It took two weeks for the skin around my lips to grow back."

He and Liz had been seniors that year, J.C. a freshman. "Liz did your makeup every morning so no one could tell what happened."

"Right." J.C. tossed the crust back onto her plate then brushed her hands off. "Look, you don't have to worry about getting Aidan to change his mind. It's not like I've always dreamed of being a candy maker. It was a spur-of-the-moment idea. Believe me, another one will come along. They always do."

He scowled at his half-eaten slice of pizza. She'd always been that way. Brimming with plans, abandoning one grandiose scheme for the next.

Perfect. He had an out. She didn't want his help. Now maybe his guilt over making her a promise he couldn't keep would ease. Maybe now he could go back to not giving a damn about anything or anyone. It sure made it easier to get through the day.

"Do you always roll over when you don't automatically get what you want?" he asked more harshly than he'd intended.

Her nostrils flared and two spots of color stained her cheeks. "No. But that doesn't mean I go around knocking my head against walls, either."

"When those other stores turned you down, did you even try to convince them to change their mind?"

J.C. shifted her chair to the side, and the cat leaped

onto her lap. "What's the point? They already said they weren't interested."

"The point is to stop taking the easy way out and fight for what you want."

"Wow," she said through tight lips. "That's great advice coming from the man who either ignores his problems or drowns them."

Other than his fingers flexing on his thigh, he showed no sign she'd just made a direct hit. "When I want something badly enough, nothing stops me from getting it."

He just no longer let himself want.

She licked her lips nervously. "Aidan's already made up his mind—"

"So we get him to change it."

"How?"

"By proving your chocolates will sell."

The cat nosed J.C.'s plate, and J.C. moved her barely touched pizza out of reach. "Except I can't give him a guarantee people will buy them."

He finished off his first slice and dug into his second. "But we can market them so they tie in with the wines. Aidan will see an opportunity to increase sales. And believe me, nothing makes him happier than increased sales."

"But I thought wine went with real food. Not candy."

"It can go with sweet or savory. We figure out which of the Diamond Dust's wines go best with each flavor." He nodded toward the crate. "I brought the wine so we can do pairings."

"We?" she asked as if he'd suggested they take jobs as targets at the rifle range. "As in, you and me, we?"

He scratched his cheek. "I was thinking me and the cat. But you'll do in a pinch."

Her lips twitched. "You might be better off with Daisy, seeing as how I don't know anything about pairing wine with...well...anything. Besides, last I heard, pregnancy and alcohol don't mix."

"You're not going to drink. You tell me about the chocolates, what's in them and we'll go from there."

"But...are you sure you can do this? I mean...you don't work at the winery..."

"I grew up working there. Dad taught us every aspect of running the business."

"Right. Of course, but it's...you've been away from it—"

"It's not brain surgery, Jane," he said, keeping his frustration out of his voice. "What's the problem?"

She methodically stroked the cat's back, one hand over the other. "I don't want to be part of anything that encourages you to drink." She cleared her throat. "No offense."

He leaned back, stretching his leg out. "I won't get drunk."

As if he had such little control he'd get wasted sipping what would probably amount to a couple glasses of wine. When he wanted to get drunk, he went straight for whiskey.

Like the bottle he'd picked up at the liquor store earlier today.

"If it'll make you feel better," he said, "I'll use a spit bucket."

"That's disgusting."

"You don't taste with your stomach," he pointed out. "So there's no reason to swallow."

"I guess not," she said, sounding unconvinced. "But there's no way I'm dumping spit."

He closed the pizza box lid and set his empty plate on top of it. "When Dad held private tastings, that was our job, mine and Matt's."

And as usual, no matter what the job, Matt had complained the entire time.

"I haven't seen Matt in years," J.C. said, her elbow on the table, her chin resting on her hand. "How is he?"

He ducked his head so she wouldn't see his frown. He hadn't realized she had any interest in his long-haired, love-'em-and-leave-'em, too-pretty-for-his-or-anyone-else's-good brother. The brother who thought J.C. had a sexy mouth.

"He's fine," Brady said. "He was home Thanksgiving."

And gone the next day. Matt came back to Jewell for the holidays and their mother's birthday, but he never stayed more than a few days.

"Not long ago, the paper ran an article about him," she said. "About his job and all the awards he's won and how one of his wines made it onto some sort of top one hundred list—"

"*Wine Spectator*'s annual Top 100," Brady said, unable to stop staring at her mouth now. "He's doing well for himself."

Giving him a half smile, as if unsure if he deserved a full one, she used the back of her hand to brush her hair back. "I'll say. Funny that he works for wineries all over the world when his family owns one right here."

No, what was funny was how at ease she was now that they were talking about his brother. How, sitting this close to her, he could smell the soap she'd used in the shower. See the tiny freckles dotting her nose. And that with her eyes bright and those few loose curls framing her face, J.C. looked fresh and soft and…pretty.

"If you want," he said mildly, "I can tell Matt to call you next time he's in town. I'm sure he'd be more than happy to get together with you."

J.C. blanched. "Thanks, but I'll pass. So far my experience with the Sheppard men has sucked." Though her words were cold, he detected a slight tremor in her voice. "I'll get the chocolates. I wouldn't want to keep you any longer than necessary."

This time when she walked away, he studied the wall in front of him. Once she disappeared into the kitchen, he tipped his head back, hitting the chair. Then he did it again.

And because his hands were twitching, because he felt unsettled and edgy, because panic was there, right there at the back of his mind, he pulled a bottle out of the case. Merlot. Not his favorite—and a far cry from the whiskey he preferred—but it would do. He just needed it to get him back on an even keel. With that promise, he took the wine and the corkscrew he'd brought and headed to the bathroom.

Where he could have one drink without worrying about J.C. and her disappointment in him.

LIZ COULD THINK OF NOTHING better than coming home after a grueling twelve-hour night shift to the smell of bacon and Carter's special buttermilk pancakes. Unless it was the sight of him standing at the stove wearing nothing but a pair of red and green checked pajama pants.

"Hi," she said cautiously. He may be making her

breakfast and, she glanced at the set table, bought her a dozen red roses, but that didn't mean either of them had forgotten the tension between them was still as strong as it'd been on Thanksgiving. "What's all this?"

A cup of coffee in one hand, a spatula in the other, he said, "It's breakfast." Liz's heart did one slow roll.

"I can see that," she said, tracing her fingertip over a silky rose petal. "But…why?"

On the Saturday mornings when Carter didn't have to make rounds at the hospital, he was usually still in bed when she got home from work. She'd slide under the covers and, more often than not, they'd make love before she drifted off to sleep.

After shutting off the stove, he transferred the pancakes to a tray and carried them to the table. "Because I wanted to do something for you." He took both of her hands in his, brought them up to his mouth and kissed her knuckles. "And because I hate this distance between us."

She squeezed his fingers. "Me, too."

"I've missed you."

She nodded. Though they'd been together the past week, they'd barely spoken. And when they did, their conversations were stilted. Overly polite. The only time they touched was when they slept. They'd wake up wrapped in each other, but it never went any further.

It'd been torture.

He sat and pulled her onto his lap. "I blew it all out of proportion, what happened on Thanksgiving. I was…" He exhaled and shook his head, his hair tickling her cheek. "I was jealous."

She couldn't catch her breath. That wasn't what she

wanted. She didn't want Carter to be jealous. Didn't want him to doubt her love, not even for a second.

But she couldn't tell him the truth, either. How betrayed she felt. The thought of Brady and J.C. together infuriated her. She couldn't even face her own sister. Couldn't forgive her.

Worse was that she'd dreamt of Brady, of the way they used to be together. The way he'd kissed her. Touched her. Made love to her.

"You have nothing to be jealous of," she promised. "Brady and I are over. We've been over a long time."

He slid one hand up to her rib cage, his thumb brushing the side of her breast through her long-sleeved T-shirt. "I'm afraid I'm going to lose you," Carter said, his eyes searching hers.

"Never." She pressed her lips to the side of his neck, inhaled his familiar scent. Caressed the warm skin of his shoulders.

And thought of how Brady had looked the other day when she'd gone to return his ring. Angry. Lonely.

Tears stung the backs of her eyes. No. She wouldn't think of him. Not when she was in her husband's arms. Not ever again. She needed to get Brady out of her system. Before she lost everything. Her sister. Her husband. Herself.

"You'll never lose me," she repeated firmly.

Shifting so that she straddled him, she trailed biting kisses up his neck. He moaned, his hands going under her shirt to smooth her back, down her stomach. She trembled and pressed against him. Kissed him hungrily, loving how solid he was beneath her. How hard. How he was all hers.

"Liz," he said, cupping her breasts. "I love you, baby."

She arched into his touch, her hands gripping his shoulders. "I want you, Carter," she told him, gasping when he grazed her nipple with his thumbnail. "Only you."

His eyes flashed and then he kissed her again. Grasping her under her rear, he stood and swept one arm over the table. Plates and food crashed to the floor, the vase of roses shattered. And as her husband laid her among the ruins of their breakfast, Liz had one man in her thoughts. In her heart.

Him.

"HAS HELL FROZEN OVER?"

Brady glanced at Aidan sitting behind their dad's large mahogany desk, his cell phone up to his ear, one hand covering the mouthpiece.

"Why?" he asked as he entered his dad's—now his brother's—office. "Did you get laid?"

Aidan grinned as he leaned back in his leather, ergonomic chair. "It's not even eight—"

"Don't remind me." Brady slouched in one of the matching checked armchairs facing the desk.

"It's just...unusual...for you to be lurking outside your hovel before— Zachary," he said, turning back to his phone conversation. "It's Aidan Sheppard. Sorry to call you so early on a Saturday but..."

Zoning his brother out, Brady tipped his head back. Aidan's Irish setter, Lily, padded over and nudged his hand until he scratched behind her ears.

Aidan needed to redecorate. The room was the same as when his father had been alive. Sunlight shone in the large window to his right, splashing light on the cream area rug and the wide board oak floor. The built-in bookcases on either side of the window still held his father's books—everything from his favorite author's political thrillers to biographies to books on horticulture and winemaking techniques. Interspersed among them were framed family photos, a few knickknacks and Tom's prized baseball trophy.

Even the bronze statue of a frog, standing on two legs, dressed in knee-high boots and tunic playing a guitar—the statue their mother had claimed too ugly to be seen in any other room—stood in the spot Tom had proudly picked out for it.

And people accused Brady of not being able to let go of the past.

With Aidan's voice no more than a soft murmur in the background, Brady let his eyes drift shut. When he'd come out of the bathroom last night, he'd been steadier. Ready to deal with J.C. and, more importantly, ready to ignore the feelings she evoked.

He wasn't sure if she realized what he'd been doing in the bathroom, how he'd gulped down one glass worth from the bottle of merlot as some sort of anesthetic. But she didn't kick his ass to the curb.

By the time he got home, he was trembling with the need for a drink. After his first shot, he poured himself another and…hadn't been able to drink it. Because he'd had too much to do to get ready for this impromptu meeting with Aidan, he reminded himself. Not because he kept seeing J.C.'s face. Not because every time he lifted his glass he felt as if he was failing himself.

His body relaxed, the constant tension that tightened his shoulders finally eased. Until the first memory hit him, hard and fast like a bullet. Thad's laughter as they drove down the dirt road. The cloud of dust kicked up from the tires. The old man who'd stood on the side of the road, his face lined and weary.

The images came faster, flashing through his mind. The explosion. The sharp pain in his knee, his head smashing against the pavement. Coming to, his leg mangled. Through the thick echoing in his ears, women and children were screaming and comrades shouting, crying out for help. Smoke. Burning bodies.

His buddy lying in the street, his eyes sightless.

Lily whimpered. Brady was clutching the dog's fur. Breathing hard, he forced his fingers open and the dog slunk over to Aidan. He gulped in air, his shirt clinging to his sweat-soaked skin.

"You okay?" Aidan asked quietly.

Damn. How long had his brother been off the phone? Resting his elbows on his knees, his head lowered, Brady nodded.

"Here."

"Thanks," he said, taking the coffee Aidan offered and downing half of it. Lukewarm.

"Want to talk about it?"

Talk? Hell, all he wanted was to forget it. "I'm good."

Aidan studied him, his hands clasped together on top of his desk. "All right," he said slowly. "But if you ever do—"

"Yeah. Thanks," he forced himself to add before finishing off the coffee. He set the cup down and tossed the folder in front of Aidan.

"What's this?"

"It's all the reasons you should reconsider J.C.'s chocolates."

Aidan took off his reading glasses. "As much as I'd like to help J.C. out, I already told you we don't have the money in this year's budget. Besides, I'm not so sure chocolates would sell well, especially with the economy being the way it is."

"Sales of gourmet chocolates have been rising steadily for the past few years," he said. "Plus, twenty-five percent of annual candy sales are made between Thanksgiving and Christmas."

Aidan raised his eyebrows. "You learn about candy in the Marines?"

"In boot camp, right after I learned how to take apart and reassemble my M16." He shifted. "I did some research."

God bless the internet.

"That what this is?" Aidan gestured to the folder. "Your research on chocolate sales?"

"Among other things," he mumbled. He loosened his neck muscles, moving his head from side to side. "Just read it."

Aidan put his glasses back on, opened the folder and began to read the top sheet. It was a far cry from a real business proposal but it was the best he could do without experience.

Brady stretched his leg out and whistled softly for Lily. She hesitated, but when he held out his hand and snapped his fingers, she walked over, her ears back, her head down.

"Sorry, girl," he murmured, rubbing her head. She wagged her tail and dropped beside him. And as easy as that, she forgave him.

If only humans were that easy to placate.

After what seemed like an eternity, Aidan set the papers down and studied Brady over his glasses. "You did all of this?"

"J.C. came up with her projected costs. My pairings."

Aidan tapped a mechanical pencil against his desk blotter. "Expensive candy. I can go to the convenience store and pick up a candy bar for under a buck."

"She's making a quality product with high-end ingredients." According to J.C., anyway. Brady had been impressed with her refusal to use cheaper ingredients. "Don't you appreciate her high standards?"

"I do. I even agree with them. But that doesn't mean I want to do business with her. What if we agree to a deal and she can't hold up her end of the bargain? Or decides she's bored and would rather move on to something else?"

"She won't." Although for all he knew, those were very real possibilities. And if Aidan didn't stop tapping that damn pencil, Brady was going to shove it up his—

"You haven't been back long," Aidan said, dropping the pencil, "so you may not realize that as sweet as J.C. is, she also has a reputation for being unreliable."

"Is that where you get all your information? Local gossip?"

"Does it matter if it's gossip if it's the truth? I don't want to take a chance on conducting business with a vendor who may or may not provide her product."

"She'll provide it," Brady said, pushing himself to his feet. He'd make sure of it. "Make one of those consignment deals. That way you're not out cash and she still gets to sell her candy in the gift shop."

Aidan closed the folder. "Not interested."

Brady linked his hands together on top of his head. Blew out a breath. "What do I have to do?"

"For what?"

He dropped his arms. "To make this happen."

Aidan smiled—never a good sign. "Work for the Diamond Dust."

"That's it?" He'd figured it'd be something…bigger. Stop drinking. Or go back to physical therapy.

Bare his soul to some shrink.

He almost wished it had been one of those stipulations. Then he could've walked away.

"There are a few provisions—"

"Of course there are."

"—such as you, and you alone, are in charge of getting J.C.'s chocolates in the gift shop. I don't care what type of agreement you make with her as long as we don't lose any money."

Brady pinched the bridge of his nose. "No pressure there."

But Aidan wasn't done. "You have to put in eight solid hours of work a day, five days a week. And the first time you show up for work drunk, the deal is off."

"You realize this is blackmail."

"Funny. In business, we call this negotiating. Take it or leave it."

Brady ground his teeth. He couldn't imagine working for his father's company after all these years. Or worse, having Aidan as a boss. And what if he had another panic attack or whatever that had been? He couldn't control when the flashbacks came. Couldn't control how he'd react.

Besides, J.C. told him she didn't need this. And he'd set up that savings account for the baby. She could dip into that anytime she needed. Except she wouldn't.

He shoved his hands into his pockets.

"When do you want me to start?"

CHAPTER NINE

"JANE MONTGOMERY? Is that you?"

J.C.—along with the rest of the people attending the Diamond Dust's Holiday Open House that Saturday— looked toward the sound of the high-pitched voice. A short, busty brunette in dark skinny jeans and killer red leather boots elbowed her way through the crowd.

"If she's not careful," Brady murmured from behind J.C., causing her to jump, "she's going to jiggle right out of that shirt."

"I can see where that would bother a guy," she said, her heart thumping against her ribs.

What was he doing here? She hadn't spoken to him since a week ago when he'd called and told her she could sell chocolates at the Diamond Dust's open houses on consignment.

"I didn't say it would bother me."

She looked up at him so quickly she almost wrenched her neck. "Holy cow. Did you make a joke?"

"I never joke about women and jiggling."

Before she could decide that yes, Brady Sheppard had indeed shown some humor, the brunette reached them. With a squeal guaranteed to ring every eardrum within a five-mile radius, she threw her arms around J.C.

"I can't believe it's really you," the brunette said,

rocking her side to side. "You look fabulous! I hardly recognized you."

Rounding her shoulders and sticking her hips back in an attempt to keep her baby bump from touching the other woman, J.C. met Brady's eyes over the other woman's head. But he held up his hands. The universal signal for, "You're on your own."

"Uh...thank you," J.C. told her new hug-buddy. "Who are you?"

The woman pulled back, squeezing J.C.'s hands. "It's me! Tina Harris."

J.C. blinked. "Tina?"

Last she'd heard, Tina worked in real estate up in Richmond, having lived there since high school. J.C. scanned the other woman head to toe. No wonder she hadn't recognized her. While she could now see Tina in the pert nose and dimpled smile, her hair was shorter and a far cry from the brassy blond she'd dyed it to in high school.

And those boobs? Totally new.

"Wow. It's nice to see you," J.C. said. "You look terrific."

"Forget about me." Tina held their hands out to the sides as if to better showcase J.C. "You look amazing."

"Thank you. Do you remember Brady Sheppard?" She stepped back to include him.

"Of course. You went out with J.C.'s sister, didn't you? You two were such a dream couple. I imagine you're married with a few kids by now, am I right?"

Though nothing in Brady's expression changed, J.C. could feel his tension.

"Brady and Liz broke up over a year ago," she mumbled.

Tina's dimples disappeared. "That's such a shame. The same thing happened to me and Mike...you remember Mike Nivens, don't you?" she asked J.C. before turning to Brady. "Mike and I were high-school sweethearts like you and Liz except we dated a few months, not years and years like you two. But after graduation, we went our separate ways. Which worked out for the best," she said with a giggle, holding her left hand out.

Good God, how did she even lift her hand with that rock on her finger?

"Congratulations," J.C. said.

"I'm so lucky. Shawn...that's my fiancé...is the best. Guy. Ever. He's an orthodontist in Richmond...there he is now." Tina waved. "Honey? Honey, we're over here!"

J.C. winced and lifted her shoulder to her ear. For such a small person, her voice carried.

"There you are." Tina's great guy came up to J.C.'s chin, had a pot belly and a comb-over that started at his left ear. He smiled and wrapped his arm around Tina's waist. "I thought I'd lost you."

"Honey, I'd like you to meet Brady Sheppard—his family owns this winery. Isn't that cool? Brady," Tina continued, cuddling against comb-over's side, "this is my fiancé, *Doctor* Shawn Connolly. Shawn is the number one orthodontist in Richmond. If you're ever in the market for braces, be sure to look him up."

Brady shook Shawn's hand. "Nothing I'd like better than driving three hours to get metal bands slapped on my teeth."

J.C. reprimanded him with a slight shake of her head.

Shawn shared a look with Tina. "I'm sure you can find quality dental care right here in Jewell. It seems like a beautiful little town."

"It is," Tina said, ignoring Brady's slight. "It was the best place to grow up, so safe…why…everyone was like family. And this is Jane Montgomery, an old friend of mine from high school. But I tell you, I couldn't believe it when I first saw her! She's lost a ton of weight."

J.C. gritted her teeth. "Actually, I didn't lose quite that much."

And she and Tina sure hadn't been more than acquaintances. Cute cheerleaders didn't hang out with chubby girls who'd rather volunteer at the local ASPCA than work on homecoming floats.

Tina hugged Shawn around his middle. "Well, however much you lost doesn't matter. You look so much better."

She didn't need to be reminded that she'd spent most of her life overweight. Especially in front of Brady.

Brady laid his hand on the small of her back and she almost jumped out of her skin. "What brings you to Jewell?" he asked the couple in front of them.

Tears stung her eyes. She blamed it on hormones. She couldn't even listen to love songs on the radio without getting all blubbery. Not because the warmth of Brady's hand seeping through the silky fabric of her dress made it easier to pull her shoulders back and pretend Tina's comments didn't bother her.

"We're going on a cruise for Christmas so we're doing the holiday thing early with my family," Tina said. "But I still need to get my sister-in-law's gift and was hoping to find it here. She's such a snob. She returns everything."

"Chocolates," Brady said.

Tina looked at him as if he'd lost his mind. "Excuse me?"

"We now carry a line of locally produced gourmet chocolates," he clarified, sounding as if he'd memorized a brochure. Reaching behind J.C., he picked up the tray of samples she'd set out and held them out to Shawn and Tina.

"None for me, thanks," Shawn said. "My teeth are like a walking billboard for my business."

"I don't have his willpower," Tina confessed, scanning the tray. "I can't pass up chocolate. Ooh…what's this one?" She pointed to a glossy dark chocolate truffle with a drizzle of white chocolate.

Brady nudged J.C. "That's cappuccino," she said. "The…uh…ganache is milk chocolate, coffee and cinnamon."

"Sounds yummy." Tina picked it up and bit into it, her hand underneath the candy to catch any loose bits. The expression on her face was practically orgasmic.

"The cappuccino flavor is one of the top sellers in J.C.'s line," Brady said.

"You made these?" Tina asked. As if J.C.'s candy-making ability ranked up there with walking on water and being able to yodel.

"It's just a—"

"Yes," Brady said, not even glancing her way. "She makes them all."

Ten minutes later, Dr. Shawn walked over to the gift wrap table with three boxes of mixed truffles. Tina waited in line at the checkout counter with a bottle each of the three wines Brady suggested made the best pairings.

And Brady was still by J.C.'s side, all silent and grim-faced in his worn jeans, faded Marine Corps T-shirt and work boots. His hair was beyond shaggy and getting close to unmanageable. She'd say he hadn't shaved in a week.

"I appreciate the sales job you did with Tina," she said.

He leaned back against the thick, wooden beam next to her table and inclined his head. The Brady Sheppard way of saying *you're welcome.*

Well, if he couldn't take the hint that she wanted him gone, she thought irritably, she'd just ignore him. Humming "It Came Upon A Midnight Clear" with the two violinists playing softly in the corner, J.C. pulled on clean gloves and arranged a trio of her extra dark truffles on the silver tray then checked her watch. With less than thirty minutes left until closing time, she wasn't sure how many more she'd need to set out, but there were still at least twenty customers milling around the gift shop and tasting room in the large farmhouse.

Two walls were all windows, with silver pendant and gooseneck lights hanging from the exposed ceiling beams. Wide, wooden beams showed where original walls stood and ancient-looking narrow boards made up the floor.

Finger foods, catered from The Old Library, the fanciest restaurant in Jewell, were presented on a covered board over three large wooden wine barrels.

"Why'd you let Tanya upset you?"

She dropped a chocolate on the floor. Picking it up,

she tossed it into the garbage can under the table. "Her name's Tina. And I wasn't up—"

"Bullshit."

Sighing, she turned, only to find him standing too close to her. "I... It's hard for me to...to know what to say when someone comments on my weight. It's... awkward," she finished, her gaze on the table.

And she hated that there were days she still felt like that overweight girl. Self-conscious. Second-best to Liz.

"Seems to me," Brady said after what had to be the longest moment of her life, "you've done something to be proud of."

"All I did was lose weight." It wasn't as if she'd graduated from college. Or gone to medical school. She didn't help save people's lives every day she went to work.

"Was it easy?"

"What?"

"Was it easy to deprive yourself?"

"It's not about deprivation. It's about making better choices." She took the gloves off and crumpled them in her hand. "Everything in moderation. Fruit instead of junk food. Exercise more."

"You still needed willpower. Dedication. Determination. And these?" he asked, gesturing at the candy before settling his right hand on the table. "They're good. Tanya—"

"Tina."

He shrugged. "She bought three boxes because they're good. Not because of anything I did."

"Well," she said, warmth spreading throughout her chest, "you sure told me."

"You don't give yourself as much credit as you deserve."

"That has to be one of the nicest things anyone's ever said to me. Except for when I was in third grade and Davey Rodgers told me my hair made me look like a little lion."

"Not a lion," he said, studying her intently. She would've stepped back except he lifted his free hand to her hair and wrapped a curl around his finger. "More like a sunburst around your face."

J.C. JERKED HER HEAD BACK, her hair tightening around Brady's finger before sliding away. She tucked it behind her ear. "So, is this how you usually spend your Saturdays?"

He fisted his hand. "I'm working."

She tipped her head and studied him. "You get paid to stand around and look…"

He raised an eyebrow. "Intimidating?"

She opened a bottle of water and gestured at him with it. "I was going to say grumpy but intimidating works, too."

"I didn't say I was happy about working. And I sold three bottles of wine, didn't I?"

"That you did." She crouched to pull a box out from underneath the green cloth covering her table. "Do you get a commission?"

"Just a regular paycheck," he said absently, his attention caught by the way her bright pink dress swirled around her knees when she straightened.

"You're working here for real? That's great. You must not be—" She blushed and concentrated on setting out more of her candy. "Your knee. It…uh…must not be bothering you as much."

And if that was what she'd meant to say, he'd kiss bin Laden's ass. "I don't drink on the job."

As per his brother's instructions, he'd been sober every day. Hungover, but sober.

"I never realized you were interested in working here," she said, choosing to ignore him.

"I'm not." He helped himself to a white chocolate truffle. "It's temporary."

"Do you still want to go into law enforcement?" At his sharp look, she shrugged. "Liz mentioned you wanted to attend the police academy when you got out of the service."

"I'd never pass the physical."

Not to mention the psych evaluation.

"Maybe if you find a good physical therapist—"

"My knee will never be a hundred percent," he said, tossing a second half-eaten chocolate in the garbage.

"I'm sorry," she said, laying her hand on his forearm. His muscles tensed under her warm fingers. "Now stop wasting my inventory."

He stepped back and her hand fell to her side. He nodded to the middle-aged couple approaching them. "Customers."

As J.C. went into her sales pitch—offering them a sample, explaining the different flavors and wine pairings—Brady edged away.

He didn't need her pity. He'd known the risks going in. Those risks were part of the reason Liz hadn't wanted him to join up. For as long as he could remember, he'd wanted to be a Marine. To be in the middle of the action.

Right. *Action.* He saw a snow-covered road carved from the side of a mountain. Heard the echoing, rat-a-tat of machine gun fire. His commander's shouts. His buddies' curses. Felt the surge of adrenaline as he dove for cover. Returned fire.

His mouth dried and his heart began to race. Taking J.C.'s water, he drained it, his fingers denting the plastic.

"I could've gotten you your own water."

He lowered the bottle. "Sorry."

J.C. regarded him seriously. "Hey, are you—"

"Another sale?" he asked, motioning to the couple walking off.

"No," she said, drawing the word out. "But they seemed to like the Turtles."

He twisted the cap back on the bottle. "Can't win them all."

"That's so inspiring," she said. "I think I'll put it on one of those needlework samplers and hang it in my living room." She moved an oblong red ceramic tray of white chocolate dipped pretzels an eighth of an inch to the left. "Is there a reason you're standing watch back here instead of…whatever else you're supposed to be doing? That can't really be your job."

"As far as Aidan's concerned, anything and every-thing he doesn't want to handle—and thinks I can—is my job."

Pam, the gift shop's superefficient manager, needed him here as much as Aidan needed help being uptight. Pam had no sooner given Brady his first assignment—making sure all the chardonnay bottles were label side out—than he'd realized that Aidan had asked him to work an extra day to keep Brady busy.

As if he were a kid who needed to be entertained or else he'd get into trouble.

He'd been about to walk out, he should've walked out. But then he'd spotted J.C. at the back of the store setting up her table.

"I like it back here."

She smacked his arm. "Yeah. For the free chocolate."

"Among other things."

She caught her breath.

And someone cleared a throat. "Are we interrupting?"

J.C. GROANED AND QUICKLY stepped away from Brady. What had so far been a pretty decent day was about to go downhill. Fast.

"Liz. Hi," she said, her voice strangled. "Wha-what are you doing here?"

Crossing her arms, Liz glanced at Brady and then back at J.C. "We ran into Lori Crandall at the grocery store and she mentioned you were selling chocolates here. I can't imagine why you didn't tell us yourself."

"Right. I saw Lori in here earlier." J.C. wiped her palms down the side of her dress. "I…I would've told you…" she lied, "but I figured you'd be…too busy…to come."

"Hey," Carter said as he joined them, a grin on his movie-star-handsome face, "we're never too busy for you."

Then he pulled her into a warm hug. Out of the corner of her eye, J.C. saw Brady roll his shoulders back as if preparing to go a few rounds.

Winner got Liz.

Luckily, if Carter had any violent thoughts about Brady, he hid them well. "How are you feeling?" he asked as he released her.

"Fine. Good. It's okay if you have to go," she told Brady in a rush. "I'm sure you have a lot to do."

"Nothing that can't wait. Aren't you going to introduce us?" he asked in a deadly soft tone as he inclined his head toward her brother-in-law.

"Not on your life." Taking him by the arm, she pulled him to the other end of the table. "Stay here. Please," she said, when he looked ready to argue. "Please, Brady."

He looked over her head at Liz and Carter. His mouth flattened. "Where are your boxes?"

"What?"

"The store closes soon. If you get the boxes, I can start packing up your stuff."

"You don't have to."

He sent another fleeting look at Liz. "All part of the job description, Jane."

J.C. felt numb. Still thinking of her sister but willing to settle for her. Well, at least he got her name right this time. "Sure. Whatever. They're under the table."

"I can't...I don't think I can get them," he said tightly, stopping her before she could walk away.

She shut her eyes for a moment. She could do this. She could act as if him sending longing looks her sister's way—after he'd touched her hair so sweetly—didn't bother her. Grabbing the boxes, she set them on the table and then deliberately turned away.

Liz, in her black skinny jeans, white top and red jacket, and Carter, with the barest hint of stubble and his striped scarf tucked under the collar of a caramel-colored suede coat, could've been in the picture accompanying one of those fashion magazine's articles: How The Perfect Couple Dresses, Weekend-Style.

But on closer inspection, J.C. could see perfection was an illusion. There were tension lines around Carter's mouth. Liz held herself stiffly. And while Carter kept his gaze on the candy display, Liz kept looking at Brady only to drop her gaze when she thought someone noticed.

"It was really…great…of you both to take the time to…support me like this," J.C. said when she reached them.

"I have to admit," Carter said, "once I found out what you were doing, I had an ulterior motive for wanting to come out here."

She swallowed and peeked at Liz, but her sister wouldn't look her way.

"I was hoping you'd have some of that chocolate bark with the cashews available," Carter continued. "The last time you gave me some to take to the office, I was a real hero."

She exhaled shakily. "Sure. I think I still have a few boxes left…" Before she could look over her products, Brady slid two, one-pound boxes down the table.

Wonderful. He could not only hear every word they said, but he wanted them to be aware he was listening.

She tried to return Carter's smile but failed miserably. "Here you go. There's one milk chocolate and one white chocolate."

"Perfect," he said, the unusual edge to his voice the only indication Brady's presence still bothered him. "Do I pay here or up front?"

"Oh, no. They're my treat."

"You can't be giving away all of your profits," Carter said.

"We'll pay for them," Liz said firmly, finally meeting J.C.'s eyes. "We insist."

"Okay, then. Thanks." J.C. swallowed but it felt as if she had one of her truffles stuck in her throat. "You can…uh…pay at the cashier."

Carter pulled out his wallet. "Looks like they're getting ready to close." He shot a glance over J.C.'s head—presumably to where Brady still lurked. "Will you be all right here by yourself, J.C.?"

She could've sworn she heard Brady growl.

"Sure. I get to keep most of my stuff here—they're going to set up a small display of the chocolate I have left to sell during the week," she said, purposely misinterpreting his question. Would she be all right alone with Brady Sheppard? "I'll be fine."

Though he didn't seem convinced, he didn't push it. "I'd better get in line, then." He kissed her cheek. "And in case we don't see you before then, good luck Tuesday."

"Thanks."

"You ready, honey?" he asked Liz.

"I'd like to speak with J.C.," she said. "I'll catch up with you in a minute."

"I hate this," J.C. blurted as soon as Carter walked away. She lowered her voice so Brady couldn't hear. "Can't we please discuss this?"

Liz frowned at J.C. "What's Tuesday?"

And that had been the last question she'd expected. "Nothing. Just…I have an appointment with Dr. Owens…"

"And you told *my* husband about it?"

"*Your* husband," J.C. whispered, her movements jerky as she swept pieces of the curly gold ribbon she'd scattered across the table into a pile, "is the only person at your house who'll talk to me when I call."

Liz drummed her fingers on the table, next to the base of a glass pedestal holding the remaining bite-size samples of J.C.'s Turtles. "What's this really about? You selling chocolate here?"

"I need extra cash. For the holidays."

"Do you really think orchestrating it so that you're around him more is going to change anything?"

J.C.'s head snapped back. "I…I didn't orchestrate anything." But…but hadn't she let him talk her out of speaking with Aidan? And then she'd jumped at the chance he'd offered to sell her chocolates at the Diamond Dust. She'd even spent the evening with him pairing the wine and chocolates after he'd been so ugly to her. "He just happened to be working—"

"Isn't that how it always is with you? Things *just happen*."

J.C. winced as she remembered how she'd tried to explain why she and Brady had gotten together.

It just sort of…happened.

"I didn't even know he was going to be here," J.C. insisted.

"You've always wanted whatever I had," Liz said, her hushed voice sounding thick. "And Brady is no different."

J.C.'s scalp tingled and she snuck a look over her shoulder. She edged closer to her sister. "I don't want Brady."

"Even if you did, he's not the right guy for you. You deserve someone who'll put you first."

She knew that. She didn't need Liz and her condescending attitude to remind her.

"Because no way a man could possibly want me after they were with you," she said, her hands fisted. "Mediocrity just doesn't cut it after you've had perfection, right?"

Liz blushed. "I didn't say that."

And then, Brady was there, his hands on her shoulders. "Your husband's waiting for you," he told Liz. "You'd better go."

Liz blinked several times, but J.C. caught the sheen of tears in her eyes before her sister walked off.

For several heartbeats, J.C. didn't move.

Brady squeezed her shoulders. "You okay?" he asked, his mouth close to her ear.

She cringed. As if he gave a damn. As if his whole show of support hadn't been for her sister's benefit. It was as fake as Liz's so-called concern.

Trembling with anger, with humiliation, she jerked away from him. "Do me a favor. The next time you want to try to make my sister jealous, leave me out of it."

CHAPTER TEN

WELL AWARE OF THE INTEREST they were getting from the people left in the store, Brady wrapped an arm around J.C.'s waist. Though she stiffened, she didn't fight him as he led her down a short hallway and into the stockroom. They'd no sooner stepped inside when she twisted away from him.

"Is there a problem?" he asked.

She stared at him incredulously. "You used me as some sort of…of…" She glanced around, as if she'd pick the right word out of the air. "Tool…to get back at Liz. Did you think she'd toss Carter aside and jump into your arms because of me? I hate to break it to you, but I'm the last person Liz would ever be jealous of."

How he'd stepped on this landmine, he had no clue. He hadn't been playing games and he sure as hell hadn't been trying to make Liz jealous.

He scratched the underside of his jaw. Playing hero brought a man nothing but grief.

Sure, he may have felt a slight surge of satisfaction at Liz's reaction to him coming to J.C.'s aid. But that only proved he was human.

And not as dead inside as he'd like.

"I don't want to get back at Liz," he said.

"Then what was with all that touchy-feely stuff? You

deliberately made it seem as if there was something going on between us."

"By telling her she should leave?"

"You touched my shoulders," she said with as much indignation as if he had pinched her butt.

Behind him, someone rapped lightly on the still-open door.

"Sorry to…interrupt," Pam said curiously, glancing between them, "but I need to get—"

"Later," Brady said before shutting the door and leaning against it.

No doubt when Aidan heard about it, he'd rip Brady for being so rude to a valued employee.

"Your fight was starting to draw a lot of attention," he said with what he considered remarkable calm in the face of her irrationality. "I thought it best to intervene before it came to blows."

"We weren't fighting. We were…having a discussion. A private discussion that you were eavesdropping on."

"Seeing how I was the main topic, I'd say I had a right to overhear."

You've always wanted whatever I had.

I don't want Brady.

J.C. rubbed her temples. "She hates me."

Impossible. Liz had always doted on her little sister. She'd been J.C.'s biggest champion.

He shrugged. "She's pissed. She'll get over it."

"That's a big help," J.C. said acidly. "Thanks so much."

"You want a shoulder to cry on," he said before he could stop himself, "try your brother-in-law."

She looked at him as if he was a few rounds short of a full clip. "What?"

"Nothing."

Damn it. Maybe his paranoia was getting worse. How else to explain him taking issue with J.C. cozying up to Liz's husband? Just because she'd been thrilled to see him and had asked Brady to back off when he'd been itching to take the guy down a peg didn't mean anything. It certainly couldn't mean that Liz had been right about J.C. wanting whatever her sister had.

Even if she had told that bastard about her doctor's appointment Tuesday. An appointment Brady had no idea about.

"You're tired…" Didn't pregnant women get tired easily? And cranky? And blow things out of proportion? "Why don't we finish packing up your stuff then I'll drive you home."

"I don't need your help getting my stuff together and I sure don't want you taking me home."

Damn but she was stubborn. And starting to seriously tick him off. "You shouldn't drive when you're so upset."

"I've been upset before," she said as she stalked toward him, "and unfortunately, I'll be upset again. But I'm still capable of taking care of myself."

In other words, he could take his help and shove it.

He opened the door and stepped aside so she could pass. He watched her walk away, her hair bouncing to her long strides, her arms swinging.

I don't want Brady.

Looked like the Montgomery sisters had more in common than anyone realized.

"I WAS THINKING we'd try that new salmon recipe tonight," Liz told Carter as she set the last of the bulging cloth grocery bags on the kitchen table. "Unless you think it's too cold for grilling."

"That's fine," he said, not even pausing as he carried the dry cleaning into the living room.

She squeezed the package of salmon fillets. If he'd at least try to keep up his end of the conversation, maybe she wouldn't have to continue with her inane chatter. The sound of her own voice was grating on her last nerve. But she couldn't shut up, either. Not when the silence was so tense. So...uncomfortable.

Not when she was afraid of what Carter would say if she'd stop talking long enough for him to get a word in edgewise.

Laying a loaf of French bread aside, she unpacked the baked chips and organic eggs. He'd been fine all day. They'd slept in, enjoyed a leisurely brunch at their favorite restaurant and then ran their errands. Up until they'd gone to the Diamond Dust, Carter had been... himself.

Lips pursed, she shook her head as she stacked yogurt containers in the fridge. Naturally he'd been upset about seeing Brady. She never would've guessed he'd be at the gift shop, let alone hovering over J.C. If she had, she would've put up a bigger fight about going there. But Carter had insisted she at least take a hold of the olive branch J.C. had extended with her daily phone calls. Though Liz wasn't ready to make peace yet, she hadn't wanted Carter to think her resistance had anything to do with Brady.

Rinsing the salmon at the sink, she heard Carter's footsteps as he came back into the kitchen.

"I'll make the marinade," she said, laying the fillets

on a clean towel, "and you can put together a salad. And do you want rice or potatoes?"

He came up behind her and shut the water off.

She laughed nervously. "What are you—"

"We need to talk."

Her stomach dropped at his serious tone, his carefully schooled expression. She kept smiling. "If we want to make it to that movie…" But he just continued to watch her. She couldn't escape what was going to happen next. "All right."

Taking her time, she patted the salmon dry and set it in a plate. After washing her hands, she put the fish in the fridge.

Carter sat at the table, his hands in his lap as he stared out the window above the sink. The evening was darkening.

What had she done? She'd been careful, so very careful, not to show any reaction to finding Brady and J.C. together.

She pulled out the chair opposite him.

"Honey, what is it?" she asked, certain she'd be better off not knowing. "What's wrong?"

He dug something out of his pocket then laid it in the center of the table between them.

A small velvet blue box.

Brady's ring.

Her lungs squeezed painfully and she couldn't draw a full breath. "Where… How…"

"Mr. Sandburg found it in your coat," Carter said quietly.

She shut her eyes. While she'd run into the pharmacy for a few items, Carter had gone next door to pick up their dry cleaning. Including her brown leather jacket, the one she'd been wearing when she'd gone to see Brady.

Sitting on the edge of her seat, she leaned forward. "It's not what you think."

"What is it I think?"

"I...I'm not sure. Maybe you see my having that ring as a way of holding on to...to him."

He linked his hands together on top of the table. "Is it?"

"No. No of course not. I...I was giving it back—"

"You were carrying it around with you in case you bumped into him?"

Her vision blurred and she blinked furiously. "I saw him last week," she whispered.

His body twitched. "When?"

"Monday."

"You weren't going to tell me."

"I didn't want to upset you." She reached out but he slid his hands back to his lap. "I tried to give him the ring but he wouldn't take it so I...I stuck it in my pocket. That's all. Look, it's so insignificant, I forgot it was even there."

She held her breath. He remained motionless, his face drawn. Had she thought his anger at Thanksgiving was bad? She'd take it any day over this.

"I saw how you looked at him."

Her blood chilled. "What?"

"Today. You kept watching him."

"I didn't—"

"And at the end, when he came up behind J.C., when he stood so close to her, you were upset."

"I was...I hadn't realized they were there..." And

that shock, along with her hurt and anger, had almost brought her to her knees. "That they were…together."

That it seemed as if they were together. Or could be.

Carter wiped a hand over his mouth. "It might not seem like it, but I'm trying to understand why you can't let this thing between Brady and your sister go. Why it upsets you so much."

Tears ran down her cheeks. She knuckled them away. "I don't know."

"If I thought it was just the fact that she was with your ex, it'd be different but…" He shook his head. "There's more to it than that."

"No. I—"

"You kept his ring. You went to see him without telling me." Carter's voice turned gravelly. "You look at him the same way you look at me. The way you're only supposed to look at me."

Stunned, tears running unheeded down her cheeks, she watched as he walked out the door. She wished she could call him back. Tell him that she needed some more time to adjust to…everything. But she'd be lying. She wasn't sure she'd ever be able to accept J.C. having Brady's baby. Or Brady being a part of her sister's life.

And because of that, she couldn't even tell her husband what he needed to hear most. That he was the only man she loved.

J.C. ARRIVED FIVE MINUTES LATE for her appointment with Dr. Owens on Tuesday to find the waiting room filled with women of all ages. Several were way more pregnant than her, and two had recently given birth—as evidenced by the newborns in their arms and their post-baby bodies. To her left, a middle-aged woman read a pamphlet on improving your sex life after menopause. And all of them were shooting glances at the corner.

She followed their gazes…and tripped over her own feet. Brady Sheppard, his left leg out straight, his hands linked on his flat stomach, watched her steadily.

Unreal.

"What are you doing here?" she asked.

"Waiting for you."

"Why?"

"I didn't want you to have to do this alone."

Her jaw dropped. *This* as in her doctor's appointment? Or could he possibly mean…? No. He'd made his stance about the baby very clear. And seeing as how he hadn't so much as mentioned her pregnancy recently, she doubted he'd changed his mind. That he'd ever change his mind.

"How did you even know I have an appointment today?" she asked.

He tipped his head to the side. "I heard you and your brother-in-law talking about it at the gift shop."

She switched her purse strap to her other shoulder. "It's…nice…of you to…think of me but I won't be alone. My mom is supposed to meet me."

He sat up. "I'll wait until she gets here."

"Oh, but—"

"Jane?" Rhonda Darcy, her round body stuffed into an impossibly cheerful set of Snoopy scrubs, stood in the doorway leading to the examination rooms. "Come on back, hon, and we'll get your vitals."

"You don't have to stay," J.C. told Brady.

She didn't want him to stay, she told herself as she

followed Rhonda down the hallway to a small, window-less room. Not after how he'd acted at the gift shop. Not when he'd heard what Liz had said to her. How her sister had practically accused her of throwing herself at Brady.

As if she'd throw away her relationship with her sister for a man. A man who didn't even want her.

"Weight first," Rhonda said.

J.C. toed off her shoes and stepped onto the scale. Staring straight ahead, she could see Rhonda's hand moving the lever to the right but couldn't make out the numbers.

And if Rhonda so much as breathed what those numbers were, J.C. might resort to violence.

Rhonda noted J.C.'s weight in a small laptop. "Hop on down." She gestured for J.C. to sit in the chair next to a metal table where she sat to put her shoes back on. "I'm sure glad we didn't call the police on your young man out there."

J.C. about fell right off the chair. "Did...did he do something wrong?"

He hadn't seemed drunk but their conversation had been brief. And as she'd learned, he didn't need alcohol to say incredibly stupid things.

"All that boy did was wait." She moved J.C.'s hair aside and checked her temperature with an ear thermom-eter. "Even when Missy told him she couldn't give out your appointment time, he just thanked her and took a seat. Didn't kick up a fuss like some folks would. But after two hours, Dr. Owens started getting nervous about him being here so long."

"Wait," J.C. said, her head coming up in surprise. Two hours? "How long has he been waiting?"

Rhonda wrapped the blood pressure cuff around J.C.'s arm. "He showed up right when we opened at nine."

While Rhonda took her blood pressure, J.C.'s head spun. Nine. It was now after four. Brady Sheppard had spent the entire day sitting in her obstetrician's waiting room.

For her.

"Anyway," Rhonda continued, hooking her stethoscope around her neck, "The doctor pointed out how you might not want him here and maybe we should call the police to escort him home. Which we can certainly do if that's what you'd prefer."

"No." She cleared her throat. "No, he's...fine. He's..."

Rhonda took a hold of J.C.'s wrist. "With both Missy and I knowing him—Missy went to school with one of his brothers, and Diane Sheppard and I go way back—so we convinced Dr. Owens he wasn't hurting anyone."

Hurting anyone, no. Confusing the hell out of her? Definitely.

Rhonda finished checking her pulse and sent her back out to wait for the doctor. J.C. walked down the hall. Just because Brady showed up here didn't mean anything. She wouldn't let herself read more into it than a sign he was curious about the baby. Or that he was crushed over her being upset with him, and he'd wanted to make amends.

She snorted softly. That would be the day.

And since she'd told him to leave, she doubted she'd ever find out.

She opened the door and sure enough, his seat was empty. But, as she stepped out of the exam room, she saw that it was only because Brady was on his feet, his expression pained as he faced her parents.

J.C. hurried over and stepped between them. "Mom. You made it." She winced at her own false cheeriness. "Hi, Dad. I hope Mom didn't drag you away from the office early."

"Your father insisted he wanted to be here," her mom said, equally chipper. Equally false. "Isn't that nice, dear?"

"Great," she croaked.

"It's not every day a man's baby girl gets to see the ultrasound of her own baby," Don said gruffly, glancing at her.

"Daddy…" She stood on tiptoe and kissed his cheek.

But when she fell back to her heels, his expression hardened. "Move aside, Jane. Brady was about to explain what he's doing here."

As much as she'd love to hear that as well, she didn't want to hold this particular discussion in the middle of one of Jewell's busiest doctor's office.

"Now, Don," Nancy said. "I'm sure Jane asked him to be here."

They both looked at her. She felt Brady's gaze, too, burning a hole in the back of her head. All of their expectations weighing down on her.

"Yes," she said. "I did. Ask him, that is." And while that might not be true, her next words were. "I want Brady to go in with me for the ultrasound."

BAM…BAM…BAM…

Twenty-five minutes later, Brady stood next to an examination table in the cold, sterile ultrasound room.

Bam...bam...bam...

If she didn't stop making that racket, he was going to lose his mind.

His head pounded. Memories circled the edge of his mind, waiting to overwhelm him. Because J.C., sitting at the edge of an exam table, kept swinging her feet, her heels hitting the metal with a resounding bam. Like bombs going off.

Brady shot his hand out and grabbed her knee. "Do you mind?"

She stilled. "Sorry."

He released her. Her skin had been warm through the soft fabric of her black pants.

"I'm nervous," she blurted. "About..." She gestured to the ultrasound machine next to the bed. "Seeing the baby."

"You worried something will be wrong?"

"No," she said so quietly, he had to lean forward to catch the rest of what she said. "That it'll make it real." She stared down at her clasped hands. "I...I don't know if I want this."

He straightened. "The ultrasound? If you're not feeling up to it—"

"The baby."

His head snapped back. He stepped around in front of her. She stared at the floor. He gently took a hold of her chin and raised her face. "Talk to me."

She pulled away from his touch. "How can I raise a child? I've never seen anything through in my life." She rubbed her palms up and down her thighs. "God, this is so selfish but...I'm not sure if I'm ready, or even capable, of committing the next eighteen years of my life to someone else."

"What are you thinking? Adoption?"

The thought of it left him cold. Of having a child out there, not knowing where he or she was, if the kid was safe. He shoved a hand through his hair. As if he had a right to be upset. As if he had the right to tell her what she should or shouldn't do with their child.

A child he'd already walked away from.

"No. Maybe. It kills me to think about giving this baby away," she said. "But I have thought about it. I'm afraid if I keep it, I'll mess up both our lives."

Damn. He should've seen this coming. All this time when she spoke about the pregnancy it was *this* baby. Or *the* baby.

Never her baby. Never their baby.

She was being torn up by the distance between her and Liz and her fears of raising a baby alone. And he'd been so focused on himself, on his own problems, he hadn't even noticed.

"Whatever you decide," he said, forcing out the words she needed to hear, "you have my support."

Words that gave her permission to put their child up for adoption. Words that were unbelievably hard to say.

"But…what about our families?" she asked in a rush.

"This isn't about them. It's about what's best for you and the baby."

She brushed her hair back and gave him a shaky smile. "Thanks."

"Could you… When you make the decision, could you let me know?"

She frowned. "If you want me to. But…aren't you leaving town? How will I get a hold of you?"

"I'll be here until after the first of the year." And when he'd made that decision, he had no idea. "But when I do leave, I'll make sure you have a way of reaching me. In case you need anything."

In case she needed him.

Before they could respond to a knock at the door, a short blonde in black heels and a red and black dress covered by a lab coat came in.

"Hello, Jane," she said warmly. "How are you feeling?"

"Fine. You were right, the morning sickness went away."

"Wonderful." She offered her hand to him. "I'm Nanette Owens."

"Brady Sheppard."

Dr. Owens opened a small laptop, scanned the screen and shut it again. "Your blood pressure's normal. Pulse was a bit elevated but that's not unusual." After using some hand sanitizer she clapped her hands. "Now let's check out your baby."

Brady eased back a step as the doctor had J.C. undo the bottom buttons of her white blouse and fold her shirt back.

"Okay," Dr. Owens said, "go ahead and pull your pants down to your hips."

He jerked his eyes up, stared sightlessly at the plain gray wall. But he could hear J.C. rustling around.

Sweat beaded on his forehead.

The doctor tucked a disposable sheet around J.C.'s pants and Brady glanced down. J.C.'s stomach protruded slightly, as if she'd swallowed a water balloon. The doctor squirted gel a few inches below J.C.'s belly button, then flipped a few switches on the ultrasound machine. After typing for a minute, she picked up a wand and placed it over the gel.

"Showtime." Dr. Owens moved the wand. Blurry black and gray images filled the screen and Brady looked away. "And there's baby."

Brady went numb. He couldn't look. He needed to keep some distance. It was his only protection.

"I don't see it," J.C. said.

"Here's the head." The doctor pressed something on the machine that made a clicking sound. "And here are the arms." More clicking. "From what I'm seeing here, I'd say you were right on about the date of conception. Baby's at seventeen weeks."

J.C.'s arms were straight by her sides, her hands clenching the sheet under her. He lightly traced a finger over her knuckle. Bent close to her head. "Breathe," he said into her ear.

She exhaled, her fingers relaxing.

And he couldn't resist any longer. He had to see. It wasn't the clearest image but he could make out a head. Moving arms and legs.

Damn. J.C. had been right. This made it much too real.

Dr. Owens worked the machine for another five minutes. When he looked over at J.C., he could've sworn she wiped the side of her face…as if she was crying. But with her head turned away from him, he couldn't be sure.

"Everything's fine," the doctor said, using paper towels to wipe the gel off J.C.'s stomach. "Heartbeat is strong, growth right on track. Do either of you have any questions?"

"When's it coming out?" Brady heard himself ask.

His neck warmed. "I mean, when's J.C.'s...what do you call it?"

Dr. Owens smiled. If she found it odd he had no clue when the baby was supposed to be born, she didn't show it. "Her due date?"

"May fourth," J.C. said tonelessly as she buttoned her shirt.

May. Where would he be then? What would he be doing? Used to be he knew exactly what his life would be like. Who he'd be with. What kind of man he'd be.

"Would you like to know the sex?" Dr. Owens asked.

J.C. stood and pulled her pants up and though he tried not to look, he caught a glimpse of the curve of her hip. "Isn't it too soon to tell?" she asked.

Brady didn't blame her for sounding incredulous. He could barely make out the baby's head, let alone anything else.

"It's early, but the baby was positioned right for me to tell..."

Brady bit the inside of his cheek to keep from saying anything. Bad enough he'd seen the ultrasound. He didn't want to know any more about their baby. Not if he wanted to walk away.

But he'd lost the right to offer an opinion.

Nibbling her lip, J.C. nodded.

The doctor grinned. "Congratulations. You're having a son."

CHAPTER ELEVEN

FRIDAY EVENING, Brady sat at his kitchen table, a bottle of whiskey at his elbow, a spotty water glass in front of him, his cell phone in his hand. He'd left the window above the sink open, hoping some fresh air would help ease the tightness in his chest. The feeling that he was suffocating.

Pressing Redial on his phone, he held it to his ear, ground his back teeth together as it rang. And rang. When J.C.'s recorded voice came on and told him to leave a message, he hung up. Turned the phone end to end a few times and then tossed it aside.

The wind picked up, blew the take-out menu from his favorite Chinese place onto the floor. The evening air was thick with the threat of rain. A storm was coming. Several, if the local weather forecaster was to be trusted. Southern Virginia was in for a long night of violent weather.

His hand shook as he poured whiskey into the glass. As a kid, he'd loved a raging thunderstorm, especially the raw power of it. If the electricity went off, all the better. He'd stare out his bedroom window, watch the sky light up. Press his cheek against the glass to feel the vibrations shake the house from a strong rumble of thunder.

He heard thunder in the distance.

His breathing felt ripped from his lungs. The nape of his neck tingled. The edge of his vision grew dark. He inhaled for the count of five. Exhaled for the same amount. And told himself that no matter how much it sounded like an IED—improvised explosive device—it wasn't.

Goddamn, he hated storms now.

He lifted the glass to his lips. Set it down again and ran a hand back and forth, back and forth through his hair.

He wanted a drink. Hell, he needed ten of them. The oblivion they promised. The relief. He needed something to get him through the next few hours while the storms raged. More to get him through the night.

Congratulations. You're having a son.

He shoved away from the table and stood. The bottle tipped. Instead of catching it, he watched dispassionately as it fell, whiskey pouring onto the table. At the last second he remembered to grab his phone. Shook off a few drops of alcohol, then tried J.C.'s number again. Still no answer.

He gripped the sink and stared out at the rain. It blew through the screen and he lifted his face, letting it dot his skin. Then another muted boom of thunder. He slammed the window shut and pressed the heels of his hands against his eyes as he bent at the waist, rocking slightly. His head pounded. His stomach roiled. Sweat soaked through his shirt as terror beat down on him.

It was bad. Real bad.

He glanced over at the glass on the table. If he drank it, he'd stop shaking. The gnawing, endless craving would end. And maybe he'd even have a dreamless night. Instead of tossing and turning. Sleeping only in the few reprieves when his brain shut down enough to pause the nightmares. He went back to the table. Sat down. Jumped back up and paced the length of the kitchen.

Last night had been the worst. He'd spent a fitful night, not falling asleep until a few hours before dawn. When he'd finally drifted off, he'd dreamt of Liz. Of the way they used to be. The way he'd always thought they would be forever.

It was their wedding night and Liz had her back to him, her dark hair over her shoulder so he could unfasten the buttons running down her gown. He'd kissed the nape of her neck, flicked his tongue out to taste her and she'd shivered. Taking his time, he'd pushed each tiny button free, trailing his lips over each inch of skin he exposed until finally the gown had slid down her naked body. She stepped free of the silk pooled around her feet and turned to him, but she wasn't Liz anymore.

She was J.C.

J.C. with her wild curls and sensuous curves and warm smile. And when she stepped up to him in his dream and kissed him, he didn't back away. He didn't wake up when, in the dream, his clothes somehow disappeared. No, he remained in that dream as J.C. pushed him back onto a large bed. As she straddled him, her breasts swaying, her eyes closed.

Then he'd woken up, hard and aching for her.

His body stirred at the memory of it.

And he looked at the spilled whiskey and realized exactly what he needed to help him get through the night.

"IN MY DAY," Grandma Rose said, "expectant mothers took care of themselves. They rested. They certainly didn't work all day and then spend all night on their feet."

As the soapy water drained from the sink, J.C. rolled her eyes at the ceramic Victorian Santas lined up on her grandma's windowsill. Funny how Grandma Rose hadn't complained about J.C. staying on her feet when she'd offered to do the dinner dishes.

J.C. dried her hands and then folded the towel. "Didn't everyone smoke and drink while they were pregnant, too?"

Like the drum roll punctuating a joke, thunder rumbled in the distance.

Sitting at her kitchen table as regal as a queen, Grandma Rose sniffed delicately. "I don't understand why you'd choose to spend your Friday night making chocolates."

"I told you, I made a commitment to the Diamond Dust." And while the commitment part usually didn't mean all that much to her, she was determined to see this project through. To just once, complete a task she'd set for herself.

"But you could be out—"

"I thought you wanted me to rest?" she asked with an exasperated laugh.

"If you were out with some nice young man, you could rest. You could have dinner. Or see a movie."

"I just had dinner, I'm too busy for a movie and from my personal experience so far, nice young men don't ask out pregnant women."

"They might if you took some care with your hair," she said, eyeing J.C.'s frizzy ponytail, "and didn't wear such awful clothes. Why, that shirt needs to be thrown out. And it wouldn't hurt you to put on some makeup."

Used to her grandma's nit-picking about her appearance—at least this time she hadn't asked her why she couldn't be more like Liz—J.C. kissed Rose's soft, wrinkled cheek. "I'd better get going. Thanks for dinner."

"Wait." Rose stood and hurried to the refrigerator, where she pulled out a plastic container. "Take some pasta home. You can have it for lunch tomorrow."

"Great." Smiling, she took the leftover fettuccine in alfredo sauce. "Thanks."

They walked past the living room. Her grandma's artificial tree, complete with festively wrapped packages underneath, was done up in blues and silver. Green garlands, white lights and silver and blue candles decorated the mantel over the fireplace.

J.C. tightened her ponytail. She'd been too busy or too plain exhausted to think about putting up her own decorations but seeing as how Christmas would be here in just over two weeks, she should get a tree. And maybe start shopping for a few presents.

In the foyer, she slipped on her pink and white polka-dot flip-flops. "I'll see you Sunday at Mom and Dad's."

Lightning flickered.

"Oh, dear. You'd better take an umbrella," Rose said, hurrying over to the umbrella stand in the corner.

"I don't need one." J.C. raised the hood of her light blue sweatshirt and, looking back at her grandmother, opened the door. "'Night," she called over the heavy rain and wind, then turned.

She squeaked at finding Brady standing on her

grandmother's porch. "Brady. God. Don't scare me like that."

"Brady?" Rose repeated sharply as she peered past J.C. "What's he doing here?"

She shrugged. Rain dripped off his hair. Ran in rivulets down his cheek. The bottoms of his jeans were as soaked as his jacket. And as usual, he was scowling.

"My grandmother would like to know what you're doing here," J.C. said.

"Evening, Mrs. Montgomery."

Grandma Rose pulled her shoulders back. "Don't you 'evening' me, Brady Sheppard. I'm not some impressionable young girl. You can't charm me."

He shifted. "No, ma'am."

"And don't for one second think that I don't know what you're after." Rose shook her finger at him. "Well, you're not going to get it. Not again. You hear me?"

He glanced at J.C. "Yes, ma'am."

"And you," she said to Jane, "need to remember what my own grandmother told me—no man buys the cow when he gets the milk for free."

J.C. considered pointing out that she'd already given him the whole farm. Instead, she nodded somberly. "No free milk. Got it."

And before J.C. could be taken to task for being cheeky, she slipped outside and shut the door. The strands of white Christmas lights decorating the porch swayed in the breeze. Cold, needlelike rain hit J.C.'s face. She turned her head and hunched her shoulders.

"Did you need something, Brady?"

He wiped the rain off his face. Stared at a point above her head. "I wanted to make sure you were all right."

"Why wouldn't I be?"

"You seemed upset. At the doctor's office." He met her eyes. "You're disappointed the baby's a boy."

"Don't be ridiculous," she snapped, then pressed her lips together. Lightning lit the sky. "Look, I appreciate you coming over here to check on me—three days after the fact—but I'm fine. And I really have a lot—"

Thunder cracked sharply. Brady shivered. "Do you think I could come up…? For a towel," he added at her hesitation. "And maybe…a cup of coffee?"

Bad idea. Bad, *bad* idea. She'd bet a week's pay her grandmother was already on the phone with J.C.'s mom. And while she could easily excuse his presence at the doctor's office as her giving him his parental rights, and their pairing wines and being at the gift shop together as purely business, this was different.

She'd have no excuse for being with him tonight.

"It's getting pretty late—"

"Please," he said quietly. Gruffly. "Please invite me up, Jane."

Slowly she nodded. Then she raced down the porch steps and into the pouring rain. Water ran down the sleeve of the hand holding her hood in place. Cutting through the front yard, she rounded the corner to the garage and climbed the stairs as quickly as possible.

At the top, her flip-flop skidded on the wet wood, her foot shooting out from under her. Her arms flailed, and the plastic container flew out of her hand as she pitched backward. Her hand hit solid wood and she latched on to the railing, the sudden change in momentum causing her to lurch forward. Her legs buckled and she twisted so she wouldn't land on her stomach. Instead, her shin hit the sharp edge of the stair. Pain shot through her. Left her gasping.

Getting unsteadily to her feet, she picked up the plastic container and glanced behind her. Brady was halfway up the stairs, his face in shadow. She limped inside and left the door open for him—Daisy wouldn't go outside, not if it meant getting wet. As she went into the kitchen, she unzipped her soaking sweatshirt and peeled it off, letting it drop onto the floor. The T-shirt she wore underneath it was wet, as well, but she wanted to check her leg before she changed into dry clothes.

After wiping her face on a hand towel, she sat at the table. "You okay in there?" she whispered, rubbing her stomach. She didn't feel any different. Other than her leg, she had no pain. No cramping.

She shuddered out a breath. Thank God.

She gingerly pulled her pant leg up to her knee. A fist-size bruise was already forming. But there was no blood. Just some slight scraping of the skin.

"You all right?"

Brady stood in the doorway, his hair matted to his head. Water dripping off him, forming a small puddle at his feet.

"Yeah. It's not so bad," she said, twisting so he could see her shin. "It hurts but I don't think there's any major damage."

"The baby?"

"Fine. I didn't hit my stomach." She stood. "Before I make the coffee, I'll get you a towel and then change."

But when she went to move past him, he didn't budge. Lightning flashed, illuminating his harsh expression. He looked...dangerous. And pissed off.

"Give me your shoes," he ordered.

She glanced down. She hadn't even bothered to kick them off when she got inside. "What?"

Another rumble of thunder. "You almost fell because you're wearing those damn things. You could've broken your neck."

"But I didn't."

He stepped toward her, his movements menacing, his expression hard. "The shoes."

"You… You're nuts," she said, edging away from him until her spine hit the edge of the counter. "Look. I'm cold. I'm wet. And I need to call the doctor to see what, if any, pain relievers I can safely take. So why don't you—"

"Hold on."

Hold on? To what…him? Not likely. Not when she just wanted him out of her way.

Wrapping his fingers around her uninjured leg, below the knee, he lifted her foot off the ground.

"Hey!" She clutched the counter for balance. "Watch it, grabby hands."

He plucked off her flip-flop and tucked it under his arm. He very carefully lifted her other leg and took off that shoe, as well. All she could do was stare as he searched through her kitchen drawers. When he finally found what he was looking for—a paring knife—she drew her shoulders back.

"You wouldn't dare," she breathed.

He raised one eyebrow. Then he held up a flip-flop, tilted his head and…with his eyes locked on hers…sliced through the strap. Tossing the flip-flop over his shoulder, he repeated the process with the second one then laid the knife on the counter and gave her a look that told her he'd not only enjoyed destroying her shoes, but he'd do it again in a heartbeat.

She shook her head. "There is something seriously wrong with you."

He closed the distance between them. Water dripped from his coat onto her bare feet. "You're the one stupid enough to wear those shoes."

She pressed back against the counter again. "At least I don't go around dismembering people's shoes."

"Damn it, you could've been hurt," he snapped, grasping her upper arms and lifting her on tiptoe.

A lump formed in her throat. He'd been scared for her. How awful it must've been for him in that split second when it'd seemed as if she was going to fall backward. How helpless he must've felt. How angry because he couldn't race up the stairs.

Thunder shook the apartment.

Brady shuddered, his fingers tightening on her arms. His breathing grew rapid.

She remembered his violent reaction that morning she'd first told him about the baby. How he'd seemed to space out at the gift shop last week.

All this time she'd thought the changes in him, his drinking, were because of Liz. Because he couldn't let her go. And maybe that was part of it. But it wasn't all of it.

"Hey, it's okay," she soothed him. She laid her hands on his chest. Under the soggy, cold shirt, his muscles tensed. His heart raced. "It's just a storm. Everything's fine."

A muscle jumped in his jaw. He slid his hands up to her shoulders. Brushing his thumbs against the sides of her neck, he tipped her head back and met her eyes. She dug her nails into his skin. His narrowed gaze dropped to her mouth.

And any hope she'd had about truly being over her feelings for this man died when he swore under his breath and then kissed her.

HIS MOUTH AGAINST HERS, Brady swallowed J.C.'s gasp. He kept the kiss gentle. Almost…reverent. He was afraid if he pushed for too much, too fast, she'd pull away. Tell him to go.

He couldn't let that happen. Not when the panic was already receding. He was able to blot everything else out because she was in his arms. Kissing him back.

He had no right to touch her, to discover that she tasted as sweet as he'd imagined. To sink into her kiss and forget how screwed up his life had become. But he couldn't stop. He needed to surround himself with her warmth. It was the only way to get rid of the fear that gripped him every day.

He slid his tongue along the seam of her lips and she pulled back slightly, but not far enough away to break contact. Forcing himself to slow down, he skimmed his lips across her jaw, over her chilled cheeks to her temple and down along her hairline.

Her skin was cold, so he rubbed her arms. Pressed closer to her as his own body heated despite his wet clothes. He wanted to tear her hair band out. Watch her shake her head so the curls framed her face. But he didn't have the patience for it.

He pressed an openmouthed kiss behind her ear. Her head fell back on a soft moan that seemed to wash over his body, caress his skin.

He kissed her mouth again. Her lips parted and the tip of her tongue touched his tentatively and about blew his mind.

He yanked her against him. Speared one hand into the damp hair at the nape of her neck to hold her still for his kiss. His other hand slid under her shirt to her waist, the curve of her belly pressing against his palm.

Deepening the kiss, he shifted his weight off his bad leg by slipping it between her thighs. She wrapped her arms around his neck, her fingers combing through his wet hair. The movement brought their bodies center to center. He hissed out a breath. Her breasts rubbed against his chest, her beaded nipples burning through his shirt.

He shifted to the side and broke the kiss long enough to wrench his coat off. Letting it fall on the floor, he raked his gaze over her and his body tightened. She was…stunning. Her lips were red and swollen, her breasts, the roundness of her belly pressing against her shirt. Her cheeks flushed, her eyes dark with desire.

He took her mouth in another voracious kiss. Grabbing her ass, he pulled her even closer. She was all soft, lush curves. And the mewling sounds she made in the back of her throat were driving him crazy. Unable to resist, he rolled his hips and almost whimpered himself. He needed to be inside her. Right now. Or else he'd lose his mind for good.

He would've dragged her down and made love to her there on her kitchen floor, was in the process of doing just that, when she stopped kissing him.

He lifted his head. "What's wrong?"

"I…I don't want this," she said, holding herself as stiffly as possible in his arms.

"Are you sure?" he murmured, unable to stop himself from trailing a finger down the smoothness of her cheek. "I want you."

She laughed harshly. "You don't want me. You want a warm body." When she pushed him, he dropped his arms and stepped back. "I'm convenient."

"What the hell is that supposed to mean?"

"It means you're looking for someone to help you through the night."

No. Not anyone. Her. But she'd never believe it.

"Is that so wrong?" he asked. "We're both adults. Both unattached."

"It wouldn't be wrong," she said with a sigh, "except you'll never be unattached. You're always going to be in love with Liz."

He wanted to deny it. Wanted his denial to be the truth, but he wasn't sure it would be. "She has nothing to do with this."

"How can she not have everything to do with this?" J.C. crossed her arms. "She's my sister and the woman you've loved half your life. What happens between us affects her, too."

"So I'm supposed to…what? Let Liz vet all the women I might sleep with? Because she sure as hell didn't ask my opinion when she decided to dump me for her husband."

"There's too much between us. Call it history or family ties…or whatever. All I know is I've already let you use me once," she said wearily as she straightened from the counter. "I'm not about to make that mistake again. Especially not for a man who only wants me so he can pretend he's with my sister."

CHAPTER TWELVE

"YOU'RE EITHER the world's most patient man," J.C. said in exasperation, coming back to the kitchen when he'd refused to leave, "or the most stubborn."

"Both," he admitted.

She'd swept out of here twenty minutes ago, no doubt hoping that if she took long enough changing into dry clothes, he'd give up, maybe even get pissed and take off. But he wasn't going anywhere. Not when she had such a messed-up view of what'd happened between them. Of why he'd kissed her.

"Here," she said, tossing him a dark blue towel and a gray sweatshirt.

He caught one in each hand. "Thanks."

She shrugged and brushed past him, close enough he could smell a light vanilla scent as she went to a corner cupboard. She'd changed into a pair of striped pajama pants and an oversize, stained shirt with a scowling Garfield holding a coffee cup above the words *I Don't Do Mornings*. She must've redone her hair because the sides were smoothed back, the ponytail higher on her head. Several curls, having escaped confinement, trailed along the back of her neck.

The skin he now knew was soft and warm and sensitive to his touch.

Squeezing the towel in his hands, he stepped back so he wouldn't pull her against him.

She turned—spray cleaner in one hand, a dry cloth in the other—and, without so much as a glance his way, went back to the table. Rain pelted the roof, its intensity waning as the storm moved past. But another one would follow. And if he was alone, he didn't think he could make it through the night. At least not sober.

By the time he'd peeled off his damp shirt, rubbed the towel over his chilled arms and chest, and dried his hair, she'd wheeled a small, three-tiered cart between the table and wall and taken a round, plastic container from the fridge.

"Thank you," she said, still not looking at him, "for cleaning up the floor."

"No problem." Since she'd left him to stew, he'd had plenty of time.

He tugged on the sweatshirt, shoving up the short sleeves. Sitting to her left, he clasped his hands between his knees. Inhaled deeply. "When I'm with you," he said slowly, his gaze fixed on her profile, "I don't pretend you're Liz. And I sure as hell wasn't thinking of her when I kissed you."

"You sure about that?" she asked, spraying cleaning solution over the table. The harsh, chemical scent stung his nose. "It wouldn't be the first time."

"Whatever I did the night of Liz's wedding, I didn't mean to hurt you."

"It wasn't all your fault." She wiped the table with brisk, rough strokes. "I convinced myself you wanted to be with me. And I kept on believing. Right until the end when…" Her voice broke, and she vigorously scrubbed the same spot. "When you called out Liz's name."

He linked his hands at the back of his neck and leaned back. Blew out a heavy breath. "Shit."

His memories of that night were blurry. Disjointed. He'd known he'd used J.C. to help him through his pain and anger. But he hadn't realized how low he'd sunk. Wincing, he shut his eyes. How low he was still sinking. Not thirty minutes ago he'd had her in his arms wanting only to shove aside his panic, to ignore the memories for a little while.

She unfolded a plastic tablecloth. When she spread the material over the table, he sat up and snagged her hand. She froze, her fingers curling. He traced his fingertip over the delicate skin of her inner wrist. Back and forth. Back and forth. Finally, she raised her head.

He wrapped his fingers around her wrist. Felt her pulse beat. "I'm sorry, Jane."

"Sometimes..." she said softly as she withdrew her hand. "Sometimes being sorry isn't enough."

J.C. DIDN'T SO MUCH as glance Brady's way as she set out what she needed—gloves, wax paper, tape, melon ball scoop, cookie sheets. After taping wax paper to the cookie sheets, she opened the container of ganache she'd made earlier. Wind rattled the windowpane.

"Won't be long before another storm comes," she said casually. As if having him sit there wearing her University of Virginia sweatshirt, all big and male and brooding, didn't bother her in the least. As if it hadn't taken all of her willpower to push him away. "If you don't want to get caught in another downpour, you'd better get going."

"Last time you wanted me out of your apartment, you told me outright."

"Fair enough," she said, pulling on a pair of gloves. "I'd like you to leave."

Scooping up a small amount of the dark ganache, she rolled it lightly between her palms, then set it on the wax paper. Repeated the process.

Brady stretched his leg out. Bent it again. Drummed his fingers on the table.

She sighed. "Brady—"

"I haven't had a drink in four days."

Her fingers tightened on the scoop and she glanced at him. Four days… She caught her breath. Four days ago he'd accompanied her to her doctor's appointment.

"Are you bragging?" she asked, keeping her tone neutral. "Or complaining?"

He slouched. "Just stating a fact."

"Oh. Well, that's—"

"I wanted to," he muttered. "Every damn day I've wanted a drink worse than the day before."

Using the scoop, she scraped a tic-tac-toe pattern into the ganache. "Maybe…maybe you need to decide what you want more. To have a drink. Or to stop drinking."

He stood. Put his hands into his pockets. Took them out again. The next storm rumbled in the distance and he hunched his shoulders.

"Don't like thunder?" she couldn't stop herself from asking.

"I've been jumpy since…" He shook his head.

"You were hurt?"

"Since I've been stateside." His expression was hard. "Sometimes…loud noises cause me to…zone out."

She frowned. "You mean you have flashbacks?"

He glared at her. "Sometimes I think about what happened back there."

There. Afghanistan. Where his friends had been wounded. Killed.

And now a thunderstorm had the power to cause this strong man to tremble. Her heart broke for him.

"Can I stay?" he asked, his tone belligerent. His feet wide, his arms loose at his sides as if ready for a fight.

"What do you mean?" If he said stay as in stay the night in her bed, she'd kick his butt to the curb—she didn't care how emotionally damaged he was.

He kept opening and closing his fist, like a gunfighter getting ready to draw his weapon. "If I go home now," he said, as if he were forcing the words out, "I'll drink. And I don't want to drink. Not tonight."

She squeezed the last of the ganache between her hands. He was using her. Again. She was his safety net. Except she couldn't save him. And even if she could, she wasn't sure she wanted to.

"Should I be your crutch?" she asked, unable to keep the bitterness out of her voice. "How about if I throw myself on any alcoholic beverages that get within a few feet of you?"

"I was thinking more along the lines of you just... talking to me," he said quietly. "Letting me keep you company while you work or do your laundry or...whatever you had planned."

She tore off her chocolate-coated gloves and dropped them into the empty bowl. She wanted to send him away. To protect herself from him. If she let him too close, he'd hurt her again. But then she met his eyes and, for the first time since he'd come home, glimpsed the man he used to be.

She had to let him stay.

"Brady," Diane said two days later as she passed him the serving bowl of green beans, "there's something important Aidan and I would like to discuss with you."

They were seated at the small table in the breakfast nook rather than in the ornate dining room—the spot for Sunday dinners when he'd been a kid. His mother sat with her back to the dark window, Brady to her left. Aidan, as always, was her right-hand man.

Spooning beans onto his already full plate, Brady raised his eyebrows. "Don't keep me in suspense."

Diane smiled at him. "How would you like to take on a bigger role at the winery?"

His fingers tingled and he set the beans down. Every week since he'd been back in Jewell, his mother had invited him to Sunday dinner. And every week he'd declined. Until yesterday, when his mother had casually mentioned she was making all his favorites.

Damn. Lured into a trap by the promise of fried chicken, homemade buttermilk biscuits and her double fudge brownies.

He picked up his drumstick. "I wouldn't."

"Told you," Aidan murmured before sipping his chardonnay.

"But why not?" she asked. "Now that you're...getting better—"

"She means now that you're not stinking drunk or hungover all the time," Aidan offered.

Diane fixed Aidan with a look guaranteed to make most men feel as if they were ten years old again. "When I need you to help explain what I mean," she said, her slight Southern accent thickening, "I'll ask."

Aidan stabbed a bean. "Just trying to help."

Brady bit into his chicken, determined not to let the topic ruin his favorite meal.

"Your father always dreamt of having his sons work at the Diamond Dust with him," Diane said.

And his food now tasted like sawdust.

"Don't waste your time," Aidan told their mother. "The only reason he's working here in the first place is because I forced him into it."

"I never pretended otherwise," Brady said mildly.

"But it doesn't have to be that way," Diane said. "Won't you at least consider it?"

He couldn't. He'd already lost Liz and any chance he'd had of becoming a member of the Virginia State Police. If he stayed in Jewell, if he worked at the Diamond Dust, it'd be like admitting he accepted the way his life had turned out.

He wiped his fingers then his mouth on a cloth napkin. "I never planned on working here. Dad knew that."

"Yes, and we fully supported your decision to join the military, but things are different now. You need to start thinking of your future."

"I am," he said. Or he would. Soon.

"Well, then, how are you going to support yourself? And what about Jane and the baby?"

"What about them?"

She seemed taken aback. "I thought you and she were...on friendlier terms."

The memory of how J.C. had felt in his arms, of how she tasted, hit him with great force. "Nothing's changed."

Except that he continued to dream about her. Had kissed her.

Even after everything he'd done, she still let him sit at her kitchen table the other night while she worked on her chocolates. She'd kept up a steady stream of chatter and hadn't seemed to mind when he'd lapsed into silence.

"Everyone in town's talking about how you spent an entire day at the obstetrician's office so you could see her," Aidan said, laying his fork on his empty plate.

Brady rolled his shoulders. Damn small-town gossip, he thought for the nth time. "It wasn't like that."

His brother smirked. "What was it like, then?"

"I think it's wonderful that you and Jane are working out your differences," Diane said, pausing to eat a bite of mashed potatoes. "Especially as I'd like to have some sort of relationship with my first grandchild. You wouldn't believe the horror stories I've heard about grandparents being refused the right to even visit with their grandchildren after a nasty divorce. In some cases where the parents were never married, the mothers disappear with the child. Can you imagine?"

Imagine? He'd been trying not to think about it ever since J.C.'s admission that she wasn't sure she wanted to keep their son.

And he'd told her she had his full support because she'd been so upset, he'd wanted to let her know he didn't judge her. And because... He swallowed the nausea rising in his throat. Because if she did decide to give the baby up for adoption, it'd let him off the hook.

She'd brought up their families and wondered how her decision would affect them. He hadn't wanted to think about it. Hadn't wanted to care.

"J.C. would never keep the baby away from you," he said.

Diane set her water down. "When relationships go bad, some people change."

"Not her."

"I'm sure you're right." Diane cut her chicken into tiny pieces before setting her knife down. "After all, it was your idea to have her sell those chocolates in the gift store. Pam said J.C.'s sales yesterday were up fifteen percent from last week."

Figuring they both needed some space after Friday night, he'd stayed far away from the gift shop yesterday. "Good." He looked over to find Aidan regarding him steadily. "What?" Brady growled.

"I find it interesting how well you seem to have gotten to know Jane."

"I was with her sister for twelve years," he pointed out. "I've always known J.C."

He tapped his fist against his thigh. Just because he'd dreamt of J.C., kissed her, and wanted to take her to bed, didn't change what'd been in his heart since he was sixteen years old.

He would always love Liz.

J.C. WAS FINISHING UP with one of her favorite customers late Wednesday morning when Liz walked into the lobby of Hampton Bank and Trust Company.

"Going to do some Christmas shopping?" she asked Mr. Carns as Liz waited in line at the end of the roped-off area.

Mr. Carns, an elderly gentleman with thinning silver hair and an easy grin, slid his money into a bank envelope. "My wife handles all the gift buying. She leaves me in charge of making sure her wallet's always full of money." He winked.

J.C. smiled. "She's a lucky woman."

"That's what I keep telling her." Hitting the counter with the flat of his hand, he straightened. "If I don't see you before, you have a merry Christmas."

"You, too, Mr. Carns."

As usual for the middle of the week, business was light. "Silver Bells" played in the background and in between each teller's window hung a swag of evergreen boughs tied with a red velvet ribbon. Behind her, Mary Jo Hanold spoke to a customer using the drive-up window. Two windows down in the lobby, Shirley Dodge counted out a deposit from one of the local grocery stores.

"Hello, J.C.," Liz said, stepping up to the window with obvious reluctance.

"It's so good to see you. I've tried calling but—"

"I'd like to cash this." She set down a personal check while seemingly engrossed in watching the hands of the large clock on the wall above the door turn. "Large bills are fine."

J.C. narrowed her eyes. "Yes, ma'am."

Other than the slight stiffening of her shoulders, Liz gave no indication she even heard J.C.

"What do you want from me?" J.C. asked as she processed the transaction on her computer. "Blood?"

"All I want is to cash a check."

"Fine," J.C. said. She was so very tired of being the only one trying to make things right between them.

She quickly counted out the cash, recounted it out loud for her sister's benefit and then tapped it into a neat pile. "Next time," she said, sliding the money across the counter, "try one of our convenient ATM locations."

Liz put the money into her wallet. "Grandma Rose

mentioned Brady spent quite a bit of time at your apartment Friday night."

"Grandma Rose," J.C. said vehemently, "has a big mouth."

"So it's true?"

J.C. straightened a stack of withdrawal slips. "He stopped by."

"Are you…are you two…together?"

Heat washed over her as she remembered how he'd kissed her, as if he could never get enough of her. Held her breast, his voice scraping along her nerve endings when he'd said he wanted her. How…relieved he'd been when she'd told him he could stay through the worst of the storms.

"No." She picked up the withdrawal slips and fanned herself. "Of course not."

When Liz didn't respond, J.C. glanced up, shocked to see her sister fighting tears. Liz must be close to her breaking point to show that much weakness in the middle of the bank lobby.

J.C. set up her Next Window Please sign.

"Don't move," she ordered and then told Mary Jo she was taking a five-minute break.

By the time J.C. had walked out from behind the teller station, Liz's eyes were dry. But she still let J.C. lead her through the lobby to the corner office they used to open new accounts.

J.C. flipped on the light and shut the door. "What is it?" she asked, taking Liz's hand. "What's wrong?"

Liz linked her fingers with J.C.'s. "Carter and I…" She cleared her throat. "We're having some…problems."

"What do you mean by problems?"

"He thinks I have…feelings…repressed feelings… for Brady."

Her mouth went dry. "Do you?"

"If you mean do I still care about Brady, about what happens to him, then yes." She tugged her hand free and began to pace. "After all our time together, how could I not? But Carter refuses to believe it's not more than that. He wants us to go to marriage counseling," Liz said, as if her husband had suggested they join a wife-swapping club.

The idea of admitting her marriage was in trouble must be devastating.

"Maybe counseling's not such a bad idea," J.C. offered.

"It's a horrible idea. We don't need it. Where would we attend sessions anyway? I could never face our colleagues after discussing our most intimate issues with one of them." Crossing her arms, Liz shook her head. "No. We don't need therapy. We'll get through this on our own. But I need you to do something for me."

The hair at the back of her neck stood on end. "I'll do whatever I can—"

"Stay away from Brady."

She licked her lips. Clasped her hands in front of her. "I told you, we're not together."

"But you've been spending time with him and I…I miss you." Liz's expression softened. "So much. But things can't go back to the way they were between us if…if Brady's in your life. And you said yourself that he didn't want any part of the baby, right?"

She remembered Brady's expression when he'd seen the baby's ultrasound—small part wonder, huge part fear. "Right, but—"

"I'm not just asking this for me. I'm asking for Carter, so he doesn't have to risk coming face-to-face with my ex when we see you. And I'm asking for you, too."

"Me?"

"You may not believe this, but I don't want to see you get hurt."

Brady's not the right guy for you. You deserve someone who'll put you first.

Someone who hadn't loved her sister first.

"Okay," J.C. managed to say through the tightness of her throat. "I won't see him anymore."

Liz shut her eyes briefly. "Thank you."

And as her sister enveloped her in a warm hug, J.C. assured herself she'd made the right decision. She'd give Brady up.

As soon as she figured out how to give up a man who was never really hers in the first place.

CHAPTER THIRTEEN

"BRADY," J.C. SAID, when she opened the door Friday evening. "What do you want?"

He raised his eyebrows and she forced herself not to wince. Well, he couldn't show up at her doorstep out of the blue whenever he liked. It wasn't fair to her. And having him standing on her doorstep, clean shaven with his recently cut hair ruffling in the breeze, didn't make keeping her promise to her sister any easier.

"There's a ten-foot Scotch pine strapped to the roof of your car," he said.

She widened her eyes. "It must've fallen onto my car when I drove home from work. Funny how I never noticed."

His eyes narrowed to slits. "How did you think you were going to get it off the car, let alone up the stairs, by yourself?"

"I didn't plan that far ahead." Stopping by the Christmas tree lot on the way home had been an impulse. It had seemed like such a good idea, spending Friday night decorating her tree. With her luck, it'd still be on her car Monday morning. "Is that why you stopped by? To tell me about my own Christmas tree?"

He studied her in that intense way of his that made her blush. "Did I do something between last week and today to piss you off?"

"You haven't even spoken to me since then. What could you have done?"

That sounded as if she'd expected him to call. She grimaced.

"So there's no reason for you to not invite me in," he said.

She lightly hit the dangling silver earring in her left ear with her fingertip, set it swinging. "Actually, there is. A reason."

"Should I guess?" he asked when she remained silent.

"I…" She swallowed. "I just got home," she said on a rush. "I haven't even changed yet."

His gaze skimmed over her black pants. Lingered on her shiny burgundy top before meeting her eyes. "I don't mind."

Her mouth dried and she stepped behind the door, closing it slightly, showing only her face through the small opening.

"Since I'm not going to see the other side of your door any time soon, you might as well take this now," he said, holding out a plastic shopping bag.

She eyed it suspiciously. "What is it?"

He pulled a large, plain cardboard box out of the bag. "Do you want it or not?"

She took it, flipped it over then back again. Letting go of the door, she lifted the lid. And blinked down at a pair of purple and white polka-dot flip-flops.

The tips of Brady's ears were red. "They were out of pink," he said almost defiantly.

"That's okay," she whispered. "I love purple."

He scowled. "I wasn't sure of your size."

"They're fine. They're perfect," she said. "Thank you."

He inclined his head, the barest of nods. "Good night."

"Wait." She stepped onto the landing, pulling the door closed in case Daisy made a run for it. "Don't you want to come in?"

"Do you want me to come in?" he asked cautiously.

She clutched the box, holding it over her racing heart. "Yeah, I do."

He gestured for her to go ahead of him and she hurried inside. Before she changed her mind.

She kicked off her shoes. "Do you want a soda?" she asked, setting the box on top of her coffee table before making her way toward the kitchen. "I think I have regular—"

"How are you going to get the tree up here?"

She placed a hand over the fluttering in her stomach. "I'll call my dad tomorrow."

He glared at the sheet and tree stand under the window. "I can't bring the tree up."

"I didn't ask you to." And then she realized what he meant. What bothered him. "Is this about your knee? Because even if I wasn't pregnant, I couldn't drag that tree up all those stairs, either."

He tossed his jacket onto the sofa. "That's different."

"If that isn't one of the finest examples of the male ego at work, I don't know what is."

"It's not ego. Not all ego. More like I hate not being able to do all the things I used to."

"So you can't haul a large evergreen up a flight of stairs. At least you can still climb them," she said, sick to death of him focusing on what he couldn't do. What he didn't have, such as Liz. "You're able to get out of bed by yourself. You can work at a job—even if it's not the one you'd always planned on. You're surrounded by people who care about you. Who are more than willing to give you a hand when you need one. And if all of those reasons weren't enough for you to thank God each and every day," she said, her face hot, her voice breaking, "I'd think the fact that you're alive would be."

The room seemed too quiet after her outburst. All she could hear was the sound of her own ragged breathing. Her pulse kicked up as Brady closed the distance between them, the surprise on his face giving way to admiration.

He stopped a few inches from her. Close enough she could feel his body heat, smell the fresh winter air clinging to his clothes. "You're right. Those things weren't enough for me. I'm not sure they'll ever be." He tucked one of her stray curls behind her ear, his fingertip grazing her neck. "But you're wrong, too. Because right now, I can honestly say I'm very grateful to be alive."

"DID YOU FIND SOMETHING to drink?" J.C. asked as she came back out into the living room ten minutes later. After her impassioned speech and his own admission, she'd bolted with the excuse of changing out of her work clothes.

Sitting on the sofa, her cat curled up next to him, Brady held up his can of soda. He watched as J.C. walked past him. She'd pulled her hair back and had on the same clinging black pants she'd worn last week when she fell on the steps and a loose T-shirt the color of peaches.

As she disappeared into the kitchen, his fingers tightened on the can. He took a long swallow. "You hungry?" he called.

She came back into the room eating from a bag of pretzels. "What'd you say?"

He grinned. "I asked if you were hungry."

She sat on the other end of the couch. "Nowadays that's pretty much a yes no matter when you ask me."

"We could order some dinner," he said casually. "Maybe get some Chinese?"

"Sure," she said after a long moment, as if having takeout with him was some sort of momentous decision. "That'd be nice." Handing him the bag of pretzels, she stood. "Let me grab the take-out menu for The Golden Dragon."

"I don't need it. I'll have a number three and a number fifteen."

"You have the menu for the Chinese restaurant memorized?"

The cat stood and stretched, stepped onto Brady's lap and lay down again. "Just the dishes I like."

She rubbed the side of her stomach. "I take it you don't cook."

"Not if I can help it."

"Me, either. Between my parents, Grandma Rose and Liz and Carter, I—" She blushed, acting as guilty as if she'd admitted to hiding Al-Qaeda operatives under her bed. "I'll go order dinner," she said before rushing out of the room. Again.

He didn't call her back. Not when he had no idea what to say to her. He knew what he should say—that J.C. could go ahead and talk about her sister all she wanted. That Liz was a part of her life and as such, she shouldn't worry about bringing her up in an innocent conversation.

Leaning his head back against the couch, he stared at the ceiling. Yeah, he should say all of that. But he'd be lying. He didn't want to hear anything about Liz. Didn't want to be reminded of her existence. Not when he'd gotten to the point where he could go all day without once thinking about her.

Someone knocked, and Brady set the cat aside and stood. He opened the door, nodded at Matt and then noticed J.C.'s tree on the stairs behind his brother.

"Thanks," he said, figuring he could manage to drag it up the last few feet. "I've got it from here."

Matt pushed the door back open when Brady tried to shut it in his face. "Don't I even get invited in? After all, I dropped everything to do you a favor."

Dropped everything, his ass.

"Favor's appreciated," Brady said, refusing to fall for his brother's bait.

When he'd called Matt's cell phone fifteen minutes ago, Matt had been at The County Line, one of the higher end bars in Jewell. And Brady sure as hell didn't feel guilty for tearing him away from a watered-down drink and whichever local girl he'd been trying to charm into sleeping with him.

"Well, appreciation's great and all," Matt said, leaning against the door. "But I'd rather have a beer."

"J.C. doesn't have—"

"Food should be here in twenty minutes," J.C. said, coming up behind Brady. "Oh. Hi, Matt." She glanced curiously between the brothers. "I didn't know you were home."

"Since I had to fly back to Australia the day

after Thanksgiving, I thought I'd come in early for Christmas."

Funny how Matt's accent became thicker whenever a female was within hearing distance. His green eyes lit as he scanned J.C. head to toe and back up again. "Jane Cleo, you get prettier every time I see you."

Brady stopped himself from laying a proprietary hand on J.C.'s shoulder. "Any women stupid enough to buy your tired lines?" he asked.

Matt grinned, his hair, too long, blowing around his face. "You'd be surprised."

"I wouldn't," J.C. said. Brady scowled while Matt laughed. "What?" she asked. "I'm just saying there are plenty of stupid women out there."

He laid a hand over his heart. "You wound me, sugar. And after I hauled your Christmas tree up all those stairs. Your very heavy Christmas tree."

At that moment, Brady would've given anything to have full use of his leg back so he could kick Matt down the steps.

"You brought my tree up?" J.C. asked, her brow knit in confusion.

"Sure did. Now, why don't you hold the door open and I'll bring it the rest of the way in."

Brady stepped out onto the landing. "Better let me help you," he said. "Seeing as how this is one of those extra-heavy Christmas trees."

He carefully took a hold of a thick bottom branch while Matt did the same. Walking backward, they pulled the tree up over the doorstep and into the apartment. The sharp needles pricked and scratched his skin. The pungent scent of pine filled the room.

"Want me to set it up for you, Jane?" Matt asked.

"No," Brady said before J.C. could so much as open her mouth.

"You sure?" Matt hooked his thumbs in his pockets and sent J.C. one of his patented grins guaranteed to charm the ladies. "I'd be more than happy to stick around."

"We've got it," Brady ground out. "Thanks for coming over."

"Yes," J.C. added, giving his brother a warm smile. "Thank you so much, Matt. This was really sweet of you."

"No problem." He walked to the door and stood on the landing. "Call me if you need anything else," he said to J.C. "Come to think of it, why don't I give you my cell phone—"

Brady shut the door. "I don't suppose you have a hacksaw?" he asked, his hands on his hips as he studied the tree. The cat came over and delicately sniffed the trunk. "We're going to have to cut this down by—"

He broke off, went rigid when she pressed against his side. Stretching up, she kissed his cheek. "Thank you for getting my tree inside."

"I didn't do anything," he said, stepping back when what he really wanted was to pull her closer.

"You called your brother when it must've been hard for you to ask for help."

J.C. flinched, her hand going to her side.

"What is it?" he asked. "Are you sick?"

"No, I...I think I felt the baby move."

"You're not sure?"

"I'm new at this, remember? Dr. Owens said I'd know what it was like when I felt it, whatever that's supposed to—" She gasped, her face filled with wonder. "That had to be it."

Brady watched her stomach, as if he could somehow get a glimpse of movement through her clothes and skin. "Does it hurt?"

"No, it's...weird. Here." Shifting so they were toe to toe, she took his hand and slid it under her snug top.

His fingers grazed her warm skin and he clenched his fist. "J.C., I—"

"Don't you want to feel it, too?"

Forcing his fingers to uncurl, he let her guide his hand to her side. Her skin was incredibly soft and he couldn't stop himself from cupping the roundness of her stomach, his thumb by her belly button, his fingertips brushing her hip bone. They were so close, he breathed in the fresh scent of her hair. Had the torture of her breasts brushing against his chest with every small move she made.

He cleared his throat. "I don't feel anything."

"That's because he hasn't moved yet." Another second passed. And another. "There! Did you feel it?"

He shook his head. "What's it like?"

"The first few times, it felt as if there were butterflies in my stomach—literally." Making a sound somewhere between a laugh and a cry, she raised her head, bringing their faces to within inches of each other. Her smile faded.

"Butterflies, huh?"

"Uh...yes... It was this...sort of fluttering," she whispered, staring at his mouth. "But now it's more of a... rolling sensation. Sort of...how you feel when you're falling..."

She lifted her hand to his cheek. Her lush breasts pressed against him, her breath washed over his lips.

And then she kissed him.

She kept the kiss delicate. Light. But in that instant, with her mouth supple and warm against his, her lips tasting of salt and a sweetness that was uniquely her, his senses spun.

Yeah. He knew all about falling.

He also knew how much it hurt when you hit the ground.

She eased back. Her smile was so purely Jane—simple and honest and bright enough to chase away nightmares—it took all his waning willpower not to yank her to him.

"In case you were wondering," she said as she adjusted her shirt to cover her stomach again, "that was one of those happy kisses."

He frowned. Happy what? And then he remembered. That day when she'd kissed him in his mom's kitchen, she'd claimed she'd only done it because she was happy.

"Good thing I was here," he said.

"It was awfully convenient. Although if I'd felt the baby move a few minutes earlier Matt would've still been here so…"

"You would've still kissed me."

She laughed. "Well, you would've had a fifty-fifty chance."

He set his hands on her waist and pulled her forward. Sliding his arms around her, he held her to him, pressing his palms against the flat of her back.

"You would've kissed me." His gaze followed the movement of her throat as she swallowed, then shifted back to her eyes. "Say it," he demanded in a soft undertone.

She gripped his forearms, her short nails digging into his skin. "I would've kissed you."

He dipped his head in acknowledgment and dropped his arms. "I'll check in the garage for that hacksaw," he said. And maybe, if he helped her put up her tree, she'd be so happy she'd kiss him again.

"THIS IS MY FAVORITE PART," J.C. said late the next night as they watched the DVD of *It's A Wonderful Life*.

"You said that before."

Tossing popcorn into her mouth, she didn't even bother glancing at Brady. Not when Mary and George were about to kiss for the first time. And, okay, she may have said her favorite part was the scene after the school dance when Mary and George walk home, but this was her absolute favorite scene.

"You're not going to cry again, are you?" Brady asked.

On the screen, George stormed out and Mary smashed the record of their song into pieces.

"I haven't cried yet," J.C. said. She may have welled up a few times, but what did he expect when she was watching the most fabulous movie ever? "But if tears bother you, I should warn you that I bawl at the end for a solid five minutes."

"Great," he muttered, slouching down even farther on the opposite end of her couch, staring at the brightly lit Christmas tree across the room.

Setting the popcorn bowl aside, she picked up her water glass and took a sip. "Are you all right?"

He sent her an unreadable look. "Fine."

"Are you sure? You seem…distracted."

He lifted one shoulder in a shrug.

She huffed out a breath, trying to figure out why he was acting like his old brooding, angry self. It was as if he didn't want to be there—although when they'd talked at the Diamond Dust's gift shop earlier, he was the one who'd asked if he could stop by. She couldn't refuse him, not after last night when he'd helped put up her tree and then had kissed her so tenderly before he left.

And for once, she hadn't felt guilty for wanting to spend time with her sister's ex. Or worried about telling Liz she'd made a mistake when she'd promised to stay away from Brady.

She paused the movie. "We don't have to watch—"

"I said I'm fine."

She crossed her arms at his clipped tone. "Yes. That's obvious."

"I just…" He ran his palms up and down his jeans. "I really want a drink."

"Oh." She sipped more water, but it did little to ease the dryness in her throat. After pulling the hem of her shorts down, she tucked her legs underneath her. "Are you going to have one?"

"If I could stop at one drink, it wouldn't be a problem now, would it?"

"No, I suppose not."

When she remained silent, he sat up. "Aren't you going to tell me not to drink?"

"Is that why you're here?" she asked, proud of how calm she sounded, how rational. "So I can stop you from drinking?"

"You don't get it," he burst out. "I don't need you to

babysit me so I won't drink. I want a drink because…
because, maybe if I get drunk," he continued, the low
rumble of his voice scraping along her nerve endings,
"I can forget how much I want you. Even for a little
while."

She caught her breath. "I…I don't…"

"It's killing me to sit here and not touch you," he
admitted raggedly, his hands fisted on his thighs.

It all made sense now. How Brady had barely looked
her way all evening. Why he'd sat as far away on the
small sofa as possible.

She knew what was at risk. Her family wouldn't
understand. Wouldn't approve. And her sister? If J.C.
followed her heart, if she chose Brady, she may never
be able to salvage her relationship with Liz.

Her heart pounding, she unfolded her legs and knelt
on the cushion, facing him. He watched her warily, his
jaw taut. Swallowing back her trepidation, she said the
words that had the power to change everything between
them.

"Touch me, Brady."

For a moment, he didn't move. Other than the rapid
rise and fall of his chest, it was as if he were made of
stone. Then he groaned and pulled her forward for a
voracious kiss. She tumbled, catching herself against
his shoulders, and still he didn't release her mouth. His
kiss was hard. Hungry. Almost punishing.

When he lifted his head, they were both breathing
hard. He kissed her jaw up her cheek to her temple and
back down again. His fingers kneaded her neck, his
other hand squeezing her outer thigh. He captured a
fistful of her hair and tugged her head back. He pressed

his lips against the hollow of her throat before scraping his teeth across her collarbone.

She whimpered and clutched his shoulders, her nails digging into his skin. He kissed his way back up her throat to her mouth again, his tongue sweeping inside to touch hers.

He straightened and combed both hands through her hair, his touch incredibly gentle. "Where's that purple top?" he asked.

"What?"

"The tank top you wore with these shorts before."

"I'm wearing it."

He stared at her black sweatshirt so intently she half expected it to burst into flames. "Under that shirt?"

She nodded and he lowered his hands to the hem of her shirt. She lifted her arms as he pulled the fleece up, his knuckles grazing the sensitive skin on the inside of her arms as he pulled it over her head and let it drop.

She glanced down. The ribbed tank top clung to each curve, hugging the mound of her belly and her breasts, her hard nipples jutting out. She held her breath as he edged closer, his leg bumping her knees. He brushed his fingertips over the fabric covering the upper slope of her breasts and she exhaled softly.

"I really like this shirt," he said solemnly, dragging his fingernail down between her breasts and back up. His cupped her breasts in his hands, his thumbs brushing back and forth over her nipples.

"I'll…" But the promise to wear it more often died on her lips when he bent his head and his open mouth was over her breast. The heat of his breath washed over her, causing her nipple to tighten even more, if that was possible. His tongue rasped against the cloth and she jerked, her hands clutching his thigh.

He raised his head, got to his feet and held his hand out.

Though her nerves battled with her anticipation, she didn't hesitate. Linking her fingers through his, she stood and led him to her bedroom.

She let go of him to cross the room and turn on the lamp on her nightstand. Brady came up behind her. Wrapping an arm around her waist, he pulled her to him, his arousal pressing against her back. Reality about what they were about to do, how it was going to change everything—again—crashed over her and she stiffened.

"I won't hurt you, Jane," Brady said, brushing her hair aside and kissing her neck.

He would. Of course he would. Eventually. Because she wasn't who he really wanted. But he did want her tonight, right now. And that would be enough.

She forced herself to relax against him and felt his own tension ease, as well. He turned her around and kissed her deeply as he backed her toward the bed, helping her onto the mattress. Straightening, he quickly toed off his shoes and stripped his shirt over his head.

Her blood quickened. He was all lean muscles and golden skin, his mouth unsmiling, his eyes glittering. He was gorgeous. And as always, she was plain Jane Cleo.

But he didn't look at her as if she were plain, but rather as if she were…special.

Beautiful.

He climbed onto the bed and lay down on his side

next to her. He dipped his head for a kiss and she sighed. No more second-guessing. No more insecurities.

She ran her hands over him. Over his broad shoulders, down his arms and back up again, then trailed her fingertips down his back to the waistband of his jeans. He was so warm. His skin smooth, his muscles flexing under her hands. Then his kiss became more urgent.

In one quick motion, he sat up, pulling her up with him. He grabbed the bottom of her tank top and peeled it off.

"You're beautiful," he said huskily. Reverently.

Warmth filled her, grew to searing heat when he eased her back again, bent his head and sucked one nipple into his mouth. She whimpered, then bit down hard on her lower lip. Her hands curled around her bedspread. With each tug and pull on her breast, desire built inside her. He moved to her other breast, giving it the same attention until she squirmed.

He kissed his way down to the slope of her stomach, his hands on either side as if holding a precious—albeit large—egg.

"Hello, baby," he murmured.

J.C. felt the baby move as if he couldn't help but respond to Brady's deep voice.

Brady rubbed the sides of her stomach a moment longer, placed a kiss just under her belly button and then slid his hands to the waistband of her shorts. J.C. lifted her hips and he tugged the material, along with her underwear, down her legs.

It hurt to breathe as he stared down at her. She squeezed her eyes shut. As much as she wanted to watch him undress, as much as she wanted to see him—every part of him—she couldn't. Her stomach turned with nerves as she waited for him to enter her. What if the unsatisfying sex last time hadn't been Brady's fault? What if she'd somehow messed up? Moved the wrong way or—

Her eyes snapped open as his hand smoothed up her inner thigh. He was lying on his side next to her, still wearing his jeans. "Wha-what are you doing?" she asked.

"Touching you."

"Why?"

"Because you're soft." He nudged her legs farther apart with his hand then pressed his nose to the side of her neck and inhaled deeply. "Because you smell good." His hand trailed along the crease of her thigh up to her hip bone, then back and forth over her lower stomach. Her pelvis contracted. "Because I want to make you wet for me."

Heat suffused her at his words, said in such a dark, seductive tone. "I..." Her breath whooshed out when he brushed his fingertips over the tight curls between her legs. Back and forth. Back and forth. She lifted her hips but he didn't deepen those featherlight touches like she wanted. "I think I'm already there so if you want to..."

"I do want to," he said with such a wicked smile, she couldn't help but smile in return.

Until he slid his hand down. It was like an electric shock, feeling his hard, work-roughened hand on her most intimate place. She gripped his wrist, tried to pull his hand away, but he didn't budge.

"What's wrong?" he asked, looking so confused and sexy, for a moment she couldn't remember why she'd stopped him.

"Nothing," she managed to squeak out, her voice about three octaves higher than usual. "I... You don't have to... I've never done this before," she said, forcing the words out. "This...part...I mean..."

"J.C.," he asked slowly, "were you a virgin the night we—"

"No! No, there were...two other guys—"

His head snapped back. "Two?"

"Three...since we should count you," she added faintly.

For several long moments, Brady just watched her. Her body started to cool and all the reasons why they shouldn't be doing this seeped back into her brain.

Until he sat up. Keeping his hand above her center, with his other hand he brushed her hair away from her face. Then he kissed her. Their lips clung for one heartbeat. Then two. When he lifted his head, he traced the arch of her eyebrow, the slope of her nose with one finger. Her resistance and her doubts melted away.

"I want to touch you," he said quietly, his hand now in her hair massaging her scalp. Before she could point out that he was touching her, he continued, "I want to touch you like no other man has touched you. Make you feel things no other man has made you feel."

He was. He did. But she couldn't say that out loud. He rubbed large circles over her stomach as he swirled his tongue around her nipple. When he bit her nipple lightly, her hips rose off the bed.

Then his hand on her stomach moved between her legs. At his slow, sure strokes, her pleasure built, almost impossible to bear. Sweat coated her skin which suddenly felt too tight. Sensitive to his touch. Her need to find relief from his talented hands and tongue grew until her hips pumped up and down. Brady once again sucked on her breast, his teeth scraping the sensitive bud the same time he slipped a finger inside her.

She teetered on the edge, but then she looked down at the sight of his head at her breast and she fell. Her back arched off the mattress and her vision blurred as her orgasm flowed through her, a rush of pleasure followed by smaller tingles of electricity. Tears stung her eyes.

And she knew that her worst fear had come true after all.

She was one hundred percent, totally and unequivocally in love with Brady Sheppard.

CHAPTER FOURTEEN

His body aching, screaming for release, Brady raised his head and watched J.C. come down from her orgasm. Her eyes were closed, her full lips parted, her heavy breasts rising and falling as she panted softly, a sheen of sweat coating her skin.

At that moment, she was the most beautiful thing he'd ever seen.

As if of its own accord, his hand moved back up to her belly. He couldn't seem to stop touching her there, where she carried their child. Couldn't get past how... hard...her stomach was. He could only imagine what she'd look like next month. Or four months from now. How much more would her body grow and change?

And did it even matter if he wasn't sure he'd be around to see it?

He rubbed her stomach, his body growing harder as she wiggled and sighed. Her eyes slowly opened. She skimmed her hand over his shoulder and down his bicep, her touch hesitant. Shy, almost.

Which made sense, considering her sexual history. Obviously neither of the two guys she'd slept with had taken the time to give her pleasure. Idiots.

And he was idiot number three for not only neglecting J.C.'s satisfaction the first time they'd made love, but by not even remembering being with her and calling out her sister's name. Make that king of the idiots.

And yet, by some miracle, she hadn't turned him away tonight. Instead, she'd trusted him with her body.

I won't hurt you, Jane, he'd promised.

J.C. stared at him, or rather the bulge in his pants. She reached out, her hand a few inches above his arousal. Behind his zipper, his body twitched.

"Don't stop," he said in a husky whisper when she took her hand away without touching him.

"I'm not stopping," she said. "At least not until I've had my fill of you."

He swallowed in an attempt to work some moisture in his mouth.

J.C. rose onto her elbow, the movement causing her breasts to sway. He lightly pinched one hard, dusky tip and she moaned. He lifted his head to take her into his mouth again but she moved back, out of reach.

"Let me," she said, nudging his shoulders until he reclined on the bed once again.

He held his breath as she laid her hand against his cheek. She stroked the side of his neck, then his shoulder and down his arm. Outlining the edges of his USMC eagle tattoo with her fingertip, her frown thoughtful. He expected her to ask him about it, why he got it, what it meant. Instead, she smoothed her hand back up to his shoulder and down his chest. Under her soft, seeking touch, his heart skipped a beat before finding a steady rhythm that quickened as her fingers traveled down to his belly button.

He inhaled sharply, his stomach muscles contracting. With as much concentration as an explosive ordnance disposal unit defusing a bomb, her other hand went to the waistband of his jeans. Both his lungs and his groin tightened almost to the point of pain. But he forced himself not to move. To wait and see what she'd do next.

"Could you take your pants off?" she asked in a rush.

He thought she'd never ask. He undid his jeans, shimmied them and his boxers down his legs and kicked them off before sitting back up.

She blinked. "Wow. That must be some sort of land speed record."

"I aim to please," he managed. Not an easy feat when J.C. stared at his body as if he were one of her candies.

"So do I," she murmured. His mouth went dry.

J.C. rose to her knees. Lying flat on his back, he couldn't watch her like he wanted so he grabbed a pillow, folded it in half and shoved it under his head, the scent of her shampoo surrounding him.

As she sat back on her heels beside him, she looked confused, as if she had no clue what to do. He almost took her hand and placed it on a part of him where he'd love for her to start. And finish. And spend any amount of time and attention on.

She leaned forward and softly kissed his scarred knee.

He jerked, his hands fisting into her bedcovers.

She lifted her head and turned to him, her hair falling to the side, the ends tickling his lower thigh. "Does it hurt?"

"No."

But he couldn't stop himself from tensing when she laid her right hand above his knee. Blindly staring up at the ceiling, a lump formed in his throat as she traced each and every one of his scars, her touch as gentle, as soothing as a summer breeze. No one had touched his knee in a nonprofessional way since the attack. He couldn't remember anyone ever touching it, touching any part of him with as much compassion and tenderness as J.C. did now.

When she was done with his scar, she caressed his thigh. Up and down, from his knee, along his outer thigh to his hip bone and back again. Each time she seemed to get more confident. And a lot bolder as she worked her way toward his inner thigh, stopping shy of his erection. Grinding his teeth, he raised his head to look down at her only to find her watching him.

As soon as his eyes met hers, she wrapped her hand around him. His vision blurred. Then she started stroking him leisurely. He about went over the edge. He hissed out a breath and fought for control. But he couldn't take his eyes off her, the sight of her pale, small hands on him and the way she watched him carefully, her eyes bright, as if there were nothing she'd rather do than touch him, explore his body.

She was…amazing. Her generosity and warmth. Her sensuality. Her beauty—both inside and out. And she wanted to be with him. Even after all of his mistakes, she still wanted him. She humbled him.

She scared the hell out of him.

He lost the ability to think at all when J.C. did some sort of gentle twisting motion that felt so damned good that he groaned.

And she smiled.

That did it.

He jackknifed up, had a glimpse of her startled expression right before he took her mouth in a hungry kiss.

Clutching his biceps, she kissed him back as he lowered her to the mattress and followed her down, supporting his weight on his elbows.

Breaking the kiss, he shifted to the side, picked up his jeans and shook them until his wallet fell out of the pocket. He flipped it open and took out a condom.

"I'd say it's a little late for that," J.C. said, the lightness of her tone unable to completely cover her underlying nerves.

He opened the packet and covered himself. "It's never too late to be safe."

Besides, though he'd gotten a clean bill of health when he'd had a physical before starting physical therapy, he didn't want to take any chances with J.C.

He settled himself between her thighs, his arms shaking with the effort to hold himself back.

"Are you sure this is safe?" he forced himself to ask. "For the baby, I mean."

"Dr. Owens said it's safe."

She no sooner got the last word out when Brady lifted her hips and slid inside her. Her body tensed, her expression unsure. He withdrew slightly and didn't move. It took every ounce of self-control not to take what he needed so badly from her.

But he couldn't find any of those things at J.C.'s expense. Not again. Not when he was finding his way to who he was. He kissed her, careful to keep his weight off both the baby and his bad knee.

He continued to kiss her until some of the stiffness left her. When she combed her fingers through his hair, he rolled his hips, filling her. She gasped into his mouth and he smiled against her lips before pulling back and repeating the motion. Again. And again until the tension built to a fever pitch. Her hands pulled at his hair, her body soft and pliant under his. But still, he could feel her holding back from him.

He lifted his head but her eyes remained closed, her hands now at his hips. "Jane." Her eyes popped open, her nails digging into his skin. "It's just you and me here," he continued hoarsely, increasing his tempo as he moved in and out of her body. "No one else I want here. Only you, Janie."

Reaching between them, with the pad of his thumb he rubbed the hard nub at her center. Her mouth opened and her eyes grew cloudy. Her body squeezed around him. She tipped her head back but kept her eyes on his as she came, her body pulsing around him. Pushing him to follow.

He gripped her under her thighs and plowed into her. Again. And again. His concern for the baby, his vow not to hurt J.C. keeping his control in check. Keeping him from taking her as hard, as fast, as he wanted.

His climax built.

"No," he ground out when J.C.'s eyes began to close. "Watch me, Jane. Watch what you do to me."

Her eyes, so dark they seemed bottomless, locked on his. With a guttural groan, he threw his head back and emptied himself.

J.C. ROLLED OVER and reached for Brady but found his side of the bed empty. The sheets cold. Shoving her hair out of her face, she glanced at the glowing numbers of the digital clock on her nightstand. Two thirty-two. Flopping onto her back again, she flung her arm across her eyes. After she and Brady had made love, he'd pulled the comforter over them both and she'd immediately fallen asleep in his arms.

Hoping he'd still be there in the morning.

She tossed off her covers. Since she was up, she may as well get a glass of water, maybe use the bathroom. Swinging her feet over the edge of the bed, she sat up and flipped on the light.

"You okay?"

She yelped and almost fell off the bed. She spun around to find Brady, wearing only his jeans, sitting on the floor, his back against her closet, one leg bent, his injured leg out straight.

"Don't do that!" Grabbing the comforter, she wrapped it around herself.

"Sorry."

She frowned. Something was wrong. And it wasn't just that he sat on her floor in the middle of the night. His expression was tight. His hands clenched.

Holding the end of the comforter so she didn't trip, she walked over and sat next to him. "What are you doing on the floor?"

"I couldn't stay." His head fell back against her closet door with a thump. "But I couldn't leave, either."

"I'm sorry, I don't understand."

"I should go," he said. "But I don't want to."

She wouldn't read more into any of this—what he said or how he acted or how he'd looked at her when they'd made love. She was going to take it one day, one minute at a time.

And she wouldn't get her hopes up or start wishing for things that weren't going to happen. Like him loving her back.

"I'm glad you stayed," she said. "But I think you'll be more comfortable in the bed."

"I can't."

"Sure you can. It's plenty big enough for two."

"No. I mean, I really can't. I have these…dreams." He faced forward and wiped an unsteady hand down his face. "Nightmares. And sometimes I get…sometimes it's like I'm…back in Afghanistan and I…I'll throw a punch or…" He shook his head, and his voice dropped so low she had to strain to hear him. "I don't want to hurt you. Or the baby."

Oh, God. Unable to catch her breath, not strong enough to face the bleakness in his eyes, she curled her knees up to her chest and stared at the floor.

As much as it shamed her, as big as her feelings for Brady were, she wanted to run. She had no idea—absolutely no clue—how to help Brady, what to say or do.

"These dreams…" She cleared her throat. "Are your dreams like the flashbacks?" The flashbacks he never confirmed nor denied having.

Sometimes I think about what happened back there.

He remained silent. She didn't press. She waited, hoping he'd open up to her. Time passed and her toes got cold so she tucked the comforter around them.

"We were on patrol," Brady finally said, speaking in a slow monotone as if unaware she was even there. "Jonesy was driving, Thad was riding shotgun, and me and Van were in the back. One minute Van was telling us about when he'd accidentally hired a male stripper to show up at his brother's bachelor party, and the next…I was coming to on the side of the road. We'd all been laughing and then…" He swallowed. "The explosion was so loud, after it was as if I was listening to everything through a filter. But I could still hear Van yelling for help. Jonesy's cries of pain."

She shivered. God, she couldn't even imagine what he'd gone through. How close he'd come to dying. "What about your other friend?"

"Dead," he said flatly, his lips a thin line. "He had a wife and two little kids and now…" He blew out a heavy breath and lowered his head into his hands. "It should've been me."

"Don't say that." She scrambled onto her knees in front of him, cupping his face in her hands and raising it so he looked at her. "What happened was horrible for you all but—"

"He should've lived," he said, bracketing her wrists with his hands. "He had people to live for."

J.C.'s eyes stung but she wouldn't cry. Not when Brady sat there dry-eyed, thinking he had nothing to live for.

"Have you considered talking to someone about this?" she asked. "A psychologist or—"

"No."

Shaken and humbled he'd trusted her with this, she pressed her forehead against his. "I'm glad you told me. But I think," she said carefully, not wanting to say the wrong thing, "you should consider getting professional help."

He exhaled shakily, his breath washing over her face. "I know you're trying to help—"

"I am. And I won't push you, I swear, but could you at least think about it?"

"Yeah," he said gruffly. "Okay."

"Thank you," she said. Then she pressed a kiss against his mouth. As she stood, she let the comforter slide off her shoulders to pool at her feet. "Come on. Let's go back to bed."

After a moment's hesitation, he accepted the hand she held out and let her help him get to his feet.

As much as she wanted to, she couldn't heal him.

But she could help him get through tonight.

BRADY CARRIED HIS SHOES as he soundlessly made his way to the bedroom door. He glanced back at J.C. She was still asleep, the covers pulled up to her chin, her lips were parted, her hair a mass of wild curls.

He wanted more than anything to slip back into bed with her. To be here when she woke up so they could make love again.

He snuck out of the room. Sitting on the sofa, he put his shoes on, grabbed his jacket from the chair where he'd tossed it last night and stepped out into the cold. His leg had stiffened during the night and descending the stairs became an awkward and painful process. But less awkward than it would've been if J.C. had woken up while he was still there.

He couldn't face her. Not now. He needed time to sort things out. Like why he'd told her about the nightmares when he'd never told anyone else. Why he'd enjoyed holding her so much as she slept.

A black Lexus pulled into the driveway as Brady reached the bottom step. Goosebumps appeared on his arms as the driver got out.

Stopping below him, Liz glanced from him to J.C.'s apartment and back at him again.

As if she had any right to try to make him feel guilty.

"You slept with her? Again?" Liz asked, crossing her arms over her red jacket.

He moved to the left but she blocked his way. Her breath turned to a cloud before disappearing. "What's between me and Jane is none of your concern," he said.

"That's where you're wrong. Anything having to do with my family is my concern. Especially when someone is using my sister to get to me."

"Get to you? Why the hell would I do that?"

"To hurt me for what I did to you or…or maybe you think if you make me jealous, I'll come back to you."

"I'm not into revenge," he snarled. "And what makes you think I'd ever want you back?"

Liz tucked her hair behind her ear, her hand trembling. "From what I understand, you've made it clear you want nothing to do with the baby. Why else are you with J.C. if not to hurt me?"

"You act as if she has no redeeming qualities other than having you as a sibling."

Liz blushed, rubbed her gloves hands together. "J.C. is plenty special on her own but I'm not blind to her faults. She's a dreamer, unreliable and can't stick with one project, job or college for more than three months at a time."

"She's also sweet and funny and sexy…" Brady shook his head to clear his thoughts.

Liz's took a step back as if she'd been slapped. "Oh, my God," she breathed. "You're in love with her."

The back of his neck tingled, like it used to in Afghanistan before a firefight broke out. As it did moments before the bomb exploded. "I'm not in love with Jane Cleo," he growled, noticing the relief in Liz's eyes.

Loving one Montgomery sister had almost killed him. And he never made the same mistake twice.

"All the more reason to stay away from her," Liz said emphatically, the breeze lifting her hair. "Before she gets hurt. I mean it, Brady. Leave her be."

Damn it, he knew that. "You gave up any say into how I live my life when you wrote me that Dear John letter."

"This isn't about you and me," she said unsteadily.

"It's only ever been about us," he said, his voice rising. "I loved you, I wanted to marry you. We'd planned our life together and then suddenly you met someone new and it's over?"

Her mouth trembled. "It wasn't like that. With Carter, I mean. I never... We didn't..."

"You didn't what?"

"I never cheated on you."

"Is that supposed to make it all right?" he asked, taking that last step, forcing her to back up. She bumped into J.C.'s car. He kept walking until he stood mere inches from her. "How long after you sent that letter did it take the two of you to get together?"

Her eyes welled with tears. "Brady, please don't..."

A car drove by but both Brady and Liz ignored it. "I deserve to know," he said, his stomach in knots. He needed to know. "How long? A week? A month?"

She wiped her fingers over her cheeks, brushing away the tears. "One."

"One week?"

She stared at the ground. "One day," she said faintly. His blood drummed in his ears. "So while I was over seven thousand miles away, thinking you and I were still engaged, thinking you still loved me, you were back here screwing another guy?"

She blanched. "I never meant for it to happen. And I'm sorry I hurt you, Brady, but…people change. Feelings…change. You need to accept it and move on."

Accept it? She'd lied to him. Used him. And the best she could do was toss him an *I'm sorry?* And now she wanted him to move on—just not with her sister.

To hell with her.

"Just because it was that easy for you doesn't mean that's how it works for everyone." He started pacing, the breeze doing nothing to calm his anger. "You have everything you've always wanted." He spun to face her and she shrank back against the car. "Everything you were supposed to have with me. Instead, I'm five months away from becoming a father to a baby I don't want with a woman I'll never be able to love because she's not you!"

Behind him, he heard a sound—as if someone had just been punched in the stomach. Brady's scalp tingled, his skin grew clammy. He turned to find J.C. in the same pajamas she'd had on last night, standing on the next to last step, her feet bare, her eyes huge. With one hand she gripped the railing, with the other she held her stomach protectively.

His panic spiked. He sensed he was close to losing something important—something he might not be able to get back.

He didn't move.

Now, he wouldn't have to worry about facing her again. Trying to keep his distance. About the feelings he had for her he couldn't explain. Things between them could end here, now, before they became even more complicated.

Before he had to admit to himself that what he'd just said had been nothing but a lie.

CHAPTER FIFTEEN

TODAY WAS SUNDAY, J.C. thought stupidly as she stood there, the wind blowing her hair in her face, causing her eyes to tear. How could she forget it was Sunday. And that on Sunday mornings when Liz didn't work the night before, she took Grandma Rose to church.

"J.C., let's go inside where it's warm," Liz said as she walked toward her. J.C. didn't so much as glance Brady's way. She couldn't. If she looked at him now, she'd never get through the next few minutes without breaking down.

Liz climbed up to stand next to her. "Oh, honey, you don't even have any shoes on."

"I didn't think I'd need them," she said absently.

Liz put her arm around J.C.'s shoulder, either ignoring or not noticing how J.C. stiffened. "Come on. We'll go in, ask Grandma to make some of her blueberry pancakes. You'll feel better after you have something to eat."

J.C. blinked. "Yes, I'm sure some pancakes will make this all better."

"At least you'll be out of the cold and away from…"

Away from Brady.

Brady, who hadn't moved since he noticed her.

Brady, who didn't want the baby. Who still loved Liz.

A sob rose in the back of her throat and she covered her mouth to hide the sound.

"None of that," Liz admonished gently. "You don't want him to see you cry, do you?"

Why not? He'd already seen her at her absolute worst and best. She was about to tell Liz exactly that when she saw the pity in her sister's eyes. Any small pieces of her pride that'd survived Brady's impassioned speech died.

She shrugged Liz's arm off. "You go ahead, I'd like a few minutes alone with Brady."

"I don't think that's a good idea," Liz said.

J.C. stared hard at her sister. "I didn't ask your opinion. Or your permission."

Liz was taken aback. "If that's what you want…"

"It is."

"All right. But remember, I'm right inside if you need me."

"I won't," J.C. said with such conviction, she almost believed it herself. "I can handle this on my own."

Looking far more hurt than J.C. thought she had a right to, Liz rounded J.C.'s car and walked over to their grandmother's house. J.C. finally turned to Brady. As she'd suspected, his hooded gaze was on her, his hands in his front pockets, his hair still mussed from her bed. From her fingers.

Brady stepped toward her, stopping when she backed up a step.

"Jane…" he said in his deep voice.

"Is this where you tell me last night was a mistake?"

"It was."

"So it meant nothing to you? Or maybe you're too big of a coward to admit it did mean something."

"I'm sorry."

"Don't," she warned, unable to keep her voice from shaking. "Don't you dare patronize me by giving me some trite apology."

He glanced down at the ground. "It's the best I can do."

Her toes were numb, her legs shaking from the cold. "No. It's all you're willing to do." The baby moved, strengthening J.C.'s resolve not to let him see how much he'd hurt her. "I feel sorry for you."

His posture grew rigid. "Don't bother."

"Why not? Isn't that what you want, what this is all about? Poor Brady Sheppard lost his one true love and his plans for the future. Welcome to the real world, Brady, where people get their hearts broken every day. Where plans fall through, jobs are lost and loved ones pass away. The world where we don't always get what we want, but most people make the most of what they do have."

"I'm trying to," he said with a definite edge to his voice as he stepped onto the stair below her, bringing them eye-to-eye. "Once my knee heals more—"

"You'll what, be whole again? Be able to act like a human, like someone who stands up and brushes himself off when he falls? Your leg is an excuse, like your drinking."

His expression darkened and he walked away, his gait uneven.

"Oh, no, you don't," J.C. muttered. Careful of the damp stairs, she didn't start jogging until she stepped onto the cold, rough cement of the driveway. She rounded the garage and sped past him to stand in front of the driver's door of his truck.

His keys jingled in his hand. "Move," he ordered.

She swallowed. "Remember when I told you I've never seen anything through because it's easier to quit when things get tough?" He inclined his head. "Well, that's only part of it." She tried to slow her breathing, to get her heart rate back to where it belonged. "The truth is, if I quit, then I can't fail."

And if she never failed, that was almost as good as always succeeding. Like Liz did.

"But I've realized," she continued, pulling the sleeves of her sweatshirt down to cover her cold hands, "that by giving up so I don't fail, there's also no chance I'll ever succeed. And if succeeding means taking risks and putting myself out there, putting my pride on the line, then that's what I'll do."

She'd do it because, right now, success was more than getting what she wanted. It was proving to herself she had the courage to try.

"Brady, I…" She took a moment to regain her composure. "I'm in love with you."

He flinched. "No. You aren't."

"You don't have to love me back," she told him quietly. "You don't even have to like the fact that I'm in love with you. But don't you ever tell me what is or isn't in my heart."

He held his head with both hands, as if to stop it from exploding. "Damn it, Jane. Don't make this harder than it has to be."

"How could I? You're the one who made love to me last night then couldn't slip out of my bed fast enough this morning. You're choosing to hold on to Liz, to what you had. Wishing for things to be different, for a life you could've had if Liz hadn't fallen in love with Carter.

If you hadn't been injured. If you hadn't slept with me and gotten me pregnant."

Brady stared straight ahead, not showing even the tiniest flicker of emotion, of reaction to her words.

Tears stung the backs of her eyes. "I can't tell you what your life would've been like. But I can tell you what you could've had. Me. And our son. You could've had a home filled with laughter and love and hope. But you'd rather wallow in self-pity."

He glanced at her, took in the tears running freely down her cheeks. "Is that all?" he asked tightly, a muscle jumping in his jaw.

She used her sleeve to dry her face. "One last thing. If you ever start thinking you'd like to be a part of our lives after all—don't bother. My son and I will be fine without you. We don't need you." She'd make sure her baby had all the love and support she could give him. Hopefully it would be enough to make up for his father's abandonment. "But I wonder, Brady," she asked softly, "how do you think you'll be without us?"

LIZ WAS ADDING FROZEN blueberries to her grandma's pancake batter when J.C. finally walked into the kitchen. Her relief at seeing her sister died quickly once she noticed J.C.'s tear-streaked face, red nose and chattering teeth.

"You poor dear," Grandma Rose said, wrapping her arm around J.C.'s middle and leading her to the table. "Sit down while I fetch a blanket."

"How about getting a pair of socks, too, Grandma?" Liz asked. Grandma Rose waved her hand to indicate she'd heard as she hurried out of the room.

"Here," Liz said, setting a tea cup in front of J.C.

"Don't worry," she added when J.C. just stared at it, "it's decaf. And I added extra honey."

J.C. picked up the cup, sloshing tea over the side. Liz was about to help her when J.C. raised the cup and took a sip.

Grandma Rose came back into the kitchen carrying two blankets and a pair of fuzzy slipper-socks. "We'll have you warm again in no time," Rose said, wrapping a fleece blanket around J.C.'s shoulders while Liz pulled the socks over her cold feet. The second blanket they laid across her lap.

And that whole time, J.C. didn't move. She didn't even blink. Liz and her grandmother exchanged worried glances.

"Hey," Liz said, covering J.C.'s cold hand where it rested on the table. "Are you all right?"

"Fine." She pulled her hand away and put it on her lap. "And you'll no doubt be happy to know that Brady's gone. Once again, you get exactly what you wanted."

Liz sat back. "Excuse me?"

"You didn't want him in my life and now he's not."

"He never should've been there in the first place," Liz pointed out. "And as I remember, you promised me you wouldn't see him anymore." She lowered her voice so Grandma Rose couldn't hear. "And yet, there he was, sneaking out of your apartment not twenty minutes ago."

And the sight of Brady leaving her sister's place after having obviously spent the night had been enough to knock the air out of her lungs.

J.C. pulled the blanket tighter around her shoulders. "The only reason I agreed to that promise was because

I was willing to do anything to get you to forgive me. But you already knew that, didn't you?"

Liz flushed hot, then cold. "Don't be ridiculous."

"And then you added in that story about you and Carter—"

"What about Liz and Carter?" Rose asked, setting a plate of pancakes in the middle of the table.

"Nothing," Liz said, her cheeks burning. She sent J.C. a loaded look, one that clearly said, "Keep your mouth shut."

"Carter thinks Liz is still in love with Brady," J.C. said with more than a hint of venom in her voice. "Liz denies it, but either she's protesting too much or not enough, because Carter thinks they need to attend marriage counseling."

"Is that true, Elizabeth?" Rose asked.

"Carter and I are fine," she snapped, glaring at J.C. "And we'll be even better now that Brady Sheppard is out of the picture."

J.C. shook her head. "You'd like to believe that, wouldn't you? You'd like to pretend that Brady is at the root of all your problems."

Liz stabbed a pancake and set it on her plate. "Pretend? Brady *is* at the root of my problems and he has been ever since he crashed my wedding."

"So rude," Rose said, sitting opposite J.C. "You should've let your father have him escorted off the premises."

"I didn't want a scene," she insisted, pouring syrup over her pancakes though her appetite was quickly disappearing.

"You really don't see what you're doing, do you?" J.C. asked. "The reason Brady is a problem for you and

Carter at all is because of you. You put him between you and your husband because you haven't let Brady go yet."

Liz set her fork down so no one would notice her hands trembling. "That's not true. Just because I don't want my sister and my ex-fiancé to be together doesn't mean I'm holding on to Brady."

"No." J.C. stood and tossed the blanket over the back of her chair. "It means you can't stand the idea of Brady moving on. Of him wanting to be with someone besides you."

"But he doesn't want to be with anyone else, does he?" she snapped, immediately wishing she could take her words back when she saw J.C.'s stunned expression. The hurt in her eyes.

"You're right," J.C. said faintly, her face white. "I'll always be second choice to him." She rubbed at her temples. "Want to know the worst part? Up until this morning, that would've been enough for me."

Liz's chest burned. "J.C., I didn't mean—"

"Not now, okay? I...I can't handle much more this morning and I..." She brought her hand to her mouth, her fingers trembling. "I'm not feeling very well."

"Let me get you some ginger ale," Rose said, going around the table to the refrigerator.

J.C. was already backing out of the room. "No. Thank you. It's just a headache. I'll lie down until it goes away."

A moment later, they heard the front door close. Liz went to the sink and watched J.C. make her way up to her apartment, her steps slow, her shoulders shaking.

"She's crying," Liz said, pressing her fingers against her eyes. "I didn't mean to make her cry." She sighed and dropped her hands. "How did everything get so messed up?"

Rose set the dishes in the sink. "It got messed up because life is messy. People are fallible. They make mistakes, say things they shouldn't. And sometimes, they even hold on to a relationship, not because they still want to be with that person, but because there's unfinished business, unresolved feelings."

"My feelings for Brady are firmly resolved." *Liar,* a tiny voice inside her head whispered. She filled a glass with water and drank deeply, hoping to dislodge what felt like a pebble in her throat. "I love Carter, not Brady."

Rose smiled and patted Liz's cheek. "I believe you. And once you realize what's holding you back from fully committing to your husband, heart and soul, everyone else will believe you, too. Including yourself."

HIS MOTHER WAS getting married.

And instead of celebrating with her, her fiancé and their respective families, Brady was hiding upstairs in his father's office—in Aidan's office—where he could drink a few beers in peace.

Lying on the leather sofa, he stared out the window at the starry sky. Bing Crosby singing "White Christmas" floated upstairs, as did the muted sounds of laughter, conversation and general revelry.

He tipped his bottle of beer at the sky in a mock toast. Welcome to the Sheppards' annual Christmas Eve party, where more than one hundred of his mother's closest friends mingled downstairs. After his mother and Al had announced their engagement to wild applause, Brady had done his familial duty for about fifteen minutes

before the press of bodies, the noise and smells—floral
perfumes, musky colognes and rich, buttery desserts—
forced him to find some solitude.

Sensory overload, he thought, drinking his beer.

But up here, with the lights off and no one asking him
how his physical therapy was going or if he planned on
sticking around Jewell now that his options were limited,
he could breathe.

I'm in love with you.

The bottle slipped from his fingers, dropping with
a thud. It rolled, spilling beer over the carpet before
he could grab it. Damn it. Damn it! Why couldn't J.C.
leave him alone? Every time he'd shut his eyes last night,
he'd relived their lovemaking, the dreams so vivid he'd
woken up reaching for her. Only to remember the look
on her face when she overheard him claiming he didn't
want the baby. That he couldn't love her because she
wasn't Liz.

He tipped his head side to side until his neck popped.
But he could still hear her voice in his head.

*My son and I will be just fine without you. But I
wonder, Brady, how do you think you'll be without
us?*

My son, she'd said, claiming their baby as effectively
as if she'd said straight out she was keeping him. And
he didn't doubt they'd be fine. J.C. was far more resil-
ient than people gave her credit for. She'd be a terrific
mother. And someday, she'd meet someone without so
much baggage. A guy smart enough not to screw up
what a good thing he had with her.

Sitting up, he finished his beer. He needed another
one. Or twelve.

But to get one, he had to venture yet again into the

party. This time he was bringing a six-pack out with him instead of one bottle.

He got to his feet as the office door opened and someone flipped the lights on.

"I thought you might be in here," Matt said from the doorway. He looked at the beer bottle in Brady's hand, his eyes narrowing slightly. "There's a pretty brunette out on the porch to see you."

Jane.

"Why didn't you bring her up?" Brady asked roughly, already on his way toward the door.

"I tried. She said she didn't want to interrupt the party."

Brady brushed past Matt and was down the stairs in a few minutes. In the living room next to the foyer, the party was in full swing. Avoiding eye contact, he paused at the front door to comb his fingers through his hair and realized as he raised his hand he still held the empty beer bottle. He stuck it under the skinny fake tree in the corner his mother had decorated all in red.

He stepped outside. Between the porch light and the white Christmas lights his mother had wound around every available surface, the porch fairly glowed, making it easy for Brady to see her sitting on the wooden swing.

Just not the woman he'd hoped it'd be.

"Hello, Brady," Liz said, stopping the motion of the swing and standing.

He exhaled. Mouth tight, he nodded.

"I'm sorry to barge in on you this way," she said, hunching her shoulders against the cold. "I forgot about your mom's holiday party until I pulled in and saw all the cars."

"Is J.C. okay?"

Liz looked at him speculatively. "As far as I know, she's fine."

"Good. That's…good." He shoved his hands into his pockets. "Do you want to come inside?"

"I'd rather stay out here if you don't mind. This won't take long."

He lifted a shoulder, then leaned back against the porch rail while she retook her seat on the swing. She cleared her throat. "Brady, I…I owe you an apology."

"Mind telling me what, exactly, you're apologizing for?"

Tipping her head back, she searched his face. "I'm sorry I wrote you that letter."

Out of all the reasons he could think of for Liz to show up at his mother's house on Christmas Eve, her apologizing for writing him a Dear John letter hadn't made the list.

"After everything we'd been through," she continued when he remained silent, "you deserved more than a letter."

It didn't matter. No apology could change what happened or bring him back what he'd lost. But maybe he could get some answers to the questions that had plagued him for so long.

"Why'd you write it?" he asked. "Why not break off things when I was home for leave that summer instead of letting me go overseas thinking nothing had changed between us?"

She clasped her gloved hands together on her lap. "I should have. But I'd convinced myself my feelings for Carter weren't serious." She lowered her head, her gaze on the porch floor. "But the biggest reason I didn't end our engagement face-to-face or even over the phone was because I knew you'd try to talk me out of it. I was afraid if you did," she said thickly, "I'd let you. And then things would go on between us the way they always had."

"That would've been so bad?"

"Not bad," she said with a shaky breath, "but not what I wanted, either." She raised her head, tears sparkling in her eyes. "I loved you, Brady, I loved you for half of my life but I…I didn't want to marry you," she whispered.

"What the hell does that mean?" he growled, not giving a rat's ass that she winced at his harsh tone. "You accepted my proposal. You wore my ring. Now you tell me you never planned on marrying me?"

"It wasn't like that," she said, getting to her feet. "I didn't even realize it myself until…until after I met Carter."

Brady stared at Liz as if he'd never seen her before. "All those times you pushed the wedding date back," he said, "because you wanted to finish college first, then med school and your residency, those were excuses not to marry me?"

"I kept thinking, hoping, something would change." She pulled a tissue from her pocket and wiped her eyes then blew her nose. "I held on to you because I loved you too much to let you go."

"You loved me," he said in a monotone. "Just not enough to commit to making a life with me."

"I was wrong. That's why I'm here. It's time I let you go for good, for both our sakes." She reached past him and he stiffened. But she didn't touch him, just set the blue jeweler's box containing the ring he'd bought her on the porch rail. "Goodbye, Brady."

He watched Liz walk away and stood staring out over the driveway long after she left. But instead of thinking of Liz and what she'd confessed, one thought consumed him.

J.C. had been right.

He wiped a shaky hand over his mouth. He'd been holding on to his past because he couldn't imagine loving any other woman but Liz. He'd thought they had the perfect love, but it had been a lie. All those years of waiting for Liz to set a wedding date, to be ready to marry him, he'd pretended everything was great because he wanted to hold on to the fantasy rather than face reality.

While he'd been focused on what he'd lost, he'd ignored what he'd gained. A chance for the life he'd always dreamed of with a beautiful, warm, funny woman. A woman who'd give him a child. A woman who loved him.

And he'd pushed her away.

Although...

CHAPTER SIXTEEN

"YOU'RE LATE."

With a gasp, Liz whirled toward the sound of her husband's voice. "Carter. You scared me."

"Sorry."

Frowning, she shut the front door and walked into their living room. Carter was slouched in an armchair staring at the flames in the fireplace. Other than the fire and the colorful lights on their Christmas tree, the room was dark.

"I thought you were going to Mitch and Kelly's for dinner," she said, taking her coat off and laying it on the back of the sofa before switching on a floor lamp.

Carter's shirtsleeves were rolled up, the top three buttons of his collar undone. His pale hair stuck up at odd angles, as if he'd repeatedly run his hands through it. "I didn't want to go without you. I wanted to spend our first Christmas Eve as a married couple together."

She crossed to him. "I'm glad. I want that, too."

"How was work?" he asked, sipping red wine as he regarded her over the glass. "You must've been busy."

Sitting on the arm of the chair, she slipped off her shoes and wiggled her toes. "You know how it is during the holidays. The E.R. was a madhouse."

"Is that why you're late?" he asked in that calm way of his. "Why you've been crying?"

She rubbed at the aching arch of her foot. Though she'd done a quick repair job on her makeup in the car, she knew there were still traces of smudged mascara under her red-rimmed eyes. And the tip of her nose was still pink.

She helped herself to his wine, took a long drink and prayed she'd done the right thing for her marriage. "I went to see Brady."

His fingers dug into the arm of the chair by her leg. "Why?"

"To apologize." She tucked a strand of hair behind her ear. "And because...we both needed...closure."

She just hadn't realized how badly they'd needed it until yesterday after J.C. had left their grandmother's house.

Carter sat up. "You apologized for breaking up with him?"

"No. For how I handled it. How I handled every-thing." She stood and wandered to the tree. Traced a fingertip over a red ball before facing her husband. "He needed to know the truth about why I wrote that letter. And I had to return his ring."

"Did he take it back this time?"

"I didn't give him a choice." She clasped her hands. "I left it there. What he does with it isn't my concern. Not anymore."

"Why?" he asked quietly.

"I...I don't understand."

He rested his elbows on his knees. "Why worry about closure now, after all this time?"

She rubbed her hands over her suddenly chilled arms. "For you," she told him simply. "For us. I want us to get back to how we used to be. And because..."

When she'd seen Brady leave J.C.'s apartment, Liz hadn't just been angry, hadn't just felt betrayed. For one awful moment, she'd hated them both.

Her throat burned with tears. "Because yesterday I realized I couldn't move on with my life until I'd settled my past. Neither could Brady."

Carter watched her, his expression unreadable. "What if we can't go back?"

Fear immobilized her for one heartbeat. Two. Then she shook her head. "I'm not going to lose you," she told him fiercely.

Kneeling in front of him, she gripped his hands. Relief made her light-headed when he linked his fingers with hers. "Thanksgiving, when we argued about Brady, you…you asked me if I still loved him and I didn't answer." She drew in a breath, then said in a rush, "Ask me now."

Dropping his gaze, he rubbed his thumbs over the backs of her hands. "I'm afraid to hear the answer," he whispered.

She brought his hands to her mouth, kissed both in turn and waited until he met her eyes. "I don't love Brady. I made a mistake, a huge one, in not telling you that before. You are the only man I love. And that is never going to change."

Carter searched her eyes and this time, instead of feeling guilty, as if she was hiding something from him, she let him see the truth.

He pressed a soft kiss against her forehead, then on each closed eye before wrapping his arms around her and dragging her onto his lap. She curled into him and rested her head on his shoulder.

"I love you so much, Liz," he told her. "I never want to lose you."

"You won't," she promised, stroking her fingers through his hair. She took his wonderfully handsome face in her hands. "I love you," she told him again.

Then she tugged on his hand and pulled him to the floor. And in the flickering glow of the fire, she showed him just how much.

WELL AFTER 1:00 A.M., when all the guests had gone and most of the cleanup was completed, Brady sat back in a recliner in his mother's family room, staring at her tree so long, the lights began to dance and blur in front of his eyes. He shook his head and blinked several times until his vision cleared.

The only reason he was still here was because Matt was freaking out about their mother's engagement. And because he wasn't in any hurry to go back to the cottage where he'd spend a restless night dreaming of J.C. Wondering if there was any way he could make things right between them again.

Yeah, even listening to Matt bitch and moan was better than that.

"You think Al would mind if I call him Daddy?" Matt asked from his spot on the sofa, his head propped up on his bent arm as he stared at the ceiling.

Aidan was on the floor, his back resting against an armchair, his dog lying next to him, her head in his lap. He stared at his youngest brother. "You're an idiot."

"Me? Hey, I'm not the one in this family who's taking the marital plunge with a guy who looks like a horse when he smiles. All those teeth can't be real. And if a man lies about his teeth, who knows what else he'll lie about."

Aidan pinched the bridge of his nose. "He's not that bad."

"He's a politician," Matt pointed out. "There's nothing *but* bad about that."

"He's retired," Aidan said. "Trust me, he's a decent guy."

"How do we know he's not after Mom's money?"

"He could buy the Diamond Dust outright—twice—in cash, and still have money left over."

Matt raised his head and looked at Brady. "What about you? Do you think Mom's making a mistake?"

As if Brady had any right to judge someone else's choices. "If she is, it's her mistake to make."

"That's such a cop-out. You don't think it's risky for a woman Mom's age to jump into marriage with the first guy who asks her?"

"He might not be the first guy to ask," Brady said, lifting his bottle of beer to his mouth. Feeling Aidan watch his every move. "For all we know, it's just the first time she's said yes."

Scowling, Matt got to his feet. "If you two aren't going to take this seriously, I'm going to bed."

"Merry Christmas," Brady murmured as his brother left the room, adding to Aidan, "I would've thought out of the three of us, you'd be the one having the hardest time with Mom getting remarried."

While Tom Sheppard had loved his boys equally, he and Aidan had had a special bond. Probably because they were so much alike.

"I like Al. More importantly, he makes Mom happy."

Aidan leaned his head back on the chair cushion. "Besides, Dad would want Mom to move on."

Seemed to be the theme in Jewell. His mother getting remarried. Liz moving on with her new husband. And eventually, J.C. would move on, as well. She'd give birth to their baby, raise their son.

I'm in love with you.

Even that would change.

And that thought turned his blood to ice. He finished his beer and stood. "Want another?"

"I'm good."

Brady tossed his empty into the recycling bin and grabbed a full bottle from the fridge. He flipped the cap into the garbage and then sat back down. "You have something you want to say?"

"Do you hear me talking?" Aidan asked.

"No. But I can feel all those waves of disapproval."

Aidan stroked Lily's head, her eyes squinting in pleasure. "I'm wondering what happened to send you back to the bottle."

"Maybe I'm just thirsty."

"I thought Jane would be at the party," Aidan mentioned way too casually for the comment to actually be casual. "Did she have other plans?"

He scowled. "How the hell would I know?"

"Thought you two were…friends."

Cold sweat broke out on his forehead. Friends. Jeez. "We're not," he said.

Aidan bent one leg, resting his arm on his knee. "You blew it, huh?"

"There was nothing to blow. She wasn't what I wanted."

"Why not?"

He froze in the act of raising his beer to his mouth. "She's Liz's sister."

"You don't want her because she's Liz's sister? Or because she's not Liz?"

"Both. Neither." Hell. He carefully set the bottle on the table. "It would never work out."

Aidan raised an eyebrow. "Your crystal ball tell you that?"

"This isn't how my life was supposed to be," he said, feeling as if the words were being ripped from his throat. "Liz and me breaking up. My knee…" The nightmares. The drinking. J.C. and the baby. "None of it's what I wanted."

"And all this time I thought Matt was the idiot in the family," Aidan muttered as he stood. "You think you're the only person whose life is one hundred and eighty degrees from where you thought it'd be? If things went according to plan, Dad would still be alive and I'd be working my way up to partner at some high-end law firm in D.C."

"You could've still had that law career," Brady said, feeling as if he were backed into a corner and the only way out was to start swinging. "No one forced you to take over the winery after Dad died. The only thing you didn't choose was Yvonne leaving."

At the mention of his ex-wife, Aidan's expression hardened. "Why don't you take responsibility for yourself, for your decisions? It's not as if your life turned out the way it has through no fault or conscious choice of your own."

Brady wanted to deny it. He hadn't wanted Liz to end their engagement and he sure as hell hadn't asked for his vehicle to run over that bomb. But, damn it, he had stayed with Liz despite her repeatedly pushing their wedding date back. He'd joined the Marines, stayed in the Corps despite the risks involved.

He chose to spend time with J.C. even though his feelings for her grew more tangled, more confused with every one of her smiles. With every casual touch or soft kiss.

He'd let himself fall completely for Jane Cleo Montgomery.

Shaken, he rubbed the heel of his hand over his heart. "You were right the first time. I definitely blew it with J.C."

"So fix it."

If you ever start thinking you'd like to be a part of our lives after all—don't bother. My son and I will be fine without you. We don't need you.

His pulse pounded in his ears. "I don't think I can," he admitted.

"Want my advice?"

"No."

"Don't let her go. Do whatever you have to do or say to convince her to give you a second chance."

Brady brought his head up at the urgency in his brother's voice. "Is that the voice of experience talking?"

"It's the voice of a man whose wife walked out on him." Aidan's expression was grim. "And because he chose not to go after her."

CHRISTMAS MORNING, J.C. and most of the other congregation joined in as the First Presbyterian's choir sang "Joy to the World" at the end of the church service. She snuck a glance down the wooden pew, past her parents and Grandma Rose, to where Liz and Carter stood sharing a songbook. They'd arrived just before services started, harried, windblown and flushed. And obviously very much together.

As J.C. watched, Carter bent his head and whispered in Liz's ear. She smiled, then caressed her husband's cheek with her fingertips.

J.C. jerked her gaze back to the songbook in her hand but the words blurred. Maybe this loneliness was her penance for coveting her sister's ex.

Or maybe she'd just been simply foolish to fall in love with someone as lost and damaged as Brady Sheppard.

The song ended and as usual, her family was one of the last to leave, thanks to Grandma Rose being in no particular hurry to get out of the pew. How it could possibly take someone so long to put on a coat, button it, pull on some gloves and dig her house keys out of her purse—because God forbid she'd have to stand outside her own front door searching for her keys—J.C. had no idea. All she knew was that by the time her grandmother was ready to go, the church was half-empty.

J.C. followed her family out of the pew. Her parents walked down the aisle with their closest friends, Sandy and Dan O'Brien, while Carter escorted Grandma Rose.

Leaving Liz standing in the aisle waiting for her. J.C. considered exiting from the other end of the pew, even took a step in that direction before sliding her purse strap over her shoulder and moving forward.

Liz's smile was bright, her eyes uncertain. "Merry Christmas," she said, hugging J.C.

Though it was petty—petty and immature and not

in the Christmas spirit at all—J.C. kept her arms at her sides. "Merry Christmas."

Liz's smile faltered. She cleared her throat then swept her gaze over her sister. "Wow, you look really…"

So help her, if Liz said *tired* or commented on the dark circles under her eyes or the pallor of her skin, J.C. was going to hit her with a hymnbook.

"Pretty," Liz decided.

"Thank you." The baby moved—he'd been rolling around like mad in there all morning—and J.C. rubbed her stomach. "I take it everything's all right with you and Carter?"

Liz glanced over at her husband, who was waiting patiently for Grandma Rose to finish her conversation with the minister. "I wouldn't go that far, but we're trying. We…" Fidgeting with the buttons on her coat, Liz lowered her voice. "We're going to look into couples' counseling after the holidays."

"That's good," J.C. said, meaning it. She stepped into the aisle, forcing Liz to hastily move out of the way. "I hope…I hope you two work things out."

She walked toward the double doors. The church had cleared out quickly. The kids were itching to change out of their fancy clothes and play with the toys they'd unwrapped earlier. The adults were either hurrying from one relative's house to another's or racing home to start Christmas dinner. Her parents were probably speeding home themselves to host their annual Christmas brunch at noon.

She'd planned to attend. Had told herself she was tough enough to survive a couple hours surrounded by family and friends. But now she was panicked at just the thought of acting as if everything were okay.

She'd go back to her apartment. Once there, she'd call and tell her parents she wasn't feeling well and wouldn't make it to their party.

"Jane, wait," Liz called, stopping J.C. before she reached the doors. "I...I want to apologize for what happened the other day. For the things I said."

"It doesn't matter."

Liz's eyes filled with tears. "How can you say that? I was...horrible. What I said about Brady..." She swallowed convulsively. "About him not wanting anyone but me..."

"All you said was the truth."

Liz opened her mouth. Then shut it as she looked over J.C.'s shoulder, her eyes widening slightly. "No," she said, "I don't think that was the truth at all."

A ripple of awareness washed over J.C. Holding her breath, she turned slowly. And there he was—Brady Sheppard, leaning against the door, looking as sullen and dangerous and lost as he had on the day of Liz's wedding.

Except...he wasn't looking at Liz. No, he was looking at...her. Even when Liz brushed past him and walked out the door.

J.C.'s mouth went dry. Shock held her immobile as he straightened and strode toward her, his step purposeful despite his limp. He looked...well...he looked awful. As if he'd slept in his clothes—or hadn't gone to bed yet. His hair waved in disarray, his eyes were bloodshot and the thick stubble on his cheeks and chin did nothing to soften the harsh lines of his face.

He didn't stop until he was so close she had to tip her head back to meet his eyes.

"You're not at your apartment," he rumbled.

She blinked. Blinked again. "No. I'm not."

"You didn't stay there last night."

She gaped at him. "How do you—"

"I waited for you."

She remembered the other times he'd waited. Thanksgiving night. At the doctor's office for her appointment. "You...you waited all night?" He nodded curtly. "I... stayed over at my parents' house. They didn't want me to be alone."

"When you didn't come home I thought..." He looked away. "I thought I'd lost you. For good. Tell me I haven't. Tell me I'm not too late."

Shaking her head slowly, she backed away. But for each step she took, he followed.

"I'm not doing this," she said, her voice trembling when she'd meant to sound confident. Angry. Damn it, she was angry. And way too raw to give him even the slightest opportunity to hurt her again.

"Please." He reached out as if to touch her face but she jerked her head back. "Please," he repeated, curling his fingers into a fist. "Just let me explain—"

"Explain what, Brady? You've made it perfectly clear you don't anything to do with me or our baby. Oh, or maybe you'd like to tell me how you'd rather be with Liz, but hey, I'll do in a pinch, right? And if it's dark enough and you pretend real hard," she said, her voice cracking, "you can convince yourself you're really with her."

"Jane...no...God, I didn't..." He looked stunned. "You know that's not true. I made love to *you* that night. You're who I want."

"It's too late."

She started to walk away.

"I love you, Jane."

She stumbled and turned around, her eyes wide. "Don't say that," she snapped.

"It's the truth. I love you."

"You love Liz." She hugged her arms around herself. "You're always going to love Liz."

"I'm always going to care about her, but I don't love her. I'm not in love with her. Not anymore." He stepped toward J.C. "You were right. I couldn't see what had gone right in my life." Another step. "You, Jane. You and our baby are what's right."

She began to shake. "No."

He regarded her gravely. "What I said that morning after we made love...what you heard..." He blew out a shaky breath. "I was scared. Afraid of my feelings for you. I didn't know what to do with them. They were... too much. Too soon. I wanted to control them because so many parts of my life were out of my control."

"Stop. Please..." Her voice was raw. Her breathing shallow. "I can't do this again."

"You said you and the baby didn't need me," he said, relentlessly, stubbornly, as he closed the remaining distance between them. He gently lifted her chin. "You may not need me, but I need you. Both of you."

Afraid to believe, she searched his eyes. Joy and love, so much love for him, welled inside her and the tears she'd tried to hold back rolled down her cheeks.

"Don't cry," he said raggedly, wiping her face, his touch unsteady. "It rips me up when you cry."

Throwing her arms around him, she pressed her face into his neck. She inhaled his familiar, comforting scent. He stilled for a moment, then with a groan, wrapped his arms around her, pulling her close, holding her so tightly, she couldn't breathe. She clung to him harder.

"Thank you," he murmured. "Thank you."

He pulled back and kissed her, his lips warm, his mouth coaxing. When he straightened, he cupped her face in one hand, his thumb caressing her jaw. His other hand went to the soft swell of her stomach, his fingers spread wide. "Tell me."

Because he still seemed so unsure, so nervous, she kissed him. Then smiled. "I love you, Brady."

He nodded and she felt some of his tension drain away. "I love you, Jane Cleo," he said, his voice husky.

And then—disheveled, contented and, if she wasn't mistaken, mended—Brady Sheppard smiled. At her.

EPILOGUE

One month later

ABOUT A MILE AWAY from the turn to the Diamond Dust, Brady took a right down a narrow lane.

"Where are we going?" J.C. asked from the passenger seat as he passed two houses—one on each side of the road—and pulled to a stop in front of a large, well-maintained farmhouse where the street ended. "Brady, what's going on? You know how your mom gets if we're late for lunch."

Lunch with his mom, Al and Aidan had become a weekly Sunday event. Things were still...tense...with J.C.'s family, and he doubted he and Carter would ever be more than stiffly polite to each other, but J.C. and Liz seemed to be making inroads.

He unclenched his hands from around the steering wheel. "We'll be there on time. I..." His throat was dry. "I want to show you something."

Grinning, she rolled her eyes. "Like I haven't heard that line before."

When he couldn't return her smile, hers slid away.

"You okay?" she asked, laying a hand on his arm. "Do you need to do some breathing exercises?"

"I'm fine." He squeezed her hand. "I'm not having an…an episode."

He'd been seeing a therapist for the past three weeks who'd officially diagnosed him with PTSD—post-traumatic stress disorder. And while he couldn't say he was thrilled with the diagnosis or having to spill his guts every week in his therapy session, the techniques he'd learned for dealing with his memories, stress and flashbacks were helping.

"Come on," he said, then hurried around the car, opened her door and pulled her to her feet.

She laughed but followed him to the wooden porch. He dug a set of keys out of his pocket. Her eyes widened. "What are you doing? Who lives here?"

"It's empty," he said, pushing open the door and tugging her into the wide foyer. He swallowed. "Want to look around?"

"Uh…sure."

Holding her hand, he led her up the stairs, turned left and walked into a large room with deep burgundy walls and white trim. "Master bedroom," he said, repeating the information the Realtor had given him, "complete with walk-in closets, bath and a balcony."

"It's very…pretty," she said, looking at him as if he'd recently suffered a head injury.

"Two more bedrooms up here." Spinning her around, he walked down the hall and into the room on the right—this one smaller and painted a sunny yellow—only to walk right out again and into the third bedroom at the back of the house. He opened the door at the end of the hall. "Closet." Gestured toward the final door. "Bathroom."

By the time he'd gotten her back down the stairs she was silent and his knee was aching.

"Foyer," he said as they passed the tiled entryway again. "That's the family room." He pointed to the large room off the foyer, then, knowing where he wanted the tour to end, he went the way they came, pointing at rooms as they walked. "Another bedroom or office, half bath, dining room."

Finally, his heart pounding, they reached the last room. "This is the kitchen."

"Yes," J.C. said, tugging free of his hold, her brow furrowed. "I can see that."

He waited as she slowly walked around, checking out the stainless-steel appliances, granite counters and built-in pantry.

"Well?" he asked, his voice a low growl when she remained silent.

She leaned back against the sink and crossed her arms. "Well what?"

He ground his teeth together. "Do you like it?"

"The kitchen?"

"The house."

She shrugged. "Yes."

He narrowed his eyes. Yes? That was it? "The asking price is for the house plus ten acres. And since it's been on the market for over a year, the owners are ready to make a deal."

"Well, if I was in the market to buy a house, that would all be good to know." Smiling, she straightened. "You ready to go? I'm starving," she added as she walked toward the door. "Do you think your mom made that potato soup I like?"

"I'm in the market."

Almost to the door, she turned slowly. "Excuse me?"

He shoved his hands into his pockets. "I'm in the market to buy a house. To buy this house." She regarded him steadily. Sweat formed at the nape of his neck, a bead of it sliding down between his shoulder blades. "I want to buy this house for you and the baby. For...us."

"Why?"

"Because I love you," he ground out, crossing to her. "And you love me."

"Yes, I do." She tipped her head to the side, looking so serene and so damn beautiful, he caught his breath. "I want you to ask me," she said softly.

His chest tight, he pulled a ring box out of his pocket and opened it. "It was my great-grandmother's," he said of the round diamond set in a platinum scrolled band.

"It's beautiful." She kept her hands clasped in front of her. She met his eyes. "But I'm still waiting for you to ask me."

"I can't kneel."

"No." Her eyes glistened. "I don't want you to. I just want the words."

"Jane Cleo Montgomery," he said quietly, taking her left hand and sliding the ring onto her finger, "I love you. I want to make a life with you and our baby." He kissed her hand, then looked into her eyes. "Will you marry me?"

"Yes," she whispered, linking her fingers through his. She cleared her throat. "Yes, Brady. I'll marry you."

Humbled, grateful, he pressed his lips against hers. Her mouth softened. He lifted his head and grinned. "I know you're anxious to get to lunch, but what do you think about christening the house before we go?"

She laughed and linked her arms around his neck. "I think that's the second-best proposal I've had today."

* * * * *

A sneaky peek at next month...

Cherish™

ROMANCE TO MELT THE HEART EVERY TIME

My wish list for next month's titles...

In stores from 16th December 2011:

❑ The Tycoon Who Healed Her Heart – Melissa James

& Daring to Date the Boss – Barbara Wallace

❑ Beauty and the Wolf – Lois Faye Dyer

& Their Miracle Twins – Nikki Logan

❑ Donovan's Child – Christine Rimmer

In stores from 6th January 2012:

❑ The Prince's Texas Bride – Leanne Banks

& The Reluctant Princess – Raye Morgan

❑ Master of the Outback – Margaret Way

Available at WHSmith, Tesco, Asda, Eason, Amazon and Apple

Just can't wait?

Have Your Say

You've just finished your book.
So what did you think?

We'd love to hear your thoughts on our
'Have your say' online panel
www.millsandboon.co.uk/haveyoursa

🌹 Easy to use
🌹 Short questionnaire
🌹 Chance to win Mills & Boon® goodies

Mills & Boon® Online

Discover more romance at
www.millsandboon.co.uk

🌹 **FREE** online reads

🌹 **Books** up to one
month before shops

🌹 **Browse our books**
before you buy

...and much more!